THE POISON KEEPER

DEBORAH SWIFT

QUIRE BOOKS

THE POISON KEEPER

I swear by Apollo Physician,
by Asclepius, by Hygieia, by Panacea,
and by all the gods and goddesses...
I will use treatment to help the sick
according to my ability and judgment,
but never with a view to injury and wrong-doing.
Neither will I administer a poison
to anybody when asked to do so,
nor will I suggest such a course...
But I will keep pure and holy
both my life and my art.

The Hippocratic Oath

PROLOGUE

PALERMO, SICILY, JUNE 1633

'Did you see her?' Duke Antonio de Verdi's voice rose from the bed in a feeble croak.

His housekeeper, the ramrod-straight Signora Fattorini, nodded, lips pursed in satisfaction. 'I waited as you suggested, in the guest chamber, and spied her through a crack in the door. She dropped something into your broth, Your Excellency.'

'Dispose of it. And have Bruno and Alessandro fetch her in.' A pause, in which he heaved himself up on the pillows and gathered enough saliva to speak again. 'No word, hear me... no word to anyone beyond these walls. Just a stomach sickness, understand me?'

He saw in her eyes, and her servile curtsey, that she understood exactly. He didn't want the court to know he had no control over his wife.

'Your Excellency, the glovemaker is due to see the Lady Valentina at two o'clock. What shall I tell her?'

'Send her away. My wife won't be needing any more gloves.'

CHAPTER 1

A SPLASH of noonday sun danced against the latticed window. Giulia paused, plate in hand, as a spider, escaping the sudden light, spooled slowly downwards on its silvery thread. If it put so much as a leg into the downstairs chamber, Mamma would kill it. Any stray crumb could pollute her work, she said. Any creature that fell into her carefully measured remedies could change the balance. Turn good to ill. Things were apt to turn into their opposite without careful attention, Mamma said, and Mamma was always right.

Fortune smiles on you today, little one, Giulia thought, *Mamma is busy in the still room.*

The spider completed its acrobatic descent and was gone, spindly legs scuttling away across the windowsill and into the blue-black shadow behind the cheese press. Giulia finished laying out the meal: yesterday's bread, wedges from a round of hard salty cheese, pickled olives and figs from Tuscolo.

She called down the staircase, 'It's ready, Mamma.'

It was their servant Maria's day off, so it was left to Giulia today to make Mamma eat. And today she was determined to make her listen.

She cocked her head. No answer, again.

Mamma often didn't hear, or pretended not to, when she was involved in her work. Giulia tucked the stray wisps of hair back into her dark coiled braids, lifted her heavy skirts and hurried downstairs, heels clacking on the stone treads. The door was shut as usual. It seemed to her she'd been locked outside this door her entire life. Only when Mamma was ready would she open it.

She remembered the time when she was eight years old straying into the still room and lifting the end of a stopper to her nose to smell it. A stinging slap to the cheek. 'Never, never do that,' Mamma had shouted, whipping the stopper away with a gloved hand, with the stark warning; 'You could die.'

Since then the door was locked until Mamma deigned to open it, and she had accepted it as the way things had to be, even though she was quite old enough to know better than to meddle with Mamma's work.

Jerking her attention back to the present, she gave a double knock, louder than necessary. Perhaps she'd be able to make Mamma listen this time.

The door swung open, and Mamma was there, angry as a wasp, a pair of red-hot tongs in her hand and a lump of something black smoking in their jaws. She hated being disturbed. 'What?'

Giulia put a hand to her nose. The heat and noxious smell of the still room had stopped her at the threshold. There was always something on the boil down here.

'Well, what is it that you must knock fit to wake the dead?' Mamma pulled down the gauze so only her sloe-black eyes were showing. The lower part of her face was covered so she did not breathe in the gases as she worked.

'It's ready,' Giulia said again.

'What?'

'Food, Mamma. You put it in your mouth and swallow it, and it stops you from dying.'

'Ha, ha. Less of that. I'm coming. What's the hurry? Nothing will spoil. I must wait until this dissolves.' She pointed with the tongs to a small charred pan bubbling over the fire.

'I'm hungry,' Giulia said, 'even if you're not.' She blew onto her upper lip. 'It's airless again down here. How can you bear it?'

'Because if I don't finish this, neither of us can afford to eat, my dove, that's why.'

'You should let me help you more.'

Mamma dropped the smoking lump of matter into the pot. 'This is delicate and needs a slow and steady hand. Better I do it. And never fear, there'll be time enough for learning this when you've mastered the kitchen simples.'

'They're mastered, Mamma, and well you know it. I can make them blindfold, every single one. You promised you'd train me in the secret arts when I was sixteen. Then you changed your mind and said when I was eighteen. And still, even now, I'm waiting.'

Mamma threw her a look that said 'not that old argument'. Giulia watched her mother hang up the tongs, wash in the stone basin, wipe her hands, repeat the procedure, and examine her fingers minutely. Then she put her gloves back on, and returned to ministering to the fire.

Giulia watched all this pother with barely disguised impatience. She was used to Mamma's excessive cleanliness, though today it made her want to scream. Mamma dealt in grains and specks – granules of matter so small they could barely be seen. Not a single ant was allowed to tiptoe into her workroom; every table was scrubbed with lye and bleached white, and she made Maria burnish the tiled floor with beeswax to a high gloss.

Giulia hovered by the dispensing table, picked up a small lead weight from the scales, then put it down again. It was fruitless to discuss this again. But the words still came out of her mouth: 'When will you train me in alchemy, Mamma? Who will make the remedies when you're too old and sick?'

'Tush. I'm hale as ever I was. Can't get rid of me yet. Anyway,

I'm far too occupied at the moment to spare the time.' Mamma shrugged and turned away again to stir the pot. 'Pass me that flask, will you.'

The sight of Mamma's bent back, with the neat grey curls poking from under her starched cap and the hunch of her shoulders, suddenly made Giulia furious. By God, she'd make her listen this time. Deliberately, she picked up the slender glass flask from the table, opened her fingers and let it crash to the ground.

Mamma whirled round at the sound of splintering glass, astonishment in her face.

'Will you heed me now?' Giulia said. 'I've asked you over and over. God in heaven, I'm twenty-three years old. More than old enough for a proper share in the business. A son would have taken over by now. Instead, you leave me toiling in the kitchen like a servant. Even Francesca has more responsibility than I, and she's not even part of the family.'

'It's because she's not part of the family that I use her. I'm trying to protect you. It's more complicated than you—'

'Oh, don't try to fob me with those excuses again. You just want control over everything. I'm weary of it, Mamma, weary of your promises that come to nothing. Weary of the whispers between you and Francesca. Weary of all the women that come here with their aches and pains and desperate faces. What are you all so afraid of? That I'll make some sort of mistake and kill someone?'

Mamma's eyes sharpened with suppressed anger. 'Who was it that burned the wax for the liverwort balm? Who forgot to add borax to the tooth dressing? Do you think I can trust you with my remedies?' She picked up a green-tinged bottle and brandished it before her. 'One drop of this has healing power. Three drops can kill. Are you ready for that responsibility?'

Giulia stepped back.

'Well, are you? No. You flare like sulphur. You're just like—' She cut off her own words. 'When you start to show a little more restraint, a little more responsibility, instead of ignoring my instructions, then it might be worth training you. You smash something for no reason and think that shows your mettle?'

'You never listen to me.'

'And you don't look under the surface of anything. You don't ask enough questions. You see the women who come here as a nuisance. You never once asked me why they come, or what they need. You haven't grasped that to know anything you must look beneath what's there, to see its soul. That this work is dark and dangerous, and not for meddling with. Now be gone from here. A hot temper has no place in my still room.'

Giulia was stung, though her heart knew there were elements of truth in the accusations. She swung out of the door, hitched her skirts, and clattered up the stone stairs to the kitchen, yelling as she went, 'I wish you weren't my mother. And you can find someone else to make your kitchen remedies.'

She heard Mamma bang the still room door shut after her, and it reverberated inside her with a longer ache. As a child, she'd loved Mamma with a fierce pride, but these days she and Mamma were like rowers each pulling the boat in different directions.

Disconsolately she laid cold meats on the two plates. They were lucky to have meat at all; most lived on coarse bread and sheep's cheese, if they could barter for it. Still smarting from the argument, she picked up an olive, rolled its soft oiliness between her fingers, and ate hastily, cramming the salty food into her mouth. She spent the rest of the afternoon packaging the kitchen remedies but there was still no sign of Mamma.

Perhaps she didn't need Mamma. Surely by now she knew enough without her? After all, she could make and sell the simple remedies by herself. Perhaps she'd take a stall in the market, like Claudia who sold the goat's cheese. Mamma couldn't stop her, though she would think such a profession beneath her status.

The thought of defying Mamma was both enticing and frightening.

After she'd put the meats under the cover, she took her large-brimmed hat against the late afternoon sun and banged the door with force behind her so Mamma would hear her go, and followed the narrow baked-earth streets towards the marketplace.

She'd need a recipe book to write down salves and simples so she could keep a record of them. Mamma had two books, one the kitchen book, which she had open access to, and the other the chymist book, never far from Mamma's side, and watched over by her as if it was a holy writ. She had sneaked a glance inside the second one to find painstakingly drawn diagrams of mandrake roots shaped like men, vipers coiled in aspic, and astrological plans of stars and planets, all surrounded by her mother's tiny writing. But no matter, today she'd begin to make her own book, and one just as interesting as Mamma's.

As she emerged into the market, the stalls were just setting up after the afternoon siesta, and the square was full of black-clad women unpacking baskets and boxes under the shade of the lime trees. She bought a sweet pastry from a woman with a face as wizened as a walnut, and stood in the street eating it, knowing that Mamma would deplore such unladylike behaviour.

She would go to Fabio's too on the way back. Fabio was the son of their neighbour, and he ran with a wild set – the boys that jostled you on the street or hung off the bridge parapets, legs dangling in mid-air. Once, when she was sixteen, a boy from the Catholic seminary had taken a liking to her, but Mamma had frowned and pursed her lips. 'Men are snakes,' she said, her eyes narrow and hard. 'Even young ones.' So the little spark of hope and excitement was extinguished.

In the marketplace she purchased two fine-looking books with papers bound together in thin boxwood covers, and this gave her an excuse to walk down to Fabio's leather shop. Fabio worked with his father, a saddler, but his father, the lazy sot, was seldom there. Supposedly repairing broken harnesses on outlying farms. Fabio had more skill in his little finger than his father did in his whole ale-soaked body. Fabio's strong fingers could carve tooled leather belts and the elaborate leather knee pads and fenders for Spanish saddles. He could incise swirling foliage and intricate geometries, and his speciality – the tooling of beautiful leather covers for books.

Giulia paused a moment outside the door to smooth her skirts, and cool her cheeks with the back of her hand. She didn't want to like him, because Mamma wouldn't approve, and besides, he wasn't of good blood. But even though she tried to stop herself, her thoughts still lingered on his slow way of smiling, on the way his eyes always seemed to be watching her when she went by. For weeks her cheeks had been as hot as embers each time she passed his *bottega*.

She calmed herself and with the books tucked tightly under one arm, ducked under the canvas awning and pushed open the door. A pungent meaty steam rose from a vat by the fire where Fabio soaked the skins in hot water to soften them for his work. Today he was bending over the bench with a hammer and punch in his hand, working on the frontispiece of a horse's head collar. He stood up as she entered, and she found herself at eye level with the point where his linen undershirt was open to reveal a small patch of bare brown skin. She shifted her eyes up to his, acutely aware of the unwanted flush rising to her cheeks.

A spark of something lit his eyes. She both wanted to look at him and wanted to look away.

'Good afternoon, Signorina,' he said, leaning his hands on the counter. 'How can I help?'

'I'm thinking of leather covers for these books,' she said, trying to sound as if it was something she was used to ordering. She placed them on the counter.

'I see. How much would you like to spend?'

She hadn't thought. She floundered. 'Oh, I'd like them to look handsome … but not be too costly.'

He picked up the first book and examined the wooden cover. 'Big enough for calfskin. And a monogram perhaps? I can show you some initials. And then maybe a border?'

'Yes, that sounds perfect.'

'Let me bring you the pattern book.' He turned away to a shelf where a number of well-used books were stacked and ran his finger along the spines.

She took the chance to tidy her hair under her hat, but he turned back too quickly and caught her doing it. She dropped her hands hurriedly, feeling foolish.

He smiled and put her book on the counter. 'You'll need the "G" and a small "d" and of course the "A".'

He'd remembered her name. Giulia d'Adamo. A regal name, she'd always thought it.

'Look,' he continued, 'this one has a nice elegant curve.' He leaned towards her to point out the letter 'G'.

Though he was dark, faint golden hairs on his arm were showing where his sleeve was rolled up. The sun must have caught his arms. Having him so close gave her a shivery sensation of anticipation. 'Yes, that one,' she said, 'and' – flipping back the page – 'this one.'

'A good choice, Signorina,' he said, his eyes hooking hers again. 'I can see how well they'd work together.'

She was warmed by his praise, even a little heated. How foolish, she thought, to be pleased at something so small. Mamma would have frowned at her for it. 'Will it cost a lot to do?' she asked.

'Ten scudi,' he said.

'Oh.' Disappointment sharpened her voice. 'I'm afraid I couldn't—'

'But as it's for you, and I shall enjoy making it, we'll make it six, shall we?'

The relief, and his conspiratorial expression, made her giddy. They smiled at each other as she took the coins from her purse and put them into his hand.

He gripped the ends of her fingers with his before she could withdraw them. 'I was wondering,' he said, 'I saw you sitting on the bench in the square last night.'

The ends of her fingers were frozen in mid-air. It seemed to stop her breath in her lungs. So he'd noticed her. She'd been watching them, the young men playing cards in the warm night air, but she hadn't dared approach them. She knew no card games. Mamma didn't believe in wasting time on such things.

He was still talking, still had hold of her fingers. 'So I wondered if you'd be there again tonight? Do you play cards? A few of us are going to meet at ten bells and play a game of—'

A draught behind her. He dropped her hand as if it burned.

Giulia turned. It was Claudia Lippini, the last person she wanted to see.

'A game? Oh do tell. I love games,' Claudia said in her husky voice. She came right up to the counter and looked down at the 'G' Giulia had chosen. 'Is this for you, Giulia?' She put her head to one side and wrinkled her nose. 'This one? Oh. It looks a little old-fashioned.' She turned the sheets until she reached her own initial. 'I'd have this, see.' She traced the letter 'C' with a long, languorous stroke. 'I think Fabio could do this one beautifully.' She looked up at him coyly and toyed with the laces on her chemise and the ends of her sun-bleached hair. Giulia noticed her neck was none too clean. She used to play with Claudia when they were children, and Claudia was three years younger, but it always felt to Giulia as if Claudia were several years older, and three times as wordly-wise.

Fabio turned to Claudia, like a plant to the sun.

Feeling suddenly plain and gawky, Giulia shrivelled. She dropped her gaze and saw her feet, encased in practical brown leather and the thin worsted of her stockings. Claudia's gown, on the other hand, was so full the hem brushed the ground.

Claudia gave Fabio a long, slow smile as she stroked her finger down the designs in the book. Fabio followed the movement as if in a trance. She, Giulia, no longer existed at all.

Should she leave? She hovered as Claudia told Fabio about the forthcoming feast day, the Memorial Feast to San Giovanni, and how she'd planned to steal a keg of wine and stay out late to join the festivities.

'Will you be in the square tonight, Fabio?' Claudia asked.

Fabio glanced at Giulia. 'Well, a few of us were going to meet up for a game of *primero*.' He looked down at the counter apologetically.

'I'll join you then, and perhaps bring a few more. The more the merrier, hey, Fabio? What time?'

Fabio's eyes shifted away from Giulia. 'We said ten bells.'

'I'll be there.' She picked up the books from under Fabio's hand and passed them to Giulia, who had no option but to take them. 'Are these yours?'

Her stare propelled Giulia to put them under her arm and hurry from the shop.

What a fool. She'd been like a marionette in front of him, all gangling limbs and stupid smile. Mamma had kept her so confined she didn't know how to talk to men like Fabio. It was all very well to read about alchemy and philosophy and humours, but she realised she had spent all her time with dead men. She had no sense of how to behave with a real-life man, especially one as well favoured as Fabio. How could she compete with someone like Claudia? Claudia's family were as poor as mice, so she had no dowry, but that didn't prevent her from giving herself airs and graces, and Claudia's outspoken manner had a way of eclipsing everyone else in the room.

And she'd been so flustered she'd forgotten to leave her books there to be covered. Fabio must think her addle-headed, to negotiate a price, give him her coins and then flee. She imagined he and Claudia would be laughing at her, and the pain was as sharp as toothache in her heart.

She was halfway down the street before she stopped, hesitated.

Was she to be so easily diverted? *Fool. Don't let Claudia rile you*, she thought. She wanted her books covered, and her custom was surely as good as anyone else's. Fabio had her money in his hand, so she'd have to brook his scorn and take them back. She shouldn't have been so intimidated by Claudia, and anyway perhaps Claudia would have gone.

She braced her shoulders and turned with a purposeful stride. If she was to be independent from Mamma, she'd need to be hard-minded. She pushed open the door and put both books firmly on the counter, ignoring Claudia who was still there, smirking.

'You'll need these,' she said. 'And I'll see you in the square at ten bells.'

Fabio's eyes widened, and he quickly suppressed a grin. Claudia's sour expression gave her a small stab of triumph. With her head up, Giulia stalked past her, giving her a brief nod, before emerging back into the sunshine.

Her elation lasted until she got back to the house and found Mamma was still at work and the meal was untouched. Damn her. She wouldn't go down again. But now she'd set herself on the road to making her own remedies. She got out the worn wooden bowl and crushed a filling for a ladies' pomander, blending ground cedar wood with cinnamon bark, cloves and jasmine flowers. When it was done, she went to the clavichord in the parlour. Music always had the power to soothe her, and today the poignancy of the notes eased her yearning heart.

Time passed and she became engrossed until the church bells from the nearby monastery rang for vespers. That time already, and still no sign of Mamma. A nervous flutter in the stomach at the thought of meeting Fabio. Perhaps Mamma was right. According to her, men were fickle and never to be trusted. She couldn't remember her father; he had died when she was a baby and nobody ever spoke of it. If they did, Mamma frowned and changed the subject, as if it were a great secret. But now she was grown, and a woman, and the time had come for her own secrets.

So she wouldn't tell Mamma that she was going to meet Fabio by the fountain in the square.

Giulia stroked a hand down the smooth red silk and smiled at the thought of the scolding she would have got from their servant, Maria, for wearing such finery in the kitchen. It was a gown she seldom wore – a vivid cherry red, trimmed with vines and pomegranates embroidered in gold-coloured thread. She'd had it for nigh on two years but had never been bold enough to wear it as it possibly contravened the sumptuary laws, being too bold and fancy for her status. Besides, Mamma's sniff of disapproval had taken the edge off her purchase and made her reluctant to parade it in front of her. Now she was to forge her own profession, she was determined to make her own choices. She'd have a stroll by the harbour too, before going to meet Fabio. She was too restless to stay indoors any longer.

Mamma still hadn't appeared, but she dare not go out unchaperoned without at least telling her where she was going. It was an old habit that was hard to break. She went downstairs to the still room, knocked on the door and waited.

When the door opened, she said, 'Mamma, I wanted to tell you I'm going out. I met Claudia Lippini and—'

'What are you doing wearing that gaudy thing?'

She tried to divert the question. 'Shall I lock up the front door? What is it you're making?'

'A remedy for black bile,' Mamma said, a glass jar full of tawny liquid in her hand. 'Where's your blue one? Where are you going dressed up like a night-walker?'

'Just the square, Mamma. With Claudia. It's cool in this silk, and it's been so hot lately.'

'That Lippini girl needs a firm hand. What are her parents thinking? Out all hours and unchaperoned. I'll be up soon, and then you can get changed and I'll come with you.'

'No, Mamma, I don't think—'

'I must finish measuring this first; one of the bishops at the cathedral suffers from melancholia and he'll pay well.' She put the flask down and lifted a piece of frankincense from the scales. 'Poor man, he wakes up every day thinking that he—'

A door banging upstairs. Clattering feet.

Mamma's friend and helper Francesca burst into the room. 'The Duke de Verdi,' she said, breathless. Her round pudgy face was rimed with sweat.

'The poor man. Gone already?' Mamma asked.

'No, worse. The Lady Valentina couldn't do it. He's still alive.'

What was this? Giulia sensed a sudden tension in the atmosphere, a hiatus like the silence before an earthquake.

A hiss of steam as Mamma shoved the hot frankincense into the flask. 'He lives? So what's all this fuss?' Then she paused, searched Francesca's face. 'Do they suspect?'

Francesca's eyes were dark with panic. 'We're lost. She has confessed everything to him. Confessed! Told him about the *cantarella*, how she's been feeding it to him day by day. I knew there was something slippery about her. Didn't I say she was not to be trusted?'

'Calm,' Mamma said. 'Go slow now. What exactly did she say to the duke?'

'Oh, she gave him a tale. That it is we who tried to poison him,' Francesca said, her hands grasping at the folds of her black widow's gown. 'Ha! She, who said she wished to see him writhe in agony for eternity for the pain he caused her. One more dose would have done it, yet she failed at the last moment. Too frightened to do it. The foolishness of it, that she should—'

'What did she say to you?' Mamma was stock still in the middle of the room, her face as grey as winter sky.

'She blames us, despite the fact she came to us and begged for it. She called me a sinner for supplying her with the poison and begged me to repent,' Francesca said. 'As if it were all our doing, not hers.'

'When?'

'Not a half hour ago, when I went to deliver the bottle. "Get out of Palermo," she said, as if it were as easy as that! To up sticks and go. And for why? Because she knows the duke will seek revenge and she doesn't want our deaths on her conscience.'

Giulia was struggling to keep up. 'What do you mean, deaths? What has she to do with us?' Giulia asked.

Mamma gestured to her. 'Giulia, go upstairs.'

No. Not this time. 'Are you saying you've poisoned someone?' The knowing was stuck in the back of her thoughts, but it was a knowing she didn't want to see.

Mamma had gone to tug Francesca by the sleeve. 'Did the duchess say she'd told him our names?'

'She told him everything. The whole of it. So now the duke's men will surely seek us out, and they are the best mercenaries in the whole of Sicily. The duchess has turned bedlam. You should see her; she falls to her knees like one possessed! Weeps and pulls at her neckerchief as if to tear it away from her throat.' Francesca's outburst stopped, as if a cork had been pulled. A pause, before the whisper came. 'What shall we do? She's already confessed to a priest, told him it was our idea, to be rid of him because he taxes us too much.'

'That much is true,' Giulia said.

'Be quiet, Giulia,' Francesca snapped. She turned to Mamma. 'The duchess begged the duke for forgiveness. Vowed she'll take holy orders, spend the rest of her days in a nunnery asking God's absolution, if he'll only spare her.'

'And will he?' Giulia asked. 'What did he say?'

'Nothing of course,' Francesca said. 'She's under house arrest whilst he decides what to do with her.'

'The wet-eared fool.' Mamma gave a derisive laugh. 'He will not forgive. What man would forgive a woman who tried to kill him? He'll see the truth and he'll finish her.'

'What do you mean?' Giulia asked. A shiver of foreboding. Mamma was pacing back and forth, her eyes flicking here and there.

'It means he will press our whereabouts from her.' Francesca turned angry eyes on Giulia. 'We must leave. Pack now and go. None of it is our doing, but we will be blamed none the less because we supply the means to do it.'

So that was it. A coil of fear wound itself into Giulia's stomach. No. She couldn't go now. She had to meet Fabio in the square at ten bells.

Francesca had begun to pull things off the shelves and load them into baskets.

'The duke won't be well enough to do anything yet,' Mamma said, but her voice wavered.

'He can speak, can't he?' Francesca said, her pale hands twining over each other. 'That's enough to sign our death warrant. He has troops, doesn't he?'

Mamma's face did not react, but that in itself meant it was serious. She came over and took hold of both of Giulia's arms. 'I'm sorry, my dove. I never meant this to happen.'

Giulia squirmed away. 'What's this about a death warrant? Tell me what's happening!'

'You know nothing, *cara*. Best to let it stay that way. But you will need to go to my sister Isabetta. She's in Naples. Stay there until I can come for you. Do you hear me?' The urgency of her voice plucked at Giulia's heart.

'No. I'm not leaving Palermo. Not today, please not today.'

'You must.' Mamma swept up a lead point, scribbled an address in her kitchen book and tore out the page.

'You're not sending her to Isabetta?' Francesca stopped loading jars into a basket and stared.

'There's nowhere else. And it's away from here, out of the duke's control.'

Francesca shook her head as if Mamma was a fool, and ran up the stairs.

'What time's the sailing to Rome?' Mamma shouted after her.

'Half after seven,' came the reply.

'And Naples?'

'Don't know, seven bells I think.'

Giulia looked at the address blankly. She had never met her aunt. Though letters from her to Mamma often arrived, she knew them by their florid handwriting and Mamma's grimaces and air of disapproval when she opened them. She, Giulia, was never allowed to read them.

Mamma had fetched a bag of scudi and now pressed it into her hand. 'I'll come with you to the harbour to take ship, then we must go separately. The sailing to Naples is at dusk. Seven bells.'

She had never been on a ship. 'But what will I tell—?'

Her words were crushed to air as Mamma clasped her in a tight embrace. Mamma's neck smelled of the metal minerals she used – of quicksilver and antimony. 'If anyone asks, you are not my daughter, not Giulia d'Adamo.'

'It makes no sense. Why can't I come to Rome with you?'

'Listen. There's no time to explain. But this is important, more important than anything else. You must go to Isabetta. Tell no-one where you have gone, not even your friend Claudia. Not even that Fabio you've been swooning over these last weeks.'

How did she know?

'And this you must remember – whatever happens, whatever I've done, whatever may come of this – I love you. More than my life, I love you.' She touched a finger to Giulia's cheek, her expression full of sorrow. 'I've failed you, and I never meant to, I only meant to protect you from this, and now there's no time to explain.'

Giulia scrambled away. 'What's to explain? It's clear enough you were helping someone to die. For money. Every week when you went to mass, when you went to confession, you had these deaths on your hands… it's evil. Despicable. How could you?'

'It was for you, and other young women like you, I did it. Those that were trapped… oh, there's no time to make you understand, things are not always as black and white as they seem.'

'Taking a life is a sin, the Holy Mother Church tells us that.' Her words came out thick and clotted. 'How can you say it is not?'

A hammering on the back door to the chamber, the one that led to the back alley. Mamma whipped round, startled. 'Just don't think ill of me,' Mamma said, caught between her and the door, her eyes full of entreaty. 'If you remember only one thing, it is this. Be kind.'

More knocking.

'Don't answer it.' Giulia's anger was gone in an instant, and fear settled in her stomach like a stone.

'Who is it?' Mamma called.

'Francesca,' the voice replied. 'The mules are saddled. We must go now. If I know the duke, he will send men as soon as he can rouse them.'

Mamma unlocked the back door with a rattle of bolts and creaked it open. The door that was always locked.

'Quick!' Francesca said. 'Load up. Try to look casual, as if we're going to market.'

Mamma grasped Giulia's upper arm in a tight grip. 'Listen. I don't care what you think of me, but heed me well. My name will bring you only misfortune now. That's why you must take another name. It will keep you safe. And you must leave here, never come back. Swear it. Swear you'll take another name.'

The reality, that they were really going to leave, that Mamma was going somewhere without her, hit her like a punch. 'I don't want another name,' Giulia said. 'I want to come with you.'

'No. You don't know me,' Mamma said. 'D'you understand? You must let Isabetta mother you from now on, that's if you need mothering. I've done all I can, you're a fine young woman now, good and clever, and you must stand on your own two feet.'

But she didn't know anything about her aunt. She grasped at straws. 'But Mamma, what about Maria?' The servant. Tomorrow she would come back to an empty house.

'There's nothing to be done,' Mamma said, as she gathered up boxes of metals and minerals. 'She will find us gone and draw her own conclusions. It won't be long before she hears a garbled version of the truth anyway. This town's full of malice and gossip.'

It was all happening too quickly. Helplessly, she stood by as Mamma swept up the box of expensive Murano glass perfume bottles and wordlessly thrust them into her hands. Clutching the clinking box, she stumbled into the reddening light, so dazzling it brought the unshed tears from her eyes. She wedged the box hastily into the pannier, scrubbed at her face with a sleeve, then ran back in for the embroidered tablecloth. She must stuff the space in the basket, lest the bottles got broken. Mamma's precious bottles. The thought brought a choke to her throat.

Mamma heaved another cloth-wrapped package into Giulia's hands. Judging by the drag of it, probably a lump of lead. Costly, and vital to Mamma's profession. Whatever profession that was. An uneasy darkness hung around it now.

The mule shifted as she dropped the heavy weight into the pannier. Back through the open door into the flickering light of the room, where the last hanging straggles of herbs made shadows on the wall. In those few moments, Mamma had been busy, and more lidded panniers already stood open on the baked-earth. Francesca had dragged a motley collection of gowns from the clothes press upstairs. Nightclothes and stiff bodices and random skirts and sleeves with the laces dangling, all squashed together in an unruly heap. She threw them all into the pannier. The draught made the hanging herbs shudder and dance.

'Take this,' Francesca said, pointing at the pannier. 'Hurry.'

Giulia slammed the lid shut and dragged it across the floor, her thin arms straining.

More followed. Mamma was throwing things into bags now. A rattling box of stone jars, the satchel of herbal tracts, the Bible, heavy as a millstone, with all the jewellery they possessed thrown in with it. This fact alone made her jittery. Mamma was always so methodical and careful.

Hands fumbling, Giulia tied the rest of their possessions onto the mules outside the door. 'What about the clavichord? Our music?' As she tried to fetch more, to save the things she thought were precious, Francesca glanced up the road.

'No more time,' she said. 'Men are coming. *Condottieri.*'

Giulia's stomach swooped. A group of mercenaries in their black leather jerkins over red and yellow were just turning into the street. Powerfully built men, armed with swords and their leather belts stuck with daggers. Francesca gave a cry and leapt on the mule from the mounting block. Frantic to get moving, Giulia pulled on the leading rein to drag the cavalcade forward.

'Wait!' Mamma cried.

What now? Mamma was dismounting again in a flurry of camphor and heavy skirts.

'Mamma, no!' Giulia shouted.

'Santa Olivia,' Mamma said, 'she will protect you.' She dived into the dark doorway, to return a few breathless moments later clutching the wooden statue that always stood on the shelf above the distilling table. Mamma went nowhere without the protection of Santa Olivia, the patron saint of the poor in Palermo, and friend to the beasts of the field.

'Here, take her,' Mamma cried, thrusting the statuette into her grasp. 'And take this.' She wrenched open the top of Giulia's chemise and thrust a heavy book down it next to her stays. The edge scraped on her bare skin, but there was no time to object. 'Remember me with love. That's all I ask,' Mamma said, taking hold of her hand to squeeze it.

Men's voices. Mamma's hand slid away; the air was suddenly cool.

'There! Stop them.' The sound of leather soles on cobbles.

'Giulia! Get up,' shouted Francesca, urging her to mount.

But Giulia, hindered by the statue, was helping Mamma onto the mule. A quick glance behind. Her throat closed tight. They were coming. With her free hand she tried to drag the mule forward.

The mule chose the moment to be stubborn.

'You there. Halt!'

She turned to see a tall, powerfully built man, his shoulders bunched around his neck, his bent nose and misshapen ear signifying more than one fight. His companions strode after, still a few paces behind.

'Halt I say!'

The order fired her into motion. 'Gah!' she shouted, waving the wooden figure to scare the mules into action. 'Get on!'

The mules shot forward in a clatter of hooves. Giulia broke into a run after them, behind her the sound of men's feet. The tail of the last pack-mule whisked around the corner. She put on a spurt but a gloved hand grabbed her by the shoulder and she was brought up short.

The man's arm was around her neck now, dragging her back. A smell of leather and sweat.

'Stay still, vixen,' he said.

His other hand was at her waist. She dropped the statue

where she stood and tried to prise his arm away. Other men's footsteps were approaching. It was now or never.

She turned suddenly and shoved the point of her elbow into the soft part of his belly. His momentary surprise was all the time she needed. She squirmed from under his arm and drew back her fist to strike him hard between the legs.

For an instant she was looking into a shocked face, then he crumpled. She heard his groan and the metallic sound of his sword hitting the stone cobbles, but she didn't wait to see what became of him. She grabbed Santa Olivia and ran, her skirts and petticoats dragging on her legs, making each stride like swimming upstream.

Up past the bakery and the back of the little church of San Francisco. Seeing two well-dressed, masked women tottering towards her on chopines, with their maids behind, she slipped past them, squeezed sideways into a narrow dark alley by the church, and watched the men pound past.

Breathless, she creaked open the heavy wooden door, crept into the cool dark of the nave and squashed herself into the confessional box. 'Holy Mary, Mother of God, pray for us sinners,' she whispered over and over.

She wrapped her skirts around her, tried to catch her breath. She cursed her pride; this gown was the worst possible colour for hiding. She would have to wait here until dark.

Should she go after Mamma and Francesca? Or should she wait for Fabio at the square?

Neither seemed safe. In less than an hour she had learnt three things: one was that her mother was somehow responsible for the attempted murder of a duke. And the second was that he would want revenge, and finally that the house she'd known all her life could no longer be her home. She daren't go back. What if the men came for her there?

Death warrant, Francesca had said. The words were like nails, snagging all her thoughts. Now she could make sense of it all, the hidden boxes of venom arriving at night, the women appearing furtively at the door. She'd always known there was some darkness welded to the light of what her mother did, but she had chosen not to embrace it, and her mother knew it. That was why she hadn't taught her the skills.

She thought there'd be time to learn it all, but now time was cheating them both. She unfolded the piece of paper from her pocket with Aunt Isabetta's address. Aunt Isabetta. A woman her mother never spoke of unless it was with a curl of the lip. Her mother would surely come for her there to explain. If any of it could be explained.

CHAPTER 2

GIULIA HELD tight to Santa Olivia, knowing Mamma would want the statue back the next time she saw her. The feel of the smooth olive wood was comforting beneath her fingers. How strange, she had never paid the statue much attention before, but the saint was holding a feather in her hand, beautifully carved and lifelike, and in the other an olive branch, like the one the dove brought back to the ark.

When her breath quietened, and her heart stopped battering against her ribs, she stood Santa Olivia on a pew and looked for something to write with. She must get word to Fabio. The book was digging into her chest, so she drew it out, recognising it straight away, even though there was no title. She scanned the first few pages. Recipes, formulae, drawings of minerals, her favourite of the vipers curled into a spiral, and written instructions all in Mamma's tight hand – her mother's precious 'chymist's book'. But no spare paper – every leaf was filled with Mamma's cramped notes.

She found a ragged quill and a stoppered ink bottle near the book for births and deaths. By the sparseness of the entries, you'd think nobody had been born or died for a long time in this parish, and this church seemed forgotten, overshadowed by its larger neighbours.

No-one would know if she tore out a page from the back to write a message.

She scratched a note quickly, still listening for the door, half her attention on the noises from the street outside. But the small church was silent and expectant, the pews dusty and the air redolent of frankincense and old hassocks. A single votive candle in a red glass flickered before the Virgin, who stared down at her with doleful eyes. Under its light, she wrote:

Fabio, I cannot meet you tonight. Something has happened and I have to leave Palermo. I am going to family in another city. I hope you will pardon me for leaving without explaining. It is not an easy story to tell. But be assured you are in my thoughts and...

What? Should she tell him how he made her feel? She could not. She was too shy to confess how he made her heart flutter.

...and if you wish you can write to me at this address.

She scribbled Aunt Isabetta's address on the paper but then had second thoughts. Could she trust him? She dare not. Her mother had insisted she tell no-one, not even Fabio, though she longed to. She ripped off the bottom of the page and fed the edge to the candle flame under the Virgin. It shrivelled so fast she dropped the last corner as the heat bit into her fingers.

Would Fabio miss her? Or would her foxy friend Claudia toss her hair at him and give him her lazy smile?

The note was unfinished but there was nothing else she dared say. She signed her name with a flourish and the drawing of a sprinkle of stars.

Maybe he might remember her then.

With a lump in her throat, she folded it in half and half again. When the sun crept a little lower across the church windows she ventured outside, looking this way and that, fearing armed men might be lying in wait. People were beginning to come out on the streets for the evening stroll, and the buildings planted deep shadows in the alleyways as, clutching Santa Olivia, she hurried in the direction of the harbour.

At the end of La Ruga Nova, she turned right into the small square where Fabio's parents ran their leatherworking shop. Even outside, the musky smell of leather was unmistakeable. There was a note pinned to the shop door, 'Back soon.' She sighed in frustration. His father often did this; his opening hours had always been unreliable.

She waited a few more minutes, but no-one appeared to open for the evening's trade, and she was beginning to feel conspicuous. She dived around the side of the shop to their house and pushed the note under the door. It was the best she could do. Perhaps it would prevent Fabio waiting in the square like a fool. She pushed away the thought that he might decide to bestow his favours on Claudia instead.

As she stood to go, she saw a dark-clad mercenary scanning the crowd in the square. It looked like the big man she had tussled with outside her house. The older man with the torn ear. Her heart seemed to flip in her chest. She shrank back against the doorway. It could be him, or it could be merely a man waiting for a friend.

She didn't care to find out. Instead she turned back into the shadows and set off at a brisk pace towards the harbour. Would Mamma be there waiting? She hoped so, for she had no luggage at all, only this statue of Santa Olivia, a purse of scudi, and the book tucked under her arm. She clasped the book tight, though it was surely as dangerous and incriminating as carrying a barrel of gunpowder. But it was Mamma's pride and joy. That and Santa Olivia. The dark and the light.

Coming out of the narrow streets into the dazzling late afternoon sun, she skirted the open space of Piazza della Marine, keeping out of the remaining sunlight which lit up her gown into a scarlet flame. She pushed the book down her bodice again so she could lift her hem clear of her shoes with one hand, and ran alongside Il Palazzo della Drana. The blue-black shadow of its tower stretched like a long finger, out towards where hundreds of fishing boats and small craft had gathered. They bobbed in the small buttonhole-shaped harbour, ready to row travellers out to the bigger ships, or to fish on the evening tide. Across the water, galleons and traders waited by the yellow stone fortress at the harbour mouth.

Past the warehouses to the Pedigrute Gate, her head never still as she searched for Mamma's familiar face. No sign of her. Hollow now, she felt like she did as a small child who'd got lost, an edge of panic sharp in her throat.

Where could Mamma and Francesca have gone? She twisted her head searching for them. The harbour bristled with masts and pennants, and red-capped men on the quayside tallying and taking money.

'How much to get to Naples?' she asked one of them.

'Fifteen scudi,' he said. 'You travel alone?'

'No,' she said, 'with friends.' The moment she said it, she felt even more alone.

She thanked him but didn't buy a ticket. She hovered by the quay, still hoping Mamma would materialise beside her, her face ruddy and smiling, her short, stout figure putting a comforting arm on hers to show her which way to go.

She found out from a stevedore that the ship to Naples would leave in less than an hour, and she must take one of the small boats if she was to make the evening sailing. She was still poised uncertainly by the wharf, unable to decide, when a disturbance in the crowd caught her attention. A group of about twenty mercenaries was approaching from the Piazza del Castello. One of them gesticulated and shouted orders and they began to fan out around the curve of the harbour. She stared just long enough to know that the big man giving orders was the same man again, the one she had grappled with in the alley.

Weakness washed over her; she thought she might faint. The men were closing in like a noose around the harbour. They'd be looking for a girl in a red dress. With Santa Olivia under her arm, she opened her purse and bought passage.

Hurry, please hurry, she thought as she climbed into the tender and sat down next to three nuns in their Benedictine habits. Other passengers boarded too, bringing leather cases, wicker trunks and flagons of oil and wine.

She glanced up to see a mercenary scanning the boats. Instinctively, she crouched down between the benches to hide. Her breath came fast, and she expected at any moment for the order to come to take her from the boat.

'Please, Santa Olivia,' she said, whispering a prayer.

Next to her the nun unfolded her woollen cloak and spread it over Giulia's shoulders. The other nun on the other side did the same. Giulia found she was enveloped in the heavy weight of their mantles. The boat tipped and rolled as it was rowed away from its moorings. After a few more breathless moments where Giulia could see or hear nothing, there was a tap on her shoulder.

'It is safe now,' a soft voice said.

She emerged to find that they were far away from the shore, the people on the quay like tiny dolls.

'Thank you,' she said, tears starting in her eyes. 'That was so kind.' She had always ignored nuns before. Thought of them as old crows.

'We saw you were in trouble,' the nun said. 'And that you

prayed to Santa Olivia. Better to act first and ask questions later, I always say.'

CHAPTER 3

THE NUNS WERE on their way to the Feast of the Sacred Heart in the Vatican in Rome, by boat to Naples, then carriage. Sister Simona, a plain-faced woman with expressive bushy eyebrows, seemed to be in charge, even though she was the youngest, and Giulia gave her a tale that her mother was ill with an infection and had sent her away to her aunt's for her health.

'With no luggage except a statue and a book?' asked Sister Marthe, an elderly woman whose habit looked far too big for her, as if she had shrunk inside it.

Sister Simona cast Sister Marthe a warning look. 'It is none of our business. Leave the girl alone.'

'Trouble with a man again, I suppose,' Sister Teresa whispered to Sister Marthe with pursed lips of disapproval. Giulia felt guilty telling lies to these women, who had helped her for no other reason than kindness.

With their company she was able to sleep, despite the night-chill and the seasickness that plagued her on the long journey. She clutched her stomach on the first night, glad she had not eaten the evening before, and fell into a fretful doze, wondering where Mamma and Francesca were, and what she could possibly tell this aunt she had never met.

Scandalised that she was travelling unchaperoned, the nuns guarded her like nesting birds guarding a chick, the whole of the next day at sea. Sister Marthe gave her a straw bag to carry her only possessions, and the youngest, the mannish Sister Simona, made them all observe prayers at the proper hours. Sister Simona was curious about how Giulia might be received where she was going. She said she knew Naples well and demanded to look at the address.

'I know where that street is,' she said, insistent that when they eventually arrived, they would guide her right to the house.

The ship berthed in Naples early after the second night at sea, so when they arrived it was just after dawn, the sun still a pinkish blur hanging low in an egg-blue sky. Giulia was awed by Mount Vesuvius, which was almost purple in this light. It stood motionless and benign, as if no fiery breath could spurt from its jaws, even though it had erupted less than eighteen months ago, raining torment on everything below. Today, Naples was bustling with traders, despite the fact the whole city could be buried tomorrow under red-hot lava if the fire god willed it.

Giulia drank it all in, her head turning from side to side so as not to miss any detail. Cats strolled from the alleys to stretch out on the warm flagstones, and horses and carts trundled lazily by with workers on their way to the wheatfields.

Sister Simona marched them through the narrow streets with their tall shuttered houses, with a 'Keep up. Keep up!' to her gaggle of followers. Sister Teresa and Sister Marthe were painfully slow walkers. 'It's near *Il Mercato*,' Sister Simona said after a quarter hour of walking, her cheeks flushed with exertion. 'An area of wealthy merchants. There are many beautiful *palazzi* close to the market. Your aunt must be a wealthy woman.'

'I don't know,' Giulia said. 'I've never met her.'

Sister Simona glanced at her two companions and frowned. 'Then we will come and meet this aunt of yours,' she said.

After a little more walking, and pleas from Sister Teresa of 'Please, slow down!' they came to a stop outside a long avenue of houses fronting a square, where traders were already beginning to set up for market.

'Is this the one?' Giulia asked, surprised. They were standing before a lofty white stone villa, with high arched windows and a balcony with an ornate 'goose-breast' balustrade. A sign in curvaceous script read 'Villa Bianca'.

'Imp... imposing.' Sister Marthe was so breathless it was the only word she could manage.

There were two stone steps up to a vast double door, with a cartouche above carved with twining leaves, and urns of overblown flowers and fruit. It seemed so strange to arrive anywhere without Mamma. Giulia was intensely aware of her lack of proper luggage, that no-one had dressed her hair, and that despite her rich gown, now somewhat crumpled, she was to all intents a beggar on the doorstep. It was intimidating. She took a breath, took hold of the heavy brass ring and knocked on the door.

No answer. The house remained shuttered. Sister Simona pushed past her to knock again, harder, but when there was still no answer, she tried the door. It was open. 'Come along.'

The nuns escorted Giulia inside into a dark hallway, with marble underfoot and gilded panelling. It was shuttered, but a heavy scent of perfume, like the pungent scent of lilies, hung in the air. Giulia breathed it in. So different from the sharp smell of physic at home.

'Excuse me,' called Sister Simona into the echoing hall. 'Is anyone there?'

'*Buongiorno?*' Giulia called, louder.

Suddenly they were surrounded. Servants, obviously come straight from their beds, appeared bearing candles and lanterns.

'What do you want?' A tight-faced serving woman wearing a plain cambric nightshift, her hair in a long braid under a cap, stood barring their way, her hand curled around a candle. She was obviously the housekeeper in charge.

'Beg pardon, but we are seeking Isabetta Boveri,' Giulia said, smiling hopefully. 'She's my aunt.'

The servants looked at her askance. 'Too early. She sees no-one before noon,' the housekeeper said.

'Then we'll wait.' Sister Marthe, glad of the excuse, plumped down on the only chair in the hall.

'All of you?' The housekeeper looked down her nose at the nuns.

Giulia turned to Sister Simona. 'There's really no need for you to wait. You've been more than kind.'

At that moment a door clicked open upstairs, and a woman's imperious voice called out. 'Can't a woman get any sleep? What's all that noise? Alessa! What in the devil's going on?'

'Your niece, mistress. She's here in the hall.'

'Niece?' the voice said. 'Don't talk nonsense. I have no niece. My family disowned me, twenty-five years since, the lousy bunch of no-goods.'

A stab of alarm. Would she be turned away? The nuns looked to each other, frowning.

A moment later a woman rushed down the stairs in a flurry of yellow silk, causing the candles to waver in the draught. Sister Simona gaped and the other nuns took a step back.

'Where is this niece?' The woman, a taller, thinner version of her mother, looked from Giulia to the sisters. 'And who on earth thought it a clever idea to admit these nuns?'

'Pardon us,' Sister Simona said. She stepped forward calmly, her shoulders braced. Anyone else would have wilted under the flashing eyes of the new arrival. 'Are you Signora Boveri?'

'Of course I'm Isabetta Boveri. How dare you wake me at this hour?'

'My apologies for the intrusion,' Sister Simona said. 'We are leaving as soon as we make sure Giulia is safe. Her mother left her to travel alone.'

'So like Theofania,' Aunt Isabetta said. 'No consideration for anyone else.'

Giulia stepped forward. 'I'm Theofania's daughter, Giulia. I'm glad to meet you. I've heard a lot about you.' A lie, but she was anxious to make a good impression.

Aunt Isabetta's face froze. She looked her up and down, and her voice came out in a whisper. 'But that's impossible. You can't be Giulia. Giulia's a child.'

'I'm twenty-three.'

'Let me look at you.' Her aunt stared at her face as if she might see through it. 'Yes, yes, you have our look,' she said, as if to reassure herself. 'The widow's peak in the hair, the pointed chin.'

'Aunt Isabetta, I'm sorry we could not give you more notice of my arrival in Naples, but Mamma said you'd be glad to give me a place to stay.'

'She sent you *here*?' She shook her head. Then she turned and paced, a frown on her face. 'But she never wanted us to meet, she said… oh, never mind what she said.'

She was slimmer than Mamma, and her face was painted in the style of a woman much younger, though the wrinkles round her eyes showed her age to be past forty. Her opulent dressing-robe was made up of swathes of yellow-dyed silk, the sleeves trimmed with gold point, and the neck tied in an elaborate bow. Beneath, she caught a glimpse of a lawn nightgown, and a garter but no stocking. Giulia stared. She was wearing jewellery to bed, something Mamma would never have permitted.

'Why?' Isabetta asked. 'Why would she send you to me after all this time?'

Giulia hesitated. She couldn't speak of the reason before the nuns and these servants.

Aunt Isabetta saw the difficulty and clapped her hands. 'Go, all of you! Back to bed. Alessa, fetch me if the viceroy's nephew wakes. You'll hear him wake when it goes quiet. He snores like a pig.' The servants melted away. She turned her attention to the nuns, who hovered silent and wide-eyed. 'I thank you for your courtesy in bringing her here. She will be perfectly safe with me, you have my word.' She held the door open and gestured for them to leave.

Sister Simona came over and took Giulia's hand firmly between her own, which were rough and calloused. 'If you ever need spiritual advice,' she said, emphasising the last two words, 'you may write to us at the Convent of Maria Assumpta in Rome.' She placed cool fingertips on Giulia's brow and murmured a blessing.

'Sister Simona, I can't thank you enough—'

'It's nothing. God bless you and keep you.'

She couldn't resist hugging each one in turn. Sister Marthe was quite dewy-eyed, and Sister Teresa echoed 'God bless you,' and the women left, leaving Giulia alone in the hall.

'Come, Giulia, follow me. And don't call me Aunt Isabetta. You may call me plain Isabetta in private, but Signora Boveri before my clients. Understand?'

An answer didn't seem to be required, and Isabetta led her upstairs and threw open lacquered doors into a large chamber furnished with curved plaster plaques and seats upholstered in cushioned tapestry. The ceiling was painted with cherubs flying in a vivid cerulean sky. Never had she seen anything so grand. The arched windows faced the morning sun, which splashed across the floor and cast shimmering eyes of light from the many chandeliers and wall sconces.

'Oh, what a beautiful room,' she said, astonished.

'It is where we receive our guests,' Isabetta said, 'though not usually, it has to be said, so early.'

She bade Giulia sit and pulled another chair up close, and leant forward.

Giulia flinched under her penetrating stare. 'I'm sorry for my unexpected arrival.'

Isabetta's décolletage was powdered white, and a heavy amethyst pendant glittered against her pale skin. 'So what's this all about? Where's my sister?'

'I don't know. They fled, but I don't know where.' She quashed the rising panic in her chest and raised her chin. 'But she'll come back for me; that I know.'

'Will she now? Why? Where's she gone?' There was a bitter tone to the words that Giulia didn't understand.

'There was trouble. Something about a woman trying to kill her husband. And Mamma was involved somehow.'

'The fool. I told her not to meddle in other people's affairs. But would she listen? No. She's been doing it for years. Inheritance powders again, I suppose.'

'I don't know. I don't understand. There were some things I wasn't allowed to see.'

'Theofania has a neat way of dealing with unwanted husbands. Her own husband, Francis, for example, though she'll deny it if you ask. Those potions she makes, well, some heal, but some – well they are designed so you will never see this life again. Such poisons we call "inheritance powders". Women use them if they want to inherit earlier than nature intends.'

Though she had suspected as much, the bald truth still shocked Giulia to silence.

Isabetta stood again. 'The authorities caught up with her, did they?' Giulia didn't need to say anything before Isabetta nodded. 'I knew they would. Who was the man?'

'The Duke de Verdi. One of the most powerful warrior lords of Palermo. He sent his men after us, we tried to run…' She broke off to gather herself. Her hands were trembling. How embarrassing. She twined them in her lap to still them. 'Mamma and Francesca took the mules. I don't know where they were going. She made me promise to come to Naples.'

'This duke, he doesn't know you are here?'

'No. Mamma said I'd be safe with you.'

'Then she's more of a fool than I thought. But let's look at you then. I'm sorry to say, you can't stay unless you earn your keep. I have my reputation to think of, and quite apart from the expense, it would look too strange for me to house a girl out of charity. Stand up.'

Giulia did as she asked.

'Walk.'

It felt strange to pace up and down, but Isabetta's commanding presence made her want to obey. Giulia pulled herself up tall and tried to walk like royalty.

When she stopped there was a strange expression on Isabetta's face. 'You look as I did at your age,' she whispered. She gestured for her to sit again. 'But I suppose you have no experience. That gown is a good colour on you, but far too provincial. Tomorrow we will ask my dressmaker to make you more suitable attire. You have money?'

Giulia held out the purse, now heavily depleted after paying for her passage across the sea.

Isabetta nodded. 'Good. But once you start earning you will rent a room from me, and pay monthly, like the others.'

The others? She saw Giulia's puzzled look.

'The other courtesans.'

CHAPTER 4

PALERMO, SICILY

FABIO WAITED for Giulia at the square for more than an hour. The whole time Claudia kept up a conversation, whilst all he wanted to do was look out for Giulia. Giulia of the expressive eyes. She fascinated him, how she was so awkward in her plain black dress, like a servant, though he knew the family had wealth enough by the size of their house. He liked the way she held her head to one side, and the way her shiny hair was plaited into loops about her ears. And it amused him the way she always talked like she'd swallowed the Bible, and flushed red when he bade her good day.

He glanced up the street as the bells struck the half hour after ten. The other men would laugh at him if they knew he was waiting here for her, but he liked her. There was something both innocent and knowing about her.

Claudia had grown bored with his taciturn responses, and his eyes that kept straying to the alley, so she had wandered over to where the group of young men were gathered under the lime trees sharing a flagon of wine. Fabio didn't join her; his eyes were watching the narrow entrance to the square. The evening was sultry, and he took off his neckerchief and flapped it before him to make some breeze.

The bells pealed eleven. She wasn't coming. The little cat. He could scarce believe it. It wasn't as if she had dozens of admirers, after all. And he, well the girls never said no to him. It was painful, the tight cramping feeling in his chest. Curse her. He told himself he didn't care, but unwilling to join in with the laughter under the trees, he reluctantly headed home. When he got home, his foot brushed against a crumpled piece of paper. He stooped to pick it up and read it. It must have been pushed under the door. He hadn't seen it before because he'd come straight from work, out of the shop and not the house.

Giulia's signature. So she hadn't forgotten after all. He hurried through the words.

She'd gone? He read it again, frowning with confusion, rubbing his hand through his curly hair. What was suddenly so urgent that it could have taken her away from Palermo?

He could do nothing that night except puzzle over it, but the next morning he got up early and made his way through the dusty streets to Giulia's house. The shutters were all closed. He vaulted over the wall behind and had a good look round. There was no sign of anyone. He hammered at the back door but no servant came.

He was creeping back around the side when he bumped into Maria Fernando, Giulia's daily maid, dressed for work, her hair squashed under her cap and an apron slung round her waist.

'Fabio!' she said. 'Do you know where they are? I can't get an answer.'

'They've gone away. I had a message from Giulia. It seems like they were in a hurry to leave.'

'Just like that? They left?'

'Seems so. Look at this.' A crate of broken jars lay by the gate.

'It's not like her,' Maria said, stooping to look. 'Something's wrong. Theofania, she is the tidiest person I have ever met. Everything has to be in its place. She would never allow broken pots to be left there, where any horse could tread on them.'

'They didn't say anything to you about any plans? Didn't say they were planning to travel?'

'No. Everything the same as always before my day off.' She sighed. 'I scrub floors, wash bottles and cook and buy vegetables. But what shall I do? I've no employment now. I can't believe Theofania would do that to me. She knows I rely on the money.'

'It's bad not to give notice. If you hear anything more, will you let me know?'

Maria shook her head in disgust. 'If you hear of any maid position going, will you let *me* know?' She ripped off her cap, tossed her hair back, and raised her hand in farewell. Then she strode away, leaving Fabio staring after her.

Fabio contemplated the morning's events as he dampened a leather belt in the barrel and took up the metal stamping tool. He drew the belt across the bench and hammered the stamp in with a steady tap, so it bit into the leather. *Clink, clink.* The noise was regular and soothing. It was a good thing he was able to do this without thinking, for his thoughts were all with the strange disappearance of Giulia's family.

Clink. He paused over his work. A mystery, and he was still niggling with it, the way a sore tooth wouldn't leave you be.

To ease his frustration he hammered harder, so he didn't hear the shop door when it finally opened. The first he knew of a customer was when a pair of slim white hands appeared before him on the counter.

He startled and looked up. 'Claudia.' He suppressed his irritation. 'Keep your hands off the table, or I might hit them with the hammer.'

She smiled. 'You wouldn't. You're far too careful.' She moved around the shop, picking up first one object and then another. He watched her move, one hand to her hip, as she swayed so her skirts swung over her bare ankles. She plucked a man's wide-brimmed leather hat from the shelf near the door and put it on at an angle over one eye. 'How does it suit?' she said, pouting and striking a pose.

'It's a man's hat,' he said.

'I know that,' she said sulkily, putting it back.

Obviously, she'd been expecting a compliment. He'd always been slow to the ways of women.

She leaned onto the counter so that her chest was far too close for comfort, and he moved back.

'I know why Giulia didn't meet you at the square last night,' she said, a sly glance from under her lashes.

'So do I. She left me a note.'

'Oh.' She pouted. 'What did it say?'

'That she's gone out of Palermo for a while. To family in another town.'

'I'm not surprised, given that they arrested her mother.' She smiled, as if it were good news.

Now his curiosity was aroused. He came out from behind the bench. 'What for?'

'Don't know. But there's rumours about her potions. They're saying it's no coincidence the Duke de Verdi was ill.' She paused as he tried to take in her words. She raised her eyebrows and sauntered away.

'Gossip, that's all. Set no store by it.'

'It's true, cross my heart.'

'Who says?'

'The duke's been ailing with night sweats and vomiting. He nearly died. But now they're saying its poison. Or witchcraft. Next thing, Giulia's mother's arrested, with her accomplice, Francesca, the woman they call La Sarda, the Turk. So what would you think?'

'That's the most foolish story I've ever heard.'

'It's true. Every word. Ask anyone. It's all over the city by now.

Poor Giulia. Imagine living with a poisoner. I wouldn't feel safe in that house, oh no.' She gave a dramatic shudder.

'Even if it were true, which it isn't, Giulia wouldn't have known anything.'

Claudia came nearer, fixed him with innocent eyes, put a hand on his arm. 'How can you be so sure? She lived in the same house, surely she heard their secrets.' She tossed her hair. 'Everyone's saying you had a narrow escape.'

He shook her off. 'What do you mean? Who's saying things about me?'

'People had tied your names together and there was talk of a betrothal. Your father was always trying to creep to that witch, thought he'd get his hands on their big house. But she didn't want a leatherworker's son and always turned him down.'

'Turned me down?' He knew nothing about this. His father had been meddling behind his back.

She came close again, whispered, 'You would never know then, if she had put some venom into your food, something invisible that would weaken you day by—'

'Don't be foolish. Giulia would never do anything like that.'

'Ah, but that's what they said about her mother, and now look. I wish there was something we could do but…' She let her words trail away. 'They say she'll be executed if they find her guilty.'

Fabio was too shocked to reply. It didn't seem real. Claudia had never liked Giulia, he knew that. They were always like two cats stalking around each other, even though they pretended to be best friends. He'd never understood why.

'Anyway, I know one thing,' Claudia said. 'Giulia's gone, and if I were her, I'd never come back. Let's forget about them. A few of us are sneaking out and going down to the sea to bathe tonight, once it's dark. Coming?'

He hesitated. But he was curious. His father wouldn't permit him; he expected his son to behave like a good Catholic boy and never look at any woman unless she was swathed head to foot in mantles and hoops that hid her shape. Despite the fact his father's eyes strayed all the time.

Claudia's lack of respect for her parents and her brazenness were an enigma that held both an attraction and a revulsion for him. 'Who's going?'

'Cecilia, Mario, Juno... all of us.'

'When?' he asked. He didn't like the idea he'd be missing out if he didn't go.

'I'll wait for you at the old olive tree by the harbour gate. Be there when you hear the bells chime for midnight.'

'All right,' he said.

She smiled and reached out a hand to trail it down his arm. 'Bring wine,' she said.

CHAPTER 5

THE DUKE DE VERDI'S PALAZZO, PALERMO

Antonio, the Duke de Verdi, levered himself up from the pillows. His arms were as fragile as straw and the push as feeble. He hated this, scrabbling for purchase on a pile of bolsters like an old man. He had been the strongest of all the men he knew, even the mercenaries, and this unlooked-for infirmity filled him with pent-up rage. The fact his body was too frail to vent it exhausted him.

He was not too weak to give orders though. His men had caught up with those witches, Theofania d'Adamo and Francesca La Sarda, as they headed for the port, and they were now incarcerated in the city gaol. There was a daughter too, who'd been a part of this vile travesty, but she had slipped their net. Not for long though.

'Lucio!' he yelled. His voice was cracked and hoarse, not the commanding voice he once had. *She* had brought him to this. That whimpering dishcloth of a wife. 'Lucio!'

The manservant came running from his position behind the door.

Antonio dragged himself upright against the bedhead to catch his breath, though he felt sweat trickle in a trail from his hairline.

'Have you found men to be tasters?'

'Yes, Your Excellency. The famine drives them to desperation. A man and a boy are in the kitchens.'

'Good. Make sure the boy tastes first. The poison will show more easily on a small body.'

An inclination of the head.

'And bring my hag of a wife here. I will speak with her again.'

'She's out, Your Excellency—'

'Out?' The word would barely come. 'You disobey my orders? I forbade them to let her go out. She only lives at all because of my favour.'

'She's making penance at church. Bruno and Alessandro are guarding her. You were sleeping. And they saw no harm in her confessing before God.'

'No harm? You would give the witch the comfort of a stay in heaven? Fetch her back.'

'They swore they wouldn't be more than—'

'Enough. Don't try my patience.' He had to try harder from this position to make his authority felt. It was impossible to feel assertive in a nightshirt. Before this cursed calamity had befallen him, Lucio would never have dared answer back. Antonio raised his voice. 'Bring her now,' he insisted, 'not in three hours' time.'

Lucio bowed, looking aggrieved, and went out as if it was a chore he could do without. Antonio slumped back, breathless from exertion, before making a renewed effort. He could do nothing lying here like an invalid. He must get out of bed. He willed himself to get stronger. The effects of the poison were abating, hour by hour, he told himself. They had to be.

With effort, he pulled back the weight of the damask coverlet and stretched one leg out of the bed. He stared at it. He'd only been ill six weeks, and yet surely this was someone else's limb – thin and white as raw pastry, blue veins crawling up the front of the bone. He eased himself to the edge of the bed and rested his weight gingerly on one bony bare foot. It held. A small triumph.

Pressing his lips together in concentration, he dragged out the other foot and placed it on the cold marble.

He was weak, but not beaten. When Valentina had confessed, he sent the physicians away. Useless bunch of leeches, they'd sucked his purse dry, and never once suggested it could be poison. Mind you, he didn't want them seeing his lack of control over his wife, it would be the talk of Palermo. So now, five days later, after fasting, and eating only food brought to him direct from the market and not from his own kitchen, he was improving.

But he must decide what to do with Valentina. It would do his reputation no good to have been brought so low by that worm of a woman. His housekeeper had been paid to leave him and keep silent, but in his position, he could not dispose of Valentina so easily, not without causing a scandal, and she knew it. Unlike his brother, Domenico, who had rid himself of one wife and had now found himself another.

Nauseous, he staggered to the basin, spat and then washed himself. In the stucco-framed glass, he saw his beard needed trimming and his skin was as grey as eel jelly. The sight of his own face, once strong-jawed but now jowly with loose skin, disgusted him. It fired his anger more. He wanted the old duke back. He struggled to the closet and dressed himself in a black leather doublet and matching breeches, though they hung loose over his wasted muscles. He could not drag on his high boots, but using a shoehorn, he prised on a pair of heeled shoes with red rosettes.

He was panting and rimed with sweat by the time he sank into the chair by the window, but he gripped the arms to heave himself more upright, braced his shoulders and took on a haughty expression.

Lucio returned shortly afterwards, but he stopped short when he saw him upright in the chair.

'I am stronger than I look, Lucio,' Antonio said. 'The will is stronger than the flesh, is that not so? What's more, I remember all those who slighted me when I was ill. Those who couldn't wait for me to die. Were you one of them, eh?' He fixed him with a cold gaze.

'No, Your Excellency. Of course not.' Lucio's face flamed red. 'Your wife waits below; shall I send her up?'

'Not yet. Bring me some fortifying wine.'

Lucio went back downstairs, and after a while he appeared, bringing the tray with a decanter and a glass containing a red wine, dark as garnets.

'Has it been tested? The boy?'

'A nod.'

'Has *she* tried it?' he asked. His faithless wife, Valentina. The thought of her made him want to retch.

'Yes.'

'The same glass?'

'Yes.'

'Then you drink,' he said, gesturing to Lucio to try it. Lucio wrinkled his nose, but then obliged before wiping the rim with a napkin and passing it to him.

'Like communion wine,' he said, giving a coarse chuckle, the first in weeks. 'Now, fetch my wife up.' He was wary of anything that passed his lips now, but he needed the strength. He downed the sweet cloying liquid and its heat rushed into his throat. He could always hold his liquor before, but now, since sickening, he had become overly attuned to the changes in his humours that such spirits brought. His head swam, but he felt something of his old vigour returning.

The door opened and his two bodyguards, Bruno and Alessandro, big-handed men, their faces scarred by fighting, parted to let Valentina come through. Next to the men, she seemed even smaller, like a weasel, squirming and pale, in an unbecoming flesh-coloured gown. No wonder he had strayed elsewhere.

'So you have been on your knees before God,' he said. 'And does he forgive you?'

Her pale eyes widened at the sight of him out of bed and in his familiar chair, and she tried to stutter a reply.

He cut her off. 'Your two lady friends have been detained at my pleasure,' he said, 'in the gaol of the Palazzo Chiaramonte.'

'It was a mistake,' she whispered. 'I told you; I thought it was a tonic. I didn't know what was in it. They are persuasive… they made me give it.'

'They made you, you say? For what gain? None. You are the only one to profit by my death, and you are the one who will pay.'

'I didn't know it was so strong,' she wailed. 'You barely acknowledged me. I thought if you were indisposed, confined to bed, I would be able to—'

'Lies. All lies. So the story changes now, does it? You're telling me you put poison in my food to make me pay you attention?' He laughed. 'D'you hear that, men? It's ever thus with women. We never get at the truth. Except this time, I have two women in gaol who will testify against you. Francesca La Sarda tells me you expressly went to them to purchase poison.' He saw by her face he had struck home. 'Don't bother to deny it. Your two so-called "friends" say that they were only following instructions from you. That you meant to kill me.' He leaned forward. 'And if you wish to see another summer, you will bring me the third.'

'The third?' She blinked watery eyes at him. 'I don't know what you mean.'

'The daughter, Giulia. Well versed in the same venal skill as her mother, I've no doubt.'

'I never saw a girl at all. It was always the other two women who came.'

He laughed. As if he'd believe that. 'If you wish for my clemency, you will find her. Bruno will accompany you whilst you search. For such women to be at large in our fine city is a sin against humanity and an insult to all god-fearing men.'

'But how can I find her? I don't know where to look.'

She was grovelling now, and it made him want to crush her underfoot – if only he could have summoned the strength. 'You will make enquiries. People will talk to a woman. If the girl is not here by the time those other women meet their deaths, you will join them in her stead. D'you understand?'

Her mouth trembled a little before she spoke. 'And if I should find her, you will let me go in peace? I was foolish. Easily led. I must atone for it with prayer and with service to the Holy Mother Church. If you let me go, you need never see me again – I swear I will live out my life in penance with the Carmelites at Santa Maria Maddelena.'

'If they are foolish enough to take such a despicable sinner as you.'

She was silent a moment. 'You will agree?' Her stupid face lit up in hope.

He shrugged.

'How can I be certain you will keep your word?'

'Your choice. It is of little account to me. You can choose to die now or take that risk. After all, if a man can marry but find out later his supposedly "innocent" wife is a poisoner, anything is possible, is it not?'

She crumpled. Just once he wished she would fight back, that she'd become an adversary worth having. But no, she was always this feeble, milksop of a woman. He should have known she would choose poison. The weak way, the way of cold-hearted women. Valentina always took the coward's way out, and he despised her for it.

'Get out of my sight,' he said. 'You pollute the atmosphere with your presence. You have until the morning to let me know what you decide.'

But she seemed too terrified to even take a moment to think about it. 'I will find the girl,' she said.

He sighed, and gestured for Alessandro and Bruno to take her away. She must know he couldn't let her live, yet she wouldn't face her fate head on but had to wheedle more time. Still, if it served him, who was he to complain?

CHAPTER 6

THE DUKE'S bodyguard Bruno Borroni waited in the shade of the large villa. A big man, he always suffered in the heat of the day. He was chaperone to the duchess and her maidservant, Filide, as they knocked on several dozen doors making enquiries about the poisoner's daughter.

He was relieved that nobody had seen the girl. Or if they had, they were keeping quiet, just as he himself was. He moved forward now and held up the sunshade as Filide knocked on yet another door. The duchess Valentina hovered behind, out of the heat, as her rank demanded.

This hunt would be a waste of time, he knew, though he would never say so. He could hazard a good guess where the young one had gone. He was one of the few in Palermo who still remembered Theofania's sister, Isabetta. In truth, how could he ever forget her? The beautiful Isabetta, who was as wild as the wind and twice as unpredictable.

The thought of her cut him with a familiar yearning even after all this time. His first love.

It was twenty-five years since he had seen her, since that disastrous night when she had turned down his proposal, saying that life as the consort of a mercenary was not for her. He'd tried to persuade her, grown hot and angry, but of course it only made it worse, and she wouldn't listen. The poppy powder had her in its dreaming sway.

After she'd gone, he'd searched for her everywhere, and when he finally found her, five years later, in a bordello in Naples, he'd wished he hadn't. Such a waste.

Had he driven her to the courtesan's life with his harsh words? The thought of Isabetta lying with other men made him want to... A snap. He looked down at the stem of Valentina's sunshade, now broken in half and dangling uselessly in his fingers.

'What have you done to that shade?' Valentina asked as she returned from the door.

'Don't know. Must've been a weak joint,' he said.

'They haven't seen her,' she said shortly. 'Has nobody seen her? How can she just disappear into the air like that?'

He shrugged, kept his counsel. If the girl was with Isabetta, it would be a precarious enough life. Valentina had shown no sign at all of trying to escape his guard. It confused him. If he were her, he would have put as many leagues between himself and the vengeful Antonio de Verdi as possible. Yet here she was, doing the duke's bidding as if they were still the devoted young lovers he remembered from years past. Perhaps that was the problem; that you could never rid yourself of that intoxication of first love once you had felt it. That somehow, no matter how vile the person, or how dreadful the deed, the first love still held you in its pincer grip.

Today was the servant's half-day off, so after Filide had left them, Bruno suggested Valentina take a few moments to drink and sit in the shade. The sun was piercing now, and there was not a breath of a breeze.

They settled on a stone bench in the dappled shadow of an orange tree. Invisible crickets rattled in the foliage near the courtyard fountain, though it was so dry there was no trickle of water from the dolphin's stone mouth. He offered her a drink from his leather flask but she waved it away. Bruno peeled himself an orange with the knife from his belt and put a segment into his mouth, savouring the welcome tang.

The duchess rested her head in her hands a moment before looking up. 'What if we never find her?'

'Why did you do it?' Bruno asked. 'Why did you try to kill him?'

She raised her head, and her gold-flecked eyes looked into his. 'He had become impossible,' she said. 'Ambition had corrupted him. He used me. Loaned me out as unpaid courtesan to his friends, those who, in return, would vote for him as Master of the Guild.'

Bruno was silent. For a woman to speak of such shame left him with no reply.

'You are shocked.'

'Not shocked at what he did, but shocked you can speak of it.'

'The aristocrats all know and think me low. Where's the sense of hiding it? I thought if he no longer existed I'd be free.'

'But here's what concerns me,' he said softly. 'Why didn't you finish it? As a fighting man, I find that hard to understand.'

'Signora Fattorini, the housekeeper, saw me administer the dose. So that was the end of it. She always was a tattle-tale. I thought I could take God's power and make it my own. Because I wanted a life, and he allowed me none.'

'But now you will certainly have no life, for he will dispose of you as soon as he has the girl.'

'I thought I could do it quicker. I thought when he became ill he would confess, make absolution to God. There was plenty of time for him to make his peace at the last. But he was stubborn and would not. He could not countenance that he would die. Such arrogance. Yet no matter how I hated him, I remembered how he was when we were young. How tender he was then. He would not take confession, and I could not condemn that boy I remembered to the eternal scorching flames.'

'What about those women in gaol, their future?'

'They are good women. I have no fears for their souls. They did not do the deed. It was I who administered the poison. They will ascend to heaven, as God promised. After all, it is not this life that matters, the Church tells us, but eternal life. What's our little span in the face of all eternity?'

'You think they would choose eternal life when they could keep this one? Think again. One of them has a daughter she loves.'

'Yes. We must find her.'

'Why? He will not let you go free any more than them. He's using you again. It's what he does.'

'He gave me his word. He said if I found the girl, he would allow me to go to the Poor Clares. It will save his face. You know my husband – he would never admit to anyone that he had been poisoned by his wife. Even Signora Fattorini has been dismissed. Better to put it down to a mystery illness.'

She was fooling herself. 'You think his word will count for anything? Even after all these years of knowing him?'

She hung her head, brushed imaginary dust from the bench she was sitting on. So she did know; she was not as stupid as he had thought. Even if she were to find Theofania's daughter, the duke would kill her. He had never shown mercy to anyone who crossed him.

Bruno touched her arm. She startled and blinked.

'Your Excellency,' Bruno said softly, 'if he will kill you anyway, why give him two deaths?' His tone was casual, but he put steel behind it. The poisoner's daughter stuck in his mind. Something about the bleakness in the young woman's face when he tried to apprehend her… well, it moved him.

'You mean, even if we find something, we should pretend we can't find her?' the duchess asked.

'You'd be sparing a young woman who has probably done nothing except be in the wrong place at the wrong time. You know he has already begun the torture – her mother and the other woman, but they refuse to tell him where the girl is. Brave.'

'Then we must keep looking.'

'Why?' He tried to keep his tone light. 'Why ruin another life?'

'I have to have hope. I look at this life, at its riches and glories. At the green of the leaves on the orange trees, and the skinny sparrows pecking in the dirt, and I have to do something. I pray and trust God will be my salvation. Because I have turned away from my sin, as the Lord asked me to do, and I have to have hope. I hope if we find her a miracle will happen. Antonio will be pleased and change his mind.'

Bruno spat on the road. 'Can a leopard change his spots?'

CHAPTER 7

DUKE DE VERDI'S PALAZZO, PALERMO

THE DUKE TOYED with the letter in his hand, mulling it over, sitting in the chair by the open window, with the bustle of the market below.

The letter was from the viceroy, Acevedo y Zuñiga, telling him that he feared riots in Naples. The last time, in 1628, the Spanish had nearly lost control of the native population. Now it showed every sign of history repeating itself, as it had in Milan. Harvests hadn't recovered since the eruption of Vesuvius, and there were shortages everywhere, but the cities were the worst. People were clamouring for bread and threatening to overturn the governor's estate if they didn't get it. The viceroy needed reinforcements. It was a flattering request. Perhaps he had remembered that he, Antonio, had been instrumental in negotiating a treaty between the Neapolitans and the Spanish. Now he'd personally asked for him to go to Naples, and the honour was a sweet one. He prided himself on always being on the winning side, yet there were obstacles to this request that would need careful thought.

He eased himself out of the chair and began to pace. The first difficulty was that it was his younger brother, Domenico, who was the viceroy's current emissary in Naples. He could well imagine Domenico's bitterness if he, Antonio, were to suddenly arrive to take control. Domenico was his least favourite brother, and they'd never seen eye to eye. Domenico was always jealous that he had inherited the title of duke and since then had apparently built his own little empire in Naples. His other three brothers, even less well favoured in the pecking order, were all in Naples with Domenico, dancing to his tune.

He drew himself up and stretched back his elbows to puff out his chest, then let out a ragged breath. The other difficulty was that he wasn't yet fit. Even going up the stairs still made him breathless. But he could get himself fit, he knew it.

Part of him relished the idea of reasserting control over Domenico. He'd ask for a few more weeks to tie up loose ends here in Palermo before leaving. In that time he'd ride daily, lift pike and musket, climb the stairs to the *terrazza* every day, and build up his stamina.

He read the letter through again. *'You are an experienced man who knows how to maintain discipline,'* the viceroy wrote. *'There is a fully-staffed house awaiting your pleasure and a cohort of 200 local guildsmen from the Armourers' Guild ready to assist you.'*

It was decided. But he would take his own men. Men he could trust, like Bruno Borroni, not these Spanish armourers he knew nothing about. Domenico was a crafty bastard, and one who got his brothers to do his dirty work for him, so he would have to be prepared for blood.

Bruno had been summoned to the duke's private quarters and now made his way there. When he entered the chamber he saw that the duke was standing up by the desk, his piles of correspondence neatly stacked. He was recovering his energy, Bruno thought. His face had lost its skeletal appearance, and his voice was crisper, though he was still leaning on the chair for support.

'Take this letter to the post,' the duke said, 'and then expedite the trial of those two old crows in the gaol. The poisoners.' He held out the letter in an imperious way, and Bruno stepped up to take it.

'We will be leaving Palermo soon,' the duke said, 'and I want them dead before we leave.'

'Leaving?'

'Don't worry, Bruno, you will be leaving with me. We have two weeks to pack and make ready.'

Bruno stiffened. He was to be uprooted at the duke's whim. He kept his face impassive. 'Shall I tell the other servants?'

'Not yet. I don't want my wife to know yet. I haven't decided whether to take her or leave her here.'

'Where are we going, sir?'

'Naples. They need more *condottieri*. Rebels are causing trouble against the Spanish rule. We've been asked to offer support to my brother Domenico, who is part of the viceroy's commission.'

Naples. Isabetta immediately came to mind. It was as if her presence were somehow at the core of everything he did despite her absence. That his love could last this long shamed him.

'I need a good man in a skirmish,' the duke continued, 'someone sure-handed and reliable.'

'You flatter me, sir.'

'Nonsense. Be honest, this cloistered palazzo life has never suited you. I need experienced men, and a good fight in Naples will do you a power of good.'

'How many men will you take?'

'Fifty men-at-arms at the outset. The rebels will be disorganised. Obviously, my brother Domenico has trouble keeping control, so a small but efficient force will be best. See to it that you check all the horses, all the harnesses, and clear out the stables. If we are to go to Naples, I need everything in perfect order.'

Bruno bowed his assent. So he was to be stable-boy now too. If he wanted to eat, he knew how to obey orders. A mercenary's life was one of unquestioning loyalty and obedience, that's what they paid him for, and Bruno always did his best to convey that impression, no matter his thoughts on the folly of the orders. Best to be impersonal – the enemy of today might be the comrade-in-arms of tomorrow.

'One more thing, Bruno. Send Lucio to me, and then make sure we are not disturbed.'

'Very good, sir.'

'And not a word to my lady.'

'Yes, sir.'

Bruno bowed his way out. Quite apart from the pain of being so near to Isabetta, Naples was the last place on earth he wanted to be. A simmering nest of organised crime known as the Camorra. Ruthless despots in rival gangs. Besides, he had no wish to go and fight another man's war, when it was street skirmishes, with no sense of honour, and no chance of glory.

CHAPTER 8

A WEEK LATER

WHEN HER HUSBAND asked her to walk with him to help build up his strength, the Duchess Valentina was nervous, but she knew she could not refuse her husband. She looked around the chamber for the reassuring presence of Filide.

'You don't need Filide today,' the duke said, 'as I will be accompanying you. I told her she could visit her mother.' Filide's mother had taken her vows a few years ago as a nun.

'Then what about Bruno? We usually have a man to guard us,' Valentina said. 'The streets are not safe for rich men like you.'

'Bruno's busy,' he replied. 'I asked him to give the stables another thorough inspection. I will be riding again soon, and I suspect things have become lax. I've asked my man Lucio to accompany us instead.'

Valentina stiffened. She'd never liked Lucio. He was her husband's lapdog, always ready to fawn over him at every opportunity.

They headed down the curved staircase, and Lucio, primped and servile, was already waiting, holding out Antonio's short summer cloak. At his feet stood a large covered basket.

'What's that?' she asked him. Lucio glanced to her husband.

'Some delicacies from the kitchens,' Antonio answered. 'Lucio will row us around to the far side of the bay where we can eat al fresco and have time to talk.'

He would talk, he meant. It was always he who talked and she who listened. But perhaps he was prepared to make a truce. Perhaps he wished to know if she had located the young woman yet, the daughter of Theofania d'Adamo. She had recoiled at what Bruno had told her, that the women were being tortured, and she was uneasy because she knew this would be awkward – the women had refused to talk and she, Valentina, had found nothing. Giulia d'Adamo had disappeared like the winter rain, leaving no trace at all.

Out into the sun, which was as sharp as knives even through her veil. She put up her shade against the heat.

'We will walk by the harbour,' Antonio said. 'I want to see which ships are in and take a look at the wharf. I have been prevented from doing it for far too long.'

He turned slightly at this and gave her a pointed look. At the same time, he increased his pressure on her arm. Instinctively she tried to pull away. But as she did so, Lucio stepped up beside her. He was sweating under the weight of the basket, which seemed to be causing him difficulty. She wished it were Bruno, not Lucio. He would have carried it with ease. Besides, she was beginning to feel hemmed in.

At the harbour they waited in the shade, whilst Lucio hired a skiff with oars and loaded the basket aboard. Antonio was looking better, more colour in his face, but with his renewed strength came her fear of him.

She hesitated, reluctant to leave dry land, but Antonio pushed her before him into the prow, so she was sitting ahead of both of the men. She remembered such outings from their courting days, but they seemed such a long time ago, in the time when she had mistaken Antonio's forcefulness for strength of character and his naked ambition for charm. She wondered if he would tell her that she was to die with the other women. Her stomach twisted, and she gave an involuntary shiver despite the heat.

'It's a fine day to eat outdoors,' she said. 'What did you want to talk about?'

'Later,' Antonio said, 'we'll talk later.'

She took out a rosary and ran the comforting beads through her fingers. When she glanced behind, it was to see Antonio staring at her with cold dark eyes. The shiver rose to the back of her neck.

'Give me the oars, Lucio,' he said. 'I need to build my arm strength again.'

After he settled himself on the bench seat and grasped the oars, she watched him take a few hard pulls before she turned to look ahead. The water was flat and glassy, a deep aquamarine over a surface of impenetrable black. The basket was in the prow. It seemed heavy for just the three of them. After a few hundred yards she turned again; sweat had broken out on Antonio's brow, yet he was pulling determinedly, a grim set to his mouth.

After he had rowed out a little further, past the tall ships at anchor and they had rounded the harbour wall out of sight of the town, she glanced back again in time to see him push the oars back into their rowlocks and wipe his face with his sleeve.

'That's it,' he said to Lucio. 'That's far enough.'

Something in his tone made her tighten. 'Where are we headed?' she said, in a voice as near normal as possible.

When he moved it was sharp and sudden. He grasped her arms in one swift movement and pinned them behind her back. The boat rocked. Waves slapped against the side.

'What are you doing?' Her voice was feeble. She tried to twist, but he had her held tight, fingers pinioning her arm like a trap.

'Do it,' he ordered.

Do what? A knife snaked over her shoulder. Panicked, she threw herself backwards with all her might, and Lucio gave a yell of surprise. The split instant of freedom gave her enough room to scramble out of reach and turn in horrified panic. A curse from Antonio. The boat wobbled in the water. Lucio thrust the knife towards her again. She crawled further towards the prow.

'Don't, you fool!' Antonio threw himself backwards to counteract the weight in the prow.

The men's faces were strangely similar. Both with an expression like they were trying to swat a fly. In that moment the world slowed to a turning wheel and she understood they meant to kill her.

Here. Now.

The world rushed back in as Lucio grabbed her again by the skirt to drag her forward. The land dipped and rose. One kick. Two. Desperately she kicked out to push Lucio away. A toe caught him in the chin and he fell backward towards Antonio, but Antonio thrust him back to his feet and he immediately staggered up and fell towards her again. The knife was at arm's length. Slashing closer.

Nowhere to go. She made an almighty effort and twisted away, launching herself into the water. Instant darkness.

Foolish. She sank under almost immediately. Above her, the shadow of the boat rippled in a dark stain. She swam away from it, breaking surface a moment for a gasp of air. Her skirts and hoops were filled with air, but they held her back, showed where she was.

Immediately, a dark figure landed on top of her. Lucio. He was a strong swimmer, unencumbered by skirts. She flailed out of his way. A nose and mouth full of seawater. Choking. Frantic splashing. A sting across her arm and the water bloomed red.

She felt two more stings as he slashed at her. She was tiring now, the weight of her sodden petticoats dragging her down. Her legs were like lead pushing against them. Another splash, and an oar hit the water just by her head.

She gasped for air, saltwater stinging her eyes, before she looked up once more to see the oar come crashing down again.

This time there was nowhere to go. Darkness exploded around her.

Antonio hauled at Lucio's arms as he clambered back into the boat. Lucio leant over the side, his face green, his doublet and breeches sluicing water into the bottom of the boat. Both shoes were missing. Antonio sighed impatiently. It was Lucio's own fault, he should have made it quick and clean like he'd told him to.

Antonio stared as the half-submerged object floated away from them, surrounded by a pinkish-red cloud already swarming with fish. Lucio's fault. It should have been easy, but Lucio had found a way to make the whole thing messy as usual.

With difficulty, Antonio hauled the oar back into the boat but then thrust it back into the water to drag the body nearer. 'Get the rope,' he said. His body was protesting, he suddenly felt exhausted. He dragged the body close to the boat, reaching out to grasp the floating skirts 'Tie the rope round her arm,' he said.

Lucio was shaking. You could tell he wasn't a military man; no officer would turn green at the sight of a death. He watched him fumble with the knots.

'Get on with it,' Antonio said.

Lucio did so with excruciating slowness.

'Is it tight?' For answer, Lucio pulled on the knot with both hands. Antonio scooped up the other end of the rope and tied it to the basket. 'Now help me,' he said, opening it.

The basket was full of rocks, and it took effort to position it on the edge then heave it overboard. The dark body was engulfed by the sea, the bubble of skirts sinking until the surface closed over as if nothing had ever been there.

Antonio dipped his hands in the water to wash them. 'They'll never find her,' he said.

Lucio nodded, though his eyes shifted uncomfortably from Antonio's.

'When we get back, pack suitable clothes as if she's travelling on a journey, but then get someone to take them to the second-hand market in Salerno.'

'Yes, sir.'

'And remember what we planned. She left early this morning on a coach bound for Rome. You were powerless to prevent her.'

He bowed his head.

'You will have to find your own excuse about why you are shoeless.' Lucio squirmed in his seat as he intended he should. The man was a fawning ass, always leaving his orders half-done. A man with no mind of his own. Fortunate really, because he couldn't turn him out of his household now. Not unless he went the same way as Valentina.

'You have seen nothing,' he said. 'Row us back to shore.'

When the Duchess Valentina did not appear for the rest of the evening, nor any of her maidservants, Bruno sought out Lucio in the duke's dressing chamber to ask where she was.

'She's gone away,' Lucio said. 'She's left him.'

Bruno stared. In the light of the candles on the dressing chest, Lucio's expression was one of a cornered fox. 'What do you mean?'

'She left early this morning. She's gone to Rome. Took all her belongings and her servants and went.'

'When?'

'This morning. I told you.' He plucked at the lace on his cuff.

Bruno walked over to him a little too close, so he looked down on his slightly-balding head. He knew how to intimidate shorter men. 'I saw her this morning and she and her servants mentioned nothing of it.'

'Maybe she didn't want to go to Naples.'

'Oh? How do you know? What did she say about it?'

He pushed his sparse hair off his forehead. 'Just that she didn't want to live in Naples. I expect she's gone to relatives.'

'She never mentioned it to me. And the duke just let her go? After all the rumours?'

'He was angry, but there was little he could do. He's not inclined to chase after her. Would you be, given what they're saying she did to him?'

'Which carrier took her things?'

'I don't know. I was out on an errand.'

'How convenient. And it's very convenient for him too, that she won't be joining us in Naples.'

Just then, the duke arrived. His pointed look seemed to have the desired effect, as Lucio stooped to pick up a pair of shoes for cleaning and went out of the door. 'A problem, Bruno?'

'No, Your Excellency. I was enquiring about which horse Lucio wishes to take to Naples.'

'What, now? At this time of night?'

'I didn't mean to inconvenience you, sir.'

'Fighting men should not be here in my private chambers.'

'Beg pardon, Your Excellency.' Bruno bowed his way out.

Valentina had never struck him as being a woman who would make hasty plans. There was something that smelt bad about this, but he knew better than to confront the duke directly. Instead, acting on his suspicions, he walked out and down towards the gaol where the two women, accused of supplying Valentina with the poison, were being held.

'Was another woman brought in this morning?' Bruno asked.

The governor, a balding middle-aged man intent on stuffing his clay pipe with greyish tobacco, assured him no other female had been arrested.

'Well, what about the two women held on charges of poisoning?'

The governor sucked with satisfaction, then blew out a cloud of pungent smoke. 'They're to be executed on Monday morning. Monday's always execution day. The crowds come to expect it. Makes up for lack of meat on Fridays!' He guffawed. 'I'm hoping the duke'll decide on pressing.'

Bruno hid his revulsion. He was all for a fair fight; death in battle was an honour. But this practice of loading stones onto the chest until the ribs collapsed and the person died of lack of breath seemed barbaric.

'Yes, came down himself last night and said he wanted it done as soon as possible, now nothing we've done has made them confess. Not even the water. They won't tell the whereabouts of the third woman, the daughter, so there's no point keeping them no more, is there?'

Bruno thanked him and walked away.

A half hour later he knocked on the door to Filide's house.

Filide answered the door, her hands floury as if she'd been baking. 'Has he let you go too?'

'No. But I wanted to know if you've seen your mistress today?'

She scowled. 'The duke gave me notice. Last night. Said that the duchess was going away and I wouldn't be needed. I'd "no longer be required" were his words. And me being with her nearly two years.' The outrage at this unfairness was written on her face. 'You'd think she'd at least give me thanks. Have they kept you on?'

'For now, yes. Did he say where your mistress was going?'

'They're bound for Naples, aren't they? I heard he's going to fight the rebels in the city, God help them. So I suppose they will employ some other skivvy when they get there. They could have told me before. I liked the mistress, I would've liked to say good-bye. Hated him though. He always looked at me like I was a louse he'd picked up from a dog.'

So Filide thought her mistress was going to Naples. Lucio had said Rome.

He was fairly certain it was neither.

It was a mystery it would not profit him to solve, he knew that much, so after he'd sympathised and wished Filide well, he returned to the house.

Already the male servants were bustling back and forth, packing up the household goods ready for the move to Naples. The hall was bare now, and his boots echoed oddly in the unfurnished void. All the tapestries had been removed for transit. Dust motes hung in the air as he surveyed the space.

He headed for his chambers below. He must begin his own preparations, though travel would seem odd without Valentina and her entourage. Few would miss her, for the duke had not encouraged friendships. That she should be of so little account gave him a hollow feeling in his gut. For he too had few friends. Men, well they were rivals or warriors to be bested. Women – well, he'd had only one love in his life and it had nearly broken him, so he wasn't going to make that mistake again.

He opened his chamber door, and Isabetta's face drifted into his thoughts, the sparkle of her eyes, the way she had called him her 'big wolf'.

No. He mustn't think of her. He was too old now, and past all that. Please God Naples was large enough so their paths would never have to cross. He'd thought he could save her from herself, but perhaps she was dead by now. Opium addicts rarely lasted long. Resolutely, he thrust open a window into the courtyard. The duke was there training, practising his sword thrusts.

Bruno watched the duke thrust and parry for a moment. The duke had lost his fighting edge, his steps were not as incisive as they used to be before his illness, but his determination was like an obsession. Pondering this, he realised the duke didn't look like a man whose wife had just left him. He looked as he always did, intent on himself.

CHAPTER 9

FABIO HAD no desire to witness the execution. But on the day, a large crowd clogged up the arteries to the square, including Fabio's street, making business impossible. A blazing July sun throbbed in a piercingly blue sky, but the heat had not deterred the huge turn-out. The crowd sweated excitedly under the brims of their hats, dabbed their necks with their sleeves, and sweltered in the smell of dust, hot cloth, perspiration and the occasional pomander.

'Come on,' Fabio's father said, slapping him on the shoulder.

Fabio reluctantly followed him into the hot press of the people pushing into the long square near the monastery, where the gibbet was usually situated. But today he was surprised to see there was no gibbet. Instead, a platform on which the Duke de Verdi and his officials were due to speak. This fact alone made the crowd pulse with excitement.

'Fabio!' Claudia was elbowing her way towards him.

Best pretend he hadn't seen her.

He stood up on his toes to crane at the duke, who was standing grim-faced, talking with the cardinal in his sumptuous scarlet robes, surrounded by a group of men in the white and blue ceremonial robes of the Silk Weavers Guild. The whole entourage oozed power, and to emphasise their importance, the dais was heavily guarded by a cohort of mercenaries in their distinctive red and yellow breeches and gleaming breastplates.

Fabio's father, in his blue linen cap, left him and muscled his way to the front, but Fabio didn't follow him. His father had drunk a skinful already, and he didn't want to get into any arguments. Father was loose-mouthed when he'd had too much and apt to spoil for a fight.

'Fabio!' Claudia again. Her hand grasped him by the sleeve to tug him forward. 'Come on, we won't see anything back here.'

'No, I can see enough. You go if you want to.'

Her face pinched in annoyance. 'I don't want to go on my own. What's wrong? Don't you like me?'

'Just leave me alone,' he snapped.

'Killjoy,' she said. And she stalked off, angrily pushing her way through the crowd. He could still see the back of her blonde head under its linen cap, edging ever nearer to where the mercenaries were holding back the crowd from the walls. A trumpet sounded, and the buzz of the crowd quietened, wondering when they would get their spectacle.

The duke came to the front of the dais. 'Fellow citizens, there can be no greater sin than to take another's life. Even more sinful if it is by stealth, as these women planned to do. Who knows how many deaths can be laid at their door when they do it in such vile secrecy? With women like these in our community, cankers that feed upon us, taking good men's money and dispensing only death, we will never be safe. I vowed therefore to make sure that women like these, who have no redeeming virtue of their sex, should receive the severest punishment.'

He glanced towards the ramparts of the city walls. At that point the crowd suddenly looked up and pointed. Soldiers, their helmets sparkling in the sun, and two women, bruised and hunched, shackled by the ankles and barely able to stand. There was a hubbub as everyone jostled to see.

At the same time the duke continued: 'As a deterrent to all who might dabble in these pernicious arts, they have been condemned to die. They will be put into sacks and thrown from the city walls, after which their broken corpses can be taken for dissection. The bone-men are welcome to try to dissect from their corpses where the evil in them resides.'

Fabio glanced around to see if anyone else found this shocking. Corpses had to be buried intact if they were to be resurrected to life on Judgement Day.

The men on the walls manoeuvred heavy hessian grain sacks over the women's heads so they were covered to the knees. Fabio felt his hands grow clammy and his stomach churn. Surely not. Someone should do something. At the same time he couldn't tear his eyes from the two figures teetering on the ramparts.

'Let it be done,' the duke cried, dropping his arm as the signal.

A strangled cry as the first woman was pushed and, arms tied, dropped headfirst like a stone. The clank of shackle and thud and crack of bone made the crowd shift back, so Fabio was pushed backwards. He had barely time for an intake of breath before the other woman was pushed. She too plummeted. But when the sack landed there was still movement. The crowd surged forward. He saw her shackled ankles, and her feet, one in a shoe, the other bare, protruding from the sack, heard a groan before the crowd set upon the sack like baying dogs, stamping and clubbing the sack until it ran red. His father's blue cap was amongst them.

He staggered away. He had known Giulia's mother and always thought her pleasant, if distracted. The thought that anyone could end this way filled him with revulsion. And where was the duchess? The one he was fairly sure had started this whole affair? There was no sign whatever of her, or her punishment.

As he went, he caught sight of the duke and the frog-eyed,

barrel-chested cardinal with the jewel-encrusted crucifix. They were smiling and chatting as if nothing untoward had taken place. He had seen hangings before, and plenty. People knew what to expect. But this? This was savage.

He strode away disorientated, as if he could not take in what he'd seen. For once he was glad he didn't know where Giulia was. Wherever she was, he was glad she didn't have to witness this. And he was sad too, for he knew the taint of it would reach her, and he feared she would have a hard life after this.

'You missed it all.' Claudia ran up to him, breathless. 'It was horrible, they—'

'Leave me be. I don't ever want to see you again. You rejoice in this... this calamity that has happened to your friend?'

'What's wrong? They tried her, didn't they? Guilty, they said. She deserved it.'

'Nobody deserves a death like that. You sicken me.'

'Oh, that's the way it is, is it? I thought I meant something to you. I gave you everything – everything a maid can give you, and you turn on me like all the rest.'

'Maybe you give it too cheaply,' he said.

He saw the barb register, and tears spring to her eyes. It made him squirm, but he was too angry to stop. He left her standing in the street staring after him.

Bruno too walked away in a daze. When the crowd had dispersed, he was charged with marching back to the palazzo as the duke's escort. The duke of course was in a carriage, shaded from the sun. Bruno simply followed the rest of the mercenaries. He barely saw where he was walking because he was thinking of Isabetta and how she would feel. Pray God she was not somewhere in that crowd. She would blame him, even though, like the rest of the duke's men, he had no idea what was to happen until it was too late to reason against it. The thought of Isabetta's sister dying in such a way sickened him. He wondered how Isabetta would get the news, and who would hold her up when it came.

'A task well done,' the duke said as they entered the cool, echoing hall of the palazzo.

Bruno inclined his head.

'If you were the daughter of that vile poisoner, where would you go?'

Bruno baulked. The question came out of nowhere as the duke was just removing his gloves and handing them to Lucio, now resplendently dressed as if for a wedding.

'I don't know, Your Excellency.'

'Perhaps Naples. It is not too far, and has a big population. They say the Annunziata hospital houses two thousand at a time. It would be easy to get lost in such a city, heh? Easy to get lost, but not impossible for an intelligent person to find.' He raised an eyebrow, pleased with himself. 'About the poisoner's daughter – you said she was wearing red. Lucio's been making enquiries.'

Lucio smirked. 'One of the fishermen at the harbour saw a young woman in red boarding a tender for the Naples sailing. He swears it was the same day.'

The duke slapped his gloves on his thigh. 'And we will be stationed there in a few weeks' time. Do you have any friends in Naples?'

'No.' Bruno shook his head. The image of Isabetta's face rose up in his mind.

'Didn't you used to correspond with a woman in Naples?' Lucio said. 'I remember, years ago, taking some of your letters.'

'Is that so?' The duke turned, with sudden interest in his tone.

'It was nothing to speak of. I used to know someone there, but it was a long time ago and we've lost touch.' He glared at Lucio.

'You could renew your acquaintance. Who is it, this woman?'

Bruno hesitated, uncomfortable under the duke's scrutiny. In these circumstances he could certainly never contact her again.

'Just someone I used to know,' Bruno said. 'We were close once, but not any more.'

'But you know where your acquaintance lives?'

'I do, but I doubt if she'd—'

'I need an advance party to see what the situation is in Naples. What the rebels' grievances are. What my brother Domenico is doing about it; how many men he has under him. You will go to Naples and look up your old friend.'

'But I—'

'Go there, and ask your friend if she has any knowledge of this Giulia d'Adamo.'

'But that's impossible if the girl's hiding. It will be like searching for a pin in the sand.'

'Nothing is impossible. When you have come back from the dead like I have, you realise that everything is possible if you have the will. Life needs to be grasped and tamed with both hands.'

Bruno dipped his head, hoping the duke could not read his thoughts. He would never reveal Isabetta's whereabouts to the duke. He would have to make a pretence, and find some excuse.

'Best go immediately, Borroni,' said the duke. 'Even with two of the witches gone, I shan't sleep well until I know that the whole cabal has been removed, like a canker from an oak.'

'Very good, sir,' he said, knowing he could not and would not. He turned to go.

'And Bruno, I shall expect you to send me the advance reconnaissance by courier.'

Bruno raised a hand to show he had heard, but he kept on walking. His anger was bottled up like beer in a keg, and he feared an explosion. People assumed a mercenary was free to choose his master. Not so. The Duke de Verdi had freed him from a Spanish gaol after a fight that had gone wrong. The duke never let him forget it, and it bit into his heart, the knowledge he could be back inside that foul cell, in chains, if he didn't obey.

CHAPTER 10

VILLA BIANCA, NAPLES

GIULIA LET ALESSA, Isabetta's waiting woman, finish braiding the front of her thick dark hair into a jewelled net. The rest hung in artful curls down her back. She played with the ivory and silk fan that Isabetta had given her, fanning it before her face. It was four o'clock, the siesta was over and people were beginning to rouse, but the stone walls still radiated heat, and it was chokingly hot, despite the gauzed windows that were supposed to let in cooler air.

Finally, her hair was finished and she stood, her stomach taut with anticipation and excitement. Two gentlemen callers were to be admitted to the chambers today – one, a merchant in silk, and the other, his friend, a wealthy widower who was looking for some diversion. Giulia was to be the diversion, and she was waiting for Isabetta to arrive to finish her training in the courtesan's art of conversation, and in how to tempt a man.

Isabetta kept asking innumerable questions about Giulia's childhood and her former life, avid for details. It made her resist and want to do precisely the opposite and tell her nothing. She missed Mamma like a constant ache, and talking about her made it hurt more. At the same time, she was overwhelmed by this new life of colour and glitter and manners and show. She was determined to shine.

She'd dressed in a new gown, one of three. Today's was sewn from an elaborately patterned cream brocade, and consisted of a tight jacket-like bodice with a drawn back overskirt that fell in heavy folds at the back. It emphasised her figure in a way that was pleasing, but was also uncomfortably hot.

The door opened, and as Isabetta swept in, Giulia stood to greet her. Isabetta stopped mid-step, as if she couldn't believe her eyes.

'You look… quite grown, Giulia.' She walked around her chair as if she was an exhibit. 'I would never have guessed you could look so… striking. But you're too pale.' She gestured to the maid. 'Alessa, fetch the beetroot juice and cochineal from my chamber.' The maid dipped a curtsey and disappeared.

'Is it time already?' Giulia stood.

'Sit again, *cara*. I have something for you.' Isabetta drew her chair close to Giulia's. From her bodice she drew out a slim parcel wrapped in green velvet and unwrapped it on her lap.

A knife. Small, sharp, and glinting in the light of the window.

Giulia stared, uncomprehending. It was no jewel, this knife. The handle was whittled from a simple piece of smooth carved wood.

'Sad, but necessary. We all carry one. If we are out, we stow it in the top of our hose or in our bodice. If we have an assignation here, then it lives under the mattress, where our hands can easily reach it. Men are unpredictable beasts. They can turn into something unexpected when the passions take them over. Sometimes, if the man is… if he's dangerous, then you may find it useful.'

'You mean, I might have to use it?' She shuddered. 'I don't think I could…'

'No, no!' She laughed. 'You think I want to kill my clients? It's not for drawing blood. It's for threatening them only. You must say you will use it... down below. It always has the desired effect – their ardour soon cools.'

'Have you ever had to use it?'

'Twice. I was grateful for it each time. The first time, I slashed a hole in the sheets to demonstrate its sharpness, and I've never seen a man pale so quickly. It gave me time to shout for help. But don't look so worried. Signor Vecci is a gentleman, and he has vouched for his friend, the widower Signor Emilio Colombo. I wouldn't let just anyone near an inexperienced child like you.'

But I'm not a child, she wanted to say. 'What must I do?'

'You need only converse, perhaps play a game of *minchiate*, make sheep's eyes to rouse Signor Colombo's ardour. Nothing more. I have told them you are not to be bought yet. Here, take it. It won't bite you!' She held out the knife.

It felt cool and weighty in Giulia's palm. She rested a thumb on the blade and immediately a bead of blood appeared.

'Quick, find something to stop it!' Isabetta fussed round staunching the blood with her kerchief. 'Don't let blood fall on your gown.'

'Pardon, Isabetta, I didn't realise it was sharp.'

'Of course it's sharp! What were you doing?'

'I just wanted to see—'

'Well don't. And be careful.'

Giulia sucked at it. It was only a small nick, but the sight of the blood had shocked her.

'Wrap the knife up again... that's right. Is it staunched?'

Giulia held out her thumb where the bleeding had stopped.

'You'll find a small leather pocket in the front of your bodice, in the stomacher, where the stiff embroidered panel sits. A courtesan's secret. We ask the dressmaker to fit it so we can stow the knife there and it won't interfere with our movement. You will get used to reading the man – if he is a man for legs or for breasts, and then you will know where to hide it – there, or in your garter.'

The knife was snug against the bodice, but she couldn't imagine ever having to use it – unless those *condottieri* came that were looking for Mamma. Even then, the thought of the blade on flesh revolted her.

Isabetta fussed around the back to tighten the laces on her under-bodice again until the knife handle dug in and Giulia thought her ribs might crack.

'Now, you are to hint, hint only, never ask, for a gift of jewellery.' Isabetta turned her to face the looking glass on the wall. 'See how your throat and ears are bare, inviting some adornment? Use your hands to draw attention to it, like so.' Isabetta rested her fluttering hands at her throat. 'It is a skill, this.'

Giulia tried the gesture.

'Oh my saints, not like that. You look like you're batting away a flea. Be graceful, a little out of reach. Inflame desire but never flaunt. And make sure to please him enough that he will make you a gift.' More instructions followed until her head reeled.

Isabetta turned to the looking glass and inspected her own complexion again, but Giulia couldn't be still. She paced the room, back and forth, growing more agitated by the moment.

All these expectations. What if she couldn't do it? She couldn't even hold a conversation with a man without getting flustered. How was she supposed to make sheep's eyes?

This talk of knives, and inflaming a man, made her jittery.

The maidservant, Alessa, returned with a lacquer-work tray of small pots and phials. The sight of them reminded Giulia immediately of Mamma, and she glanced at the statue of Santa Olivia that she had put in pride of place on the table near the window. She had heard nothing from Mamma since leaving Palermo, and a sharp twist of anguish made her grip the silk of her skirts into her fist.

'Best not to play with your skirts like that,' Isabetta said. 'They'll crease.'

'I was thinking of Mamma, of what she'd think of me if she

could see me.'

'She'd be outraged. But then if she sends you to me, she can't be surprised at how you'll earn your keep. It's the oldest profession in the world, and a good one. Call it an education. It has never harmed me, and you never know, you might develop a taste for it, as I have.'

'I miss her.'

A flash of annoyance in Isabetta's eyes. 'She won't have forgotten you, I know that much. You were all she could ever speak of. When you were small, she called you *passerotto*, little sparrow, and never stopped telling me how clever you were. How you were the first girl to be able to read her herbal tracts, and how hard it was to keep you out of her workroom.' A bitter expression made her forehead crease. 'You were always the first in everything according to Theofania. Such a prodigy. And all thanks to her tutoring.'

Giulia wasn't sure whether or not to smile.

'Her perfect daughter, hey? Take cheer, she would write to you if she could. And you know what she's like – stubborn, not afraid to speak her mind. She'll fall saddle side up. Now, let's make me proud, shall we?'

Proud? She knew what Mamma would think of her in such a tight-waisted gown with her throat all exposed, and proud wasn't the word.

A commotion below. Isabetta hurried to the door. 'They're here. Quick, rouge your cheeks and redden your lips. I'll go and greet them.'

Another anxious turn in the stomach. A look in the glass showed a stranger. A dark, startle-eyed woman in a low-cut gown of pearl brocade. With a few dabs of a brush, her lips became fiery red. Too much?

There was no time to rub it off. The door swung open and Isabetta entered, followed by two men. Giulia curtseyed low as she'd been taught. Obeisance and humility, and at all times '*grazia*', grace, her aunt had insisted, which was the opposite of what men expected of women who were paid for their favours. Behaving like royalty would 'establish the courtship rules,' Isabetta had said.

Both men took the cue and bowed, but their eyes were fixed on Giulia, so she was forced to drop her gaze again, though not before she had seen that they were indeed well dressed in the latest style, velvet breeches and doublets, with broad collars of spotless white linen.

After the introductions, they sat for refreshments and conversation. Signor Vecci, a rotund man in his fifties with a greying point of a beard, did most of the talking. It was clear he was taken with Isabetta by the way every opinionated sentence was directed at her. The only time he stopped regaling everyone was in order to cram another almond biscotti into his mouth.

The other man, younger, was a widower, long-faced and beardless, dressed all in black, his hair hanging limply to his shoulders. His eyes roved the room, lingering on a fine marble sculpture of a naked Venus set in an alcove above the door. He averted his eyes and returned them to her, but there was something closed about his expression. Perhaps, if he'd been widowed, it was grief. She found his gaze somewhat disconcerting, and she touched her hand to her hair.

'And where do you come from, Signorina Tofana,' Signor Vecci, the older man, asked.

Signorina Tofana was the name she had chosen for herself, for it still bore traces of her mother's name, Theofania.

'Catania,' she answered. Catania was the second-largest city in the region, under the shadow of Mount Etna, and far enough away from her mother's reputation in Palermo. 'I was schooled there – in Latin and Greek, and in music,' she said. 'Would you like to hear me play?' To escape Signor Colombo's scrutiny, she gestured to the clavichord, which stood open by the window.

'Where in Catania?' the pale-faced Signor Colombo suddenly

spoke.

She gave an impression of nonchalance, though she was sure the lie showed in her eyes. 'In the middle of the city itself,' she said airily. She tried to remember the name of the street Isabetta had suggested, but she was flustered and it wouldn't come.

'In the centre? Tell me where, I might know it.'

'I have not been home for some time…' She felt heat rise to her face. She looked helplessly to Isabetta, but Isabetta had become engaged in a whispered discourse with Signor Vecci, and she couldn't catch her eye.

'But Signora Boveri told me you've only been here a few weeks. Have you been travelling?'

'Yes,' she said with relief, 'to many different places.'

His eyes narrowed. 'And you come from Catania? Do you know the Church of Sant'Agata?'

Of course she did not, but she nodded anyway.

'My brother's home is on the same street. In fact, it is our family home.'

She nodded again, feeling a fool, but she had to show some sort of agreement.

He stood up. 'There are no houses on that street, only a monastery. You lie. You've never been there, have you?' he said quietly.

'Your lie was the first,' she said. 'You lied on purpose to catch me out and make me feel small.' Angry at being discovered, she hurried over to the clavichord and began to play random notes that disturbed the silence.

'Precisely as I expected,' Colombo said bitterly.

Vecci made soothing noises to him, but she ignored them both and settled to play a toccata by Merulo, so that further conversation was impossible.

As the plangent notes filled the chamber, the tension in her shoulders released. This, at least, she could do. She was supposed to charm the Signor, and he had seen through her immediately;

she had failed in the first few moments. To release that feeling, she played with verve, almost anger.

When she finished, Vecci stood and applauded. 'Bravo. That was marvellous.'

'I concede you play with some musicality, Signorina Tofana,' Signor Colombo admitted, 'even if you are not from my home city of Catania.'

She gave a half-smile and stood up.

'Come, Signor Vecci,' Isabetta said, giving him a little nudge, 'I will take you to show you my new painting, *Diana the Huntress in The Forest*, and leave these two to get to know each other.' She cast Giulia a meaningful look as she escorted the older man out through the door.

Giulia wanted to call her back but knew she could not. When she turned, Signor Colombo had also risen from his seat.

'I shall leave now. To tell truth, I have no wish for your company,' he said, sweeping his hat from the table. 'I never wanted to come. I came only because my good friend Vecci insisted. He said it would dull my grief, but as I suspected, it has only made it worse. He said you were an innocent, but I should have known what you'd be.'

'And what is that, sir?'

'A whore like Isabetta and the rest of her birds of prey.'

'You do Isabetta a disservice. She's a woman kind enough to take me in when I had nowhere else to go.'

'Vecci said you were a virgin, but I see now I've been taken for a fool. God help me, it was a mistake to even cross the threshold. My wife would turn in her grave if she could see me here.'

She took a step towards him, heat rising to her face. How dare the men discuss her so? 'I have never lain with a man in my life, Signor Colombo, and I assure you that when I come to choose who shall have that honour, it will not be you.'

Her words were intended to sting, and they hit their mark. He was silent a moment, his lips trembling. Finally he said, 'Then what is a well-bred young woman like you doing here? In this place? Why are you not with your family?'

'There are people in my home town who wish me harm. It was safer to be incognito.'

'Who would wish you harm? You have accomplishments, that's clear enough. Why not choose a godly life?'

'Some of us are not able to choose. A calamity struck my family, and I had to abandon my home and leave behind everything I knew. Isabetta is offering me the chance to start again.'

'Is there nowhere else?'

'If there was, do you think I would be here?' She felt emotion rise in her throat. 'In a whorehouse? No. It has not been easy to start anew with nothing in a strange city with nothing familiar in sight and where I have not even a single friend.'

The words seemed to touch him. He sat down again on the red upholstered chaise. 'My apologies. I have lost my courtesy these last weeks. You are right. Starting again is hard. In the eruption of Vesuvius a year ago we lost all our livelihood. Our whole estate was turned into a smoking heap of charred embers. The roof of our oil warehouse fell in with the weight of ash. Then it rained and a landslide buried what was left. No roads to the coast were passable. In the space of a week we were left with no stock and unable to trade. So yes, I know how it is to lose everything.'

'You have done well then, sir, for you look prosperous now.'

'Prosperous but unlucky. I started the business again in the city, but I seem to attract calamities. My wife has been dead only three months, and I am only now realising that she will never return and somehow I must start again once more.'

'Let us hope there's an end to it, and no more calamities will come.'

He shrugged. 'Why would it matter? I have nothing left to lose. I have money, yes, but no life. In the last months there was no time to plan – Elena was so ill, and all I could do was struggle day to day, fetch her medicines, deal with the servants, talk to the physician. Afterwards, I was so angry I could not bear to speak to anyone. It seemed wrong, that her servants were alive, whereas she…' He paused, swallowed. 'After she'd gone, the maidservant had no-one to dress, so I had no more use for a maid. When the maid went, the cook went… and then the rest of the women… all except Anna, who is too old to go. It's such an empty house now, it tears my heart.'

What could she say, to a man who had lost so much? 'I'm sorry for your loss.'

'My business is suffering because I cannot give it my attention. It all seems so pointless. And I cannot show my emotion in public, it is not expected, no matter how much it hurts. Vecci said I must get over it and start to live again, but I don't know how. I miss Elena every moment.'

'What was the matter with her?'

'The white lung disease. She grew thinner and thinner, her breath rattling like shells in a jar. People said it was the ash. That she'd breathed in the fumes from Vesuvius. Whatever the curse was, I could do nothing. I had to watch her failing day by day, until she was barely a person at all, just big tortured eyes in a pale skull. 'Help me, Emilio,' she whispered to me in the last days. She meant, help her to die. But how could I?' He leapt up and covered his eyes with his hands.

Giulia didn't speak. She was reminded all too painfully of Mamma. Mamma would have known the right medicine to give, in the right quantity.

'Of course I couldn't,' he said, talking away from her, to the wall. 'Even though she begged me. Impossible, when she was the one thing that made my life bearable.' When he turned back, his eyes were wet. 'I was too selfish. I wanted to keep her. Poor Elena, she should have gone before; I could have saved her days of suffering. What sort of a man am I, that I could have put her through that?'

'She will have felt your love,' Giulia said, more softly. 'She will have known that you couldn't shorten the journey, that it would be a sin for you both. Did a priest come? Did she go peacefully at the end?'

'I don't know.' His anguish showed in the way he paced, shaking his head as if to rid himself of it. 'The doctor came in the morning, then I went out, I was going to buy flowers, you see. Jasmine for the scent, and some big white lilies I'd seen in the *mercato*. Elena loved them, and the scent of flowers took away the scent of the sickroom. But when I returned, she was so still. Not a breath in the room. I knew she was gone straight away. It was as if she'd deliberately chosen to go without me. I couldn't even show her the flowers.' He turned away again and pressed the hem of his sleeve to his eyes. When he turned back, his expression was stricken. 'I didn't mean to tell you so much.'

'Signor Vecci is wiser than you know. Grief seems a large burden to bear alone. Perhaps you need to talk. And you are mistaken – Isabetta tells me a courtesan is not only for one thing. A courtesan can be many things – a confidante, a companion, even someone to share a jest.' She hoped she was right. 'Sit again,' she said, patting the space next to her on the upholstered chaise. 'I ask for nothing. Only your company. My aunt will be angry with me if you leave so soon, and we can simply talk. You can tell me about Elena, she sounds like an extraordinary woman.'

'Very well. But I must have your word that you do not tell Signor Vecci that I could not press you to… that we…'

'Nothing said or done in this chamber will ever go beyond these walls.'

He put his hat down again and sat. 'Would you play for me again?' he asked.

'Of course. What shall it be? How about *Gagliarda Napoletana* by Valente? A very pretty tune.' She walked to the clavichord again and struck a few notes. 'Do you dance, Signor Colombo?'

'No. My feet don't know how. I never have and never will.

Not even with Elena. But I'll hear your galliard, nonetheless.'

She played several more bright melodies for him, and he listened attentively. 'I keep thinking how much Elena would have loved this music,' he said.

Giulia merely nodded and continued to play.

At one point when she turned, she saw he was weeping, but she ignored it. *Let him weep*, she thought, *there is nowhere else he can do it.*

After the bells rang the hour, a soft knock. Giulia leapt to her feet and ran to answer it. Signor Colombo turned his back so the others could not see his face. The door swung open and she ushered Vecci in, with Isabetta following behind, her hair mussed and dishevelled, her lip paint smeared. She caught Giulia's eye and raised her eyebrows.

'She plays well, eh Colombo?' Vecci said. 'We could hear the clavichord right through the house. And I was thinking, if you like music, perhaps you would both accompany us to the salon of my great friend, Ferdinando de Ribera, for the June masque. It will be a fine entertainment, will it not, Emilio?' Signor Colombo nodded his agreement. 'There is to be a quartet, with some singers. The viceroy, Acevedo y Zuñiga, will be there, and the papal vice-chancellor, Barberini.' He looked round, as if all these illustrious names should make an impression.

'August company indeed. I will certainly be there,' Isabetta said. 'I will wear my new pearl and amethyst necklace.'

Of course, the men looked to Giulia's neck immediately and saw it was bare. Aunt Isabetta was certainly working hard to encourage the idea of a gift.

'But we shall see you at church before then, shall we not?' Vecci said.

Isabetta nodded. 'Of course. I shall try not to laugh when Father Girolamo tells us again that the meek shall inherit the earth.'

'You're wicked, Isabetta.' Signor Vecci grinned and winked.

CHAPTER 11

VILLA BIANCA, NAPLES

OVER THE LAST few weeks Giulia had become used to the business of entertaining men with small conversation and harmless coquetry. Isabetta had supplied her with several more elderly clients, most of them widowed merchants from the city. They were rich men who wanted female companionship, but without the added trouble of another wife or more children. The other courtesans were envious.

'How come you get all the ones who can't get it up?' asked Bella.

'The richest ones too,' Elvira complained.

She supposed it was because she was Isabetta's niece, and she sometimes caught Isabetta looking at her with an odd expression of pride. Quickly masked, of course. Just yesterday Giulia had accompanied a Jewish goldsmith to a banquet at his brother's house. The banquet was lavish, with nine courses of fish, fowl and meats.

The thin servants watched the meal with hungry eyes and wiped their salivating mouths. When the meal was done, they rushed in rather too quickly to clear away, and presumably devour, the leftovers. Giulia guarded her tongue well, smiled and kept her opinions to herself even though it was clear that Naples was a city of two halves, the haves and the have-nots.

Today she was on the arm of Emilio Colombo for a night at the opera, dressed up and powdered to look like an aristocrat, swaying through the city streets in her client's fine gilded coach. Isabetta's dressmaker had remade three of Isabetta's old gowns into newer styles, and Giulia wore them with pride, never having worn such fine silk before.

They were just passing the Piazza Falcone when a ragged crowd surrounded the carriage, jeering and throwing handfuls of dung.

'Bread, bread!' they shouted.

Something landed in her lap, and she jerked back. When she glanced down, it was to see her new skirts spattered with filth. She brushed the dirt from her lap as Signor Colombo leant out of the window and yelled a curse.

'They pour in from the villages,' he said, 'in search of their grain. They grow it, but then the landowners ship it to the cities or to the armies fighting the French. Either they starve, or we do.'

'What can be done?'

'Little. There is not enough bread for all. We just have to hope for a better harvest next year, then there will be fewer beggars to disturb our streets.'

Mamma would have had sympathy for them. She treated the rich and the poor alike. As the carriage rattled along, she wondered what Mamma would think if she could see her now.

Oh Mamma. What had you done?

She only had one eye on the opera. Her inner eye replayed a conversation she had earlier with Isabetta. She had questioned Isabetta about Mamma, but all Isabetta would say was, 'Be patient. She'll come for you when she can, and besides, do you not like it here, with all the attractions of Naples?'

But she couldn't forget Isabetta's earlier blurted confession that Mamma could be in gaol, and she longed to know where she

was, whether she was safe, whether she worried about her
daughter's life in this city of courtesans and thieves.

She tried to be cheerful, smiled at Signor Colombo's friends,
complimented his choice of entertainment and flattered him.
Fortunately, Colombo did not want more than an escort, his wife
being so recently passed.

'Your mind was elsewhere,' he said to her as she thanked him.
'You barely spoke all evening. And I got the impression you didn't
hear a single word I said.'

'Oh, but I did. I'm sorry, Signor Colombo. I was listening.'

'Good. Because I pay you to listen. And you may call me
Emilio.'

She was silent then. He asked her to use his name as if she
were a friend, but now she saw that all the same, he saw her only
as a service he could pay for.

Back in her room and missing Mamma, she took the chymist
book from under her pillow and drew a finger lovingly over the
leather cover. Scuffed and well worn, it was stained with
different liquids and was brown at the edges with use. She had
never told Isabetta about this book. She sensed she would not
approve because whenever she brought up the subject of
Mamma's business, Isabetta frowned and changed the subject. At
the window, where the moon slanted through, she opened it up,
and the sight of Mamma's tiny handwriting made her stomach
twist into a knot. Such a mystery here in these pages.

She studied the tiny drawings of minerals all based on the *tria
prima* – something Mamma had referred to often, the three
guiding principles of sulphur, salt and mercury. Sulphur, the
fiery; salt, the bloom of the earth; and mercury, the strange liquid
that was half water, half metal and was worth more than silver.

Some tracts were clearly copied from someone else – a few
were annotated with the name Coçar, a man who she knew had
been a Paracelsian and the physician to Felipe II. One part that

fascinated her was about '*smoaks*' – the making of a gas which was both a vital spirit and a liquid for inhalation.

These unfamiliar remedies engrossed her. But the one that drew her attention the most was the one labelled '*aqua vitalis*' a remedy for heart flutters and indigestion.

In tiny letters after it, the words were written '*aqua morta*'. Deathwater.

'*Take care. One drop to cure, three drops to kill.*'

She paused, looking at the words on the page as if they might change into something else. But no. They remained stubbornly there.

Had Mamma sold this *aqua morta* to Duchess Valentina de Verdi?

A sharp knock at the door below.

She snapped the book shut and pushed it under the pillow.

She went to the balcony to lean out of the window to see who it might be. A group of men had clustered around the front door. Dark-clad men armed with swords. Two of them carried the sort of picks a farmer might carry. Except these were too finely dressed to be farmers; they had the look of the mercenaries she'd run away from in Palermo. Something about their belligerent stances made her stiffen and withdraw. She feared it might be something to do with her mother. Perhaps someone had found out she was here and had given her away? Her mind raced. She had told nobody, not even Fabio.

She heard Alessa answer the door but crept out onto the landing to listen to what the men wanted. The torchères had not been lit, so she was able to listen in the shadows without being seen. Alessa ran up the next flight of stairs to fetch Isabetta. Giulia shrank back against the wall as she saw Isabetta hurry down, a panicked expression on her face. One of the men stepped forward, did not bow or remove his hat as most of their clients did. She could not see his face from here, not from above, shadowed as it was by his hat. The man held himself stiffly, she could see that by the way his arms were held slightly akimbo.

With this man, though, Isabetta was a different person. Gone was the imperious, arrogant devil-may-care attitude, and instead Giulia saw a person cringing and cowering. Isabetta was protesting about something in a low voice and shaking her head. She looked very much as if she might be begging.

Giulia daren't go closer to the banister for fear of being caught eavesdropping, and the conversation was in low voices, but the manner of the men was threatening, the way they leant forward, eyes fixed on her like a pack of wolves. Alessa was sent upstairs and returned with a bag of coin, but when their leader looked inside, it seemed to make him even more angry. One of the men raised the pick and brought it down on the wall, where it ripped down a tapestry along with a chunk of plaster.

Shocked, Giulia moved further out of sight. Isabetta hurriedly pulled out her dangling pearl earrings and dropped them into the man's hand. When it remained outstretched she unhooked the fragile emerald necklace from around her neck and passed it to him.

In return, he took hold of her by the throat, his face a hair's breadth from hers. 'God will bless you,' he said. 'Earthly trinkets have no value when our reward will be in heaven. Here, take it.'

He gestured to one of the others, who handed her a small package. Isabetta took it, but her hands trembled. 'Thank you,' she said.

The crisis, whatever it was, seemed to have been averted, and to Giulia's annoyance they retreated to the salon, out of earshot. But they were a fair time in discussion, and she wondered who these people were, and why Isabetta was so afraid. She waited until they returned to the hall, Isabetta paler than usual, a strange set about the mouth.

'Tomorrow,' Giulia heard him say as he turned to go. 'I will send her tomorrow.'

Who was this man? Who would he send?

She tiptoed away. The thin veneer of polite Neapolitan life suddenly seemed to mask a more dangerous darkness.

The next day, Isabetta was smiling and dreamy, a strange faraway look in her eyes. She told her that Signor Vecci was bringing another friend, a special guest, a woman.

Giulia had a wild hope it might be Mamma. So she dressed carefully; now she was used to being tight-laced, and to spending time on coiling her thick black hair into elaborate curls and making up her face, but she was barely finished when the bell rang in the hall.

She waited in feverish excitement. It wasn't long before she was summoned to the parlour, where Signor Vecci was holding court over Isabetta. He was his usual self-satisfied and rotund self, full of garrulous talk.

Beside him, Isabetta had her 'client's expression' on her face, one radiating smiles. Her voluminous hooped skirts swished as she dipped and swayed, so it was a moment before she even noticed the girl behind them who was doing her best to shrink into the floor.

'This is Signora de Verdi,' Signor Vecci said. 'Agnese is the wife of a very old friend of mine, Domenico de Verdi.'

The name. De Verdi. Like the duke from Palermo. But surely this was just a coincidence? The shock was followed by the awful ache of disappointment. Not Mamma. Just this thin girl. When Giulia finally remembered where she was, she gave a half-curtsey.

'Good morrow,' Giulia said. The girl Agnese was very young to be already wed, perhaps fourteen years, with a porcelain-white, heart-shaped face and an aura of intense misery. Her thick bronze-coloured hair was pulled back under an elaborate head-dress that glimmered with a criss-cross of pearls. A wealthy wife then. She had a servant with her, who now emerged from a chair by the door – a sour-faced woman of middle age, who fixed Giulia with a scathing expression.

Agnese looked down at her feet at Giulia's greeting.

'Agnese wishes to learn the clavichord,' Vecci said, 'so of course, I thought of you and recommended you. Signora Boveri agrees, so what do you say? Will you instruct her, Signorina Tofana?'

'I would love to.' Oh, the joy of that, rather than the dread of being forced to play games of the bedchamber. 'Do you want to start today?'

'Of course today—' Isabetta said, but Agnese showed no enthusiasm or change in demeanour. Instead, she studied the floor.

'One hour's lesson then,' Vecci said. You can send Signora Gauci to find a boy to take a message to Signor de Verdi. I told him we'd send word if she was to stay.'

Signora Gauci curtseyed to him, with a disgruntled expression, as if it was too much trouble.

'Please ask the boy to tell my husband I will be an hour here,' Agnese said, her voice quiet and high.

The Gauci woman went out, followed by Isabetta, who was instructing her where to find a messenger boy, leaving Agnese alone in the room with Vecci and Giulia.

'Excellent, excellent, I'll leave you to begin,' Vecci said, bowing his farewell, in a hurry to follow Isabetta.

The girl stood awkwardly in the middle of the room, like a lost island in a huge sea.

'Come,' Giulia said, 'bring up that stool, and we can sit side by side.'

Agnese was looking about the room, taking everything in. Giulia saw her eyes fix on the statue of Santa Olivia that she had placed on a shelf above the clavichord.

'You like my statue of Santa Olivia?' she asked. 'Do you have a favourite saint?'

'I hate them all,' she said.

Giulia ignored the prickly response and beckoned again, and Agnese did as she was asked.

'You have no servants,' the girl said. It was a statement of fact.

'No. And I need none. The women here chaperone each other.'

'I wish I needed none.'

'Perhaps you have a bigger household than we do,' she said.

Agnese shook her head. 'No. It's just they watch me every moment. My husband's spies.' The words were full of venom.

Giulia didn't know how to respond, so she opened a sheet of music and propped it on the stand. She pointed to a simple set of notes on the top line and played with one finger.

'Now you,' she said.

Agnese picked out the notes with ease.

'Good. Now these.'

Again the girl found the correct notes.

'Both together?'

Agnese obliged, playing the run of notes three times over. 'Oh,' she said, eyes alive, 'it sounds so sweet.'

The lesson progressed as Giulia introduced playing with all the fingers and set some exercises and scales. She glanced over at Agnese on the stool beside her; she was flushed with effort and excitement. She looked like a different girl from the one who had come in earlier. How a little joy had transformed her!

Just after the quarter bell, Isabetta pushed open the door and led in a gentleman in dark clothing. Giulia and Agnese stood as he entered, though Agnese reverted to the cowering look again, which made Giulia look twice at the man who had just arrived. The same surly servant, Signora Gauci, slunk in behind him. Agnese's eyes were already cast at the floor. She seemed to shrivel into herself, as if she wanted to hide inside her clothes.

'Signor de Verdi,' Isabetta said, in a way that indicated his name should mean something important. His servant hung by the door.

'Sir,' Giulia said, dropping a curtsey. The word of deference slipped from her lips, though her mind was a whirl of confusion. Surely this was the same stiff man who had taken Isabetta's jewellery last night?

Signor Domenico de Verdi was a broad-set man of about forty years, with a flat nose that had maybe once been broken. His black hair was slicked back with oil, and there was a slight twist to the mouth under his well-trimmed beard. His doublet and breeches were dark but well made, his ruff small and stiffly starched. A well-off merchant, by the look of him, but one who was still holding himself as if his clothes pained him, and he was looking down his nose at her.

Giulia held his gaze, determined not to be intimidated. 'We have had an enjoyable lesson.'

'Signora Gauci told me my wife was here and had already begun her lessons. You may show me what Agnese has learned,' he said. 'It is not often I have time for diversions like music.' He smiled without showing his teeth, and his gaze travelled the length of Giulia's figure, as if noting every measurement.

She glanced to Agnese. Both of them knew instantly it was some sort of test to be passed. Giulia opened the music at the exercise they had been playing and pointed to the notes. Agnese played, but it was mechanical, as if she no longer felt the joy of playing. But she made no mistakes, and when she had finished, she bowed her head and was still.

'Most satisfactory,' Signor de Verdi said. 'You will teach her hymns and sacred music, yes?'

'Whatever she wishes to play,' Giulia said.

'No. Not songs. Only hymns and psalms, I think, not common tunes. Sacred music for the glory of our Lord.' He turned to Agnese. 'You enjoyed your lesson?'

'Yes, husband.' The voice was barely audible.

'Then you will come again on Friday. Three times a week for the agreed sum.' The latter was addressed towards Isabetta, who was tight-lipped. Strain showed round her eyes.

'Now, Signorina Tofana, you may play me something, something to inspire the soul.'

He was a man used to being obeyed. Giulia didn't like being told what to play, but she couldn't refuse; Isabetta would be angry if she did. But it was astonishing how quickly Signor de Verdi had taken over. He was a man who took control of a room by his mere presence, and by some sort of menace that lay concealed beneath his urbane exterior.

As her hands flowed over the notes, she caught Agnese watching her with a strange burning look in her eyes, but she ignored it and focussed on the tune, a madrigal by Marino. It was a simple but touching piece that showed off her technique well, but she was aware that de Verdi was ignoring his young wife, and his eyes were fixed only on her playing. It filled her with discomfort. When she had finished, he brought his hands together in a leisurely clap that felt more insulting than enthusiastic.

'Well, I see you can play,' he said.

'Thank you,' Isabetta said, smiling at him, as if the compliment were for her, and the whole atmosphere in the room were not as volatile as a wild horse.

'It's agreed then,' Signor de Verdi said. 'My wife will come three times a week until she reaches Signorina Tofana's standard.' His expression said, *and don't let it take too long.* 'Come, Agnese,' he said, 'pick up your gloves.'

Agnese seemed fixed to the spot until he put his hand on her back. She flinched, as if his palm were red-hot, but he swept up her gloves from the chair by the door and continued to propel her out of the room. She walked like a wooden puppet.

'Farewell, Signora de Verdi,' Giulia called out, but Agnese didn't turn.

As soon as they were out of the room, Giulia let out a sigh of relief. A tension had gone with them.

'Is he related to the Duke Antonio de Verdi? The man Mamma supposedly poisoned?'

'His brother.'

'You jest.'

'I hate him,' Isabetta said. 'But he is too powerful a man in the city to cross.'

'Does Mamma know he's here in Naples?'

'I've no idea. Probably not.'

'Did he come here last night?'

Isabetta looked at her sharply. 'What do you know of it?'

'Nothing. I just… happened to be passing the top of the stairs and saw a man take down our tapestry with a pickaxe.'

'Forget you saw that. You must say nothing to anyone, do you hear me? If he hears a word against him from us, we will be closed down… or worse. He's a man who believes hell is waiting for women like us, but at the same time he finds us irresistible. He gets rid of his own guilt by charging us a fee for existence.'

'But that's wrong. Can't you do something about it?'

'The last courtesan who tried disappeared without trace and her premises were shut down within a day. He told the viceroy he was cleaning up the city.'

'Why does he want me to teach his wife then?'

'Some notion of his about having sacred music in his home. He's a man obsessed. He's funding an enormous church, in the new style, sacred to Santa Fina. He will stop at nothing to build it – he wants it to be the most impressive church in Naples, and the fee we pay him to keep this house open goes towards that. He says it is only fitting that whores like us should pay penance.'

'But that's simple extortion!'

'But extortion sanctified by the Church. Cardinal Bono, who is only too happy to have another church funded by a man like Domenico de Verdi. More visible power for Rome.'

'I'm not sure I want to be involved with a man like him, especially if his brother is the Duke de Verdi of Palermo. What if they should talk of me?'

'Be very clear, Giulia. You have little choice. I tried to avoid doing business with him, but… I have my reasons. Besides, Vecci was insistent, because Domenico de Verdi was leaning on him too. So it is Vecci we have to thank, if thank him we must.'

'That poor wife! She's only a girl, but at least she'll be easy to teach. She has a good ear for music.'

'Well, teach her quickly is all I ask.'

CHAPTER 12

GIULIA WATCHED Isabetta go out early to fetch yesterday's broadsheet from the market square. Saturdays were always far too busy for reading, but there was time on Sundays. Giulia observed her from the window, drawing all eyes as she usually did, in her blue well-corseted gown and carrying a sunshade lest her face become freckled. As always, Giulia was keen for her return, awaiting her second-hand peek, hoping for any sort of news of home. Isabetta could never wait until back in the house to read it, so she walked with only one eye on the passing carts and mules, and the other on the paper.

Giulia smiled as a watermelon-seller with a donkey had to haul it to one side as Isabetta, oblivious, stepped into its path. The fruit merchant yelled something at her, but she did not even hear him. In mid-step, she stopped dead, transfixed by some item of news.

For a long moment Isabetta stared into space, her expression stricken, then looked at the paper again. Then up at the house, to her very window. Giulia moved back out of sight but could still see Isabetta crumple the sheet tight between her hands, as if to squeeze the breath from it. Abruptly, she turned on her heel and walked away from the house, her gait unsteady, until, bending double, she leant against the wall of a neighbouring building.

It was bad news. With dread, Giulia watched her unscrew the paper again and read it as if she would suck every nuance from the words before she let it drop. Isabetta's face transfixed her. It was set into an unseeing mask, and unsteady as a sleepwalker, she headed back towards the house.

Giulia retreated from the window and prepared herself for morning mass. The summoning bells were already pealing, but there was no sign of Isabetta. The women waited impatiently, fanning themselves in their Sunday clothes. When Isabetta appeared, she was red-eyed and her face was puffy even though she had put on a lace mantilla with which to hide it. She would not catch Giulia's eye.

'What is it?' Giulia whispered. Panic engulfed her.

But Isabetta merely shook her head brusquely and strode on ahead.

The women arrived at the Church of San Giovanni late but caused the usual stir as they entered the church. This was a regular entertainment that the congregation looked forward to. After all, there were five courtesans to gawp at, including Giulia; the others were Bella, Elvira, Maria and Anastasia, but also their three female servants, who attended mass with them. The courtesans were dressed formally, like aristocratic ladies in well-cut high-necked gowns. Today, Isabetta hadn't advised them, as she usually did, to tantalise possible clients by leaving some hair showing, as if carelessly, under their veils. But nonetheless, they had all done so, following the usual routine.

The courtesans' chatter was subdued, and as she followed Bella's fiery red ringlets into the pew, she was glad she could dip her head so her own mantilla covered her worried expression. Isabetta, oddly taciturn, led them into the back two rows, and in their elaborate hooped skirts, they took a while to settle.

The service was long and the morning warm, and Isabetta sat

rigidly beside her, staring into space. In this light, she looked older, her forehead and upper lip etched with fine lines despite the ceruse. When a tear trickled from the corner of her eye, Isabetta did not bother to wipe it away.

'*Dominus Vobiscum*,' the priest intoned.

'*Et cum spiritu tuo*,' Giulia replied. She inhaled the frankincense and took comfort from the familiar chant of the congregation's responses. It soothed the deep sense of dread at whatever ailed Isabetta.

The priest, an elderly man, almost dropped the chalice when he was to pour the communion wine and raise the host. One wrist was stiff and swollen to double the size of the other. Neither of the altar boys seemed to notice, or offer help, and the priest was left to struggle alone.

On the way out, they were forced to stand and wait for the rest of the congregation to leave first. The over-curious expressions of the merchants' wives, and the fact they were last into the church, and last to leave, showed their lack of status, she knew. They were not quite citizens like the rest. But when they reached the doors, Father Girolamo, the priest, was waiting to greet them nonetheless.

'This is Giulia,' Isabetta said, her voice strangely cracked. 'She's staying a while with us. She's my... my niece.'

He gave her a nod of acknowledgement, seeming oblivious to the tension. 'I can't clasp hands with you, my dear,' he said. 'I had an accident on the way to church yesterday. I wasn't looking where I was going and I tripped and fell. Foolish. My hand won't close properly.'

'I saw your wrist was swollen,' Giulia said. 'It could be a sprain. Do you mind if I look?'

'Not at all.' He held out his wrist obligingly.

She ignored Isabetta, who was exerting a slight pressure on her arm to pull her away to where the others waited, fanning themselves by the building opposite, under the shade of the purple bougainvillea.

The priest's arm and hand were inflamed and she felt the bones gently. He winced, but as far as she could see, it was just a sprain. 'Have you tried a poultice of linaria?' she said. My mother used to say that was the best to bring the swelling down and stop bruising.'

'Come away, Giulia,' Isabetta snapped. 'The man doesn't want your mother's quack remedies.'

Giulia ignored her. 'Try adding arnica for good measure. You can make it yourself with a pestle and mortar and a little goose fat.'

'Ah. I will try it. Thank you for your advice,' he said seriously, and he smiled at her with his warm hazel eyes as Isabetta pulled her away.

'The old fool. They should get someone younger,' Isabetta said. Her words were sharp and angry. 'I'm surprised no-one has died of boredom in there.'

Giulia kept on walking. Talk of herbs had made her nostalgic for Mamma. She wanted to work in the kitchen again, and she longed for the smell of fresh greenery instead of the overpowering perfumes of Isabetta's salon. She turned. 'Where is the nearest apothecary?' she asked.

Isabetta frowned. 'Leave it be, Giulia. Sins can't be wiped out by pandering to an old priest, and besides, it's closed on the Sabbath.'

'I can always ask someone else,' she said, jutting out her chin.

Isabetta took her by the arm, her face inches from Giulia's. 'Listen hard, Giulia. I don't want you following in Theofania's footsteps, do you hear me? She wouldn't listen either, and look where it led her.' Isabetta's anger seemed close to tears.

Giulia stepped back. 'What's the harm? It's only a kitchen remedy for an old man with a bruised arm.'

Isabetta leaned towards her, stabbing her finger in the air.

'She was just the same, God rest her. Stubborn as a donkey.' She threw up her arms. 'Do you want to travel that road? Risk your life every single day? Be arrested and flung in gaol?'

The words hit her like stones. The whole cavalcade of women had stopped and were waiting, staring as they argued in the street.

'Where's Mamma? You know, don't you?' A choke came to her throat.

'Best you forget about her.'

'Tell me. Is she in gaol? Is that what you think?'

A pause. Isabetta turned away, curled in on herself like an old woman. Then she began to shake. Sobs wracked her shoulders.

'What is it?'

'Leave me be!' She pushed off any attempt to soothe her. But then she brought herself under control with a heaving breath. 'She's dead.' Her eyes were streaming but her words were flat. 'The duke executed her. Why else has she not come for you? She'd have climbed a fiery Mount Vesuvius to get to you if she could, the silly fool.'

Giulia swayed. The pavement seemed to tilt, her heart squeezed in her chest. 'Who told you?' Then light dawned. 'Oh no. It was the news-sheet, wasn't it?'

'I feared this would happen, that she would get the blame for some rich aristocrat's vindictive heart, but to die in such a way...'

'What? You've got to tell me—'

'It's over.' Isabetta cut her off. 'I wish to God it were not. But there it is. And best not to dig. You don't want to know the details, truly you don't, and you must keep your mouth shut. Shut, d'you hear? Unless you wish to be tarred with the same brush. Like mother, like daughter, they'll say. And that's the last thing my sister would want.' Isabetta marched on ahead, but then swivelled, her expression bitter. 'Actually, no. The last thing she'd want is that you turn into a courtesan like me.'

CHAPTER 13

GIULIA PRESSED her eyes tight shut. She hadn't slept. Thank God she was not to entertain a client until evening. It was no use, she had to get up. Her eyes were full of grit, her head ached, and she couldn't think of eating for the churning in the pit of her stomach. With the dawn light came the careless chattering of sparrows and the cheery shouts of market traders setting out their stalls. She dressed without thinking, took a wrap and went out into the dawn. She must find out the truth about Mamma.

She went to the stallholders who were setting up their wares for the day.

'If you please, have you got a copy of Saturday's broadsheet?' she asked.

She was ignored or dismissed with a shake of the head. Most people were unable to read, and they stared as if this woman with the unkempt hair and dark circles under her eyes was losing her senses. Finally, a middle-aged widow setting out vegetables in rows took pity on her. She gestured her to her husband, who was puffing at his pipe, deep in conversation with another trader hunched over a stall selling prints of famous paintings.

She went over and asked again. 'I can pay,' she said.

This caught his attention. He scrabbled under the trestle table. The paper was soiled and had obviously been used for wrapping something else. He smiled knowingly at her, smoothing it out over a copy of a print of *The Courtesan's Lament*, a lurid depiction of the ills and diseases that might befall courtesans if they did not repent.

She handed over coins and took the paper. Mouth dry, she strode away.

Back in her room she spread it out on the coverlet and began to read. An hour later the sheet lay on the bed and Giulia had stared at the wall for so long she did not know what the time was, but the noon sunlight had crept in through the window. She was bone-chillingly cold even though it was midsummer and the sort of day where butter melted in the crock. She struggled to move, a kind of torpor had set in, a sense of being set outside her own life. As if she was watching herself pick herself up from the outside.

Inside her head, the vision of Mamma's death replayed over and over, like a nightmare that wouldn't stop. The fact of having to imagine it, to try to see what Mamma's last terrified moments must have been, to imagine the musty smell of the hempen sack, its dark texture, Mamma's dread at what might come. Then to imagine the fall through empty air, the ground crashing up too soon, shocking out her last breath.

The man who had ordered this had chosen for her a death with no dignity. She would make sure the Duke de Verdi remembered that. That a man should have such control over anyone; that he should rob her of even the chance to look out over her city one last time, to take one last look, filled her with fury.

Giulia braced herself upright, stood and pressed her palms against the edges of the window that faced towards Palermo. Dark feelings swirled around her like smoke, filling her nostrils, creeping into the crevices between thoughts. Mamma thought her too flighty and irresponsible for this work, too young. But not now. She had aged a lifetime in one day. A sacred task, her mother called it, this power over life or death. And now, she was the last in her line. The duke should have been dead at her mother's hands, not this other way around. And now only she was left to bring the power back to herself and wreak retribution on the duke's head.

She would learn how to make the *aqua morta* and complete her mother's task, and when she did, she would make sure he knew precisely who held his life in their hands. The moment she made that decision, the rest of the palazzo fell weirdly quiet. She could hear no birdsong, no cicadas. The sounds outside stilled. Only her breath, like a rasping tide; the life flowing in and out.

She took the chymist book from under her pillow, suppressing the choke in the throat that it brought. She understood now why Mamma kept her away from the workroom and would never tell her what she made, would never give her the secrets of her special 'aqua'. The starched pages of the book drew her, like a puzzle that needed to be solved. She creaked open the book to the section marked *'Banes'*. Lists of different kinds of venom, from tree frogs, from Egyptian vipers, from salamanders and scorpions. And lists of different types of bezoar stones that were the antidote. Where could she get these things? She would need to know more. Why hadn't she listened when Mamma was alive?

Mamma? Her thoughts reached out into infinite space.

She thought she sensed a silent presence. Turning, she saw nothing, but then movement caught her eye. A spider, hanging from a thread in the corner of the window. She remembered watching a spider just before the duke's men came to the house...

She walked over to watch it. It must mean something. *Everything means something*, Mamma used to say.

She was seized with a sudden desire to know, to understand what had driven her mother to such a dangerous occupation. What was it all about? She was at a loss to understand it. She would go to the apothecary, see if she could begin to fill in the missing pieces. She could make something for the priest, Father Girolamo. It would be a beginning, at least.

Going down the back stairs to keep out of Alessa's view, she stepped out into the warmth of the afternoon. Isabetta and Bella had had clients last night and were sleeping in, though how Isabetta could still take a lover after yesterday's news, she hardly knew. That the sun should still rise the same felt wrong, with Mamma no longer in the world. She hadn't eaten, and it gave her an eerie floating sensation. She had never considered that her mother wouldn't always be there, at the crux of her life, cajoling and nagging and telling her what to do.

The ordinariness of putting on a hat and tying it seemed strange when she was so close to death that she could almost touch it. The apothecary would be both a safe place and a dangerous place. Would Mamma want her to risk ending the way she had? Isabetta had been clear – her mother never wanted her to have the life of a courtesan.

Mamma's words came back, that life is not black and white. *But it is*, she thought. There was only one way she could go, and her feet were already moving in that direction.

She stopped a gourd seller on a mule to ask him the way to the apothecary, and he pointed a gnarled finger down a side street towards the church of Santa Maria del Carmine. She soon spotted the iron sign of a pestle and mortar jutting above a shuttered window, with the name *Aromatorio Ruggieri*. Her eyes kept leaking tears, as if they knew more about her mother's death than she did herself. She brushed the tears away, bit down on her trembling lip. She must rally herself.

As she arrived, a man and woman in dark clothes emerged from the door to unfold the shutters and pin them back. The window had no glass but was open to the street, with a counter stretched across it made of wood bleached white by scrubbing.

'*Buongiorno*,' Giulia said, the words like chaff in her mouth.

'A good day indeed,' the woman said, smiling. She was a flat-faced, heavy-set woman with a capable manner. Giulia watched as she propped up the awning to keep the goods from the sun. 'Just a moment,' she said, 'and we'll be ready for business.'

Giulia read a notice attached to the door. '*Wanted – boy for apprentice. Enquire within.*' They must be well established to be able to afford to take on someone else. She wished she could be that boy, instead of one of Isabetta's 'signorinas'.

Inside, the woman's husband, thinner, with the sort of stoop that suggested he spent his life reading, was laying out bundles and pots for collection on a long shelf. Each one was labelled with a name in spidery script, so she guessed these were medications ordered by the physician for his clients and were awaiting collection. The number of bundles and the well-organised interior assured her this was a well-licensed business.

Rose sugar, quince paste, oil of sweet almonds. Each label was like a stab. Her mother used to have rows of jars like these in the still room. Just like at home in Palermo, the higher shelves were stacked with the more valuable metallic powders such as gold, iron powder, and a blue glass flask marked *argentino vivo*, the living silver, that Englishmen named after the slippery messenger god, Mercury.

'How can I help?' Signor Ruggiero asked, barely glancing up, intent on weighing a bright yellow substance on his balance. Powdered turmeric. Easily recognisable. She watched as he tipped the powder into a cone-shaped packet and put it aside.

'I want some ingredients to make a poultice,' Giulia said. 'I thought linaria and arnica. I have some olive oil at home to bind it.'

'Ah, so you know a little.' He looked up to take her in. 'Who taught you? Your mother?'

She flushed, took a deep breath. 'I must have read it some-where. I like making remedies.'

He nodded vigorously. 'I also. When I was a small boy I was very poor, so I used to mix remedies from mud and leaves I found on the street. Only later did I discover that these items do actually have a curative power – when used correctly of course.' He laughed. 'Now I do nothing else but mix mud pies.'

'It sounds like a good life for you.'

'The best. Now, I do have my own special remedy for bruis-ing.' He went to a shelf in the corner where many *bussolotti*, the small wooden pots used for tinctures, stood in rows, and he brought one out. He opened it, but then, seeing her face, closed it again. 'Oh. I guess you would rather make your own.'

The woman bustled up and gave him a playful slap on the arm. 'Now, Matteo, don't go encouraging her. You know the *Sanita* doesn't approve of unqualified people supplying remedies. You'll get her into trouble.'

'It's only a paste for bruises, Camilla. It'll do no harm; this girl knows what she's about.' He winked at her.

'Thank you,' Giulia said. 'Yes please. It's for the priest at the Church of San Giovanni.'

'Ah, our own Father Girolamo,' the woman said. 'Yes, we know him; he's in a few times a month for the slippery elm for his digestion.'

'Camilla! How many times have I told you not to give out information about our customers?'

Camilla Ruggiero just shrugged and smiled, her husband's words sluicing away like water through a sieve.

'I saw your notice,' Giulia said, 'for an apprentice. Would you consider taking on a woman?'

'A woman?' Matteo looked doubtfully at his wife.

'No,' she said, banging her hands on her leather apron for emphasis. 'We don't have suitable accommodation. A girl could never sleep in that damp dispensary. And we need someone worth training, not someone who'd be off into wedlock as soon as any young blade threw her a smile.'

'Who is this woman you're thinking of?' Matteo asked.

'Actually, me. I'd be cheap to train, and I have a little knowledge about herbs and—'

Camilla broke in. 'No, it's a boy we're after, isn't it, Matteo? A good strong boy.'

Her husband sighed. 'Just fetch me a clean wrapper.' As she went, he leaned over to Giulia. 'She's got her heart set on a boy,' he whispered with a shrug.

Camilla returned a moment later with a piece of brownish paper, and Signor Ruggiero laid out the dried herbs on it for Giulia's inspection before wrapping it and tying it with twine. 'That'll be two scudi,' he said. His eyes were still apologising.

Giulia handed over the money and picked up the parcel.

'I hope to see you again, Signorina…?'

A fractional pause. 'Tofana.' The name was even more important now. Not quite Theofania, but a name to remember her mother by. 'Signorina Tofana.'

As she went out she could hear the man, Matteo, berating his wife for being so rude. 'You think we can afford to drive custom away? You should have let her down more gently…'

CHAPTER 14

BRUNO HAD BEEN in Naples a week, arriving by boat and staying incognito in a small run-down hostelry near the harbour, and he'd made a good assessment of the state of the city. A city full of struggle; narrow streets infested with beggars and whores, the harbour areas unsafe to walk alone, unless you wanted to be accosted at knifepoint. A stink of poverty and corruption under the glitter of Spanish extravagance. Years of experience and a sharp eye had kept him out of trouble. He had found out too that the Camorra, the syndicate of organised crime, was rife in the city, and that Domenico de Verdi was always the man at the black heart of it. The duke would need to know this, Bruno thought; that his brother was a man used to getting his own way through threats. Two brothers tarred with the same brush.

Before leaving for Palermo again, he could not resist a glimpse of Isabetta, though he knew this was like picking at a scab that would not heal. She had not been hard to find. Her bordello was well known among drinking men. Isabetta's salon was known as the *'piccolo gioiello'* – 'little jewel' – by her sea-faring clients, for the prices for a courtesan's company were lower than in bigger establishments. The fact she priced herself low made his chest tight.

So now he'd been on watch outside the Villa Bianca for a few hours, sitting at a roadside stall that sold small beer and sausage. He watched from this vantage point as several young women in gaudy apparel came and went, clinging on the arms of wealthy men.

When one of the women came out alone, he stopped her. She simpered up at him, blue eyes guileless, tugging at her long red hair, obviously touting for custom.

'Is this where Isabetta Boveri lives?'

'That it is, sir.'

'Is she at home?'

'She's with a client.' The reply was a stab to the heart. So she was still actively plying the trade after all these years. He wondered if she had aged, as he had. 'My name's Bella,' she said. 'Are you in need of company, good sir?'

He took a moment to drag his thoughts back. 'No.'

'Don't be shy, sir. If you knock on the door, you will find many girls… you can choose, eh?'

'No. I don't need a courtesan. Leave me alone.' His angry voice made her step away from him, before she shook her head in puzzlement and scurried across the square.

His feet seemed glued to the ground. He still couldn't move away from the house, was curious for a glimpse of Isabetta, just to see her after all these years. As the afternoon light grew golden, and long shadows stretched across the square, the door opened and a couple stepped out.

He would know her anywhere. The graceful slender neck; the way she tilted her head to one side to listen. His grip on his sword tightened and he eased himself further into the shadows. The man she was with was old, even older than he, sixty perhaps, with a rounded belly only just constrained by his tightly buttoned doublet. The sight of him hurt.

They passed by on the opposite side of the street, oblivious to him. She was so close he could almost leap up and touch her. The pain in his chest bloomed until the ache seemed to take over his whole body. She was still as beautiful. She hadn't aged at all. But not once had she written to him, despite all his letters, not once. He was forgotten. For this… this short fat pig of a man.

As they walked away arm in arm, he began to reason with himself. He didn't care. He had never really cared for her. She was lost, lost to the scent of the poppy and a life of whoredom. On impulse he walked over and knocked hard at the door.

A serving girl in an apron answered it. 'Yes, sir?'

'I'm looking for a girl—'

'Full today. So it's appointments only, sir. You'll have to send word to Signora Boveri and ask for an invitation.'

'No. I'm not looking for… that. I'm looking for a friend, a young woman called Giulia d'Adamo.'

'Well we've no-one here of that name. We've a Giulia, but that's not her family name.'

'This Giulia, is she the niece of Signora Boveri?'

'What is this? Why do you want to know?' He had insisted too much and the girl was growing suspicious. She started to close the door. He put his boot there.

'I have some news I wish to give her. Please tell her I'm here. My name is Bruno Borroni.'

'I can't just let you in. Write to her. Ask if she'll see you.' The door pressed against his foot.

'I'll make it worth your while.' He opened his purse and brought out a glinting gold scudi.

The girl put the money deep in her apron pocket. 'Bruno, was it? If you wait, I'll fetch her down.' He stood back and the door shut in his face. He heard the bolt grate home. So he waited, shifting from foot to foot, glancing back over his shoulder, half hoping, half dreading that Isabetta would return. He remembered the woman Giulia, the daughter of the poisoner, running from

them in the cobbled street near her home, remembered her eyes,
startled like a young doe. And he couldn't forget how she'd
floored him with the sharp point of her elbow. Something about
her face bothered him, but he couldn't say what.

When Alessa called her from the hallway, Giulia dried her eyes
and put away her handkerchief. She had been reading her mother's book again, marvelling at the information collected between
the pages and how much care Mamma had taken to set it all
down. And who was it all for, but for her? She had become
curious to try some of these powders. The desire to wreak
revenge was still strong, but she needed practice, and how could
she get that here?

She heard Alessa calling her again and went out to see what
she wanted.

'There's a man come to speak to you. A stranger. Says he's a
friend of yours.'

Her heart leapt. Had Fabio found his way to her here in
Naples?

'Did he give a name?' she asked eagerly.

'Bruno something. Big tall man, battered face.'

Giulia's excitement melted away into a wariness. 'Where
is he?'

'I left him by the front door. Did I do right?'

'I don't know. I need to look at him. I don't know any men in
Naples, only Signor Vecci and Signor Colombo, and my aunt's
clients. He's not a client?'

'Never seen him before.'

'I'll go out the back way and walk around the side to see if I
recognise him.' She followed Alessa down the stairs. 'Pass me one
of those masks.'

Fashionable Neapolitan women often wore masks to shield

their faces from the sun or at festivals and feasts when everyone celebrated incognito, so Alessa fetched one down from the shelf by the door and Giulia slipped on the mask, tying the ribbons behind.

In a few moments she was out of the servants' door at the back and around the side. She kept in the shadows until she could see him – a tall, broad-shouldered man with his back to her. A leather doublet and breeches despite the heat, and strong muscular legs. He was pacing up and down by the front door. His back view didn't look familiar.

But then he turned and she knew him immediately. She couldn't forget the man from Palermo who had chased her from her home. It was him; she was certain. About forty-five years old. Same well-worn face, with the broken nose and torn ear. If she hadn't known better, she would have thought it a kind face.

Mouth dry, Giulia turned as slowly as she dared and sauntered away. As soon as she rounded the corner she ran inside and bolted the door behind her.

She ripped off the mask and returned it to the shelf. 'Alessa, I do know that man. If he comes again, turn him away. You didn't tell him I was here, did you?'

'No. I'm not so stupid. When strange men call, they always have to have the permission of the Signora.'

She went back to her chamber and watched the man from behind the shutter. She heard him knock again and was relieved that Alessa kept her word and did not answer it.

After a few more minutes the man Bruno crossed the road to stare back at the house. He must know she was here, even if Alessa denied it. Or why had he come? Her breath became shallow. Keeping a little back from the window she watched him observing the house. He showed no sign of leaving, and the thought of being trapped inside the Villa Bianca with him spying on her was a development that filled her with fear.

Nearly an hour passed, and still he was there, like a lion

watching his prey. Then all of a sudden he moved out of sight, into the ever-darkening shadows. She moved closer to the window, just in time to see Isabetta returning from the city on the arm of Signor Vecci. They must have been shopping, for a pretty little serving boy was following behind carrying a number of well-wrapped parcels. Isabetta still looked pale, but she was putting on a brave appearance for lucrative clients like Vecci.

The man in the shadows was barely visible, but she could just make out his profile as he watched Isabetta and Signor Vecci arrive. Downstairs, the door banged, denoting Isabetta's return. The man emerged from the shadows and stared a moment more at the house, then he strode away in long loping strides, as if to put as much distance as possible between him and the house. It was almost as if he was waiting for Isabetta to come in before he could leave. But why?

She would have to tell Isabetta, because Alessa was sure to mention it, and her aunt would blame her, for there was no doubt at all that the duke's men had somehow tracked them down. She had told no-one, not even Fabio.

Isabetta disappeared with Signor Vecci into her private chambers and did not re-emerge. Giulia had no clients as her friend Emilio was meeting some men about reviving his oil imports. She kept gazing out of the window, imagining she saw that man Bruno still lurking in the shadows.

Finally, she saw Signor Vecci leave, and she hurried up the stairs to Isabetta's chamber. The door had been left open, so she knocked softly. No answer. She saw the bedchamber lit with guttering candles, saw the rumpled bedsheets and discarded clothing, and realised Isabetta must be in her dressing room.

'Isabetta?'

No answer. She went to the dressing room door and pushed it ajar. Isabetta was there, reclining on the day bed, a long bamboo pipe in her hand. Still she did not turn, but the room smelt strange, of something bitter. On the armoire was a scatter of stoppered bottles, and the package she had seen Domenico de Verdi give her in return for her jewellery. She called her name again and now Isabetta turned. Her eyes were enormous, deep and black, but glazed.

'Ah, Giulia,' Isabetta's voice slurred. 'Come sit by me.'

'A man came,' she said. 'A man who chased me when they came for Mamma.'

'Men are always coming here,' Isabetta said lazily. She held the bowl of the pipe over a candle flame, then put her mouth to the pipe to inhale.

'No, you don't understand. This is a man who knows who I am. A mercenary called Bruno Borroni. He's one of the Duke de Verdi's men.'

Isabetta's eyes found focus and she pulled herself to upright. 'What did you say his name was?'

'Bruno Borroni.'

'It can't be.' She rubbed her face as if to bring it back to life.

'You know him?'

'Oh yes, I know him.' A pause. 'If it's the same man.'

'A big man. In middle age, but strong. Half his ear missing.'

'He lost his ear fighting the Spaniards in Lombardy. There is no love lost between us now. We had a falling out because I couldn't tell him ..' She put down the pipe, sat up straighter. 'Oh my Lord.' She pressed her forehead into her hands. 'Did he see you?'

'No. But I saw him. I wore a mask to get a closer look.'

'You're sure he didn't see you? I can't believe he was here. It's almost as if… never mind. That's all in the past. And he did not approve of this.' She waved her hand over the detritus on the armoire, the pipe still streaming a thin trail of blue smoke.

'Will he come back? Will he bring soldiers?'

'I don't know. I don't know how he feels about me. He was full of bitterness last time I saw him. I can't blame him for that. We were very close… once. I rejected him.'

'How would he know I was here? I told no-one.'

'If he is in the pay of the duke I can see it might be possible. He used to write to me, so he knows my address, and that Theofania was my sister. He will have worked out she might send you here. Or the duke might have written to his brother.'

Her breath became shallow. 'What shall we do?'

Isabetta stood up and went to the window. The back of her hair was grey at the crown, where the dye had grown out, and flat where she had been lying down. She stared out for a moment, then turned. 'I don't know. I can't think straight. But he's a danger. Warn Alessa, and if he comes back, tell her to send him to me.'

That night, Giulia briefed Alessa, explaining that if the man returned, he must be shown to Isabetta at once rather than sent away.

By the morning she was on tenterhooks, alert to every passer-by outside, and fearing every noise, but Bruno Borroni did not return. So in the afternoon, remembering her promise to take a salve for Father Girolamo's arm, Giulia set to work in the kitchen, much to the consternation of Isabetta's kitchen maids, who told her it would ruin her hands. If she was to follow in Mamma's footsteps, she must make a start and learn all she could.

But by late afternoon, still no-one had knocked at the door, and the smell of olive oil and the leafy smell of the herbs, which should have been soothing, only seemed to choke her. Perhaps nobody would come? But then why had the duke's man been watching them?

Fear and these tangled thoughts made her almost forget that the business still had to go on, and despite everything, she was supposed to be playing escort to the lonely widower Emilio that night.

Tonight's event was at a grand villa – the Palazzo de Ribera. What if the Duke de Verdi's man, Bruno Borroni, was there? The thought that there may be spies watching wherever she went made her shudder. She concentrated on grinding and folding the green matter into the oil.

Take a deep breath, she told herself. Put the past behind you. Think only of Father Girolamo, the priest. It would be a relief to be in the presence of someone closer to God. Perhaps he would find some relief from her efforts when she took the poultice along. She would ask Mother Mary to intercede for her, to cloak her in some kind of veil of protection.

The church was quiet and empty. Suddenly awed, she lit a candle for Mamma's soul in the fusty darkness. It seemed selfish now to pray for her own protection.

A noise made her startle and look up.

Father Girolamo had come in, and now he was polishing the brass fender around the votive candles. She saw he was still using his left hand, whilst his other hung useless. She slipped from the pew, dipped her head and genuflected in the aisle, before going to speak to him.

'How's the wrist feeling?' she asked.

'Ah, Signora Boveri's little niece. Giulia, is it?' He held it out ruefully. 'Can't complain, my own foolish fault. Better than Sunday, anyway.'

She held out her basket. 'I have made you a plaster; it should help soothe it. I realised you could do little for yourself with that wrist paining you so.'

He smiled. 'That's so good of you to think of it.'

'So perhaps if there's somewhere…?'

'Come through to the vestry.'

She did as he asked, and they exited from the cool church through a side door to the dark-panelled chamber. Soon she had him sitting at a table with his arm outstretched whilst she layered on a plaster of herbs, secured with a strip of muslin and wrapped tight.

'You look pale,' he said. 'Is there something you wish to tell me? You surely did not come here just to fix my arm.'

'It's nothing,' she said, 'just a little tired.' She couldn't tell this old priest about Bruno Borroni, or about Mamma's death, or how it came about. He would be shocked that anyone could have such a profession. He would think her a witch, tainted with the devil. 'I'm just tired,' she repeated, aware her thoughts had been drifting.

His eyes said he didn't believe her excuse, so she looked away, sad that she had deceived him. Lying to a priest did not come easily to her Catholic soul.

She applied herself to wrapping his arm and securing it. When she had finished, she said, 'Sit in the sun for a half hour so it can set, and then you should be able to do all your usual tasks. Leave it for two days before cracking it away.'

He lifted his arm and turned it to examine the work. 'Feels better already,' he said. 'How do you like Naples?'

'A beautiful city. But so much new building. There are masons on every corner.'

'So there are. But I meant, how is it with your aunt?' He wasn't letting go of the subject.

She saw his attention stray to her red eyes and she twisted her fingers in her skirts. 'It is… it is not what I'm used to. But beggars can't choose.'

'No?' He gave a shrug of regret. 'Where is it you've come from?'

She stood up hurriedly. 'I've just remembered, I've an appointment with a client. I must go.'

'Thank you,' he called as she reached the door. 'I hope to see you in church again. Always good to have new blood.'

CHAPTER 15

GIULIA WAS ON EDGE, her emotions like a sea, swelling and subsiding. Isabetta, grim-faced, had laid out evening attire, and now the reality hit hard, that they would have to dance and act as if grief had not touched them. De Ribera's carriage arrived for them after sunset and they trotted through the torch-lit streets, towards the palazzo, sitting stiffly in their finery, afraid to smudge their painted lips and powdered cleavages. Giulia was glad of the paint today for it hid her red and prickling eyes. Isabetta was also subdued, but she squeezed her hand in hers. It was meagre comfort.

When they arrived at the Palazzo de Ribera, footmen in gold-braided doublets appeared to escort them to the door. Giulia lifted her green damask skirts from the dust and looked up to a vast edifice of pale stone, crowned with typical Neapolitan red pantiles. Multiple roofs rose over colonnaded walkways. They walked towards a main entrance through a passageway hung with tendrils of jasmine and bougainvillea. From indoors, the sound of viols and the beat of tambours drifted out on the moist night air.

Inside, she was greeted by the lugubrious Emilio, who gave

her a solemn nod but took her arm and guided her to a seat near where the musicians were playing. She was relieved to be in his company, a man in mourning who had lost someone too. It felt disrespectful to Mamma to be in this glittering evening attire, but to mourn would be to risk the inevitable question, to which she could have no answer.

Isabetta raised her eyebrows at her, to tell her she'd noticed Emilio's attentions. Giulia lifted her hand in a wave. Tonight, Isabetta was sparkling, almost over-bright. Of course, it was a front, a mixture of the effect of the poppy and the wine. How was it she hadn't noticed Isabetta's strange surges of exuberance before?

Emilio brought Giulia a warmed wine and a plate of sweet-meats and sat beside her. 'I'm glad you're here,' he said, 'or Vecci would be pairing me with one of them.' He indicated two women behind him with a flick of the eyes. The women were two elderly women in black mantuas, who must be at least seventy years old. She smiled back at him. It was good to have a friend.

They sat companionably to listen to the music, but despite his portly friend Vecci's encouragement, Emilio couldn't be persuaded to dance. 'I'm poor company, aren't I? I keep thinking of Elena, and it doesn't seem right to be dancing so soon.'

'I understand,' Giulia said. 'I don't feel much like dancing myself.' After a moment of watching the dancers twirl past, she asked him, 'You are in the oil import business. I wonder if you know who controls the import of perfumes and apothecaries' supplies?'

'That would be Guiseppi Romano. He's over there. Why do you ask?'

'I have an interest in perfumes,' she said. 'Especially unusual ones.' She hoped this would serve as an explanation. She decided she would try to catch Romano's eye and perhaps engage him in conversation. Her mother used to have a supplier, an importer of rare spices and minerals.

Her plans were interrupted by a voice from behind her. 'As your companion doesn't seem to be dancing, may I have the pleasure?'

A man came round in front of her, made a forward bow, clicked his heels together and held out his hand. Agnese's husband, Signor Domenico de Verdi, brother of the duke. Again, she was struck by the fact he seemed uncomfortable in his immaculately cut doublet and breeches. She recoiled, stiffened, and looked around for Isabetta. She was too far away to catch her attention.

'I have only just arrived so—' She began to make excuses.

'Come, let's dance.' He was insistent; his hand was still extended.

Emilio gestured for her to go, saying, 'Do, I'm not very much in the mood.'

Domenico de Verdi waited, still as a statue, but imperious. He was older than Emilio, and in this light his flat broken nose made his eyes appear too far apart. She imagined him wearing a laurel wreath like a Roman emperor. Her hands were sweating. She wiped them surreptitiously on her skirts and glanced round to see if she could spot Agnese.

'Shall we?' It was a reprimand.

Everyone was staring. He glanced to his hand, which was still hovering before her. Afraid it would be suspicious to refuse, she took it. He grasped her firmly and led her out onto the floor for a lively allemande. The music was already playing, and after another bow, they were caught up in the steps.

'Is your wife here?' Giulia asked, struggling to find natural conversation. 'She has a natural skill for the clavichord.'

'I'm glad to hear it. No,' he said shortly. 'She doesn't go out in the evenings.'

His tone forbade more questioning. So she gave herself up to the dance. Her companion danced very precisely, his steps almost staccato, his arms extended correctly. Obviously he was an experienced dancer, and she did her best to match him with her *glis-sades* and *courantes.* His face however showed no joy. It was as if he treated dancing as a profession at which he must excel. Nevertheless, he bowed to her again at the end of the dance and said he would have another when she had had time to rest awhile. It wasn't that he asked her, no. He just assumed she would agree.

She said nothing and returned gratefully to her seat. Emilio patted her arm. 'You didn't tell me you dance so well,' he said.

'I used to enjoy it,' she said, watching Domenico de Verdi walk away. *Except with him*, she thought.

'It makes me wish I could join you,' Emilio said, 'but I'll stick to watching, thank you. More wine?' He held the decanter over her glass.

'No more, thank you.'

'Domenico de Verdi dances well, I see. I have only ever seen him at the Exchange, and he drives a hard bargain.'

'I know little about him. What business is he in?'

'He runs the Silk Dyers Guild, and commands an army of mercenaries from all over the provinces. He rules the guild with an iron grip. It's why our Naples silk is so much more expensive than the new cheap stuff from Holland, and we've been losing trade these last six months despite its better quality.'

'I don't understand.'

'The dyers are the last part of the process,' Colombo said. 'If it's unfashionably dyed, it won't sell, no matter how much work the silk producers, weavers and finishers put into it, and Domenico de Verdi's attachment to sombre colours is driving prices down. The weavers keep trying to make him change his methods, use more fashionable colours, but the man won't budge. He despises fashion, thinks it is ungodly, insists on the subdued colours you see him wearing himself. If the dyers protest, then they lose their employment. He claims it's not his methods losing them trade, but that his suppliers, the silk weavers from Messina, have become too expensive.'

'I see.' She looked over to where Signor de Verdi was in conversation with two other men. He was looking down his nose at the other two and was clearly dominating the conversation.

'His wife is coming to me to learn music,' she said.

'His second wife, you mean? The girl?'

'Yes, Agnese.'

'Oh, is that her name? The first wife ran off somewhere. They had no children, but it still caused a scandal. No-one's heard of her since. Her parents created quite a disturbance over it, but de Verdi was implacable, said he was the wronged party, and that the wife was faithless and unreliable. This new one's father died unexpectedly, so she inherited everything. Of course, Domenico de Verdi has total control of her lands now. He likes his gold, they say, and he's a man who wants to make his mark. He's building himself an extravagant church on the Via Principale with a monstrosity of a marble tomb, all pomp and show. He's a complicated man, prone to sudden outbursts of ire. They say he hates everybody and everything, except the church, and even the bishops must be careful.' He paused as the dancers on the floor moved off and the musicians began another slower dance. 'Look out, here he comes again.'

She watched as Signor de Verdi turned away from the men and walked towards her. She saw them glance at his back and then whisper to each other with frowns on their faces.

He smiled and held out a hand. There was something about him, some charisma that was compelling. His eyes were stormy grey, the colour of the winter sea, and his hair flecked with grey at the temples. Her fear of him gave the encounter an uncomfortable excitement; she was both repelled and awed by the fact he had chosen her.

His grip on her back was firm. His eyes continued to stare above her head as though he were dancing with a wooden doll.

At the end of the dance, he led her back to where Isabetta was waiting for her. 'I'm afraid I cannot stay,' he said, bowing to

Giulia. 'I have a little business to attend to, but I hope to see more of you, Signorina Tofana.'

She dipped a low courtesy under Isabetta's watchful gaze.

As he was leaving, Isabetta approached him with a worried look, and Giulia saw her begin to argue with him. Isabetta glanced back, as if they were discussing her, and it made Giulia's face so heated she had to fan herself with her hand. But whatever Isabetta said, it was rejected by Signor de Verdi with an impatient wave of the hand.

Moments later, his manservant swirled a cloak around his shoulders, and it was then she realised that many of the young men standing at the edge of the room, and by the door, were his entourage. They looked like a fighting force, despite their silks and velvets. When he left, it was as if the whole room exhaled.

Isabetta returned. 'If Domenico de Verdi says he would like to see you again,' she said tersely, 'then you must make it clear you are available, and send him to me.'

'Yes, Isabetta.' She was very still. 'I beg your pardon, but is that likely?'

'Domenico de Verdi is a powerful man, one of the most respected in Naples,' Isabetta said. *But not well liked*, Giulia wanted to add. But Isabetta was continuing. 'He and his younger brothers are kingpins in this city. It would be a feather in your cap, and for our establishment, if you were to be his consort.'

'Even if his elder brother is responsible for Mamma's death?'

'Keep your voice down. We cannot afford likes and dislikes. Especially not where Domenico de Verdi is concerned.'

The truth dawned. 'You're afraid of him. And he's your supplier, is he not? He brings you your poppy, and that's why we can't afford to offend him.'

'Hush. Have you no sense?' She took hold of Giulia's arm and dragged her close. 'If he wishes to see you, then we will oblige him,' she said, 'as we do the rest of the men in this city who can pay.'

'But what about his wife?' Giulia asked. 'It will surely be awkward, if she is to be my pupil.'

Isabetta shook her head impatiently. 'Wives are of no account. Men still like their pleasure, married or not. And this one we must treat with kid gloves.'

'I saw you give him your jewellery, and I knew then there was something amiss.'

'It's not just for myself. It's for the girls. The Camorra control the whole of Naples, and Domenico de Verdi controls them. So I pay for his protection too.'

'But surely he is exactly the kind of man we need protection *from*?'

'Perhaps in Palermo that might be true. But not here in Naples. And with his brother, Antonio's men after you, we may yet need him and his protectors. But be careful, Giulia, tell him nothing of your past. Keep it well hidden, for if you don't, he will find a way to use it against you.'

CHAPTER 16

WHEN BRUNO GOT BACK to Palermo after the ship from Naples, the vision of Isabetta on another man's arm still had the power to make him angry. He paced his spartan chamber in the lower part of the palazzo, torn between the idea of protecting Isabetta and betraying her. Should he confess to the duke that he knew where Giulia, the daughter of Theofania d'Adamo, lived? The masked woman that had run away when he went to inquire at the Villa Bianca – he could swear it was her, though he had no proof, just an instinct. Some familiarity about the way she moved.

On the one hand, if he told the duke, he would gain credit and advancement, and it would hurt Isabetta to know it was he, Bruno, who had betrayed them. It would go some way to salving the hurt that Isabetta had caused him all these years. He imagined her frightened face when the duke knocked on her door, with him, Bruno, at his right hand and a cohort of armed men behind him.

On the other hand, to tell the duke where they were would mean he was condemning them both to death. They would both die; he was under no illusion about that. The duke had no mercy in cases like these. Valentina was dead, he was sure, for no more news had come of her.

When the summons came from the duke to go to him, he still had not decided what to tell him. From moment to moment, he wavered. His boots rang out a hollow rhythm as he walked up the long flight of stairs and down the dimly lit corridor to the well-guarded door of the duke's apartment.

The guards shuffled aside with a nod of acknowledgement, and Bruno stepped into the airy chamber.

'I received your message,' the duke said. 'So my brother is an arrogant bastard, is he?'

'Seems so,' Bruno said. 'He is feared all over Naples, though lately there's been rebellion against his measures to keep control.'

'Then we'll take plenty of men to assist him. We have the viceroy's authority and we'll use it. Ready the arms and armour we'll need, and warn the men we depart the day after tomorrow.'

'Very good, sir.' He turned to go.

'Borroni?'

Yes?' He hated the way the voice stopped him in his tracks, like a performing monkey.

'The other matter. Did you find this Giulia d'Adamo, the poisoner's daughter?'

The sight of the duke's peevish expression was enough to decide him. He could never hand Isabetta over to him. This man enjoyed holding power over him for the sake of it. It felt good to have some power of his own.

'No,' he said, 'there's no sign of her in Naples.' Never had a lie felt so sweet.

Domenico de Verdi picked up the heavy glass paperweight and, taking deliberate aim, threw it hard at the wall, where it cracked the plaster, resulting in a shower of dust. He watched it with grim satisfaction.

'Get that wall replastered,' he said to his servant, Enzo.

Enzo, who was trying to look as if he hadn't noticed the Signor's temper, stood by his desk and tried to peer at the letter that had obviously caused this outburst.

'You might as well know,' Domenico said. 'The viceroy is sending me an assistant.'

Alarm made Enzo's eyes widen. 'What? I'm your assistant. You don't need one. You have plenty of men.'

'Not a servant, fool. Someone, in their sainted wisdom, has reported that Naples is a seething ants' nest of unrest, and he wants to send a "saviour" to do something about it.'

'But all is under control. Everyone knows that if they want a quiet life, one unmolested by your men, they must obey your laws and those of the Camorra.'

'Well I wouldn't have put it quite like that, but yes, you're right.'

'Who is this "saviour" they're sending?'

'My brother.' He couldn't keep his disgust from his voice. 'The Duke Antonio de Verdi from Palermo, and a group of his bone-head mercenaries.'

Enzo sucked in his breath.

'Make no mistake, apart from the fact he's an aristocrat, it's a military force. My brother must have bribed the viceroy somehow to get himself sent here. He's always shoving his nose into my affairs. Can't bear it if I make a success of anything. But I fear his interference may make it hard to go on as we have been, and this will mean less financial reward for us all.' He let it sink in. Enzo, like all his servants, was paid better than most serving men in Naples.

'What can we do?'

'Nothing. I rely on the viceroy's goodwill. I don't want to give him any cause for concern. So you will take down a letter for me, a polite, amicable letter, assuring Acevedo y Zuñiga that we will give his envoy, the Duke de Verdi, the warmest possible welcome. Of course, when my brother arrives, we will certainly have some sort of welcome ready for him. One that makes it abundantly clear exactly who is in control of Naples.'

After a week, although no more visits came from Bruno Borroni, Giulia's tension never completely dissipated. She prayed that pursuing her was simply too much trouble. She chafed at the life of a courtesan, though she was fortunate compared to the other girls. Emilio was her most regular client, and he paid only to talk and listen to her play. Her aunt was certainly dispensing favours, but at the same time she seemed to be afraid to show Giulia any warmth or affection. And it was exhausting pretending to be someone she was not.

Since her mother had gone, she felt as if she were behind a wall. She could not explain that, as two women alone, their life had been so much entwined, so close, that now she was centreless. The only world she properly knew was Mamma's world; that of mortars and pestles and the smell of charcoal and burning.

Today, though, a light in the day. Agnese was to have another lesson.

'The last time I came here,' Agnese said, after she'd removed her mantle and gloves, 'the sound of the hammers plucking the strings stayed with me for days. I couldn't get that lilting melody out of my head.'

'Well, I have a new piece for you today,' Giulia said. 'It's a round, and we can play it together. A pretty little tune; it goes like this.' She picked out a few notes and repeated them line by line until she had built up the whole tune, then she urged Agnese to try.

Agnese's fingers were long and slender, and she had a good stretch for reaching the notes, but her left hand was weighed down with a signet ring and several other heavy jewels. As Giulia watched her play, she marvelled at how her clothing seemed to be so restrictive, that it was like a kind of armour, a façade so that the girl herself disappeared and only a carapace remained.

'Signora Gauci said she's not collecting you today.' Giulia had no wish to meet Agnese's husband again. He played on her mind; the fact that his brother had caused Mamma's death.

'No. Domenico will come for me at the end of the lesson.' The way she said his name denoted no affection.

'How long have you two been married?' Giulia asked.

'Six months, maybe a little more. Seems like longer. My guardian arranged it: Signor Vecci. It was less expensive than the convent after my parents died. He thought the money should go somewhere – "not to a bunch of avaricious women" were his words.'

'What happened to your parents?'

'Mother died in childbirth, the babe too. They waited too long and she was too old for it, they say. Father just a few months after. He choked on an olive stone. No-one was there to help him.' Her expression dared me to laugh. 'Such a small thing, and yet it cut off his breath. I was out at the market watching the Commedia dell'arte. I should have been at home helping my father. If he hadn't died, so much would have been different…'

'You say you nearly entered a nunnery. Would you have wanted to take holy orders?'

'Oh no, not then. Now – in a heartbeat. Would I had known then what I know now…' She paused, turned to look at Giulia. 'You see, Signor Vecci was intent on this marriage because it gave him leverage with Domenico. And in Naples that's a valuable thing.' She sighed. 'But now… well, I'd sell my hair for a life for a the nunnery of Sant'Orsola.' She trailed her fingers across the run of notes, before glancing at the music sheet and starting the piece again from the first bar. 'My fingers won't move quickly enough for the last few notes,' she said, as she tried for the third time.

'Don't worry,' Giulia said, 'it will come. You just need to practise. Regular practice is the key to everything.'

'I wish I could practise every day,' Agnese said, 'but there is no instrument at the Palazzo del Mare.'

'Perhaps you could ask your husband to buy you one... as a gift,' Giulia ventured.

Silence, and a small shake of the head. 'A gift?' She gave a sarcastic laugh. 'His gifts are always a transaction. Never freely given. He would demand something in return.' She tailed off, began to play again to end the conversation. After several more attempts she stopped. 'Giulia, where did *you* learn to play so well?' she asked.

'Our house was always full of music. My mother played the clavichord and she taught me, when she could be persuaded to leave her work.'

'She must be very proud of you. I miss my mother so much. We had an argument before she died. Over whether I should finish my tapestry. Can you believe it? Something so small, yet sometimes it causes me such pain I can't speak.'

Giulia felt a lump rise to her throat. Mamma's scolding voice came back to her, *you never look beneath the surface.* She felt her lips quiver, so she had to swallow and turn away.

A gentle touch on her hand.

Startled, she swung back to face Agnese. Their eyes met and a thin current of understanding passed between them.

'Friends, yes?' Her touch on Giulia's arm was like a feather, quivering and hesitant.

'Of course, friends!' Giulia said, pushing aside her disquiet about the de Verdi family. 'Now play that again.'

The hour passed all too quickly. The door banged below and then the sound of Isabetta's ingratiating voice floated up the stairs.

It must be Domenico de Verdi arriving. She exchanged a rueful look with Agnese as men's footsteps came upstairs and along the marble corridor. When the door swung open Giulia and Agnese stood to greet him.

'Don't stop playing for me,' he said, gesturing for his manservant to wait by the door and coming over to stand next to the clavichord. 'I take it there is progress today, Signorina Tofana?'

She kept a cool, calm manner. 'Agnese has natural ability, but she would progress more quickly if she had an instrument at home so she could practise.'

Signor de Verdi raised an eyebrow and picked up a sheet of music from the stand. He perused it slowly, making her wait. Then he looked up. 'Not yet,' he said. 'When she is able to play more fluently, then perhaps. Music should soothe the soul. It's a busy household, and we do not want to be distracted by irritations.'

Irritations. So her music was that to him. She felt anger surge up inside her, but she saw Isabetta's warning look and pushed it down. 'As you wish, sir,' she said, intending to acquiesce, but then she heard herself say, 'but she will certainly become proficient if she has her own clavichord, and she will surely need one eventually, so why not order one now? There are many choices to be made, about the decoration and the marquetry, and it all takes time.'

He was frowning. She saw his lips tighten; he was obviously unused to being challenged.

Isabetta picked up her ample skirts and swished closer, interceding with a nervous ripple of laugher. 'I'm sure there'll be time for all that later, Giulia.'

He gave a brief nod. 'I will give it my consideration,' he said. 'Now. I want to hear her play.'

Agnese faltered, playing more hesitantly than she had before, as if a different person had taken her place on the stool. No wonder her husband thought she was making little progress if this was all he saw. At the end of the phrase she struggled to complete it.

'Try it again,' Giulia said encouragingly.

After another botched attempt Agnese shut the lid. 'I can't do it.'

Domenico de Verdi strode over and put the lid up again. 'You can, and you will. I am not paying for you to waste Signorina Tofana's time. Now play.'

She played again, but this time her husband took down the sheet of music when she was not quite all the way through the piece.

'Come. I have business to attend to.' The music stopped abruptly and Agnese stood and followed him.

'Signorina Tofana, Signora Boveri,' He bowed farewell. Agnese's eyes stayed downcast. Giulia's heart ached for her, but she was also angry. How could she stomach this overbearing husband who was at least twenty years older and seemed to allow her no freedom at all?

CHAPTER 17

ISABETTA PICKED up a horn spoon and carefully measured out a few grains of the powder into the pipe before screwing the lid shut. Heating it over a flame released the smoke. A few long inhalations, and she was calmer, less fractious. Giulia arriving like this had brought back the past, and now her memories would not lie quiet. Truth be told, she was afraid.

The thought she would never see Theofania again seemed impossible. Though she'd been estranged from her sister for more years than she cared to count, she always thought the rift would be mended one day. But now that day would never come. The poppy was a comfort, though she needed more of the stuff now than she used to, and it all cost money. There were occasions when she regretted the life she'd chosen, the days when she couldn't buy the powder and life became its true unbearable self. On those days she knew herself to be an addict and a whore, and a woman rotten from the inside out.

She thrust these thoughts aside and was just dropping a little belladonna into her eyes when she heard the faint rap at the downstairs door.

Bella's client, she thought. She'd let Alessa go to deal with him. She continued to make up her eyes, rimming them with charcoal powder and adding a ground of pearly seashell to the lids.

A clatter of shoes. 'Beg pardon,' Alessa said, 'but it's a boy. He brought this.' She held out a sealed letter. 'It's from Domenico de Verdi.'

Isabetta froze. 'How do you know?'

'The livery, mistress. It's his green and gold. The boy's waiting for a reply.'

Not another demand for more money. She couldn't survive without her poppy powder. She tore off the seal and read the message.

By favour, to book me an appointment with Signorina Tofana. I am free this evening after seven, or on Thursday at the same time. I will take her to supper by the harbour and then we will return to your chambers. Please ensure a private room is available on our return. My boy has my purse. You may keep it as proof of my good intentions.

Signor Domenico de Verdi.

So polite. It was as if he had never stood on her doorstep like a bull, and taken her throat in his hands. As if he'd never used a pickaxe on her best tapestry. As if his cursed stick insect of a brother had never pushed her sister to a crushing death. What to make of it? She didn't know, except that it was the worst possible invitation. Why must his eye have fallen on Giulia?

She clenched a fist, knowing it couldn't be refused. Even for the sake of Giulia, her own flesh and blood. Nobody refused Domenico de Verdi. Even his name struck fear into every Neapolitan's heart.

'Wait.' She pinned Alessa with a glare, though it was hardly her fault. Then she took quill and ink and wrote a hasty reply. *This evening at seven with Giulia Tofana. Appointment confirmed. S Isabetta Boveri.*

'Take the boy this,' she said.

Giulia was just seeing Emilio out of the door when Isabetta caught her in the hall. Her aunt's face was strained, and Giulia feared Bruno Borroni had visited again. 'What?' she asked.

'You have a new admirer,' she said.

Giulia took a step away. 'Who?'

'Domenico de Verdi. He will call for you tonight at seven.'

'What?' She stared at Isabetta, so rigidly corseted in her green silk damask gown, her face carefully applied to hide her age.

'He will call for you at seven,' Isabetta repeated.

'No. You can't make me. I have a client already. Emilio was going to stroll with me down to the port. Can't one of the others—'

'He particularly asked for you, and you know he's a man of… some influence.'

'But what shall I tell Emilio?'

'Emilio is of little consequence,' Isabetta said. 'Just tell him you have another appointment and rearrange it for another time.'

'I can't do this,' she protested. 'Not when he's the brother of—'

'Put aside your thoughts about his brother.'

'Put aside those thoughts?' She was outraged. 'Put aside the thought that he is from the family that murdered my mother; that threw her from a rooftop in chains?'

Isabetta blanched. 'Domenico de Verdi may not be like his brother.'

'No? He treats Agnese like a servant, and I saw the way he bullied you when he came here—'

'Listen to me,' Isabetta said, through gritted teeth. 'What did I tell you? You saw nothing that night, and if you value your life, I don't want to hear it ever again. *Comprendo?* Whatever your opinion of him before, he is now a client. And an important and wealthy one.'

Giulia stiffened. She did not want to be a rich man's plaything. Especially this man. She wanted to learn Mamma's skills. If she had that knowledge, some sort of power over men, perhaps she'd be less afraid. Yet with no home and no money, she had little choice except to study where she could.

As if to read her mind, Isabetta said, 'If you wish to remain here, you will obey the rules of my house.'

Giulia swallowed her retort. 'I beg your pardon, Isabetta, I didn't mean to sound ungrateful. But it's a shock. I never thought I would… with that man.' She resigned herself to the inevitable. Perhaps Isabetta was right; she shouldn't think he was like the duke. He was a religious man after all, and perhaps he'd be more pleasant when she got to know him. 'What does he expect of me?'

'Just your good company for supper. But he has asked for a private room, so you know what that signifies. Treat it as an honour.' She didn't need to say the words – if you want to stay alive – but the sense of them hung in the air.

Giulia nodded, though inside her stomach recoiled. She thought of little Agnese. They were friends. What would she think if she knew?

'Come along then,' Isabetta said, striding ahead of her. 'I'll give you the sponges, the pigskin sheath and the douche. Best be protected. It's the one thing I insist on; we can't afford any mistakes. And let's hope once is enough, and then it will be over.'

She was quiet as Isabetta led the way up the stairs to her chamber, an opulent suite on the top floor, with tapestry drapes and a bed draped in Milanese lace. Isabetta pulled open a drawer stocked with the necessary items. There were many be-ribboned sheaths, laid out in rows. It made her feel faintly sick, that all these were to be worn by different men. If they could be persuaded to wear them at all. Many of them did not like the subject broached, hence the sponges and pottery douches with their narrow spouts.

'Practise with the douche this afternoon,' Isabetta said. 'It will give you a feeling for the act with de Verdi. God knows, I wouldn't have asked it of you, but we have no choice.'

Giulia turned the douche and the sponge over in her hands. How had it come to this? She thought of Fabio, young handsome Fabio, of the long eyelashes and muscled arms, of how she used to long to be near him. Signor Domenico de Verdi, with his stiff manner and eyes like stones, made her feel the opposite, as if her flesh wanted to shrink away.

'It's only natural to be apprehensive,' Isabetta said. 'Just follow his lead, and for all that's holy, look as though you enjoy it.'

'I thought my first time would be with… with… a man I choose.'

'You'll get over it. For most courtesans, it is the same. At least you have full knowledge of what will occur. Many women have no idea, and it comes as quite a shock.'

'I'm grateful for your instruction, Isabetta. I just wish it was someone else. He scares me.'

'We treat all our clients equally, the ugly ones and the handsome. That is why the business pays. Now,' she took hold of Giulia's chin in her hand and lifted it, 'You must make sure you please him.' She pinched her gently on the cheek, but her eyes were insistent. Giulia gave a hesitant smile.

'Here,' Isabetta said, 'you can use some of my perfume. Choose one.'

Giulia took in the array of perfume bottles on Isabetta's table. They reminded her of Mamma. 'I miss Mamma,' she said, her voice a choke. 'What would she think of me, dining with… with that man?'

'Try not to think of her today,' Isabetta said, but her eyes shifted away, and she grabbed the nearest bottle. 'Try this,' she said.

Giulia lifted the stopper and inhaled. The scent of roses and cinnamon brought back memories of home. She wished Mamma were here now to slap her and tell her not to touch, like she had when she was eight. Tears pricked, though she stuffed her sleeve to her eyes.

'Don't, you'll make your eyes red,' Isabetta said. She thrust a handkerchief at her.

Giulia blew her nose and picked up a random bottle. 'I'll take this one,' she said.

'Go on and bathe then, and I'll send Alessa down later to dress you.'

Giulia dipped a curtsey and the first thing Signor de Verdi did was to present her with an emerald and diamond necklace in a velvet-lined box. Isabetta's eyes grew large as she helped her fasten the clasp and then surveyed the way the cold mass hung over her collarbones. Giulia felt the weight and expectation of such a gift and it made her uncomfortable. Had this jewel been extorted from some other citizen, the way de Verdi had taken Isabetta's necklace? Like the night he'd ripped the tapestry from the wall?

He had brought two manservants with him, and their dark, silent presence, always walking a little behind them, made her uneasy. Their swords clinked against their scabbards, and the thud of their heavy boots reminded her of her flight from Palermo. What sort of man needed such a bodyguard simply to stroll by the sea?

But Domenico de Verdi ignored his men, looking only at her. He maintained an air of detachment as he talked of music and the new churches that had been built since the last earthquake and eruption.

'I heard tell of the earthquake,' she said, struggling to find an easy topic of conversation. 'What a terrible tragedy. Were you living here in Naples then?' she asked.

'No. My parents were. People say the city crumbled around their ears, but then the sea itself grew as tall as a mountain and crashed in to complete the destruction. A wall of water no-one could escape. They both lost their lives for the sins of others.' He gritted his teeth, shook his head. 'Those years were nothing but pain. No sooner had the city struggled back to life than Vesuvio bared her teeth and the mountain erupted once more into a living hell. Flows of hot lava and torrents of liquid ash. Nobody who saw that could have any doubt that it was a punishment. The sins of the citizens of Naples had finally drawn God's wrath. No more dreadful vision of hell could be imagined. But enough. I do not like to talk of that day. It is ill fortune.'

He walked briskly then, ahead of her, a stony look on his face. She dare not ask him anything else, and they progressed in silence. It was as if even asking the question had soured him towards her.

When they reached his residence, the Palazzo del Mare, an arcaded building over three floors, his manner had reverted to politeness. The building was like a fortress, enormous walls with rows of darkly glinting windows, and guards at all the gates. There was no sign of Agnese or any female servant. He took her wrap and escorted her up some outside stairs to a table on a stone-flagged terrace overlooking the bay.

'Oh.' It was one of the best views in Naples, with the curve of the harbour laid out before her. Over the water were spread all the little boats with their oil lamps burning, and the warehouses around the harbour glimmered with the glow of torches. Above, the stars winked in a sky of lapis lazuli. It should have enchanted her, but she was too apprehensive about his company to enjoy it.

She sat down stiffly, searching for an appropriate subject. She recalled that Isabetta had said he was a devout man. 'Is the Silk Dyers Guild taking part in the San Gennaro procession?' she asked. 'I have never seen it, and I'm looking forward to seeing if the miracle occurs this year.' The miracle of San Gennaro, when the saint's dried blood, preserved in an ampoule in the church, would mysteriously liquefy again, thus guaranteeing prosperity for the city for another year.

He sat opposite and gestured for a servant to bring wine. 'Yes. Of course San Gennaro would not let us down. My guild will be at the head of the procession.'

'I would love to see the miracle of the blood.'

'You will not be allowed close to it. Women are forbidden. As daughters of Eve… well, you understand it would not be appropriate.' He meant that women were still considered unclean. And as a courtesan, she would be doubly so in his eyes.

She looked down and concentrated on the plate of olives, dried meats and sheep's cheese before her. Signor de Verdi talked of how his men would scourge themselves with pads of nails until they bled. A penance, he said for their sins.

During the rest of the meal, the servant kept bringing more flagons and Signor de Verdi insisted she drink. The wine was strong and bitter, and as red as the blood he was describing. Each time her glass emptied a little, he would fill it again, until she shook her head, covering the bowl of the glass with her hand.

Her body had begun to feel grainy, as if her limbs were dissolving. She mopped a napkin to her forehead. The jewel around her neck seemed to be growing heavier. Her thoughts swam as he continued to tell her about the preparations his men were making for the San Gennaro procession, about the heavy gilded statue they would carry through the streets, and the penitential robes they would wear. He was gazing at her now with a peculiarly intense expression. She saw him lick his lips like a lizard as his eyes travelled over the jewel resting against her bare throat.

Overcome by heat and faintness, knowing by instinct she must get home, and soon, she attempted to stand. With horror, she found her legs were so unsteady she had to lean on the table. The plates rattled as she grasped at the tablecloth to keep from falling.

'I must go,' she said.

'Here, my arm,' he said, hauling her to upright. Her head felt too heavy for her neck, and she found she had to lean on him, for she was too giddy to stand without help. The steps down from the terrace stretched away in a shifting blur, and all she could think of was the relief that she would soon be back at Isabetta's.

There must be something in the wine, she thought. *I cannot be so drunk.* She was used to wine from when she was a child, but this felt different, a bitter aftertaste hung in her mouth. She thought of Isabetta's poppy. Oh, the irony of it, that she, daughter of Theofania d'Adamo, the most notorious poisoner in Palermo, should find herself duped in such a way. She willed herself to stay alert.

He was steering her now. How foolish that she should have to be half carried down the stairs. She glanced back; the two bodyguards were still with them. What must they think? It shamed her that they might think her inebriated. Into a sedan. The bodyguards paid the bearers then watched as they went. The swaying made her sick to the stomach.

At the Villa Bianca he pushed her out and she almost toppled onto the pavement. Then in through the doors, where Alessa was expecting them. Alessa curtseyed low to Signor de Verdi and gestured for them to follow.

'I think I'll go to my chamber now,' Giulia slurred. 'I feel a little unwell.'

'This way,' Alessa said, ignoring her and leading the way with the flickering torch up to the first floor. With a strong grip on her shoulder, de Verdi propelled her up the stairs. She was too tired to protest; all she wanted to do was to lie down and stop this swimming in her head.

Alessa pushed open a door to a chamber illuminated by candles, where the scent of beeswax was as heavy as pollen in the air. An ornate four-poster bed draped in crimson silk took up most of one wall.

A click as the door closed behind them.

She was alone with Domenico de Verdi.

'Now you will do as I say,' he said, 'and cleanse yourself of sin, as I am paying for the privilege.'

He let go of her arm, and she almost toppled but managed to totter to the bed. She hoped it would soon be over and she'd be able to sleep. She let herself fall back against the pillows, longing to close her eyes, but she dare not take her gaze from his face.

His features seemed to take on the sharpness of a falcon as he approached.

'Get off the bed,' he said.

She sat up, alerted by his tone. It had changed from one of politeness to one of cold anger.

He swooped in without warning, roughly grasped her arm, and with one swift movement he dragged her off the slippery silk counterpane. She tumbled to the floor with an ungainly crash.

'On your knees,' he said, pressing her shoulders down as she struggled to rise.

'What's the matter? Why…?'

She felt a boot in her back as she tried to stand. She struggled to a crawl until another boot came down on her wrist and she fell headlong. Her face was pressed into the grooved floorboards. To her side she could see his boot grinding down on her wrist.

She struggled to right herself but something hit her with force in the ribs. She curled into a ball. The thought came that her dress would be ruined, but immediately her frantic mind grabbed onto another thought – the knife in her stays.

'Now pray,' he said. 'Confess to God that you are a filthy whore.'

'No,' she said, twisting around to face him. 'It's not true. I've never been with a man. You are the first, I swear it.'

'Virgin or not, you carry that first sin with you, like all women. The sin of the snake in the Garden of Eden. Prostrate yourself before God,' he said. 'Beg for his forgiveness. Ask Jesus to wash the sins of Eve away.'

Another kick made her cry out. She had to stop him. She prayed out loud. 'Father, I have sinned...'

He took his boot from her wrist and she was able to sit up and gasp for breath. She had to get away. If she could get to her feet, she could run. But she was nauseous, and the room was moving round her in a suck and swell like ocean waves.

She got a foot to the ground, and a hand, but he shoved her back to the floor. 'Kneel,' he said. 'I want to hear you beg the Lord's forgiveness.'

Humour him, she thought. *Look for a way out.* Clasping her hands together, she began to pray again, wild incoherent words. 'Our Father, who art in Heaven, Hallowed be thy name...' Unsure whether she was praying because she was too terrified not to, or because she hoped Jesus would really save her.

She kept on repeating the words, eyes squeezed shut. When she opened them, he had unlaced his breeches.

No. Not that. She couldn't do it. Not for him.

She leapt to her feet.

Not quick enough. He was there, smelling of bitter wine and sweat, pressing her against the door, his breeches undone. 'Harlot,' he said. 'Down on your knees.'

Fear sharpened her thoughts. She reached inside the stiff front of her bodice and drew out the knife.

'Move again,' she said, thrusting it towards him, 'and you will no longer be a man.'

Shock made him take a step back. The knife was between

them, its edge close to his belly. She grasped the door handle behind her and turned it, and as soon as she'd got it open a crack, she turned and scraped her way through, slamming it behind her. Disorientated, she clutched the banister rail. Down the stairs.

A clatter as the knife fell from her grip onto the marble-tiled landing below. She ran down, tumbled down the last steps. A crack as her elbow hit the floor. She grabbed for the knife and plunged inside her chamber. Panting, she turned the key in the lock. The lock was supposed to keep the servants out, but now she could see its other use. She would take no chances. She pushed a chair against the door.

Her heart was still battering hard enough to jump out of her chest. The chamber moved round her as if alive. She forced herself to think. Would Isabetta come and help her?

She wondered if her wrist was broken, but when she squeezed it, she couldn't feel broken bones, just swelling and bruising. It throbbed a dull ache; her scraped elbow stung. Pressing her ear to the door, she could hear nothing until she heard de Verdi's voice in an imperious shout. 'Signora Boveri?'

Just his voice made her push the chair further against the door. His tone brought Isabetta's footsteps running.

Giulia leant her back to the door, hoping the lock would keep him out.

'The girl insulted me,' she heard. 'She actually dared to refuse me.'

'I'm sure not,' Isabetta protested. 'I'm sure there must be some misunderstanding—'

Isabetta's protests were cut off. 'She threatened me. Did you know that she had a knife? Do you allow your whores to carry weapons? I have never in my life heard of such a thing.'

'Signor de Verdi,' Isabetta said, her words tumbling over each other, 'please, what can I do? Why not take one of the other girls? Bella will look after you, please, sir, come this way.'

Footsteps retreating. She guessed she'd taken him into the

salon. More angry voices that she couldn't hear. Pleading from Isabetta. Giulia shivered as she heard them return and the clomp of his boots as he crossed the hall.

'Your trading licence is revoked as of now,' he said, 'and Signorina Tofana will pay with her life for daring to threaten me.'

'No, wait!' Isabetta entreated.

In vain. The door banged as he left.

CHAPTER 18

SLOWLY, Giulia untied the laces of her gown, sliding each of the points through the eye. She stepped out of it, noticing how there was a dusty bootprint across the back, and it made her shudder and fling the bodice away. How long before her aunt came to her to find out what had happened? She had no wish to talk to her, or to any of them. All she wanted to do was to bury her head under the pillow and sleep, and to wake in Palermo, back with Mamma in her old life.

No sooner had she undressed than the door jumped and shuddered. Isabetta was trying to get in.

'Open this door!'

It was so tempting to ignore her. Giulia's head was throbbing; the shock made her wary of any more confrontation.

'Giulia! Open it at once!'

She would have to face her some time. Reluctantly, she pulled back the chair and turned the key. Isabetta stormed in. One look at her face was enough to show how angry she was. Her eyes were as sharp as glass, unclouded by opium.

'What the hell have you done?' she said. 'His men will come and break the place up—'

'I can't do it. Not with men like him.'

'Why not? What happened? What did he ask you to do?'

'He wanted me to pray and—'

'Only pray?' She laughed, but it was a hard, mirthless sound. 'What is so bad about that? I've been tied and whipped, and worse, and you complain because he makes you pray?'

How could she explain? It was the fact he had tried to mix something holy with something... something ugly. It was the sneering expression on his face, the way she'd felt shame flood over her. 'I thought he'd kill me. If I hadn't had the knife, I don't know what I would have done.'

'Did you use the knife on him?' She grabbed Giulia by the upper arms. 'Tell me.'

'I had to. I'm telling you, he would have killed me.'

'It was for blaggards or drunkards, young men too hot for their own good! Not for Camorra men like Domenico de Verdi.'

The room swam, making her sway again. 'He tried to make me—'

'You don't know what you've done!' Isabetta shouted. 'It's a death sentence. Girls like you just disappear! I'll have to go and see him. He'll wreak some sort of revenge on you unless I can stop him.' And with that, she swept from the room.

That night Giulia fell into a dreamless sleep, her body flaccid as though drugged. She woke with a start and the queasy feeling that something bad had happened, before she remembered it all.

She dressed in a panic, noting the bruises on her ribs that bloomed like dull grey roses. She knew instantly she could no longer be a courtesan; that she could never face another night like the one before. The vision kept returning, making her gasp for breath, that suffocating feeling that she was about to die, de

Verdi's boot in her back, her thrashing arms thudding against the wooden floor.

She put her hand to her mouth, tried to calm herself. Mamma would have known what to do, would have comforted her. But every day that passed without her was like a splinter in her heart, a niggling pain that wouldn't go away. She needed her now, more than ever, to just fall into those arms and be hugged and comforted. Why had she been such a selfish daughter, never appreciating what she had?

She was filled with remorse. She longed so intensely for her old life that it made her clutch the wall to steady herself.

'Calm,' she spoke to herself. 'You must be calm. Think what possibilities are open to you.' She forced herself to breathe deeply. After a few moments she found some resolve.

She went to the gilded desk and took up a quill and uncorked the ink. Mamma had said to tell no-one where she had gone, but surely she could trust Fabio? If she wasn't to be a courtesan she would need another living. Perhaps her mother's legacy could be salvaged.

Fabio,

I know it is a long time since heard from me. I am sorry I didn't meet you in the square that time. I am...

She hesitated before writing,

...I am with relatives in Naples. I write to ask you a favour, though I know it may not be easy. I know my mother is dead, but I would like to know what happened to her house and all her effects that were left behind. There are some things from my childhood I would like to reclaim, and some books my mother treasured. These things should by

rights come to me, yet I need to know if it is safe, or indeed wise, for me to return and claim them. Whatever they say of her, I know her to have been good and kind. If you are able to give me any assistance, please send word to me care of Father Girolamo, at the Church of San Giovanni. I am sorry to ask this of you, but there is no-one else I can trust.

I remain as always, your loyal friend
Giulia

CHAPTER 19

PALAZZO DEL MARE, NAPLES

DOMENICO DE VERDI watched his wife, Agnese, from the window, his rosary beads passing idly through his hands. Signora Gauci was with her and would tell him later where she had been. Agnese no longer held his interest, not now she was no longer a virgin and had lost the holiness of the immaculate Mother Mary. That was why he had thought that Giulia Tofana, the niece Isabetta Boveri had been protecting, might be exactly the sort of woman he sought.

He'd been told she was too innocent for a man like him, but the threat that he would withdraw her opium supply soon changed Boveri's mind. She was lying of course. The girl was a harlot, like the rest, and vicious with it. She'd duped him. He shuddered at the thought of that knife.

Methodically, he began to count the beads as they ran through his fingers, hearing their comforting rattle. Was it so wrong to long for a woman who would make proper penance? Who would appease God's wrath against the human race? Someone to kneel before him, flagellate themselves, as he did. But Agnese had refused to pray. She refused to wear the hair shirt he asked her to wear, so now he had to use his fingers around her throat to force her to put it on. Agnese had withdrawn from him on the inside, and this angered him more than anything else, that she could move within herself out of his control. That women took their original sin so lightly enraged him. For it would be him, and men like him, that would pay when God brought down his judgement.

He wished he had not taken such a disobedient, sinful wife, but he'd needed her dowry to build the foundations of his church. He turned to the portrait of Santa Fina here in his personal apartment, which hung as a reminder of his duty. If only all women were like her, God would cease his punishments of fire and earthquake. She was truly a holy woman, a woman who had loved God so much that when she was ill, despite her pain, she remained so still that her flesh rotted to the board on which she lay. The flesh meant little to her, only the spiritual life, and after she died, the sweet smell of violets perfumed the room. He gazed at her upturned ecstatic face in its lambent glow. A true holy woman, ready to atone for her role in the fall of mankind. Agnese seemed to lack any sense of true repentance.

His reverie was interrupted by the arrival of heavy boots. He turned; a cohort of his men stood to attention. He looked them over. 'All is in readiness?'

'Yes,' Mario said. 'I have designated guards all around the walls.'

He was expecting his brother, Antonio, now lording himself as the duke. He had assembled his best men – the heaviest, strongest and youngest – and now they were an impressive sight as he went down to brief them in the loggia. He checked their positions, making sure that the whole palazzo would be covered by armed men. There must be no mistake about who held the power here.

When his brother had landed at the port the day before yesterday, the viceroy had requested a welcome party to meet him. Antonio would have expected a pageant, but following a strategy designed to show how little importance he held in

Naples, Domenico had instead sent his man, Enzo, with just one other servant. Apparently his brother had not been pleased at such a meagre reception, but that was as it should be. He wanted to receive him on his own terms, in his own palazzo.

Domenico took the stairs up to his apartment two at a time to prepare himself. He had oiled his hair and was dressed in his most sumptuous doublet. He had made sure the candelabra were lit, and an impressive portrait of him hung just behind his chair, on the opposite wall to Santa Fina. He had staged it well, he thought to himself.

A few moments later, having briefed the men, Enzo knocked and entered the large first floor chamber where Domenico was waiting, bringing with him his younger brothers and two more of his men, all fully armed. 'He's here,' Enzo said.

'How many men?'

'A small cohort of mercenaries. No match for ours.'

Domenico nodded. 'Send him up. We'll make sure he knows Naples has no need of him.'

When Antonio arrived, Domenico smiled and stood and held out his hand in greeting.

Antonio was impressively dressed in the finest figured velvet, with an immaculate lace ruff, despite the morning heat. A slim-shouldered man, well over six feet tall, he had been impressive as a youth, and much taller than Domenico, but now he looked gaunt, his face white and pinched.

So, thought Domenico, the illness had really taken its toll. He drew back his shoulders and clapped his brother on the shoulder, aware of the height difference; that his brother was still taller, and that each was weighing up the other.

'Good to see you, Domenico,' Antonio said.

The other brothers approached and were greeted effusively one by one.

'This is my right-hand man, Bruno Borroni.' Antonio indicated his companion, who was an even larger man – a man with a battered face that looked as if a dog had chewed it. 'He will command the men at my disposal. We are glad to be able to offer you assistance.'

The man Bruno surreptitiously glanced around the room, obviously assessing Domenico's armed men.

Domenico gave the big brute a nod of acknowledgement and gestured Antonio to a chair.

'I'd rather stand, thank you,' Antonio said.

'As you wish,' Domenico said lightly, feeling obliged to stay standing himself.

'The viceroy has received reports of growing rebel activity in Naples,' Antonio said, 'and he is anxious to suppress it before it becomes more widespread. He has sent me to offer you my assistance and put my men at our joint disposal.'

'Antonio, old boy, I'm afraid you've been misinformed. There is a small amount of rebel activity, but nothing my men cannot deal with. The viceroy hasn't been to Naples for six months or more, and things have changed. You will find our city quiet at night, and my men well able to keep the peace without any outside help. I'm afraid you've been sent on a wild goose chase.'

So this was the moment. He waited, studying Antonio's face. Would he capitulate for an easy life?

'Perhaps the viceroy is ill-informed, but if that is the case, I will investigate on his behalf and remedy it.' Antonio had drawn himself up even taller, and his eyes gleamed with the cold light of battle.

The supercilious bastard. Ready to bully him again, just like when they were boys. Domenico felt his temper rise.

'He has had letters from Neapolitan traders,' continued Antonio, 'letters claiming they are being charged protection money against a growing number of rebel gangs. Your name has been mentioned more than once in this connection.'

Domenico attempted a laugh. 'You know how it goes, Antonio. My name is always mentioned. Hardly surprising when I control the biggest guild in the city. Naturally, my men do all they can to keep the peace, and sometimes, yes, that involves suppressing criminals who would exploit the people of Naples.'

'I assume you take money for offering protection against these gangs?'

'No, no. You misunderstand the purpose here. My men take a small payment, a nominal amount only, but it goes direct to a building project for a new church, an agreement that pleases the people, and is a way to increase god-fearing behaviour. No better way to bring good from a bad situation, is there, brother, than to build something to God's glory.' How come he was defending himself? How had it changed around so he was the one on the defensive?

Antonio screwed up his mouth, as if he'd swallowed something distasteful.

Domenico took a moment to pause, stroll around the room, his territory. The sight of his Camorra men gave him renewed vigour. He decided to take the bull by the horns. 'Antonio, why are you here? I fail to see what use your mercenaries will be. They have no local knowledge like my men.' He gestured around. 'As you can see, I am perfectly adequately staffed, and any interference from an outsider will just provoke the rebels more.'

Antonio raised his chin. 'Why do you tolerate them at all? My aim is to eliminate these rebel gangs entirely within three months. That is what the viceroy has tasked me to do, and I shall expect your assistance to do it.'

Domenico curbed his anger. He mustn't lose favour with the viceroy. Damn his brother. Why did he always have to put his nose where it wasn't wanted? If Antonio had his way, his church to Santa Fina would never be built. He shrugged. 'My men are already fully engaged in keeping Naples safe. They will continue to do that. I don't see what use you can be.'

'I have a document here that says the Avvocata Quarter is the place of most unrest, so my men will begin there.'

Domenico felt the strength of his brother's will, like an implacable force. He'd always been able to bully him, the combination of being the eldest then gilded with the title of duke to boot.

'They will begin patrols this evening,' Antonio continued. 'I look forward to your full co-operation.' It felt like an order. 'I expect to see your men patrolling on the street after curfew alongside mine. When I'm established in Naples, you will join me for dinner, yes?' Antonio did not bow, but raised an eyebrow at his big-boned servant Borroni to summon him, and strode out, leaving Domenico staring in his wake.

Antonio had made him look like a fool, ordering him about like that. Him, Domenico de Verdi, being told what to do like a servant in front of his younger brothers. Of course, Antonio had the title on his side; and he played the aristocrat card every time. He glanced around the chamber. His younger brothers, Luca, Angelo, Stefano and Gino were giving him the sort of look that meant they were sorry for him.

'What are you gawping at?' He turned his venom on Enzo. 'Find me a map of the Avvocata Quarter. We have work to do.'

As they walked back to the duke's residence, the Palazzo de Constantin, Duke Antonio turned to Bruno. 'What did you think of him?'

'He's a man used to getting his own way, isn't he? He doesn't like us intruding on his territory.'

'He's always been awkward, held a grievance against me for being the eldest. As if I could help it! That's why we couldn't bear each other as boys. But come, they tell me he's building a church; it's this way.' He gestured Bruno onwards down the street towards the centre of the city. 'They demolished a beautiful part of the old walls to make way for it. Philistines. But I thought we'd take a look.'

Although still under construction, under its wooden scaffold, the white stone church loomed over them, three storeys of ornately carved columns and archways. A pediment above the main doorway was supported by cherubs with a plaque over it bearing the inscription 'I H S' the monogram symbolising Jesus.

'Excuse me.' Two men straining to carry a marble slab between them shuffled past. The whole thing was constructed using only the finest materials. Dozens of labourers huffed and puffed in their sleeveless jerkins to heave lumps of elaborately carved stone into position.

'Just shows his ambition,' Antonio said. 'This is no small undertaking. He might say his protection charges are small, and act as if it's all a charitable enterprise, but he hasn't fooled me. I know that the so-called rebels are his men. It's a well-known ruse.'

'What will we do if he doesn't co-operate? If we can't get him to stop?' asked Bruno.

'Get him to stop? Why would we want to do that? No. We need his contacts. We simply want to get the whole business under our control.'

Bruno looked surprised.

'What's the point of coming to Naples unless we can turn it to profit, eh?' Antonio gestured to the church. 'Let's see if we can look inside.'

They approached the main doorway, which as yet had no door in place, and peered through into the cool interior. Two dusty-haired men were laying patterned tiles on the floor.

'Careful, sirs,' one of them said, looking up from his work, 'the mortar's not yet dry.'

'We're looking for Domenico de Verdi's new tomb,' Antonio said. 'He told us to come and look.'

'Ah yes, over there in the basilica. Very proud of it, he is.'

The tomb itself was a huge marble edifice mounted on lions' feet, with kneeling statues of weeping women, probably the three Marys, bending over it.

'It's bigger than the altar,' Bruno said.

'He wants to be remembered. It's so lacking in refinement. Look, he's even got his coat of arms carved there. This must have cost half of Naples to build. He overreaches himself.'

'So what do you want us to do?'

'Lead the men to keep close to his men; don't let them out of your sight. This evening we'll be right outside his palazzo to follow wherever they go. Have our men ready to split up into groups if necessary. Make sure our men always outnumber his. It's time my brother was put back in his place.'

'Yes, sir. I'll see to it. Will you be joining us?'

Antonio hesitated. He did not wish to admit how tired he felt. The strain of meeting Domenico and his brothers had already taken its toll. 'I fear not. I have some paperwork I must do.'

'I understand,' Bruno said.

Antonio did not like to admit weakness. It made him angry, reminded him of the cause of his illness. 'In the daytime you can search the apothecaries,' he said. 'It is a shame your friend has never heard of the poisoner's daughter. But if Giulia d'Adamo is plying her mother's trade she must be employed somewhere. I want to know if any apothecaries in Naples are employing a Giulia d'Adamo. All women are to be questioned thoroughly.'

CHAPTER 20

MEANWHILE, on the other side of Naples, at the old Church of San Giovanni, Father Girolamo eased himself into the dark cubbyhole of the confessional box. His bones ached and his knees made a disconcerting grinding noise whenever he sat down. Oh, for some slippery balm to ease his knees. Maybe that little courtesan Giulia would have something for it. His wrist was much better since her plaster.

He inhaled the musty smell of the curtain that covered the grille where the penitent must speak and drew it back with a rattle. There had been no-one outside when he came in, so please God it would stay that way. An hour's respite from planning another sermon would be a relief. He suspected he'd said all he had to say in his lifetime on the lessons in the Bible. Still, duty was duty. He'd already heard confession for an hour before the early mass and now here he was again.

It was noon and the heat made him drowsy. He leant back on the cool wood and closed his eyes, let his face sag. All these years and he'd heard the same stories over and over. He had learnt to recognise lies when he heard them, by the over-enthusiastic admittance of minor misdeeds. Sadly, there were no new sins under the sun. Just the same old ones, appearing in different dark disguises.

He let his thoughts drift, chewing over the problem of the state of the poor of his parish after an eruption and five bad harvests, and the rumour of plague further south in Catania. And the fact that through all these disasters he must promote the goodness of the Lord.

A click of the door and a rustle beside him. Someone had entered the box. It was a woman. A man did not have skirts that rustled so. He sighed inwardly. He hoped it wasn't Signora Mantelli again to say she'd stolen another loaf from the bakery. She'd already said six Hail Marys this week, but nothing would deter a hungry woman with children to feed. He steeled himself.

A young voice, a quiet voice. 'Bless me, Father, for I have sinned.'

He leaned forward, unable to place the voice. He knew the voices of all his parishioners, although he had to pretend that the sinner was anonymous. This was a young woman he didn't know from church, yet her voice had a certain familiarity.

'It has been a week since my last confession, but I cannot go again to Father Costa. He has heard my confession and absolved me too many times, and yet still God gives me no answers. Why does he not hear my prayers? Why does he allow men to use women so? I pray to the Virgin Mary but how can she understand a man like Domenico? Although I try to turn the other cheek when my husband mistreats me, I cannot.' A quaver in the voice. 'I... I fear for my life.'

'In what way do you fear for your life?' Domenico. A husband called Domenico. He was still trying to place the voice.

'He likes to... I cannot. I cannot say.'

'No-one will hear but me. I am bound by God's secrecy.'

'He likes to... use a whip. A scourge to beat out my sins.' Now the words came thick and fast. 'I cannot escape him, and one day I swear I will die. At first he was telling me I was a sinner, and making me do penance. Kneel to pray forgiveness, put on a rough vest under my clothes to remind me of my sins, crawl across the floor on my knees—'

'You talk of sins. What sins are these, my child?'

'I know not what I have done, except for the sin of being a woman, to be a cause of the fall of Adam. He used to punish me for my sins with rough treatment, beatings and slaps. But now it is darker, like he wishes me dead.'

'But these sins are—'

'Please help me. He expects me home within the hour, so I have little time.' The urgency of the whispered voice commanded his attention.

Domenico. A cold fever rushed through him. He knew suddenly who was speaking. Little Agnese, the girl who had married his neighbour, Domenico de Verdi. Her voice continued, as if she was blurting everything in a great hurry. 'Please, Father, you hear confessions every day. I keep wishing there is someone who will kill my husband. I wish he is dead. I know this is a sin. If I find a way to remove him from the world, I swear I will take it. I dream of it. I dream of the moment when they lower his coffin into a tomb and close the lid. He is building his tomb, and I cannot wait for him to fill it. Because if I can't kill him first, my husband will kill me. I know it is wrong, but the thoughts keep coming. There cannot be a worse hell than the one I live in now.'

Her panic and distress was like a wind; it blew through the grille, sending a shiver up his spine. What could he answer?

'You did right to come to me,' he said, grappling for some sort of solution to the problem. He recalled his old mentor, who had schooled him in these awkward circumstances. 'God in his mercy sees more than we do. The most important thing is to cleanse yourself of sin. Cleanse yourself of these murderous thoughts. It is not for us to question the sins of others, only our own, so we can become pure and holy in God's sight.'

There was a sob so close to him that he instinctively reached his arms towards her, but of course the partition was between them.

'You must pray, pray to Santa Priscilla and San Aquila, the patron saints of married couples, to intercede with God and bring harmony between you, and you must...'

The door clicked and he felt the rush of air, and then he heard her footsteps running on the stone flags. He heaved himself to his feet and stumbled out after her, ready to call her back, even though he knew this broke the unspoken canon law of anonymity. But by the time his knees had obeyed his instructions, the girl was already hurrying out of the courtyard. He was about to pursue her when he found he was face to face with Brother Ignatius, the monk from the abbey close by, with whom he had never seen eye to eye.

'Comforting those in need again, Father Girolamo?' he said, a slight smile hovering on his lips. 'Your parishioner has fled, I'm afraid.'

Father Girolamo regarded his round, pasty face with dislike. They were the same age, but nature had treated Brother Ignatius better, his skin was smooth and plump, there were no worry lines around his eyes. His curiously bland expression had always been a source of irritation.

'Confession can be hard for some people,' was all Father Girolamo said. He wondered what the saintly Brother Ignatius would have done with such a confession. He longed to confide in someone, but Ignatius he knew was the wrong person; he knew from experience that Ignatius would only use it somehow to make him look bad. Ignatius was angling for his parish and would push him out if he could.

'You don't seem very busy,' Brother Ignatius said in an accusing tone. 'I wanted to speak with you about the refectory roof. The cardinal said he'd asked you to repair it three months ago, and something must be done before the rainy season.'

He sighed inwardly, reluctant to deal with this minor problem whilst the major problem of Agnese was still on his mind. 'Yes, yes,' he said, 'I'll do something about it this week.'

A loud crash. Followed by a strange ringing noise so loud they both stared at each other wide-eyed. He hurried to the door, but Brother Ignatius was first out into the square. By the time he arrived Brother Ignatius was standing stock still in a crowd that had gathered in a silent circle.

He pushed through the crowd, elbowing them aside. The bronze bell from the church tower had fallen. About six feet tall, one side was misshapen where it was embedded in the cobbles. The clapper was a silent tongue resting against the skirt of the bell. It was a wonder nobody had been killed.

Brother Ignatius pointed to the strands of frayed rope still wound around the hanger. 'I told you that bell should be checked, yet you did nothing about it.'

The sight of the bell, the enormity of it, the impossibility that it should have fallen at all, had awed the crowd to silence. Father Giro-lamo's legs began to shake. *Must be the shock*, he thought. The scene before him swam before his eyes, and he staggered over to a bench under an orange tree, where he sat with his head between his knees.

When he sat up, Brother Ignatius offered him a kerchief. 'You're sweating,' he said, with a faint note of disapproval.

'I don't feel quite myself,' he said.

'I'll fetch Brother Bernardo from the infirmary,' Brother Ignatius said. 'He'll give you a sedative draught.'

He didn't need a sedative, and he hated Ignatius treating him like an old man, but he was too shaky to object.

When Brother Ignatius had gone, he put his damp forehead into his hands, inhaling the smell of hot cobblestones and dirt. What would he do if he had no living any more? No parish, nowhere to live? A column of ants paraded past his bony toes in their worn sandals. And Agnese, what should he do about her? Oh for the life of an ant, with the only decision to be made to just follow your leader. He looked up. More people had gathered around the bell, exclaiming and wondering.

An omen. He could only see it as an omen. Was God telling him something? Should he have answered Agnese differently? He'd failed her, he knew. And Domenico de Verdi, what to do about him? Catholic law forbade him to tell another living soul. Yet if he believed someone was in danger, he had to intervene.

He stood up. The bell would have to wait. The maintenance always had to wait. *This was his trouble,* he thought. *People were always needing him more than the buildings.* From the corner of his eye he caught sight of two brown habits coming down the street. Brother Ignatius and Brother Bernardo. With an effort he sprinted around the corner out of sight and plunged into the dark interior of the fishmarket, where he hid behind a column.

He waited amongst the stink of fish until he was sure they would have given up looking for him. He'd go over to the Domenico de Verdi house straight away and see what could be gleaned about Agnese from the servants.

The Palazzo del Mare was an ostentatious balconied brick building, more like a fort than a house, built around a vast courtyard and patrolled by Domenico de Verdi's men, who were dressed as noblemen but by the look of their muscular torsos were all bodyguards. The front looked over the harbour and had two towers like lookouts. Father Girolamo went around the back of the house by the stables, to where a small set of stairs led up to the servants' apartments and a narrow door in a covered colonnade. He knocked and waited. The door opened, and their square middle-aged housekeeper, Signora Gauci, answered, hair scraped back under a white linen cap.

'Father.' She glanced about his person looking for clues as to why he was calling. Usually, if he went door to door, he had a collecting box in his hand.

He shrugged, smiled. 'Can I come in?'

'If you want the mistress, she's resting.' Her face was sour.

'No. It was you I wanted to see.'

'Me?' She frowned, as if he was going to ask something unpleasant.

'Just being neighbourly. It seems I don't spend enough time getting to know my parishioners.'

'Oh. Well, we're not your parish any more, Father. Master usually goes to Santa Maria La Nova now, mistress too. We all do. They have the bones of San Leonzius there.' Her tone was accusing.

'Still, we're neighbours, isn't that so? I just want to talk to you, get to know a bit more about who lives here.'

She still looked disgruntled but held the door open for him to enter. He realised he was sounding too curious, like the Inquisition. He tried to think of another approach.

He sat down at the table in the kitchen, which was scattered with crumbs, and she plonked a jug of watered ale and a cup before him. The way she did it made it perfectly clear he was an intrusion. He could hear the scratch of a scrubbing brush, and the slosh of water from the scullery, amid the faint tang of lye.

'Well?' Signora Gauci said, still standing.

Suddenly he remembered the bell. 'We had a mighty disaster this morning at the church, you'd never believe it. Our bell fell from the belfry. It's resting in the square at the moment. We can't call the monks to their prayers any more without that bell.'

He sensed her impatience as she waited for him to get to the point.

'I'm alerting everyone so they know the bell won't tell you the hour, or when to come to mass. It will be a while before it can be melted down and reforged.'

'Oh, I see. Well, if that's all—'

'You'll tell your mistress?'

'When she wakes, yes.'

'And how is she, the mistress?'

He saw the Signora Gauci's face close off, like a shutter being slammed against the sun. 'She's well. Just as you would expect. Why?'

He couldn't tell her she had been to confession or what she'd said. 'Just... it occurred to me that she's very young to be married... to have that amount of responsibility.'

'Pah. Many young women are married sooner. I was. I was married at twelve years old to Domenico de Verdi's personal valet.'

Ah. So that was it. She already had loyalty to Domenico de Verdi, and none to the girl. Father Girolamo slumped. He could think of nothing further to say.

Sensing the conversation was at and end, Signora Gauci gathered up the pile of sheets resting on the chair by the door. 'If you'll excuse me, Father, I'll take these up. Finish your ale, if you like.' The invitation was without warmth.

He nodded and watched the woman go. Strange how he had taken a dislike to her. He reminded himself to be charitable.

No sooner had she gone than the connecting door to the washroom opened, and a girl stuck her head into the room. 'Master treats her badly, the young mistress.'

'Is that so?'

The kitchen maid ventured further in, a pale-faced ghost of a girl, with gingery hair and a frightened expression. She pushed the damp wisps of hair from her face. '*She* wouldn't tell you anything, that Signora Gauci. She's just as bad as him.'

'Tell me what you mean.'

'She's terrified of him.'

'Who? Signora Gauci, or the mistress?'

'Both. Everyone. Well, mostly the mistress. Since she came she's just got thinner and thinner. She's not allowed to go anywhere, not even to the closet, without one of his servants attending. She looks so miserable, and at night when I'm fixing the dishes in the kitchen, I hear her praying out loud.'

'That's good to hear. God will surely answer her prayers and—'

'No, Father. It's a horrible sound. It's not a normal prayer, it sounds so desperate, and at the same time I hear her weeping, and the sound of him shouting and the sound of a whip hitting the ground. It echoes all through the house, but they all ignore it. How can they, when it would tear out your soul to hear her? And I fear for her. Once she didn't come down to eat, so I took her a tray, and there were bruises on her neck the size of horseshoes.'

'Is there nobody who can protect her in this house?'

'The servants are all too frightened of him to do anything. One of the servants left, but he had him arrested because he tried to say a bad word against him. The man's still there, accused of stealing. I shouldn't even be talking to you.' She glanced over her shoulder, as if Domenico de Verdi might appear at any moment.

'Who else knows about this?'

'No-one. We're not allowed to talk to anybody from outside the house or we lose our position, or worse.'

'Worse?'

'People disappear. Like a chambermaid that used to work here. He says they've run away, or left for work in another city, but I'm not so sure. We never hear from them again, and they never come back.' She hesitated, rubbed a hand across her mouth. 'Don't tell anyone I said so, though, will you, Father? Please, don't tell. All I know is, woe betide anyone who tries to go against him.'

'Will you tell me if you think she is in danger?'

'I don't know, Father. If they find out I've been talking to you I'll lose my position. But I do know I feel sorry for the girl. She's younger than I am, and although her family were aristocrats, her parents died and she has no one. She had a fortune though, I know that much. I watch her sometimes, and her eyes are so full of fear and worry. And she scratches herself with a kitchen knife when she thinks nobody is looking. Great red weals across her forearm.' She sighed. 'Of course, she doesn't know I exist, why should she? I'm just a kitchen maid. But I tell you, I'm so glad to be standing in my own shoes not hers.'

'Don't forget to come and tell me if—'

Signora Gauci appeared again in the doorway.

'Still here, Father?'

'No, I'm on my way.' He stood. 'Your maidservant was just about to show me out.'

As he left, he heard Signora Gauci scolding, 'Cettina, you lazy sow, get back to work.'

That night, he prayed harder than ever. The bell was on his mind, the fact their calls to the Liturgy of the Hours were suddenly silent. But what haunted him was the girl Agnese, locked in the palazzo not one hundred steps away. He could imagine he heard her screams and cursed his Catholic vow that he could do nothing about it except pray for her. Prayer suddenly seemed pitifully inadequate.

CHAPTER 21

WHILST FATHER GIROLAMO was at the Palazzo del Mare, Giulia had been taking her letter to Fabio to the staging post so it could be sent by courier. She had tied a mask over her face and had put on a short silk cloak to protect her shoulders from the sun; she did not wish to risk being seen by de Verdi. When she came back from the market, there was a large trunk standing in the lobby.

'What's all this?' she asked Bella.

Bella's eyes evaded hers. 'Ask Signora Isabetta.' Then she stopped midway up the stairs and said, 'I think you'll find it's all there.'

Giulia looked more closely at the bag placed on top of the trunk and saw the statue of Santa Olivia. She opened the bag further and saw a pair of her shoes, ones that Isabetta had given her when she arrived. She pulled open the trunk. It contained her gowns, her chemises, all her underthings.

With a feeling of foreboding in her stomach, she ran up the stairs and rapped at Isabetta's door.

'Why are my things in the hall?'

Isabetta stood and faced her, one hand pressed to her chest, gathering her day-robe about her. Her face was puffy, her eyes bloodshot. She sighed. 'We have no choice.'

'Is this Domenico de Verdi's doing? I might have guessed he—'

'I went there this morning but his servant told me that I couldn't see him. I had to wait. He was having a meeting with someone from Palermo. His brother. Antonio, the Duke de Verdi.'

The name was like a sword blow. It almost felled her. Giulia took a step back. 'The Duke from Palermo's here in Naples?'

Isabetta's grim expression was enough of a reply.

'Do they know I'm here?'

'I don't know,' Isabetta said. 'Domenico de Verdi was not in a good temper. Oh, I tried to mollify him. Made promises, crawled. But it did no good. He was about to send men here to arrest you, but I told him you'd already gone. You must leave as soon as you can. Bella has packed your things.'

'You'd blame me, when—'

'When Domenico de Verdi has a vendetta against someone, he rarely fails. I told him I'd terminated your employment. He says if my women are found to be carrying any sort of weapon, even a bodkin, he will close me down for good and—'

'He threatens you again, is that it? And you let him. Because he supplies your poppy powder, is that it?'

'I'm sorry.' Then more quietly, 'You don't know what it's like. The struggle… I can't live without my powder.'

Giulia turned away in disgust and found herself staring at the mess of Isabetta's unmade bed.

'Antonio, the duke, will be on on his side, you realise that?' Isabetta said. 'A death sentence already, with your family history. The de Verdis will press charges against you for attempted murder, and no-one will dare oppose them, two such powerful men.'

Giulia rounded on her, a cold shiver causing her to take a gasp of air. 'Are you saying you'll just put me out onto the street?'

'It's the only way. The safest way. Find a passage out of Naples as soon as you can. But don't tell me where you go, or Domenico might force it from me. His men use all kinds of torture to extract the information they need.'

Giulia could only stare. Her own aunt was refusing to offer her protection.

'My sister should never have sent you here,' Isabetta said. 'She cossetted you too much, kept you away from the real world. I kept telling her, but she wouldn't listen. She always thought she knew best.'

'Oh that's right, blame Mamma. Blame me, blame anyone but yourself.'

'It's for the best, Giulia, you have to see that. I'm thinking of your safety.'

'My safety? When you'd just push me out with nowhere to go?' The chamber suddenly seemed like a refuge, its familiar clutter of phials and pots, its hairbrushes, the scatter of powder on the surface of the table.

When she looked up again, Isabetta's eyes were fixed on her with a strange pleading expression. It was confusing, this blowing hot and cold, as if she loved her one minute and hated her the next.

Isabetta turned away to the window. 'I'm sorry, but I have to think about the others. Eight people's livelihoods depend on me, and I have no other trade,' she said. 'What would you do in my place?'

'Don't put the burden on me!' Giulia's chest heaved in outrage. 'What would Mamma think?'

Isabetta swivelled. 'Theofania was fool enough to risk her own death, even though she knew you depended on her,' Isabetta said, her voice hard and sharp. 'I'm sorry, Giulia, but if you had only obeyed our client, Domenico de Verdi, we would have none of this. If we have trouble, it is because you caused it.'

'I caused this? You twist it so it's my fault?'

Isabetta seemed to brace herself and harden her tone. 'You must find somewhere else to go. You must see, I cannot protect you.'

So it was over. She was to be alone. With one venomous look at Isabetta, she braced her shoulders and walked from the hall. As she got to the top of the stairs she called back, 'My mother trusted you, and a fine sister to her you turned out to be. I hope you fry in hell.'

Twenty minutes later she dragged her trunk outside the door and was on the street clutching the straw bag Sister Marthe had given her when she first arrived in Naples. The bag was weighed down with the statue of Santa Olivia and Mamma's book she had retrieved from under the pillow. She had toyed with the idea of leaving the trunk behind, as she didn't want to keep anything belonging to Isabetta. But then she hardened. She must be pragmatic, think of the future. She'd need money, and she could always sell the gowns if she needed to.

Shaken, and still boiling with rage, she summoned two boys from the street and had them take her trunk to the only place she knew might help her, a failed courtesan. The church and Father Girolamo.

In her chamber at the top of Villa Bianca, Isabetta crumpled, crouched in a chair with her knees pulled up under her, hugging herself and rocking. That had been hard, to turn her out like that, no matter that it was for her own safety. For the first time in her life, she got down on her knees and sobbed for the woman she'd become. Why was she so weak?

She needed someone strong, someone like Bruno, to lean on. If she were to know where Giulia had gone, she feared she'd crumble under pressure from Domenico de Verdi or his brother, Antonio, the duke and tell them.

Why hadn't she Theofania's courage? Theofania had always been like a tiger caring for a cub.

But look where it led her. The voice of the devil on her shoulder.

'God keep Giulia safe,' Isabetta prayed, to a God she'd long since given up on.

She tried to resist the poppy, but after a few more hours of sweating and shaking she was reaching for it again. She had no willpower, and the thought made her despise herself.

CHAPTER 22

Giulia hesitated outside Father Girolamo's house, which stood on the corner next to the row of larger *palazzi*. Built of old yellow stone like the church, it was joined to it but had its own separate entrance through a walled-off courtyard. By now it was dusk, and the street lamps were being lit by the shopkeepers for the evening opening, the streets smelling of burning tallow and oil. The boys dumped her trunk by the door, and she paid them their tip. She rapped with the solid iron knocker, and Father Girolamo came as soon as she knocked, his wrinkled face peering out through the crack in the arched oak door.

'I need a place to stay,' she said without preamble.

He opened the door wider, looked down at her trunk, which the boys had dumped on its end, and frowned. 'You'd better come in. Here, let me help.' He dragged the trunk inside, before ushering her in to his small sparsely furnished parlour, redolent of old incense mingled with pipe smoke.

'I'm disturbing you,' she said, casting a glance at the table where books and papers towered in untidy heaps atop a pile of old news-sheets.

'Not at all,' he said. 'But is there a servant with you, a chaperone perhaps?'

'I'm afraid not,' she said. 'I came because I can no longer stay at the Villa Bianca and I have nowhere else to go.'

'I see.'

The fact that he didn't ask her questions made her want to answer them.

'One of the men...' She paused, unable to get the words out. They were stuck somewhere between her heart and her throat. She looked at Father Girolamo and his kindly face and simply could not say the word. 'I can't go back,' she said.

'So you came here.'

'Isabetta won't let me stay, because the man... well, he took a dislike to me and is threatening her with closing down her business if I stay.' She knew this was an over-simplification of events, and indeed Father Girolamo wrinkled his brow in a puzzled kind of way.

'A man has somehow come between you and your aunt, is that right?'

'Do you promise not to tell anyone if I give you his name?'

'Secrets told to me are sacred if you wish it. You have my word.'

'Domenico de Verdi. He is your neighbour.'

The priest sagged, sat down, and pressed his hand to his temple. 'De Verdi. Yes. I know him.'

'His wife, Agnese, comes to me for lessons in music. Or, should I say, she did. But she's afraid of him too. I wish I had never come to Naples.'

'Be calm. You will be safe here. I have some bedding and you can lie down by the fire.' He went over to the door and locked it, shunting across both bolts.

He eased himself slowly into a cushioned chair. 'Your parents...'

'Both dead. And there was some trouble at home. I swear I

have done nothing wrong, but there are men searching for me from the Duke de Verdi in Palermo. One of them came here to Naples. If they find me, they will kill me, I know it. And now his brother Domenico is searching for me too.'

Father Girolamo sat back in his chair, rubbed his beard. 'Many problems then with this family. You are sure you have nothing you wish to confess?'

'Too many things to count. And trouble seems to follow me.'

He gave a slow nod, his beard creasing on his chest, his eyes assessing her. As a priest he must be used to discerning truth from lies. Could he see from her eyes she was telling the truth? She knew it sounded fantastical: soldiers out to kill her; another man wanting her blood.

'Why don't we read a few passages of the Bible together?' he said. 'That usually solves most problems. Would you like to choose a verse or two?'

It can't solve this, she thought. But he handed her the Bible and she opened it randomly at a passage from the psalms and tentatively began to read, as he lit his pipe.

'Unto thee, O Lord, do I lift up my soul.
    O my God, I trust in thee: let me not be ashamed,
    Let not mine enemies triumph over me...
    Shew me thy ways, O Lord; teach me thy paths.'

The act of reading aloud calmed her. After a while, he took over the reading, and his soft voice and the smoke from his pipe made her drowsy. Soon the tension left her shoulders and she found herself falling asleep.

∾

Father Girolamo piled up all his sermon papers into a heap on the desk and checked the *couvre feu* was over the coals before retiring to his bed.

By the morning he was still worrying, trying to fathom what to do about the courtesan Giulia Tofana. But Giulia was already up and dressed. He eyed her warily. A woman in a priest house dressed in an elaborate gown like that would lead to gossip, if not worse.

As he stirred his morning ale, he remembered that his house-keeper had left her old work clothes behind, in the clothes press – the ones she used for scrubbing the tiled floors. He hurried to fetch them.

'Here,' he said, handing her the pile of garments. 'These might make you less…'

'Less of a courtesan,' she said.

'Well, not exactly, but less noticeable.'

'Thank you, Father. I've been thinking, I saw a notice a few weeks ago in the apothecary's for a live-in apprentice. At Ruggiero's. Do you know if they have someone yet?'

'A boy, they were after. That's what Camilla said; since the famine they've been swamped with incomers from the country, with all manner of ills. But I don't think they'd countenance a girl.'

'I know. I asked. But maybe they'll be more inclined to take me now, if they haven't got someone. If I go there, will you vouch for me? They might trust you.'

He saw immediately that this would solve several problems, if he could get Camilla to agree. Though Matteo always thought he was in charge, it was actually Camilla who ruled the roost.

'I can write you a letter of recommendation,' he said, 'if that would help?'

~

The shutters were still closed when she got to the Ruggieros', but she knocked anyway, with Father Girolamo's newly penned letter in her hand.

Camilla appeared at the door tying her cap over her grizzled grey hair. 'Yes? Is someone ill?'

'No. Pardon me for coming so early, but I was hoping you'd still need an apprentice,' Giulia said, running on before she could be interrupted. 'I have a testimonial here from Father Girolamo, and he says you've been uncommonly busy and need an extra pair of hands.'

'Oh, he did, did he?' She looked to Giulia, assessing her. 'We've seen you before.'

'Yes, I asked about the apprentice position and talked to your husband. I have some skills already.'

'I remember.' The door was still only half-open, and Camilla was frowning. 'We'll think about it. I'll have to ask my husband later,' she said firmly, making to close the door.

'Won't you ask him now?' Giulia asked, desperation in her eyes.

'I don't know… he doesn't like to be rushed.'

'Father Girolamo thinks it's Providence, you needing someone and me having the skills…' She held out the testimonial and Camilla unfolded it, scanned it and sniffed.

'I fixed his arm for him,' she said.

It was a gamble, but Camilla finally sighed, beckoned her over the threshold and said, 'Wait there.'

Giulia waited in the dimly lit corridor that led to the shop, with the smell of spices and the sharp scent of lavender drifting from inside.

She could hear the distant rise and fall of Camilla's voice arguing, and her heart sank. After only a few moments Camilla was back.

'Matteo says he trusts Father Girolamo's judgement.' Her face said *she* certainly did not. 'He's willing to take you on. Seems like he took a shine to you when you came last time. You're lucky. He doesn't take to people easily.'

'And I can start today?' A leap of hope.

'I suppose so, as long as you don't mind hard work, and a trestle in our chamber. We've no other space.'

'Thanking you so much. You don't know how much this means to me.'

'Oh, go on with you,' Camilla said, but she looked secretly pleased. 'You know you've bent our arms. But maybe the Father's right. The great Lord God works in mysterious ways, and perhaps He has sent you, and who are we to turn away His gift?'

Giulia let out her breath. She vowed not to waste this chance. She had employment and a place to stay. Camilla, meanwhile, was looking at the letter again and shaking her head. 'That priest could persuade the back legs off a donkey.'

'I'll work hard, Signora Ruggiero,' Giulia said. 'Thank you for taking me on.'

Her face softened. 'Well, it's done now; we'll just have to get used to each other.' She went to a cupboard. 'Here, you can have one of my old skirts,' Camilla said, handing Giulia a homespun skirt, linen chemise and a loose front-fastening bodice. 'That skirt you're wearing's fit only for the pig bin. And I recognise it. It was the Father's housekeeper's. Can't have you looking like a pig girl.'

Camilla showed her to a damp back storeroom where she could change. The room was dark and confined with no windows. Giulia hesitated at the door because she'd always had an aversion to tight, cramped spaces. She forced herself to go inside and shivered in her underthings as she discarded one set of clothes for another. As she stepped into her new clothes she hoped they would provide enough of a transformation. After all, there would still be the De Verdi brothers looking for her.

She slipped the knife into the pouch under her apron, for she never went anywhere without it. She wouldn't tell Isabetta where she was. Isabetta's betrayal still ate into her, corrosively, like vinegar flooding a cut. She was finished with the Villa Bianca and that life. At least here she could learn the apothecary skills she needed and follow in Mamma's footsteps.

In the new clothes she felt different. They were baggy and comfortable, and immediately nondescript.

'Do you often get city merchants in the shop,' she asked when she emerged, tucking her heavy black hair into the new linen coif and tying it under her chin.

'Not often,' Camilla said. 'Dealing in trade is beneath them. Wealthy men always send a servant. Why?'

'No reason.' She thought of Bruno Borroni, the duke's servant. She would keep indoors, and as far away as possible from Domenico de Verdi's waterfront palazzo, but she would try to discover if his brother, the duke, was staying with him.

The memories of the night as Domenico de Verdi's courtesan were blurred, but she could still taste the bitterness of the wine and feel his boot on the bones of her wrist. She'd hoped in time his wish to wreak vengeance on her for disobeying him would die down and he might forget about her. But now, if his brother was here in Naples, there'd be scant chance of that. Mamma had seen to that. She took a deep breath and fashioned her apron strings into a neat bow.

Camilla smiled at her appearance with approval. 'Very tidy,' she said, looking her up and down. 'Here we run a clean shop, everything tried and tested according to God's great principles. And you'll earn your keep right enough. Matteo will show you the basic blending, and you'll work in the still room at the back, not at the counter unless we're busy.'

She exhaled in relief. She would not have to risk meeting Domenico de Verdi again.

'I have to say, you certainly look different in that nice clean apron, and without all that paint on your face like last time you came.'

She felt herself blush and wondered if she had really looked such a harlot as Camilla was implying.

Matteo appeared then from the still room door. 'Ah, she's here. Our little helper.'

His fatherly smile was reassuring, though it made her feel about five years old, but she followed him through to the still room behind, where he was making a 'simple' by the maceration of herbs in olive oil. 'Here,' he said, 'you continue with this, whilst I sieve this balm I'm making.'

'What's it for?' she asked, pounding the pestle down with both hands.

'A balm for scab and itch,' he said. 'Widow Scarlatti's children have some sort of infection. But before you start, you must pray.'

She stiffened, recalling the scene with Domenico de Verdi.

'We will ask San Rocco that God will work through us for the greater good.'

He tugged open a cupboard under the counter, where a sliding shelf held a worn and threadbare dark blue cushion. In the niche above was a half-size statue of San Rocco – a young man in a wide-brimmed hat, carrying a staff and gourd, accompanied by a wide-mouthed dog. The smiling dog was immediately reassuring.

'See?' Matteo said, patting the dog's head. 'Only San Rocco. Patron saint of apothecaries and dogs. I call the dog Amico, for his friendly face.'

'Most lifelike,' she said, crouching down for a better view. 'I have a favourite saint too. Santa Olivia.'

'I'll clear a shelf for her in the shop. So before beginning to mix any remedy, you must say a prayer to your Santa Olivia. Or to San Rocco. It will remind us that it is not we who heal, but God, heh?' He eased himself onto the cushion with some difficulty. 'Bad knees,' he confessed, before gesturing to her to join him.

She nodded and knelt beside him on the cushion. Already she

felt a gnaw of guilt, knowing the blackness in her heart. Here was the place she'd learn her mother's poisoning skills and avenge her death.

Her gaze roamed around the workshop. Much of it was already familiar to her from her mother's still room, but Neapolitan physic was more advanced and there were many vessels on the shelves labelled with foreign names she did not recognise.

Once Matteo stood up again, they began, and Matteo gave her a guided tour of the shelves, pointing out where the different unguents, balms, plasters and cerecloth were stowed. He passed her a mortar and had her mix a paste for treating cold humours from wax, camphor, olive oil and red lead. He watched closely as she did it, her eyes watering from the camphor fumes, until the *cerotto* was ready.

Each time that day, before beginning any process, she was nudged to kneel, and if she did not, Matteo would wag a finger at her until she complied. He himself must have been up and down from that cushion twenty times, despite his creaking knees. But his insistence on this little ritual pricked at her conscience every time.

She knew she needed skills she hadn't yet learnt if she was to become a mistress of poisons like her mother. But she was patient. Dogged even. And after all, it was in her blood.

Whilst she was in the back room, she heard Camilla's cheerful voice dispensing opinions, gossip and unasked-for advice to customers, alongside the preparations Matteo made, and it gave some comfort, until one of the customers mentioned that there was a new aristocrat who had just taken over the Palazzo de Constantin, and his russet and gold livery was everywhere.

Russet and gold. The Duke de Verdi's colours.

The Palazzo de Constantin. She must remember.

At the end of the day, she washed down the dispensing table like Mamma used to, as Camilla locked the door and sank into the only chair behind the counter. Hearing the bolts, Matteo came through and gave Camilla a hug. 'Good business, heh, wife?'

'Busy. My feet are aching,' Camilla said. 'Let's give thanks and then get away upstairs.'

'Giulia took to it like she was born to it, though,' Matteo said. 'She's like someone we already trained.'

Even Mamma had never complimented her like that before. The warmth spread in a flush to her cheeks.

Camilla pursed her lips. 'Who did you say your mother was?'

She was taken aback by the question. 'My mother's been dead a long time now,' she said.

As she'd hoped, this stopped further questioning.

The next day, in her noontime siesta, Giulia put on a hat against the sun, pulled low so it hid her face, and went to take a look at the Palazzo de Constantin where she'd heard Antonio, the Duke de Verdi was in residence. A muleteer carrying leather jugs of water pointed out the correct building. She was unsurprised at the palazzo's faded grandeur. A four-storey marble-fronted edifice, of yellowing stone, with huge peeling shuttered windows overlooking the vegetable market.

She walked around the back of the building to the trades-man's entrance. There, the sturdy wooden gates were wide open, and there was already much activity with covered carts bringing supplies of provisions and many servants unloading baskets of fruit and boxes of corn. She watched a dray full of barrels of wine unloaded, and by the number she realised it was going to be a big household, and that he was intent on a long stay.

Perhaps if he was so fond of wine she could find a way to taint it.

After watching a while and taking careful note, she returned to the front, determined to catch a glimpse of the man who had killed her mother, upended her life, and caused her so much pain. She took up watch there until she could wait no more. Camilla and Matteo would not be impressed if she was late back.

The next day she was there again.

The third day, she had not been there long when a man stalked down the steps from the covered balcony and into the light. A man she recognised. It was the older *condottiere* who had been watching her at Isabetta's – the rugged-looking man called Bruno who had chased her from Palermo. Something about him arrested her, some fascination with his features, as well as fear. He paused to wait, and a few moments later, a group of men emerged flanking a tall thin man in elegant attire – a pearly white lace collar around his neck, and a tall crowned hat.

By the attitude of the fawning courtiers, and his resemblance to his brother Domenico, in the high forehead and straight set of the eyebrows, this must be the duke. But he was taller and thinner, like a stalk of reed. She set off to pass him in the other direction. As their paths crossed, she curtseyed and stepped aside. She tilted her head so the hat would not shadow her face. He had never seen her before, but she wanted him to remember her. She looked up at him, her heart battering, and smiled sweetly.

He acknowledged her with a brief irritated nod, enough time to signal that he had no idea who she was, and that she was in his way. In that one moment she took in the fact he was wearing an unusual pendant.

A bezoar stone, the antidote to poison.

An elaborately mounted stone of dull ochre, the size of a blackbird's egg, it dangled from his neck on a gold chain.

She moved out of his way, her gaze fixed on his. He frowned, and the eyes in his pale face had small lines around them and an expression of suffering that she did not expect. She pressed her lips together, dipped her head to hide her face once more. This was the man who had killed her mother. Anger fizzed in her veins.

She would not forgive him. And one day he would pay, with a death even more painful than the one her mother had endured. As he passed he glanced back, as if to say, who is this woman who dares be in my way? After he'd passed, she walked slowly around the palazzo, taking in the servants' entrances, the doors to the underground wine cellar, the stables behind, the gate to the courtyard. She committed it all to memory.

'That man,' she asked one of the harassed-looking female servants at the gate, 'was that the duke, from Palermo?'

'Yes. You looking for work?' She looked her up and down with an assessing gaze.

'Maybe. Does he need servants?'

'Not yet. He's going back to Palermo. In a month's time though, he's moving his whole household here. Then they'll be looking for more staff. Come back then.'

A month. Enough time for her to find a poison and work a plan.

CHAPTER 23

PALERMO, TWO WEEKS LATER

IN THE LEATHER shop in Palermo, in the purpling light of dusk, Fabio had stopped work. Instead, he paced back and forth in the light of the dimming brazier, wondering what to do. Every now and then he glanced at Giulia's letter lying like a fallen bird amid his leatherworking knives and punches.

Should he write back? He'd enquired about her old house and discovered the contents had been looted by the duke's men for anything valuable. A bonfire had been held in the garden, where they burned clothing, bedding and whatever was left, including paperwork and any will, if it had existed. He did not look forward to telling Giulia that, nor that the house was now forfeit and had been let to the overseer in the duke's olive oil producing factory. He didn't want to hurt Giulia, and replying to her letter would undoubtedly cause her pain. That was bad enough. But then there was Claudia.

He felt a sliver of guilt. Claudia had been an almost constant presence in the workshop. He thought he'd done with her after the execution, but she kept appearing just the same, despite his harsh words. It made him despise her, but she was brazen and bold, and the sway of her hips and her suggestive glances held an illicit appeal that was hard to resist.

Ruminating, he sprinkled water from the pail by the door and began to sweep the leather shavings across the floor. It was time to close for the evening, and his belly was rumbling with the thought of supper.

He could do nothing, of course, and pretend Giulia's letter didn't exist. But there was something about Giulia, some mysterious pull about her that meant he couldn't forget her. But even if he did write, what could he tell her? Nothing. Better she did not know the details. His mind veered back and forth in indecision.

As the brazier's coals grew grey, the darkness in the workshop grew deeper, but still Fabio didn't light the candles. He stood for a long time, holding the broom, listening to the chirrup of the crickets outside and the tolling of the bell for vespers from the church in the square.

Finally, he swept the shavings onto a board and emptied it into the waste-barrel. Then, unable to resist, he lit a single candle, took parchment and quill, and sat down to write to her.

The jangle of the shop bell. Oh no. Not a customer now, not when he was just about to lock up.

Claudia was in the shop before he could get to the door, her presence filling the room.

'What are you doing?' she asked. 'It's very dark in here.'

Giulia's letter was still on the counter. His eyes darted over to it. Could he hide it? Too late. Claudia was sharp and had already spotted it.

'Another order?' She picked it up between finger and thumb, wafting it in the air.

'Yes,' he said, snatching for it, but she ran away, teasing him with it.

He tried again to grab it from her, but she turned her back and he saw her unfold it. Her back stiffened.

She spun round. Her eyes caught his. 'Is that who you were writing to? That Giulia d'Adamo?'

He didn't answer.

'I thought you liked me,' she said.

'I do,' he said.

'Then why are you bothering with her? Her mother was a witch who poisoned the duke. Do you really want to be mixed up with that whole foul business? What would it do to your reputation? Imagine if it got out.'

She toyed with the letter, keeping half an eye fixed on him.

'I wasn't writing to her, I was writing to my cousin,' he said, taking the unfinished letter from the counter and screwing it into a ball.

'I see.' She kept her gaze on his reddening face. He hoped it was too dim for her to see the flush. 'Then you won't mind if I—' She held Giulia's letter over the candle flame until it flared into ash.

He leapt to save it but was too late.

'What a pity,' she said. 'Now it's gone.'

'You shouldn't have done that,' he said.

'I was only saving you from yourself,' she said. 'Forget her.' She moved closer to him and snaked a hand up around his neck, lifted her mouth close to his ear and whispered, 'I came to see if you wanted another swim.'

His mouth was dry. The last time, she'd enticed him naked into the sea and let him touch her bare waist before she swam away. He felt the familiar excitement, half pleasure and half pain, fire his loins.

'Yes,' he said. 'When?'

∿

The next morning Fabio rolled over in bed cursing himself. Bedding Claudia had been easy. Too easy. He had taken her as she'd wished, under the olive trees by the shoreline, and the sticky sand and salt was still in his hair. She would think him beholden to her again now, and he cared not a bean for her. His mind was on Giulia d'Adamo and her letter asking for his help. He couldn't get Giulia out of his head, though he wished he could. The fact she was the daughter of the poisoner added to her appeal in some odd way.

In her place he would be the same. He'd want to know about his mother's property. This morning his father was away again buying hides, or so he said. Fabio knew it was just an excuse to spend longer at the tavern. But it meant he would be alone in the shop.

He glanced around. The shop was full of minor repairs – leather buckets that needed the handles fixing, broken ox harnesses and saddlery, and now he had finished the bindings for Giulia's books, he longed for something more challenging to do, anything to take his mind off the disaster of Claudia and the death of Giulia's mother.

By mid-morning his mood had evaporated under the intricacies of stitching leather. He paused and rubbed his finger, which was calloused from using the awl, before returning to the task of the bridle in front of him.

When the door opened he startled and looked up, half expecting to see Claudia, but it was a small elderly man wearing a dusty cloak. His moustache was thick and black, though his hair was sparse and grey. He was empty-handed so it wasn't a repair. Fabio smiled.

'Good morrow, sir, how can I help?'

'Are you Fabio Pasello?'

'Yes, that's me.'

'A good strong young man. And you do decorative leatherwork, yes?'

'What did you have in mind?'

'Can you show me an example?'

'I don't have much in the shop, I mostly work to commission.' A thought occurred to him, 'But wait… I do have these.'

He reached under the counter and drew out the books that he had covered for Giulia. Since she went away he had been working on them in his spare moments. They were nearly done now, riots of curling leaves and foliage, with colours of the flowers picked out in leather dye, and her initials glistening with burnished gold leaf. Of course, he'd spent far too long on them, and they were too elaborate for her to afford, but making them had made him feel as if he could make up, in some small way, for the terrible fate of her mother.

He put them reverently on the counter. The man reached out a gnarled hand to stroke them. 'Beautiful.' The fingers were bony and as knobby as old olive trees. 'Did you make the designs yourself?'

'Yes. I like to draw.'

'Hmm.'

He traced the texture of the leather for so long that Fabio became uncomfortable. 'What sort of work are you after, sir?' he asked.

The man looked up. Tears were in his eyes. 'I remember when I could do work like this. But now my hands won't let me. My name is Alfonso Garcia, and I came because I was curious about you. I saw one of your saddles and asked who had decorated it, and they told me it was you.'

'You? You're Garcia? From Naples?'

A nod.

Fabio's eyes widened. 'Really? I looked into your shop once, when I was very small, but my father pulled me away…' He tailed off, unable to continue for fear of causing offence.

'Because I'm Spanish I suppose.'

'I suppose. Times were different then.' He paused, thinking back to his scrawny nine-year-old self. 'But I've never forgotten your shop. There was a screen there, carved in leather with lions' heads and a coat of arms. It was like magic. I didn't think anyone could make such a thing in leather.'

'Ah yes, the screen. I had such pleasure tooling that. But I can't make those things any more, even if—' He pulled himself up short, shook his head as if to rid it of some memory. 'My hands are too stiff now to do it. But yours are not. I have many commissions but cannot fulfil them. My reputation is becoming tarnished now that my work is less fine than it was. I need someone like you, someone young and strong.'

'You are offering me work?'

'If you want it.'

'Have you no apprentice?'

'I had an apprentice, but he would not stay.' His eyes shifted away. 'It would mean you coming to Naples, staying in my house.'

'Oh. I don't think I could do that. My father you see…'

Signor Garcia put a bony hand on the counter. 'I would pay you well, and you would be making beautiful leather wall panels, decorative trunks, carved leather masks for carnival, scabbards twining with serpents. You will never get a better offer in your life. Your father will understand. He wants the best for his son, yes?'

It sounded simple. And yes, his father did want the best for him, as long as that was regular solid trade with a good Italian merchant. His father didn't hold with fancy work, or with the Spanish, whom he still regarded as invaders even after all this time.

'Think of it,' Garcia said, 'you can make more book bindings like these, and live in the centre of the city making work for princes and popes.'

Fabio looked down at the books, at Giulia's initials. He would love to give her these as a gift, and Giulia was in Naples somewhere, near a church where a Father Girolamo was a priest. He'd read her letter so often he remembered, even though Claudia had burned it. He could find Giulia, tell her about her mother's house himself. It seemed too much like fate to ignore.

'You agree?'

'I'd need to talk to my father.'

'You won't regret it. Nine scudi a week. Come at the end of the week. Bring your favourite tools.'

'And what's wrong with what I do?' His father's jowly face was set in a scowl.

'Nothing, Father,' Fabio protested. 'It's just that I like doing decorative work, and this will give me more chance to do it.'

'You can do decorative work here.'

'Not like at Alfonso Garcia's.'

'You mean you'd rather work for some filthy Spaniard than for your own father?'

'It's not like that. I just—'

'What will people think? My own son gone to work for someone else?'

Ah. Now we were getting to it. It wasn't about what was best for him, but all about keeping Father's good name in Palermo. It made Fabio even more determined to go.

'I'm not asking you, Father, I'm telling you. There is more business in Naples, and my prospects will be better. I'd rather go with your blessing, but if not, then I'll go without it.'

'Then go. Stab your old father in the back, like you always have.'

'That's not true. You've always left the hard work to me, whilst you spend your days drinking yourself stupid in the taverns. That's why you can only do basic repairs, because you can't be bothered to lift a finger to do anything else.'

'Hogshit. I travel miles to buy those hides, and all you do is ruin them with your fancy fiddling.'

'At least I'm doing something. How many bridles have you repaired in the last month? One. Think the business can stay afloat without me? Well just you try. I'm going where my work will be appreciated.'

The door opened and his mother came in. A slight woman, brisk and dapper, she had her sleeves rolled up and flour on her apron. 'I heard shouting,' she said.

'Fabio's decided to leave home.' His father spat out the words.

'What?' His mother's eyes flicked from Fabio to his father.

'Thinks he's too good for us.'

She stepped forward, intent on soothing him. 'Now, now, I'm sure that's not—'

'I'll be packed and gone by the morning.' Fabio felt the tight hard knot in his chest bring water to his eyes at the sight of his mother's stricken face. 'If you want to know why, ask him.' He jabbed a finger towards his father, who stepped up, his fists raised.

'You little sack of piss!'

'Yes, Father,' he shot back, 'the answer to everything. Your fists.' And with that, Fabio stormed out, slamming the door behind him.

Later, after he had cooled off, he returned, slightly shame-faced, to the house. The door was locked. He walked around the back but he couldn't get in there either. Bastard had locked him out.

A whisper from above. 'Fabio.'

He looked up. His mother was leaning out of the window. 'He won't let me come to the door.'

He saw she was dangling his favourite leather holdall from the window. He held out his arms and the holdall dropped into them, heavy as a baby.

'Your tools,' his mother said. 'A little money and a few other chattels you'll need. Those books you were working on. Write to me. I wish you well with Garcia, he was always a man well regarded for his skill, despite... Well, I'll try to visit as soon as the heat's gone from your father's temper, but you know what he's like. He'll—'

She glanced over her shoulder and suddenly the window shut and she was gone.

He guessed his father had called her.

'God bless you,' he said. 'I'll come back when I've made my fortune and take you away from him, see if I don't.' But there was no-one to heed his words. He turned and, with a heavy tread, walked away.

CHAPTER 24

NAPLES

WHEN HE DESCENDED from the tender, after more than a day's travel by ship, Fabio stretched his stiff legs, hitched his bag over his shoulder, and made his way out of the harbour. Glad to be on dry land, he strode down Via Medina, admiring its tall stucco buildings. This was a place he could *be* someone, he thought. He asked the way to Via Speranzella, and now he was heading down a side alley towards the sign of the hide and mallet. Naples sweltered, airless and dusty. Particles of pumice from the last eruption still clung to windowsills, balconies and railings, and lodged between the cobbles, giving everything a silvered look in the hot noonday sun.

Garcia – Fine Leatherwork, he read on the long wooden sign above the three narrow windows. The same sign he remembered, except that there was only one window to look through now, the others had been boarded up. The door looked as though someone had splintered the bottom of it with a shovel.

This didn't look like the flourishing business he was expecting. Last time he came, there had been trestles outside with goods on display, and a boy touting them to passers-by. The street was quiet, most of the shops had their shutters up. He pushed open the door and was greeted by the familiar smell of leather and woodsmoke.

A brazier to heat the irons was alight in the corner and Signor Garcia was in his shirt sleeves, bent over the glow, a striped cotton cap on his head to catch the sweat.

'Fabio?' His surprise turned to a wide smile and a clap on the shoulder. 'I didn't expect you so soon.'

'No time like the present, I thought. Beautiful day, isn't it?'

'All the better now you're here. Look, I've already made space for you here.' He led him by the arm to a long workbench down one side of the shop. On the bench was a travel trunk with a domed top, but the top was smashed, the leather torn.

'What happened to this?' he asked, reaching out a hand to feel the damage.

'An accident. It fell off a cart.' The answer was throwaway, but something about it didn't fit. It looked as if it had been deliberately holed. Fabio let it go, though, and began to hang his tools on the pegs provided.

'Can you fix it?' Garcia said. 'I'm not much use with woodwork now. Too much stiffness in my fingers. You'll find wood and veneers in the back room, and new hide to match.'

'Who did the decoration?'

'Simon, the apprentice.'

'He has some skill. It would match better if he did the repair. It looks like an expensive item.'

'Simon's left Naples. And it's for Cardinal Bono – see the inscribed crosses and the eye of Almighty God on the top? He wants it by the end of the week, and it's been a month's worth of work already.'

Fabio examined the chest again. 'I'll see what I can do.' This down-at-heel place wasn't what he'd hoped for, but he couldn't go back home. After all, he had his pride. And Garcia had warned him that his business was not what it was since he had grown older. He, Fabio, would build it back up though – make Garcia and Pasello the best leatherwork business in Naples.

As he worked, stripping off the damaged leather and replacing the broken lid, he was already thinking of himself as a partner.

The day wore on towards dusk, and he became engrossed in the work. It took some skill to imitate another worker's hand, but he had plenty of energy and applied himself with vigour. As he tapped the hammer to chisel the curling vines around the cross, he let out a deep sigh of contentment. This was certainly better than repairing stirrup leathers. Behind him, he could hear Signor Garcia shearing strips from a hide to make handles.

When the door flew open both men startled.

Three dark-clad men seemed to take up all the space. Fabio looked to Alfonso, who had backed away towards the door to the storeroom, setting down the leather he was holding as if it might bite.

Two of the men were shouldering iron picks, though their clothes were fine velvets, and they sported fine-tooled leather shoes with silk rosettes. They looked nothing like farmers ought to look.

'It's not the end of the month yet,' Alfonso said. 'You said the end of the month.'

The tallest of the men ignored him and gave a long slow glance around the room. 'We collect in advance now.'

'Since when?'

'Since I decided,' said a broad-shouldered, dark-haired man with an expressionless face. His clothes were sombre but impeccably cut. 'And you are?' he asked, his eyes fixed on Fabio.

'This is my new apprentice,' Alfonso said. His cotton cap was in his hands now, where he was twisting and wringing it.

Fabio stepped forward, smiled. 'Fabio Pasello. I'm not an apprentice. I completed my apprenticeship with my father in Palermo.'

The other man didn't smile, but he looked him up and down as if assessing his worth. 'So this business has two guild workers, not one?'

'Yes. No. I mean...' Something seemed to be stuck in Alfonso's throat.

'Good. Then the fee for protection has gone up. This month it is seventy scudi.'

'But I can't pay that, de Verdi. You know I can't.' Alfonso's face had become gaunt; his cheeks sagged.

Fabio had the sense he'd stepped into something he didn't understand. He swallowed and waited, every muscle taut.

'How much is in the cash drawer?' The man Alfonso called de Verdi pointed to the set of drawers.

Alfonso moved towards the cabinet as if to protect it. 'Really, nothing. Just a few scudi to buy upholstery tacks and polish.'

The two other men elbowed him out of the way. One of them pulled the drawer out and crashed it down on the table in the middle of the room.

The noise sent a bolt of panic up Fabio's spine. The room was suddenly filled with fear.

'Count it,' de Verdi ordered.

One of the other men fingered all the cash from the drawer into a purse, counting as he went. 'Fourteen scudi, sir.'

'Then there are still fifty-six owing for this month. You know what happens to men who do not pay.' He raised his hand and gave a silent signal to one of the men.

Without warning the man smashed his pick down on the trunk that Fabio had been working on.

Fabio leapt towards him. 'What in hell's name d'you think you're doing?'

'Oh dear,' the man said, smirking. 'An accident. Sorry, it just slipped.'

'You can't do this. It's deliberate intimidation.'

'Be careful with your accusations, apprentice,' de Verdi said, coming closer. 'Signor Garcia pays us to protect his property, isn't that right? There are thieves and thugs out there. Unless you have protection your property is vulnerable. Now, Signor Garcia didn't pay for our protection last month, and look what happened. Two windows smashed and a hole in his sign. Could be worse next time, but as long as he pays, my men will prevent any trouble. We will return in a week for the rest of the payment. Have a pleasant day.'

The men turned and he followed them out, closing the door deliberately behind him.

Fabio turned angrily to Alfonso, who had slumped in the only available chair. 'I suggest you explain.'

'I suppose you'll want to go now,' Alfonso said. 'I can't get anyone to stay.'

'Who are they?'

'Signor Domenico de Verdi and his brothers.'

'We had a Duke de Verdi in Palermo, a tyrant of a man. Are they related?'

He shrugged. 'Don't know. They're a notorious family in Naples. He started by controlling the silk weavers and dyers, taking protection money to keep them in business and stop his rivals from competing. Then about six months ago he started to expand into other guilds. Now he and his men are everywhere.'

Fabio ran a hand over the damaged trunk. 'In Christ's name, can nobody stop him?'

'If you try, you disappear in the night or your warehouse burns down, or you wake to find everything smashed. He has a bunch of thugs under him – they call them the Camorra. Hard men and ex-mercenaries and convicts. If you don't pay to protect yourself, they come calling. Of course, you're paying him to keep his men away. We tried writing to the viceroy, asking him to send someone to stop Domenico de Verdi, and they say he is sending someone, but so far nothing has changed.'

'And does everyone in this street have to pay?'

'If they want to stay in business. At first I thought I could keep paying, but the cost keeps rising each month, and because I'm older and earning less, it's harder to pay. And they scare me. I wake each night in a cold sweat wondering if they'll have paid me a visit in the night.'

Fabio shook his head. 'You should have told me.'

'I know, I see that now. I was desperate. I thought if I had a strong young man here to protect me, it might make him think twice about hounding an old man. But it was foolish; I can't expect anyone else to fight my battles for me.'

Fabio turned and put a hand out to the trunk again, feeling the splintered wood, the torn edge of leather with his thumb. 'Did they do this before?'

Alfonso didn't need to answer, he just bit his lip.

'A whole afternoon's work ruined.'

'You'll go back to Palermo then.' Garcia's shoulders bowed and his head hung.

A picture of his father came into Fabio's mind. The smell of ale on his breath, and the way he only took on the simplest of tasks. He couldn't go back there. It was a matter of pride. 'How much work have we this month?'

'Quite a few commissions. A set of leather chair backs and seats, another folding screen, the fronts for some altar cupboard doors.'

'If I do these, will we have enough to pay the protection money and then still make a profit?'

'If the work is high quality, then yes.'

'Then I'll stay. But only on condition we find some way to stop this de Verdi. There is strength in numbers, no? We will call a meeting of all your neighbours and work together.'

'No. Oh no, we can't do that. It's too dangerous. If de Verdi finds out, we'll all suffer the consequences.'

Fabio was fired up with enthusiasm now. 'But we can't let him terrorise us like this, we have to stand up to him. How many apprentices are there? How many men can we muster? With enough of us, I'm sure we can be ready next time he comes and give his men a lesson they won't forget.'

Garcia's expression was doubtful. 'They have Cardinal Bono and the Church on their side. And half of Naples.' He passed Fabio another sheet of leather. 'Repairs first. Crazy ideas later, right?'

Fabio took up the leather and set to work, but the notion had stuck fast. He'd get all the neighbourhood together; they weren't going to be intimidated by Domenico de Verdi's threats.

CHAPTER 25

GIULIA HAD BEEN WORKING with the Ruggieros for about three weeks, and they had settled into a routine. Giulia enjoyed Matteo's company. He was a fount of lore about herbs, tinctures and balms. Determined to follow in Mamma's footsteps, she gleaned as much knowledge as she could from him.

One day he mentioned a particular poison called 'black madness' – a mixture of thorn apple and henbane.

'Tell me what it's for,' she asked.

'It's what the Borgia poisoners used. You'll have no use for it.'

'I'd still like to know what it's for.'

'You have no-one you wish to dispose of, do you?' His eyes twinkled.

She laughed with him but later looked it up in Mamma's book. There it was, under 'Inheritance Powders'. Would it be strong enough to kill the Duke de Verdi, or should she try to make the *aqua morta* her mother had used instead?

When all the dispensing and measuring was done, Giulia was left alone in the apothecary's whilst the Ruggieros took their early midday meal. During this time she examined the properties of the herbs and spices in every jar and made surreptitious notes.

She hated it when she was interrupted, but customers often came at this time before their afternoon siesta, so the shop was kept open and Giulia had to take her meal and rest later.

Today she was wiping the counter which fronted the street until it squeaked. Satisfied it was perfect, she turned to the statue of Santa Olivia, as she usually did, and gave her a gentle wipe with her damp cloth. Camilla had let Giulia place her in an alcove alongside some of the bigger jars. Seeing her there gave her resolve. The saint reminded her of Mamma. She was worried though; how could she test out her poisons? She'd heard of these things tested on dogs, but one look at San Rocco and she knew she could never bring herself to do that.

She was about to replace the washcloth in the pail when two familiar figures headed down the narrow passage opposite, straight towards the shop. She recognised them instantly: the sturdy, square Signora Gauci striding ahead, despite the fact she should be behind, and the pale, willowy Agnese.

If Signora Gauci saw Giulia there, she would surely tell de Verdi. They must not see her. She backed into the dispensing room out of sight. Maybe they would not come here. She held her breath.

The brass handbell on the counter rang.

It made her jump, though she half expected it.

It rang again. Signora Gauci had never been patient.

'Giulia?' Camilla's voice from upstairs. 'Are you there?'

'I'm here,' she said in a low voice. 'Can you come down a minute?' She heard the sigh before Camilla's feet clattered down.

'What is it?' Camilla asked.

'I can't serve these people,' she whispered.

Camilla gave her a long hard look. Another sigh of frustration, but then, anxious for her customers, she elbowed Giulia out of the way and, pushing through the doorway to the counter, addressed them with a 'Good morrow, ladies.'

Signora Gauci explained in her nasal voice that she wanted a few ounces of blue dye for a white under-chemise that had become stained but was too good to throw away.

'I have some,' Camilla answered, 'but it's in the back.'

Giulia moved further away from the door. The next moment, Camilla brushed past her to fetch the dye, shaking her head with disapproval as she went. Though she would have loved to see Agnese, Giulia could do nothing but wait for the pair to go. A jingle of coins and then Camilla's polite 'thank you for your custom' completed the transaction.

Camilla puffed back into the room as if full of steam. 'Now, what's all this about?'

'I'm sorry. It's not easy to explain, but I know those people, and I don't want them to know where I live.'

'We cannot afford to upset the de Verdis. They hold Naples in an iron fist. Matteo has already had some sort of argument with the husband.'

'Then I pity him. Domenico de Verdi is not a man to argue with.'

'What do you know?'

'Nothing, only rumours,' she added hastily.

'Matteo will not give up his principles. "Only God rules me," he says.'

'What did they argue about?'

'De Verdi says there are gangs of thieves in Naples targeting businesses like ours. He wanted us to buy protection. Matteo refused. Said the threat was over exaggerated. But it worries me. What if de Verdi's right? But what is he to you? Why wouldn't you serve them?'

'It's not Signora de Verdi, but the maidservant, Signora Gauci, that I do not trust.'

'Why? What have you done to her? I knew there was something fishy about the way that priest foisted you on us—'

'No, Camilla, I swear. I've done nothing. The master... he—'

The bell again.

'No excuses now. I want to eat my meal in peace. We'll see what Matteo has to say about this later. Now shoo.'

Giulia pinned a smile to her face, smoothed back her hair under its cap and strode out to the counter. On the other side, a familiar face was staring back at her.

'Agnese? Where's Signora Gauci?'

'So you *are* working here.' Agnese smiled a triumphant smile. 'I saw your statue of Santa Olivia. She used to sit on the shelf near the clavichord. I used to say prayers to her in my head. Fanciful, I know, but I think she could hear me play.' She looked up at Giulia with troubled eyes. 'I miss our lessons. There is little left now for me to look forward to.'

'Agnese, I miss you too. It's good to see you, but you mustn't tell your husband where I am. It's on account of him I left – he has set a price on my head.'

'Why? What did you do?'

'Threatened him.'

'You? How?'

'With this.' She drew the knife halfway out from her hanging pouch so the blade showed, then slid it back into place.

Agnese's expression showed no sense of shock, but her mouth tightened. 'I wish I had your courage.'

'No, you don't. And I'm not brave. I ran away. I wouldn't dare actually use it.'

'So, he tried to hurt you too. I thought he might. He paid you too much attention at our lessons. I wanted to warn you. If women look too pretty, he wants to hurt them. He wants them to pay, or to atone for it somehow through prayer. It's a quirk in his nature.' She glanced furtively behind. 'Look, I haven't much time, but I need to talk with you. Please? No-one else will help me.'

'I don't know. I don't think I can do much—'

She glanced over her shoulder. 'I left my gloves here on purpose, hoping to see you, but Signora Gauci will be on my tail soon if I don't hurry back. She's waiting at the end of the street.

Come to the well near the Santa Maria La Nova tonight during vespers. Domenico never comes to night-time mass – but he makes Signora Gauci take me, and she always falls asleep halfway through the sermon. I'll have about a quarter bell of time to talk before she wakes for communion.'

'No, Agnese, I can't. What if your husband should decide to—'

'He won't,' she called, already hurrying away, clopping on her high chopines, her skirts swinging.

'Who was that?' Camilla called.

'Signora de Verdi forgot her gloves,' Giulia said.

She was in the dispensary preparing a salve for burns, her mind only half on the task, as she wondered what Agnese could want of her, when just before two o'clock, there was a shout. 'Gentleman to see you,' Camilla said.

The words made her stop what she was doing instantly and spy through the crack in the open door. She exhaled in relief. Not Bruno Borroni or Domenico de Verdi. Instead, the black-clad figure of Emilio. How did he know where she was? Warily, she went out to greet him.

At the sight of her, in her plain apprentice's garb, his eyebrows shot up. 'So I've really found you. It took some searching, I can tell you. Isabetta wouldn't tell me anything. In the end, I bribed Father Girolamo and he told me where you'd gone. He was exceedingly reluctant, I can tell you, and he swore me to secrecy.'

Giulia's heart sank at the thought she had been found so easily, and that Father Girolamo's mouth was not as tight as she'd thought.

'Promise me you won't tell a living soul where I am.'

'Is it that important? Why?'

'I refused Domenico de Verdi. Now he wants me dead.'

'You've got some courage. I'd lay bets no-one has ever dared say no to him before. Wish I'd been there to see his face.'

'No you don't. It's no jest.'

'Pardon me, I meant nothing by it. I'm just surprised. Will you no longer be working for Isabetta then?'

'No. We… parted company because of it. I work here now.'

'Oh, that's disappointing. This place seems a little unsuitable…' He glanced around as if its homeliness offended him. 'No matter. But I shall miss your company. Isabetta offered me Bella, but I have no interest in the others. I shall miss our conversations.'

'And I yours.'

He leant his elbows on the counter. 'But perhaps we could meet sometimes. It is a trial to be alone so much of the time.'

'We can meet any time. In fact, I shall be free presently, so if you have nothing pressing to do, perhaps we could stroll a little now? As long as it's away from the Palazzo del Mare and the harbour.'

He drew out his purse but she stayed his hand. 'No, Emilio, I'm not a courtesan now. We can just be friends.'

'Me? Friends with you?' He frowned, as if being friends with a former courtesan was unthinkable. But he waited whilst she told Camilla she would return shortly, and Emilio reassured her he would bring Giulia back in a half hour. As they went, she felt Camilla's eyes on her back the whole way.

She took his arm and steered him out of sight. 'We'll be the subject of gossip if we're not careful.'

He shook her off his arm. 'You look like my servant dressed like that.'

'Then let people think it.'

'Had you really nowhere else to go?'

'I have some skill in the apothecary's art. At one time, I planned to set up on my own, selling simple remedies and perfumes, but then life threw me in another direction. That won't be possible now, as I haven't premises or the funds.'

He was silent. Giulia followed him as he wove between the pedestrians, apparently deep in thought.

'This way,' he said, veering off to the left. Now his walk was purposeful, energetic. She had to scurry to keep up. A few moments later, he stopped. 'This is it,' he said.

She looked at the door he was indicating. The house ran the length of the street.

'My house. Come in for a look. I won't detain you long.'

She followed him up broad stone steps and through a gilded front door which he unlocked with a weighty-looking key. The inside of the building was cool, shuttered and cavernous. At least eight doors led off the central hallway. He pushed open one of the doors, and it led to a huge room about thirty feet square, with a low arched roof. Six circular wooden covers rested on the stone floor.

'My business,' he said, pointing at one of them. 'As you know, I used to trade in oil. I made a tidy fortune that way, until the eruption of Vesuvius cut off all the trade routes. I imported oil of Apulia from Gallipoli and brought it here to Naples. Below your feet are the cisterns where it would rest. That one for *oglio mosto* – unclarified oil – that one for pure oil.' He bent to pick up one of the lids and gestured for her to look inside.

She peered into the darkness to see a dark shaft. A waft of something rancid. She stepped back.

'It's empty,' he said. 'I haven't the heart to start again, though I hear the oil ships are coming in again now and the roads are cleared. But after Elena's death, I just kept wondering what the point was.' He slid the cover back with a scrape on stone and pulled open another. A glance showed rough stone steps leading downwards.

'What's down there?' she asked.

'It links to the tunnels underground. Elena suggested we

should build it in case there was another eruption or an earth-quake.' He stood up, brushing the dust off his hands and onto his breeches. 'She'll never use it now.'

'Let's hope no-one has to.' She tried to strike a more cheerful note. 'Perhaps one day you will feel like trading again.'

'My needs are simpler now, and I have enough of a fortune to spend my time in better ways. I am much concerned with Elena's tomb at the Church of San Gaudioso. She is interred there. It was what I wanted, for her to be interred with others of her rank. They have a process there of preservation, of honouring the body's mortality and the soul's immortality, with a famous artist immortalising the remains in a fresco painting.'

She nodded, feeling that Emilio dwelt on death rather too much. But she followed him as he led her through the door back to the hall and into a chamber opposite, a salon, through which shafts of light played across shrouded furniture.

'You see,' he said, 'I don't use it now. Come. I'll show you the rest.'

She followed him through lofty silent spaces hung with unlit chandeliers.

A small, wizened woman suddenly appeared from one of the doors. 'It's all right, Anna,' Emilio said, 'my guest won't be staying long.' He turned to Giulia. 'My servant. She's too old to let go, but she doesn't do much.'

Anna meanwhile had returned into the bowels of the house.

In a smaller salon, the chairs were uncovered, and a large portrait hung above the elaborate fireplace. 'My wife,' he said hoarsely. 'Elena.'

The woman in the portrait was haughty, her head tilted slightly back. She was no beauty, her mouth too wide, her nose too long. An amused smile played on her lips, as if having her portrait painted were a ridiculous idea. Her hands rested one over the other, the rings sparkling in paint.

'Nobody can replace her. But I have an idea.' He set off again, through another set of interconnecting doors, until he came to a set of smaller rooms, darkly panelled, with lower ceilings and the furniture stacked in the corners.

'These are the physician's apartments,' he said. 'And they could be yours, if you wish.'

'But—'

'No, hear me out.' He gestured around. 'They need some attention, but they could suit you. For your business. You said you wanted to have your own apothecary's shop, and see, there are shelves through here.' He threw open another door to a shelved cupboard. The shelves were stocked with a good stock of basic remedies, but the bottles furred with dust. 'When Elena was ill, I paid for the physician to live here, so he could be on call when we needed him.'

She was staggered. 'I have no money to afford to rent an apartment like this.'

'You can have it gratis. All I ask is something simple. That you keep me company some evenings so we can continue our conversations. I will buy a clavichord too, if you will play for me sometimes.'

'No. I don't think—'

'It's a terrible thing, loneliness. With you here, I feel I could begin to live again.'

'But what would people say?'

'Nothing. No-one needs to know about our arrangement. As far as they know, you are simply renting the apartment from me. I can shut the connecting door to my house and lock it with a key, the way I did with the physician. You would be obliged to do nothing, except to meet and talk every so often.'

She was torn. A place like this would make it easier to experiment, to follow in her mother's footsteps, away from Camilla's sharp eyes. 'It will change us, Emilio. I don't want to be obliged to anyone.'

He stood mute, stubborn. 'You are turning down my gift?'

'I appreciate the offer, but I don't want it.' She saw his face close off. 'I mean to say, I can still keep company with you, be friends, but not... not for this.' She gestured around.

'Very well. I only thought of you. I hate to see you as a servant when you deserve so much more.'

'Camilla and Matteo are good people. Though my circumstances are poor, they treat me with respect.'

Silently, they walked back through the connecting doors into the opulence of Emilio's house. Their footsteps echoed through the corridors and the hall. The diminutive Anna didn't appear.

He pulled open the front door. 'I will escort you back to the shop,' he said.

But as they went, the conversation had ceased to be easy, he no longer offered his arm, and when they arrived at the Ruggieros, he bowed stiffly and went without a goodbye.

She had offended him by refusing, and it made her feel like she had lost a friend. All afternoon she worried about it. Camilla had to snap at her twice for daydreaming over the pestle and mortar. At least she still had Agnese, though the thought of Domenico de Verdi finding out about their meeting tonight filled her with foreboding.

That night Giulia crept out from her makeshift cot, anxious not to wake Matteo and Camilla, whose hunched forms were visible through the curtains of the bed, the covers rising and falling with their breath.

Barefoot, she snatched her clothes from the chair where they were folded and carried her shoes downstairs to dress by the light of a taper, careful not to knock any jars or pots as she went. It took longer than ever to dress and slip on her outdoor shoes. Once out of the door, she breathed more easily and hurried from light to light along the cobbles, looking over her shoulder in case she should be set on by the thieves that Camilla had warned her about. And indeed Naples at night was no place for a lady alone; the taverns spilled noise onto the pavement and beggars crouched groaning in doorways. She had to be quick to dodge them as they stretched out to tug at her skirts for alms.

In the distance a ship's bell clanged, and cats yowled and hissed in one of the impenetrable alleys. Way above her, some-one's washing, forgotten, swayed ghost-like in the faint breeze. All the time she was aware of the secret labyrinthine world that existed beneath her feet, the shadow Naples Emilio had told her of, carved from the soft *tufo* rock. Even the thought of those dark tunnels made her palms sweat and her stomach queasy.

Approaching the church she hesitated. What was she doing? This was something that could only lead to trouble. Yet little Agnese was relying on her and she knew how it felt to be friend-less and alone in this city. She, Giulia, had only had to endure one night with Domenico de Verdi, whereas Agnese had to be subject to his temper and perversion every hour of the day.

She put steel into her step and strode on until she could see the outline of the stone steps to the sunken well. Nobody was drawing water, but people were filing into the church, where the great door was sandwiched between two other buildings that jutted into the thoroughfare. The procession was mostly women, but there were some men too, spindly moving shapes, dressed in the customary black. Near the tail-end of the procession, Signora Gauci and Agnese shuffled towards the door, heads bowed. Though they were veiled, she could recognise their shapes. To her great relief, there was no sign of Domenico de Verdi himself.

She did not follow them in, but waited, feeling rather foolish under the balcony of a nearby building, far enough out of the light not to attract attention, but near enough to see if anyone came out. The night air was warm and moist, mosquitos danced with their hissing song around her head, but just as she was becoming impatient the door opened and Agnese hurried towards her. They headed for a brake of trees at the edge of the square and sat on a low wall.

'I heard tell of an apothecary once that could mix a draught that would make a person sick,' Agnese said.

Giulia knew immediately what Agnese was asking. 'Is that so?'

'Your shop is full of poisons. I can see them myself on the shelves. Antimony, mercury, milkweed. I need something to make a person sick. So sick they must take to their bed. Then perhaps I might have some space to breathe, to decide what to do.'

'Your husband is a watchful man. Even if you could find a way to administer it, he would suspect poison immediately, and your life would be forfeit.'

'No. I heard of a woman in Palermo that had a poison that was so subtle nobody could detect it. A liquid, transparent like drops of rain.'

Giulia remained silent.

'I've tried asking the Church, but they will do nothing. I've seen six different priests. Do you know what it's like to confess? To tell the priest what Domenico does to me, and still they do nothing? They are all the same. They cannot help. They send me away to pray, and I can't. Praying is what *he* makes me do. Prayer has become something to make me tremble. I can't pray, because I can't believe I'm praying to his God, don't you see?' She rested a hand on Giulia's.

Giulia stared down at it. 'He has made you lose your faith in God?'

'I have emptied my faith from myself on purpose because I can't bear the idea of a God who watches and does nothing. His God has no mercy in his bones at all. I have shrunk away from his God so far that I can't find him in myself any more. Not a single spark.'

A silence. The mosquitos buzzed.

Giulia rubbed her wrists, remembering. At length, she said, 'How are you thinking to achieve it?'

'Something in his food that can't be traced. I've heard there is something, a potion with no taste. Have you the skill to make such a thing? You would only supply the medicine, you need never know if I give it.'

It sounded simple, but she knew that once out of sight, the concoction would never be out of mind.

'I trust you,' Agnese said. 'You're my friend, and you know what will work. Please. Just to give me a little respite. Perhaps then I'd be able to get away.'

She squeezed Agnese's hand, and as she did so she saw that the sleeve had ridden up. Agnese's arm was covered in a criss-cross of silvery scars. She lifted it into view with a questioning look.

Agnese withdrew it and shrugged. 'I try to cut myself. I always think, this time I'll make it so deep I'll die. But I'm a failure. I cannot find the willpower to leave this life. But the pain of the cutting soothes me.'

'You must not. They say to die by your own hand is a sin. We must have faith. God sees everything, and who knows why he lets cruelty and suffering blight the lives of so many of us? Perhaps he will take this into his own hands and find a means to punish your husband for his misdeeds.'

Agnese gripped Giulia's hand again so tight she could feel the nails in her palm. 'But what if we *are* the means?'

Giulia closed her eyes. The thought stuck like a barb. It was a thought she had owned herself, whenever she thought of Mamma's death at the hands of the Duke de Verdi. A long moment's pause before she opened her eyes and looked into Agnese's earnest face. 'How can we know?'

'We cannot know, you're right,' Agnese said. 'But I think of it as a war. A righteous war against an oppressor. Men have their wars, why shouldn't we women have ours?'

'This poison. The physic is new to me. If I could make such a thing, would you swear not to blame me if it does not have the effect you intend?'

'I swear it. A secret only we know.'

The silence around them deepened. In the distance the voices from the church were singing Mary's Canticle, the Magnificat. The words drifted through the night air, saying that the proud will be brought low and the humble will be lifted up, that the hungry will be fed, and the rich will go without.

Agnese leapt up, breaking the spell. 'I must go. The singing always wakes Signora Gauci.' And she was away, running pell-mell towards the church.

Giulia watched the door open to the light within and Agnese slip inside.

'Glory be to the Father, and to the Son, and to the Holy Ghost,' came the voices. 'As it was in the beginning, and now, and ever shall be, world without end. Amen.'

A sting to the back of the neck. She slapped hard at it and her hand came away with the mosquito and a smear of blood. The duke had crushed Mamma like she had crushed this insect. She could do this; she could help Agnese rid the world of Domenico de Verdi. It would test her skill. No need for a dog or any innocent creature. Here was the trial she needed, and if it worked, his brother, the Duke de Verdi, would be next.

CHAPTER 26

THE NEXT DAY Giulia could not help but examine all the poisons in the apothecary's shop with new eyes. Many toxic substances were in the remedies they provided. Even the belladonna eye preparation could be harmful, and so could the white lead face cream that they made from real lead and vinegar. She prayed before Santa Olivia because Agnese's miserable expression would not leave her thoughts. But when she thought of Agnese, the memory of Domenico de Verdi burned too, catching her unawares, making her heart thud, squeezing a tightness in the ribs that never loosened.

Camilla caught her measuring hemlock powder into a twist of paper.

'What's that? What do you think you're doing?'

'Nothing,' she said. 'Just practising measuring out powders.'

'Without gloves? You must never touch the powders on that shelf without gloves. And the gloves are expensive – made from the skin of newborn lambs. I won't be wasting them unless a customer is here. They take a long time to wash and dry and are easily torn. What were you wanting to practise with hemlock?'

'Is that what it is? I thought it was hyssop.'

Camilla raised her eyes skywards and let out a sigh. 'Read the labels more carefully. I can't be watching you every minute.'

But it seemed she did want to watch her every minute, because she never left her alone in the dispensary after that.

That night, when she retired to her bed and Camilla's snores were loud and even, she lit a stub of a candle and took out her mother's book. Now she read it in earnest. Had this Duke Antonio de Verdi been like his brother? Had Mamma tried to help all those women with her remedies? She tried to recall her mother's words before she left. Now she was gone, there was a gaping hole in her life where Mamma's strong opinions used to lie.

The crackling pages of the book gave clear instructions based on the humours of the individual sufferer. Giulia had been close enough to Domenico de Verdi to cast a bet he was a choleric. A man who craved dominance, and a man who could be a natural leader. The ancient Greeks believed cholerics to be violent, vengeful, and short in temper. Domenico de Verdi exactly.

Still awake in the dark watches of the night, she kept returning to the *aqua morta*, deathwater, with a fascination she couldn't explain. One drop to heal, three drops to kill.

Scorpion venom, arsenic, nightshade.

These were what she would need. Her head nodded, and she fell asleep. At one point she thought she heard something, but dismissed it as beggars in the street outside. She heard Matteo get up and pad downstairs to investigate the noise, but she paid it little attention. She pushed the book back under her pillow and slipped her cap off her hair, preparing for bed.

An almighty crash from below. She leapt to her feet, dazed. Had she imagined it? A moment whilst she listened. Then, the faint catch at the back of the throat. Smoke.

She threw open the door to find the stairs full of fumes. Shouting and thuds against the shutters. The splinter of wood.

'Matteo!' Camilla's voice from behind her.

Giulia was still dressed so she felt her way downstairs, hand to the wall, just as Camilla came pushing behind her. The front of the shop was invisible because of a dense pall of smoke. One of the shutters had been prised off and lay on the floor. On top of it was a rock tied to a bundle of smoking material, rags and straw.

Giulia was first there, and coughing, she stamped and crushed the flames under her shoes. She looked around for Matteo, but there was no sign of him. Behind her, Camilla, barefoot, her nightdress wrapped in a shawl, was flapping her arms to dispel the smoke. 'Matteo?' she called.

No answer. Where was he? Giulia pulled at the front door. Open. Matteo must have unbolted it and gone outside. Giulia hurried into the street, looked up and down, but there was no sign of anyone. The street torch still glimmered above the Ruggieros' door. But then she heard a groan.

She turned to find Matteo tightly curled under the window. His nightshirt was up around his knees.

'Here,' Giulia shouted, crouching down. 'He's here!'

Camilla rushed out and fell to her knees to take hold of him, 'Matteo? Can you hear me?'

'Careful,' Giulia said. 'Something might be broken.'

Gently, they eased him onto his back, but his head lolled and his ear oozed blood, a dark stickiness in the dim light.

'My foolish Matteo, what have they done to you?' Camilla took hold of his hand, but it hung flaccid between her fingers. She massaged it roughly, as if to warm a child who'd been out in the cold.

His eyes opened a crack but then closed, and a tear leaked out onto his cheek. His face was a mass of bruises.

Slowly, painfully, they carried him inside, past the smoke-damaged shop and into the dispensary where they hastily cleared space for him to lie on the dispensing table. He was so thin. She'd never realised before.

Once candles were lit, Camilla, her hands shaking, ran back

and forth fetching every sort of ointment for the bruising, as Giulia soaked a rag in brandy to cleanse the wounds on his head. Neither spoke; they just assessed the damage and did what they could.

Meanwhile, Matteo lapsed into silence. His nose was broken; the only sound was his breath rasping through the swelling.

'We'll need help to get him upstairs,' Giulia said.

'Do we have to move him?'

'He'd be more comfortable in bed. Shall I fetch the d'Agostinis from the ironmongery next door? They have two sons who might help.'

Before long, the sons were carrying Matteo up the twisting stair, and word had spread. The whole street came to see what they could do to help.

Camilla told them about the shutter being torn off and the stone through the window.

After they had taken Matteo upstairs, the neighbours hovered in the dispensing room. 'Did he pay de Verdi's men the protection money?' asked d'Agostini, a huge mountain of a man with hands like hams.

Giulia shook her head. 'You know what he's like. He refused.'

'He should have paid,' one of the sons said. 'Saving a few scudi is nothing compared to this.'

'It's the principle,' Camilla said. 'That's what he cared about.'

'Principles are no good if you can't work,' d'Agostini said.

'I can't believe anyone would do this to Matteo,' Giulia said. 'It's not right. Isn't there anything we can do to stop it?'

'People are too ashamed to admit they've been bullied. De Verdi's men came to us last month, but with two sons to support, I couldn't afford the fight.'

Giulia felt anger rise in her like a black tide. If a man this size was frightened of de Verdi's men, then there was no hope of the likes of Camilla and Matteo fighting back. The men were still talking to Camilla, asking her to keep them up to date with news of Matteo and offering to help in any way they could.

They were good people. They didn't deserve to be living in such fear.

Naples was sick, and Domenico de Verdi was causing the sickness. Prayer was useless against this pestilence.

If she had the remedy, for the good of all, she should use it, and soon. She did not sleep that night; instead, she opened her mother's book and turned to the page marked *aqua morta*.

The next day Camilla was wan and pale, but determined that business should go on as usual. 'It's what Matteo would want,' she said.

Matteo had come round, but he was obviously distressed, confused, and in severe pain. Camilla hurried to give him a sleeping draught, which he could barely swallow, and eventually he slumped back to sleep. Giulia was set to watch him and make sure he was comfortable.

It was mid-morning when she heard the bell on the counter and men's voices. The fact they were men made her wary, for it was so often the female servants that made errands, not the men. The voices went on for some time before leaving.

A few moments later Camilla appeared, ashen-faced. 'That was de Verdi's men. They asked if I needed protection.' She swallowed back tears. 'What was I to say? What *could* I say, with him lying here?' She gestured hopelessly at Matteo. 'I know he wouldn't want me to pay, but I had to say I would. I couldn't refuse.' She looked imploringly at Giulia. 'I couldn't risk them coming again.'

'I know,' Giulia said, laying a hand on her shoulder. 'I know. I would do the same. But it can't go on. Someone has to make a stand.'

'Well it's not going to be me,' she said. 'I just want him well and back to how he was. Big fool of a man.'

'How much did they want?'

'Forty scudi every month.'

Giulia sucked in her breath. The same as a finished apprentice's wages. That amount would be hard to find. She clenched at the unfairness of it; that Camilla should work so hard and then have to hand over her takings to ruffians like these.

'We can't pay. Not with Matteo the way he is.'

A sinking feeling told her what was coming. 'You'll manage somehow.'

'And I don't want the worry. I am sorry do this, Giulia, but I'm going to close the shop,' Camilla said.

'Why not take a little time to think about it?'

'I can't keep you on. It's too much responsibility. I have Matteo to care for, and I can't feed another person if the shop's not paying.'

'But what will I do? Is there no alternative? I can work, keep the shop open; I can—'

'You have served no apprenticeship. You have no papers that vouch for you, except the recommendation of that foolish old priest, and the authorities would close us down if they found out. Besides, my heart's gone out of it. The feeling that every coin that comes over my counter will end up in those bastards' pockets. I'll be sorry to see you go, but we can't keep you on here.'

'But what about all your customers? Where will they go?'

Camilla shrugged, biting her lip. 'Matteo is my main concern now.'

CHAPTER 27

IT WAS A DISASTER. If de Verdi was to be stopped she must have access to a place to work and equipment to do it with. There was only one answer she could think of. The next morning she braved the searing summer heat to go to Emilio's Palazzo di Fiori. She found it again easily, the biggest and most elaborate villa on the whole street.

Her knock resounded into the space behind, and moments later the toothless Anna opened the door. 'I'll fetch Signor,' she mumbled, leaving Giulia standing on the threshold.

He was clearly surprised to see her there, but she launched in, before she lost the courage. 'I have thought again about your most generous offer,' she said, as the sun beat down on the back of her neck. 'And if it is still open to me, and you are agreeable, I'd like to take the apartment.'

'Come in, come in.' Emilio beckoned her inside. She saw he was still dressed in faded black, that his beard needed trimming, and there was a stain on the front of his doublet. 'Let's get out of the heat,' he said. He paused in the lofty hall and turned to face her, his eyes bright with enthusiasm. 'I'm so glad. I have been melancholy with nobody to speak with these last weeks.'

He led her through to his parlour, and after he had summoned Anna again, he offered her a glass of Madeira wine in a dusty glass. She explained the situation at the Ruggieros: that Matteo was unable to work and the shop was closing. 'Of course, when Matteo is recovered they might change their minds, so it need only be temporary.'

'If the Ruggieros are closing their apothecary's shop, I spy an opportunity – there will be nowhere for their clients to buy. You said you wanted to open your own premises, and of course I see that my apartments will be ideal.'

He had credited her with more business sense than she possessed, but she nodded. 'In time perhaps.'

'No time like the present. No point waiting till the iron's cold. You'll need to buy stock of course. How much do you need?'

Was he offering her a loan? She baulked. 'Well, at the Ruggieros' there was a demand for pigments for painting, spices for cooking and preserving, and midwifery supplies – you know… simple remedies that women need. And the ladies like their rare perfumes, and purifying pomanders. But I'll start small, with just a few nosegays of herbs, lavender water and so on.'

He was silent a moment, seeming to weigh it up. But then he smiled. 'Yes, you will need the best quality ingredients. I see that. Would one hundred and fifty scudi be enough?'

Something in her leapt at it, then crashed. He was really offering her money. But it was too generous, too easily earned, and being a courtesan had taught her that no gift came without a price.

He saw her founder, and her discomfort seemed to amuse him. 'We will sign an agreement,' he said. 'My investment to be paid back at the year's end, with half the profit.'

So it would profit him too. She exhaled.

'I could stretch to a little more.'

'No, no.' It was all happening too fast; she felt as if there wasn't time to think. But the thought of all the stock, of being able to buy whatever she needed was too tempting to resist. 'If you are sure,' she said, 'then that amount will be ample, and I'm more than grateful.'

He stood then and refilled her glass. He seemed to have grown in stature, like a bladder filling with air. 'And now for my part of the bargain. In return for the rental, perhaps you will keep me company in the evenings on alternate days: Mondays, Wednesdays, Fridays and the Sabbath. Tuesdays, Thursdays and Saturdays can be your own.'

She put down her glass. This was too much. She had never imagined such a formal arrangement. She had imagined she and Emilio would meet now and again as friends, but this was something completely different. She saw that he was wanting to impose his rules. She sensed their friendship was tipping over into something else, yet she needed everything he was offering.

Her mother's words came back to her: 'You never look beneath the surface.'

Emilio was waiting. She put aside her doubts, took a step in the dark. 'Very well,' she said. 'I agree.'

Now he refilled her glass and chinked his to hers. 'An agreement that will suit us both admirably.'

He took a key from a drawer in the side table. Under a table draped with a Turkish rug was an iron-bound chest. He took out two bags of coin and let their weight drop with a rattle onto the table.

'Here,' he said. 'Watch me count out the amount so that you know it's correct.'

She would have trusted him, but he insisted in painstakingly counting every coin. She saw now the businessman in him, and it was like meeting a stranger. Afterwards, he made her sign a writ with the loan and called Anna to witness it by marking the document with an X. The arrangement was more formal than she had anticipated and the way he had prepared it discomfiting.

When she took the weight of the bags in her hand, she

realised she was shaking. She would have to make this endeavour succeed. She had nowhere to put the coins, so she stood help-lessly, with the two pouches dangling from her hands.

'I see I'd better loan you a bag too,' Emilio said, jestingly. As he passed to go to another room, he laid a hand on her shoulder. Emilio had never touched her before, and his palm felt heavy, like an obligation.

He returned carrying a burgundy-coloured reticule with a silver chain handle. 'It was Elena's,' he said. 'She has no more use for it now where she is. But we shall have to see about getting you a servant. You can't be wandering the city carrying your own purchases.' He sounded as if he was talking to a child. She felt the shift of power move towards him, and panicked.

'No.' Her voice was a little too strident. 'No. I mean, perhaps in time I'll be able to afford someone. For now, this money will need to pay for stock.'

'As you wish,' he said, though she got the impression her response was not the grateful one he was expecting.

When she finally left, she was both elated and uneasy. But now she had her own dispensary, she would begin work on the *aqua morta* immediately. Under the sign of the flowers, she would call herself Signorina Tofana, at the *Aromatario di Fiori*.

IN THE AVVOCATA QUARTER, in the cramped apartment of the paper merchant, the young men had gathered, bringing with them all the small arms they could muster. Fabio fingered a dagger that he had been given by his mother as a coming-of-age present. Several older men leant up against the walls observing the proceedings.

'Do we know who the Camorra's target is for tonight?' Fabio asked.

'They came to my paper shop yesterday and demanded protection money,' said a wiry merchant with a face as creased as the paper he made. 'I refused, so I fear I may be on their list.'

'I paid what they asked,' a tall, well-dressed man said from behind him. 'I'm Gallio, the vintner from Monte Oliveto. But I think it's too dangerous. Domenico de Verdi's men are brutes, dirty fighters who'll stab you in the back soon as look at you. We won't be a match for them.'

A few mumbles of agreement.

Fabio swivelled to look at him. 'Are you saying we should just let them ride roughshod over us? Lose most of our income to them, just because we are too afraid to stand up for ourselves?'

Gallio stuck out his long jaw. 'You saw what they did to Matteo, the apothecary. He's still ailing, after all this time. And in the last month they've burned down the silk weaver's house and threatened my neighbour the tailor with breaking his knees. I say leave it alone.'

'Yes, none of us want to finish up like Matteo,' said another. 'The shutters are still up on his shop.'

'But he was a man on his own,' Fabio said. 'There are twelve of us here in this room.'

'Eleven,' said Gallio. 'I won't be fighting. I just came to see if you were going to make more trouble, when we've enough of it already.'

Fabio paced the room in frustration. 'But Signor Gallio, if we all stick together we can make a difference. They'll think twice about targeting us if we make it a lot of trouble for them. We might need to do it only once or twice, just until they see we are a force to be reckoned with.'

Gallio snorted. 'What? A bunch of fishfry like you, with a few rusty tools?'

'You dare to insult us?' Fabio said. 'Here are young men sworn to defend your property and you treat them with so little respect? Shame on you.'

A few of the younger men cheered and raised their fists. A gangly young apprentice called Dante, with a big gap in his front teeth, drummed his boots on the ground.

'You know nothing about this city and its history,' Gallio said. 'You're an incomer. You just walk in and think you can tell us all what to do. Well, I'm not prepared to listen to your foolish ideas. When you've all had your heads staved in on account of this fool here, don't tell me I didn't warn you.' Gallio grabbed his hat from the sideboard and banged the door as he went. They heard him clatter all the way down the stairs.

Fabio broke the silence. 'Anyone else want to join him?'

A few more of the older men sidled sheepishly out.

'He's scared,' one of the others said, Petruchio, a blond lad with a red face and the beginnings of a beard. 'I saw them in his wine shop when I was going to get my jug filled. They had him pressed backwards over the counter with a knife at his throat. I ran away, quick, I can tell you.'

'Yet you're still here.'

'Only because it makes me so bloody angry.'

'Who's with us then?'

A bigger shout of approval. The biggest cheer of all came from Dante, who had been gazing admiringly at Fabio for the whole meeting. His cheer went on so long it was faintly embarrassing.

Fabio broke in over him. 'Then we'll leave Gallio to defend himself, the coward. We meet at Dellucci's paper shop at dusk. Be well armed. We'll wait for de Verdi's men there.'

The men crowded together in the stock room in the dark. Signor Dellucci was nervous, and he fidgeted from foot to foot like a cat on an anthill.

'No!' he cried, when Fabio lit a flame in the paper store so they could see what they were doing. 'Do you want to burn me down?' His voice had the edge of terror and madness in it, so they all huddled reluctantly in the dark. Sheaves of paper wrapped in cloth stood waist high in the corner, but they dare not sit there either for fear of damaging the stock.

In the front of the shop, ready for the evening customers, Signor Dellucci's hands shook slightly as he sliced a knife through some quartos of writing paper. A few customers had already been in, taken paper or parchment, and the men in the back were getting restless.

'What if they don't come tonight?' Petruchio asked.

'Then we come back tomorrow,' Fabio said.

'Yes,' Dante said. 'We do what Fabio says, come back tomorrow.'

'What a waste of an evening,' Petruchio said. 'I could have been earning a few extra scudi at the harbour unloading cargo.'

'You want to stop this profiteering, don't you?' Fabio said.

'Yes, but—'

They fell silent as another customer arrived. They heard Dellucci give a pleasant, 'Good evening, gentlemen.'

Fabio reached out his hand to tap Petruchio on the shoulder. In the dark he could see by the whites of their eyes that everyone was ready.

'I believe you have a purse for me,' the voice said.

'Yes I do,' Dellucci said, 'but it's in the back.' He opened the door and made a cutting motion across his throat with a finger.

This was the agreed signal. In one body they flew out of the back room, their eyes blinking in the light of the sconces. The three men in the shop were outnumbered, and taken by surprise, one of them fell immediately, clubbed over the head by a cudgel. The others drew their swords and retreated onto the street. The rest of Fabio's friends hurled themselves out into the street in pursuit.

There was no sign of Domenico de Verdi, but his men were well muscled and brawny, their sword thrusts efficient. Beside them, Fabio's friends were wild. Their anger made blood sing in their veins. Furiously, they battled de Verdi's two men up against a wall.

'What now?' Petruchio yelled.

'Don't kill them, just beat them,' shouted Fabio.

'Beat them!' echoed Dante, who was hopping from foot to foot doing nothing at all.

Fabio pushed him aside and was about to join the fray when the clatter of more men running made Fabio glance back. To his horror, the street was rapidly filling with dark-clad men. Where the hell had they come from?

In shock, Fabio recognised the livery. The Duke de Verdi's men from Palermo. Only then did he realise there really was a family connection.

An army. And they were bearing down on them with ferocious speed.

Grunts, screams, the clash of metal. The paper merchant was down, knocked out by a sword hilt to the jaw. The cobbler swung his hammer wildly, but it was an unpractised swing and he overbalanced himself. Two of the duke's men laughed and pinned him to the wall with a dagger through the doublet and a hand to the throat.

'Run!' Petruchio shouted, but his voice was silenced as he was stabbed in the shoulder and dragged away.

The rest of Fabio's men scattered like grains cast from a sieve.

'Fight on!' yelled Fabio. But it was no use. There was nobody left with him. Everyone else had scarpered or was lying in a bloody heap on the ground. Even Dante, who had stuck to him like a horse-fly to a horse, was gone.

The duke's men turned their attention to him. Fabio set off at a run. It was hopeless. He was outnumbered. Out. He had to get out.

He sprinted towards the harbour, searching frantically for a hiding place, cloak flapping, dodging down the narrow alleyways. A quick left turn. Had he lost them? He paused, listened, twisted to look over his shoulder. Behind him, a man, faster than the others, was gaining on him – a heavy man with a torn ear and broken nose, blood from a gash on the face. He could hear him panting.

He forced his legs into action. Left. Right. Lungs on fire. Twisting down the passages to the harbour, between two tall buildings. He leapt down the stone stairs to the dockside and dived into the crowds of people strolling and walking along the quay.

Two men carrying a sedan chair cursed him as he almost

careered into them, but he kept it between him and his pursuer, hoping he couldn't be seen.

His breath came in gasps, but he tried to calm it. Finally, he ventured to look out from behind the sedan chair and saw the duke's man further down the street, twisting this way and that, eyes searching every alley.

Fabio walked briskly in the other direction. His heart pounded uncomfortably under his jerkin. But worse was the twist of guilt. At his urging, his newfound friends had followed him into the fight, yet he was the only one who was walking free and uninjured towards his lodgings. His footsteps slowed. How would he tell Alfonso Garcia they had failed?

He had hoped to build himself a reputation for helping the honest man. Instead, he had wrought the reverse. None of them would ever trust him again.

He had a sudden longing for home, for his carefree life in Palermo. For swimming in the sea with Claudia, who always came back despite his offhand treatment of her. But he knew he couldn't go back. He was too bull-headed to admit failure to his father. He would have to go to Alfonso's and face what was coming. But tomorrow he would find Father Girolamo, who Giulia had talked of in her letter. Perhaps Giulia would be glad to see him. He'd always thought of her with a tingle of interest, and the comfort of a woman's arms was just what he needed right now.

CHAPTER 29

GIULIA WAS able to find out where the glassblower traded, to purchase bottles for her perfumes. At the market she questioned the stallholders until she could find a supply of the plants she needed for sweet pomanders and perfumes. Lavender, rose and lily for their scent, but also the dark contrary plants – hellebore, monkshood, nightshade. There was an ancient walled botanical garden on the other side of the city that grew medicinal plants. Old Laslo, who owned it, made her tread carefully around the plants that could harm as well as heal, warning her of the dangers of each one. It amused her, as she recognised them all and knew exactly what they could do. How his eyebrows raised when she took samples of them all the same!

The more she learnt, the more fascinated she became. She finally began to understand what had interested her mother so much. As she carefully preserved the specimens in oil or alcohol and then began to extract their essences through boiling and distilling, she grew to love the rhythm of her own breath in this solitary act of alchemy. The transformation of one thing into another by the means of heat was endlessly fascinating.

She took on a serving girl, Barbara, a girl of about fifteen years, known to everyone as Bab. Bab's mother said she had been too slow to birth and that made her slow to learn. She could not read or write but was biddable and trusting. Giulia warmed to her flat, open face and wide smile immediately. Bab would not care what secrets were held in Emilio's Palazzo de Fiori.

She took Bab with her on her excursions at dusk, when she met the feluccas bringing in spices from the galleons moored at sea. When ships came in from Morocco, she bought precious metals such as arsenic, antimony, and lead, and Bab helped her carry them home. In her dispensary, her mother's book was always at her elbow, and now she felt she knew her better in death than she ever had in life.

At first, the evenings with Emilio were pleasant. Emilio was anxious to hear about her day, how the business was going, and what she had been doing. She of course was exhausted, working all day on her salves and perfumes, and trying to establish herself as an authority of women's remedies, whilst working late into the night on her secret distillations.

Many men did not like their wives to buy from a woman, but it undoubtedly helped that she was in the Palazzo de Fiori, such a large elaborate building. She came to realise that Emilio went nowhere, did nothing. He seemed to exist solely in his shuttered-up house, mourning the death of his wife, Elena.

Her own presence was a novelty that soon wore thin, she realised. Her main activity was to read long poems from Virgil or from Tasso to him. She had the impression he hardly heard the words, and after a few weeks, she began to find the house oppressive and his company stultifying.

But this particular evening she arrived to find him in a different mood.

He handed her a glass of wine. 'I'm celebrating,' he said. 'I've just met a man who wants to repair my ruined warehouses by the harbour, with a view to renting them.'

She took the proffered glass. 'What good news.'

'The best since the eruption, but business in Naples is still slower than before Vesuvius. Of course, I don't need to go back into business, but his enthusiasm has made me wonder whether I should.'

'Is it someone I know?'

'No. He's just come to the city. I met him at Vecci's house. A very influential man – the Duke de Verdi, Antonio, elder brother of Domenico, the silk merchant. He's taken up permanent residence here.'

So the duke was living here in Naples now. Her mouth had become as dry as sand.

'You've heard of him?'

Her face must have betrayed her. 'One of my customers told me of him, that he was to be sent here.'

'He's staying in the old Palazzo de Constantin. I passed it today on my way back from Vecci's and it looks like a whole army has come with him.'

'What does his brother think?'

'Vecci said it was not the most cordial of meetings, although the viceroy expects the two brothers to work closely together.'

She tried to keep her face impassive. 'Do you know why the duke's here?'

'They say to offer support to his brother in dealing with rebellion and lawlessness in the city. The house is well guarded. Anyone would think we were at war. Vecci says Domenico de Verdi is not too pleased with his brother's arrival, thinks he's treading on his toes. Vecci sides with Domenico of course, because they have a long association, and Domenico garnishes his bread. But in my opinion the duke's a better man. Domenico was becoming a problem, like with your friends at the apothecary's. The Camorra is getting out of control. Domenico's men threaten many small traders in the poorer areas, and of course they have no wherewithal to resist. His elder brother will press a lid down on all that.'

'What's he like, the duke?' She could not resist asking.

'A gentleman. Very refined, and seems extremely knowledge-able about Naples. But there are some things he didn't know. I had to warn him about the underground caverns and tunnels. He'd heard of them of course, but had no idea they were so extensive, and that they could be used as hideouts for rebel forces. I was telling him how those beneath my house were used to smuggle barrels of brandy from the port to the city. He should explore them, I said. You don't know Naples unless you know the warren beneath it.'

The thought of it made Giulia uncomfortable. She imagined the duke's men swarming like rats through these underground mazes. She turned the conversation. 'I had several well-connected clients myself today,' she said. 'Two women came from Cardinal Bono's private apartments. They wanted the best perfumes I had to sell. Each bought several phials in the most expensive glass bottles, and if they show them to the other women in his residence, it will be an excellent recommendation.'

Emilio frowned. 'Those women are whores,' he said. 'I can't bear their simpering painted faces, thinking life is to be wasted in licentiousness and lust. They encourage the Church's corruption. To them it is a joke as the cardinals gamble over cards, grow blowsy and bloated on wine, and corrupt the small boys who serve them. Those harlots taint a man of God and will surely do nothing for your reputation. Do not serve them again.'

It was like a slap in the face. She had no words. She just sat silently. He was giving orders as if he expected them to be obeyed. And she had no recourse against him, as she was effec-tively in debt to him by one hundred and fifty scudi.

Meanwhile, as he continued to rail against the rot in the Church, Giulia's thoughts were on the Duke de Verdi and the steeping of the *aqua morta* she had been making for Agnese. Arsenic, scorpion venom, the juice of raw aconite, and the secret holy ingredient known only to her and Mamma. The scorpion venom had been difficult to source, but now she thought she had the answer in a young boy who, desperate not to starve, would risk his life to catch scorpions for a small fee.

If all went to plan with the manufacture, Agnese would only need to deliver three drops to Domenico de Verdi's food every day. Just three drops. She would get the glassblower to make a long glass dropper, of the type used to dab perfume on the wrist.

If it worked, and Agnese was finally free of Domenico de Verdi, then she would find a way to deliver the same death to his older brother, the duke.

CHAPTER 30

DAWN WAS JUST BREAKING as Giulia began work in the curtained-off alcove where the dispensing table and shelves afforded her some privacy for consultations. She was anxious to distil the preparation before customers interrupted her work. A message from Agnese lay on the counter, in the pinkish light from the window. It had come with Cettina, the kitchen girl, last night, and was just a few words.

I am not allowed to come out without Signora Gauci. But Father Giro-lamo often calls at our back door collecting alms for the poor. I beg you, I am counting on you for remedy. I can't go on. Do not forget me.

It was signed with an initial 'A', with a flourish and a picture of a musical note.

Giulia thought of Agnese cutting her wrist, and she wished she could make the potion quicker, but she dare not rush the process. She had obtained most of the ingredients but was waiting for the last, a delivery from the urchin, Nino. She took up the letter and held it over the flame of the candle, where it shrivelled to ash.

Scorpion venom. It could heal and harm. A poison to tame a poison. And Domenico de Verdi was certainly a poison. According to Mamma's notes, that's what was needed.

Meanwhile, the more mundane tasks had to go on. Now she was established, the same skills her mother taught her were increasing her reputation in the city for antidotes against banes, miasmas and venoms. Now the grape harvest was here, there was a steady trickle of demand for her balm against wasp stings, and camomile sunburn cream, as well as the ever-popular Venice Treacle she was making today.

Venice Treacle had tested her skill. It had to be a smooth paste despite its seventy different ingredients. Giulia pounded the heavy pestle down into the stone mortar and scraped it around the sides, grinding the herbs into the honey base. The sharp smell of cinnamon tingled in her nostrils, followed immediately by the stench of rotting viper flesh, black and greasy, which could never quite be disguised.

Giulia stepped away and took a deep breath of fresher air. She was about to pick up the pestle again, when the door banged shut and a ragged street boy ran in. He put a wooden box by Giulia's feet. She glanced down at it from the workbench, where it gave an ominous rattle.

'Oh, marvellous! How many?' she asked.

He grinned, ''Bout thirty?'

'Good work, Nino.' She took a purse from her hanging pocket and emptied a few coarse coins into his outstretched palm.

His eyes widened in delight.

'No stings?' she asked.

He rolled his eyes as if the very thought was ridiculous.

'You're a treasure. Same if you bring me more next week.'

He grinned, and clutching his fistful of gold, he shot out of the door into the sunshine on bare brown feet.

She wiped her hands on her apron and lifted the box warily onto the table. Through the bamboo slits the black mass of writhing scorpions rattled against the sides. Milking them would be dangerous, and need much concentration, but the venom was a powerful poison and commanded a very high price. An Arab trader had taught her mother how to hold the scorpion with tongs and to tickle it with a stick until it gave up its venom, one precious pearly drop at a time. When she was a child, her mother had sometimes let her release the scorpions back into the scrub-land behind Palermo.

Scorpion venom would be the last ingredient in the tincture for Agnese. She hoped it was as undetectable as her mother's notes maintained. Mamma was never far from her thoughts. She missed her but dare not let her mind wander that way, or the memories would rise up and drown her. She still had nightmares about a sack descending over her face, and on bad nights she'd wake with her pillow damp with sweat.

She collected together a few ingredients she had set aside, along with a glass bottle. She was just about to open the rattling cage, when there was a knock, and Bab came to tell her a lady was at the door. The introduction was unnecessary as Camilla burst into the chamber like a small whirlwind.

Giulia hadn't even had a chance to remove her apron and the fine chicken-skin gloves she had purchased to protect her from the venoms.

'I thought I'd come,' Camilla said, as her eyes travelled around the shop assessing every detail. 'I thought you'd like to know Matteo is much better.' She continued to stare at the hanging herbs and the well-stocked shelves.

Giulia whipped off her apron and dropped it over the scor-pion cage, pushing it under the counter with her foot, hoping the dark would quiet them. 'Oh that's good news,' she said. 'Give him my fondest wishes.'

'He's sitting up in bed now demanding food, though he still finds it hard to eat. He lost several good teeth, you know.'

'He didn't deserve it, a good man like him,' Giulia said. 'He's fortunate he has you to take care of him.'

'It's been more than three weeks since. You could call in to see him,' Camilla said, a slight note of accusation in her voice.

'I will. I was going to. It's just there was so much to do to get everything ready here. I worked day and night.'

'It looks like it.' Camilla prowled around the shelves, her fingers reaching out to touch the neat rows of labelled bottles. 'An older man, was it, who gave you the money for all this?'

'A loan.' She resented the implication in Camilla's tone.

'Oh.' She peered at the packages labelled with customers' names. 'I see you're making the indigestion remedy we used to make for Father Girolamo. Did you remember to add the chamomile this time?'

'He says it's very effective. It's just the way you used to make it, Camilla.'

'But it probably isn't as well blended.' She continued to range around the shop with a faint air of disapproval, until she saw the candle was still burning under one of the retorts and a clear liquid was dripping out of the glass tube to which it was attached. Giulia moved protectively in front of it. 'What are you making?' Camilla asked.

'A sedative,' she said shortly. 'One of my mother's old recipes.'

Camilla tried to peer past her, but Giulia remained where she was.

'Would it be any use for my Matteo?'

'Not that one, no.' Heaven forbid. A few drops would kill. She reached under the counter and drew out a small jar of ampoules. 'These might help though.'

'What's in it?'

'Just willow bark, a natural painkiller, with a bit of clove oil to ease the pain in the mouth. My mother used to give it for toothache.'

'Matteo wouldn't trust that. He likes his father's remedies,' Camilla said belligerently, arms folded over her chest. 'Never did like to try anything new. Not anything from an *untrained* source. Anyway, I expect it's expensive.'

'There'd be no charge. Not for you and Matteo. You taught me things I couldn't have learnt anywhere else. I miss Matteo telling me always to pray before making anything.' She pointed up to the shelf above Camilla's head. 'But see, Santa Olivia is still watching over me, keeping me on the straight and narrow.'

Camilla seemed to relax then. 'You'll come and see him, won't you? He can't understand why you've gone, and why I shut the shop. He's muddled now. The blow to the head has addled him, yet still he wants to carry on. Of course, we can't, and anyway we've got competition now.' She couldn't keep the bitterness from her voice.

'It's not competition, Camilla. I'd always recommend you, if you were open.'

'Well, we're staying shut. Matteo's lost his sense, and I want to sleep safe in my bed at night. There's no rich patron to look after us.'

The words hurt. Poor Matteo. She would visit him that evening, and take her tooth balm, even if Camilla would not. When Camilla had gone, Giulia held her breath and braved the box of scorpions.

She added the scorpion milk to the liquid bubbling in the glass. When it had cooled, she slowly decanted it drop by drop into the glass perfume bottle. She was careful not to touch the bottle or contents with bare hands, and sealed the bottle with hot wax.

Aqua morta. Just the way Mamma had made it.

CHAPTER 31

WHEN DUSK FELL, she took the small flask, wrapped well in a tied cloth, to Father Girolamo. She could not risk going near the Palazzo del Mare, so she had to rely on Father Girolamo as Agnese had suggested.

After they'd exchanged pleasantries, she held out the package. 'I wonder if you'd be so good as to take this sedative to Signora Agnese de Verdi,' she said.

'Is it from Matteo and Camilla?'

'No. Haven't you heard? Matteo has had an accident, and they shut down the shop.'

'Oh the poor fellow,' he said. 'Is it something I can help with?'

'No. He was attacked outside his shop by Domenico de Verdi's thugs about a month ago.'

'Again?' He let out a ragged sigh. 'Domenico de Verdi is a thorn in Naples' side. This senseless violence has to stop. I hear tell that people are even paying men to guard their properties at night now, it's got so bad. What's the world coming to? His ruffians are everywhere, not like in my youth, when everyone left their doors open and even women could walk safely at night.'

'Camilla was telling me Matteo's not been right in the head since then. He's in a bad way and can't work any more.'

'So who made the sedative for Signora Domenico de Verdi?'

'I did. I made it up myself. Camilla is looking after Matteo, so I have opened a small apothecary in the Palazzo de Fiori. Emilio Colombo is my patron.'

'Oh. Not Matteo any more then?' He still did not take the package. He was staring, as if he could see through her.

She held out the package again. 'Agnese did want this as soon as I could make it.'

At last, the old man took it. 'I have a feeling...' – he paused, stroked his beard in a pensive way – 'a feeling that Domenico de Verdi's violence extends to his household too.'

'This will help.'

'What is it?'

She felt the words come out of her mouth. 'Just a sedative.' She lowered her gaze.

He looked at her with a penetrating expression. 'Is it something strong?'

She moved away from him, but then she turned, and said lightly, 'Better if you can give the medicine direct to her. Not to Domenico de Verdi or to his servant, Signora Gauci; Domenico de Verdi doesn't approve of anything he has not arranged himself.'

'I see.' There was a silence. He did not look at the package but at her. 'I hope Agnese is not thinking of taking any drastic action.'

She felt her face grow hot and knew her cheeks must burn red. 'I have to help her, Father. The church will not intervene. And there is nobody else who can.'

'The church does its best,' he said stiffly. 'The potion is for him, is it not? Do not answer, then I need not have heard it.'

Giulia turned away. Something about Father Girolamo's face made it impossible to hide.

'Think,' he said. 'Is it really necessary? Though Domenico de

Verdi's name seems to be on everyone's lips, and never with anything good, if you cause him harm, it will be a heavy burden for you to bear.'

'I cannot let Agnese down. She has so few friends, and she doesn't deserve to live in such fear.'

'Can it not wait? The viceroy has sent someone to curtail Domenico de Verdi's activities. Someone from Palermo. They fear a rebellion. Especially as harvests were so poor last year and stomachs are empty. Why not see if things settle?'

'The man they have sent is his brother. He is, if anything, worse. Domenico de Verdi's activities in his own house will not be subject to outside control and Agnese fears for her life every single day.' She paused a moment before speaking. 'You forget. I know what he is like. If we do not help her, she may take another, even more sinful, way out,' she said. 'We have to choose. Her life or his.'

'No. It is not for us to say. God chooses.' He pressed his hand to the back of his neck as if to relieve tension there, before he turned to look into her eyes. 'But I believe you care for her, and I will deliver your package. After that, it is in God's hands.'

His eyes were blue, and they seemed to hold a blessing.

'Thank you, Father. I must go now. Camilla called in and asked me to visit Matteo.'

'Tell her I too will call on her tomorrow, and in the meantime, the Ruggieros will be in my prayers.' He paused. 'As will you.'

Giulia walked out of the Father's house and broke into a run. What had she done? Given Agnese a poison so deadly that it would make de Verdi sicken and die, day by painful day, just as her mother had when she gave the duchess a draught for his brother. Was she doing good or evil? The thought pounded through her head as she ran. Now the priest knew and was complicit in her plan. She had unwittingly made him an accomplice.

Her feet thudded on the hard-baked ground, her skirts flapping against her ankles. She told herself she ran to reach Matteo and Camilla quicker, but she knew it was because she had become mistress of life and death, just like her mother. And in that moment of fear and exultation, she had never felt more alive, or more afraid.

Father Girolamo watched Giulia run across the square and neatly side-step around the fallen bell. It had been there more than a month, but he hadn't found anyone to move it. It was just one more thing to worry over. But she was a conundrum, that girl, always in some sort of trouble, and you never knew what she was thinking. He glanced down at the package. He knew he shouldn't tamper, but he carefully unwrapped the stoppered bottle, careful not to touch as soon as he saw the package also contained a thin pair of gloves. A roll of paper fell out. Gingerly, he unrolled it and read the neat printed instructions.

'Three drops daily,' it said. 'Handle only with gloves. Add to wine or cordial. God be with you.'

So God came into this, did he? It was sealed with wax; exactly as he thought – not a perfume or sedative, and no label to denote its contents. He held it up by its wrapping to look at it. A clear liquid that could be anything. Giulia was fond of Agnese, he knew, and he was sure she wished her no harm. He suspected he knew what the philtre contained, but suspicion was not certainty. Until he had proof, he must turn a blind eye and a deaf ear. In his heart, his conscience writhed like an insect caught on a pin.

So Agnese de Verdi had a friend. That was good. Nevertheless, he must be careful. It would throw unwelcome light on the relationship between him and Giulia Tofana if he delivered a medicine and the man died. At least if this was as lethal as he thought it was. He was beginning to have second thoughts. Domenico de Verdi and his clan of thuggish brothers arranged the very beatings that fuelled their protection racket, and he'd been hearing about it for months, men seeking forgiveness for their thoughts of revenge. He didn't hear confessions from half of Naples for nothing.

He could just deliver the bottle. He couldn't know what it was, could he? He heard himself protesting his innocence to the Inquisition.

But if it was poison, he would be blamed. That mustn't happen.

He took down one of the bottles from the cupboard in the alcove where he kept the Manna of San Nicolo. This was supposed to be filled with sweet resin from the saint's bones, and the bottles were ubiquitous with priests all over Naples. Credulous fools that believed in this stuff. How much saintly elixir did they think a saint's bones could produce? Hadn't he himself seen the bishop collect this same sap from the cypress tree? So he was sceptical. Some mysteries were mysteries, he knew, but some were just the play-acting of the Catholic Church designed to draw a few more fools into the fold.

He transferred one of the labels to the new bottle, wrapped up the bottle again and retied the raffia string and tucked it in his basket. So now, no-one would know where the bottle came from. Every priest in Naples, and half the civilian population, had bottles exactly like this. He gave a little laugh. For a priest, he would make a great criminal.

The stucco on Domenico de Verdi's house gave off a wall of heat and cast a block of shadow onto the dusty road. Father Girolamo took a deep breath before knocking, anticipating the sour face of Signora Gauci. He had an excuse ready in the form of the collecting box. But he need not have worried, because it was the ginger-headed Cettina who opened the door.

'Ah, Father.' She grinned up at him. 'Who are you collecting for today?'

'The hospital of the Sisters of Poor Clare,' he said, stepping in.

'Shall I fetch mistress?'

'If you would.'

'Who is it?' Signora Gauci's voice from the scullery.

'Just Father Girolamo collecting for the Poor Clares.'

'Tell him we gave last week,' Signor Gauci shouted.

Cettina gave him a rueful expression but hurried away, leaving him in the kitchen.

A few moments later, Cettina reappeared, accompanied by Agnese, whose white face showed dark shadows under nervous eyes. She was painfully thin in her dark velvet bodice, her collar-bones jutting above the neckline.

He pressed the wrapped bottle into her hand. 'Manna of San Nicolo,' he said. 'A holy gift,' he whispered. 'From your friend, Giulia.'

'Is it—?'

'The Manna of San Nicolo,' he insisted. 'It has the power you seek.'

'Thank you, Father.' Her eyes filled with tears as she tucked it into a hanging pocket in her skirts. 'Send Giulia my—'

'I thought I heard your voice, Signora. What are you doing in the kitchen?' Signora Gauci said, appearing from the scullery with a basket of crockery under her arm.

'I wanted to donate to the Poor Clares,' Agnese said. 'They do such good work.'

'We gave last week,' Signora Gauci said. Then, turning her eyes on him, 'You shouldn't call so often.'

'Pardon me for saying so, but the sick need help every week, Signora.'

'It seems to me that as your neighbours we get called on rather too frequently,' she said. 'You could walk further afield. Cettina, show Father Girolamo out.'

'God be with you, Father,' Agnese said.

'And also with you.' He didn't wait for the emphasis in his words to sink in, but he turned and walked away, the sun burning down on his silk cap. Strangely, he felt better. As if he had actually done something useful.

Feeling more cheerful, he set off for home and a quiet evening preparing the sermon. As he approached his house though, he saw a young man peering in through the window. The man had his nose up to the glass and was shading his eyes against the sun.

'Yes? You are looking for me?'

The man smiled and removed his cap to reveal coal-black curly hair. 'I'm looking for someone, a friend of mine. She gave me this address.'

'And who might that be?'

'Giulia d'Adamo. I'm from Palermo. She wrote to me and told me I could find her here.'

'I know no-one of that name.' Could this be one of the men searching for Giulia? How had he found her address? And the family name – it wasn't the one he knew.

A warning echoed in his blood. She'd said they would kill her if they found her. He rubbed his head, tried to appear vague. 'No, it's not meaning anything to me. Tell me the name again.'

'Giulia d'Adamo. She told me particularly to look for her here.' The young man had a peculiarly intense expression. It decided him.

'No. I know nobody of that name.' Should he ask for an address from this man? No, if he did it would amount to saying he knew where she was. 'Try asking at another church,' he said.

'But—'

'I said, I don't know her.' He unlocked his door and stepped inside, closing it firmly after him. He watched the curly-haired youth go from behind the crack in the shutters.

The encounter worried him though. The name. D'Adamo. It was oddly familiar. Where had he heard it? He paced the floor back and forth over his worn carpet, where he usually paced when he thought about his sermon. D'Adamo. Like Adam and Eve from the Bible. He'd heard the name before.

He went to the table where the pile of news-sheets sat. He never threw anything away. Everything had a use. He sat down, got out his eye glass and searched the pages, scanning for the name.

He was three sheets down when the name jumped out at him.

Women executed in poison plot. Theofania d'Adamo and Francesca La Sarda were executed today after plotting to poison our illustrious patron, the Duke de Verdi. The daughter of the family, Giulia d'Adamo, is also under suspicion and must be apprehended immediately. Anyone with information about her whereabouts must contact...

Holy Mary, Mother of God. His stomach gave an unpleasant lurch. It was far worse than he thought. This was no dabbler helping a friend. She was a professional – brought up to it; the daughter of the Theofania d'Adamo of Palermo. And he had sent her to work in Camilla's apothecary. Not only that, but he had delivered a bottle of physic made by her to Agnese de Verdi, wife of Domenico, the most dangerous man in Naples.

They were already looking for her, and now he was an accessory. Hadn't he just labelled the bottle with Manna of San Nicolo? And just now, someone from Palermo had been looking for her. He shivered. The Inquisition's torture chamber had just come a little nearer.

CHAPTER 32

ISABETTA LET THE PIG-FACED MERCHANT, Vecci, kiss her hand before he got into his scarlet-topped carriage and drove away. She wiped her hand down her skirt and was about to turn and go up the stairs into the Villa Bianca when a man stepped in front of her.

Though it was years since she'd seen him, she'd know that face anywhere, and it caused her to falter and bring a hand to her throat. Bruno Borroni.

In an instant she took in that his features were more lined, that he had filled out, that he was no longer the youth she had known all those years ago, but a tough man with an unhappy frown. A cut from a recent fight ran across one eyebrow, still scabbed. Nevertheless, her heart jolted. Her first instinct was to run. She tried to step past him, but he moved in front of her again.

'What do you want?' she asked, struggling for control of her emotions.

'I've come about Giulia d'Adamo, your niece.'

'Then you've come to the wrong place. She no longer lives here.'

A woman passed with two cages of songbirds on a yoke, and he was forced to step aside. Isabetta made to go, but a moment later he was there again, his hand on her arm. 'She was here before. I saw her. Where has she gone?'

'I don't know.' She shook him off. 'Leave her, Bruno, let her go in peace. Why are you hounding her?'

'You lie. You know where she is, you must. Don't try to cover for her because I'll find out the truth soon enough. I am under the Duke de Verdi's orders. He wants revenge for what your sister did to him.'

'He's had his revenge. My sister is dead. Why does he want Giulia? She knows nothing. It should be his wife he is punishing. She's the one who caused it all.'

'His wife is missing. Probably dead at his hand. He's a ruthless man.'

'And you are prepared to do his dirty work and sacrifice an innocent girl for money.' She used the words she knew would hurt. 'I thought you were better than that.'

She saw she'd made an impact by the way he winced and tried to hide it.

'If I fail in this task the duke will send me back to gaol in Spain. Besides, he already suspects you are harbouring her.'

She felt everything stop. 'How does he know?'

'Because one of the servants told me he's been tracing the family records. How long will it be before he find out Theofania had a sister, and that she's in Naples? He will be on your tail as soon as he has the address. I came to warn you – for old times' sake.'

She was listening now, because with those few words, he'd somehow summoned the past.

'I care about what happens to you, don't you see?' he said. 'I'm offering you a chance to escape the duke's wrath and a probable death sentence. If you tell us where she is, he will be lenient with you.'

She was already shaking her head before he finished. 'I can't. You don't know what you're asking. You have no idea.' A strange strangled laugh escaped her lips. 'You must leave it, Bruno, or you'll only hurt yourself.'

He took hold of her by the shoulders, and his face was full of pain. 'What's happened to you? You're not making sense, Isabetta. You've taken too much of that damn poppy.'

The self-righteousness of the man. She felt her anger rise to match his and wrenched herself away. 'I've never been more clear in my life. Leave the girl alone.'

'Tell me where she is.'

'I'll never tell you even though you pull me through red-hot coals. I don't care if I die for it.' She shrugged her shoulders.

'Then you are a fool.'

'No, not a fool. Because she means something to me. Because I care for her. Because she's my daughter.'

She saw the words hit him like a blow. He took a step away.

Her breath was ragged now. 'You think I left you because of the poppy? No. That was what I told you, because it was easier. It's because I was unwed and having a baby, and you were so intent on your soldiering career I knew you would not stay home to support me.'

'For Christ's sake, Isabetta. Doesn't she know?'

'No. Theofania agreed to look after her because she was barren, but her husband would not accept Giulia and treated them both ill.' Isabetta paced. 'Of course, we always meant to tell her once she grew up, but somehow the time never came. And Theofania was adamant it was better for her not to have a courtesan as a mother. And Theofania grew to love her so much, and as time went on… well, I hardly knew my daughter. Not until she came to Naples. And then I had to pretend. How could I tell her then? She was grieving. It wasn't a good time to give her that news.'

The big man seemed smaller now; his head was bowed as he took it in.

'So you see now why you must not try to find her.'

'Because she's your daughter.' His words were whispers, wondering. Then his voice suddenly rose in outrage, 'I thought you were faithful to me. What bastard dared to—'

She raised a hand to stop him, saying the words he had to understand. 'No-one. I was faithful.' She raised her eyes heavenwards, shook her head. 'It's you, Bruno. She's not just my daughter, she's yours.'

CHAPTER 33

FABIO GAZED at the sign on the front of the shop. This was the third apothecary he'd tried, and so far no-one had heard of Giulia d'Adamo. It was a gamble, that she might be working at one of them, but the only thing he could think to do. The priest Girolamo obviously had no idea who she was, and he'd sent him away as if he was a ruffian. This apothecary looked even less hopeful than the rest. *Aromatario Ruggieri*. A sign at the door read 'Closed', though the upstairs window was open and he could hear voices from within. One of the shutters at the front of the shop had been holed and now it was patched, badly, with two planks. He nearly didn't knock, but then he thought, *Why not? Nothing to lose*.

His knock brought a square-shouldered woman to the window. 'We're closed,' she said.

'I'm not looking to buy anything. I just want to know if you can help me find someone. A girl called Giulia.'

'Giulia, you say? Wait a moment.' He heard her clatter down the stairs.

A moment later and the small door creaked ajar, and her head stuck out.

She surveyed his face, the bruising and black eye. 'Were you one of those at the paper merchant's then? Do you know Petruchio?'

'We were ambushed.'

'So Domenico de Verdi's men got you too.'

'I managed to run. The others weren't so lucky.'

'So I heard. Jacquetta from the pottery told me. Said a bunch of young apprentices got themselves leathered.'

'I'm not an apprentice, I'm a time-served man.'

She stepped out into the street. 'Have you heard anything about what will happen to Petruchio? Jacquetta's half-crazed with worry. She thinks they might transport him. Fancy taking on the Camorra. Whoever's foolish idea was it?'

'How were we to know that the Duke de Verdi's men would join him? We were outnumbered.'

'You were fools, you mean. Where is it you work?'

'At Garcia's, the leatherworker just off Via Speranzella. But I've only another quarter hour before I need to be back. I was hoping you could help me. I'm looking for a girl called Giulia. She's a friend of Father Girolamo.'

'Giulia Tofana, you mean?'

His heart leapt. Tofana? It wasn't her family name, but he it was close enough to her mother's name, Theofania. It had to be her. 'Do you know where she is?' he asked eagerly.

'She used to work here before my husband had his… accident. How do you know her?'

'We grew up in the same town. She's a friend.'

'I couldn't keep her on. We couldn't afford it now Matteo can't work. Next thing we know, she's got the gall to set herself up in competition. She lacks experience if you ask me. She sells women's herbs, midwifery supplies and trifles like that. She calls it an apothecary, but she's not a proper apothecary, not like this one. It's at the back of the Palazzo di Fiori. That's what she calls herself. *Aromatario di Fiori.*' She sniffed, as if the name offended her.

'Where's that? Is it close to here?'

'Over the other side of the Montagna district. She's no proper shopfront like ours, just a side door, and she's only open odd times. There's a notice on the door telling you if it's open. I don't know why there's this sudden interest in her. Another man came looking for her too – an older man, a soldier-type. Is he a friend of yours?'

'Doubt it. Not if he's part of the militia. I've seen enough of soldiers for one week.' He gave a quick bow of farewell and turned to go.

'Hey, don't you want something for that eye? I've got a nice—'

'No thank you,' he called, already halfway down the street. 'I'll be on my way.'

The sharp scent of lemon balm and geranium filled the air as Giulia tipped the multicoloured petals into the box. A benign mixture this time, one to fill ladies' pomanders now the heat was on the city and the stench of drains and rotting ordure had become unbearable. It was so hot that Bab had taken an early siesta and was lying in the corner of the dispensary, her pink face glistening with sweat as she slept. The customer waiting at the counter, an elderly lady who'd been fanning herself with a black lace fan, closed it as Giulia tied up the box and handed it over.

Taking the money, Giulia looked down to feel in her pouch for change. When she glanced up again, a man had entered and was waiting behind her customer.

Fabio from Palermo was there in her shop. She couldn't stop staring; it was like a mirage, something unreal from a past she'd almost forgotten.

He was scanning round the dispensary, eyes ranging over the scales, over the pestles and mortars lined up in different sizes on the shelf. As he looked, so did she, taking in his bruised face, the fact his hair had grown longer, that he had a beard. Yet she would know him anywhere by the flutter it set off inside her chest.

She saw him read the labels of the customers' orders, each one wrapped in paper with the name. She saw him pause at the parcel for Agnese, Signora de Verdi, and bend to read it more closely. Agnese had ordered more of the *aqua morta* only a few days ago.

'My change?' the woman asked.

'Oh. Oh yes.' Giulia handed it over. But at her words Fabio turned to look at her. Her eyes caught his. An awkwardness as they both gave hesitant smiles.

She fumbled the change, dropping it on the counter. The woman scooped it up with a curt 'Good day,' picked up the box, and went out.

'It smells good in here,' he said, coming nearer.

'It's the season for it,' she said, eyes now unable to meet his. 'Lavender and geranium. What did you do to your face?'

'It's nothing.' He reached a hand to touch the bruising. 'Just a street brawl I got caught in. About your letter – I would have come earlier, but I couldn't find you before. That priest, Father Girolamo, he said he didn't know you.'

'I changed my name. Seemed best. The duke's people are still searching for me, after what my mother did.' The thought of the *aqua morta*, even now perhaps bleeding in Domenico de Verdi's wine, hung in her thoughts like a shadow.

'I got your name from the Ruggieros. They said someone else was looking for you too, a soldier, but they hadn't told him where you were. They don't trust soldiers.'

Bruno Borroni. Would she never be free of him?

'I'm sorry, but there's nothing left at your old house. It was all stripped, and the house itself has been made forfeit to the duke's estate.'

'What?' She remembered what she had asked him to do. She had almost forgotten it. A stab of disappointment. 'Oh. I didn't think there would be. I just hoped…'

'I was so sorry about your mother,' he blurted.

'Were you there when they…?'

He nodded. A silence. Giulia blinked away the troubling image in her head. 'You came all the way to Naples just to tell me this?'

'No, I was coming here anyway. I left home and I'm working at Alfonso Garcia's. Best leather tooler in Naples, so I'm still at the old trade. Been there a little more than a month now.' He glanced round the shelves again. 'I'm surprised you're still doing this…' he said. 'People might think—'

'I know what people might think.' She bridled at the inference that she should not. 'Mamma taught me well, and I have to earn a living.'

'I didn't mean…' He stopped, started again. 'I have your books. Those you asked me to re-cover. You paid in advance for them, so I finished tooling them. Maybe we could meet later and I can hand them over.'

She said yes without thinking. And when he'd gone the shop seemed instantly emptier, as if he'd taken some vital essence with him. She began to frantically mix more potpourri, aware of a disturbance within her, like the low rumbling of an earthquake.

What was she doing? She couldn't get involved with Fabio now. It wouldn't be fair. She had crossed some line into darkness and danger, and because of it she needed to be in control. Her mother had said all men were snakes, and so far she had been proved right. Yet the thought of meeting Fabio was irresistible. And he'd sought her out, taken considerable trouble to do so.

But was he trustworthy? He had a wild streak in him that she sensed was both attractive and hazardous.

They met the following evening at the lemonade stall in the main square of the *mercato*. Giulia took Bab with her and kept her own

head and face well shadowed under a lace mantle until she saw
Fabio arriving, carrying a cloth-wrapped parcel under his arm.

She pulled back the mantle, but he was already making his
way towards her, to the cluster of wooden stools and tables
under the striped awning. She left Bab to sit close by, where she
amused herself watching a caterpillar creeping on the low branch
of a fig tree.

Fabio sat and unfolded the cloth. She caught her breath.
Surely she hadn't paid for such exquisite work. He had tooled
and gilded each book with her initials in different styles, with
wreaths of flowers and herbs around the borders and over the
spines.

'They're beautiful,' she said, quite overcome that he should
have thought enough of her to produce such a gift.

'I enjoyed making them. What will you use them for?'

An innocent question, yet she felt the danger in it. 'To write
my herbal remedies. To make a note of special mixes for particular clients. But they look so fine, I hardly dare use them.'

'Use them,' he said. 'And where everyone can see them. They'll
be a good recommendation for my work.' He placed a hand over
hers on the table. She did not pull away and his touch seemed to
reach everywhere, like a river current, flowing up her arms and
down to her feet, until all her senses seemed kindled into flame.

'Tell me about Palermo,' she said, to cover her confusion. 'Is
there grain enough for everyone there?'

He talked animatedly about Palermo, about the olive harvest,
about the herring fishermen who plied their trade off the coast,
about the acquaintances they both knew, but all the time his hand
grew hotter and more damp. His knee pressed against her thigh
under the table. His eyes looked deep into hers, their black
depths inviting.

When the church bells clanged the hour, the spell was broken.
The raucous cacophony of sound prevented further conversa-

tion. 'I have to go,' she said. Tonight was one of the nights she'd promised to sit with Emilio. 'I have a client.'

'At this time of night?' He drew her closer to whisper over the bells.

'Women often come this late, after their chores are done.'

'In that case I'll walk with you.' He threw some coins on the table to pay for the lemonade and led her back towards the Palazzo di Fiori.

Giulia covered her head with her mantle again, keeping her head down and a sharp eye for Borroni, the duke's man. After a few steps, Fabio's arm came around her shoulders. It felt good, like a protective shield, and she realised nobody had touched her, or hugged her in affection, not since the nuns had left her at Isabetta's.

As she reached the *Aromatario Fiori* though, she pulled away. She must not let herself get involved with Fabio.

He took hold of her arm. 'What is it?'

'Nothing. It's just… I don't know if—'

He put a finger to his lips. 'Sshh.' He pulled her close into his arms and placed a gentle kiss on her lips before letting her go. The moment seemed to reverberate like the bells; she could still feel its note long after he'd gone. She hesitated on the threshold, savouring the feeling.

It was then she glanced up. On the balcony above, Emilio was staring down at her. Abruptly, he turned and went indoors.

CHAPTER 34

IT TOOK Giulia a moment to regain her equilibrium and cool her face by fanning her burning cheeks. A glance in the looking glass showed eyes that were feverish bright. She closed them and took a few deep breaths. Tonight was Wednesday, a night she should see Emilio. She would have to face him, she knew. How much had he seen? She should have left Fabio at the market.

She prepared herself and tried to appear calm, but as soon as she saw Emilio's face, her mood sank. He was standing by the window, but he turned when she entered. His expression was tight and he had obviously been waiting for her.

'I don't think I can have been clear,' he said. 'I don't wish my premises to be used for any sort of entertaining.' He shot her a hurt look. 'You said your business was with women only.'

'It is, Emilio.'

'Then who was that man who was on your doorstep earlier?'

'An old friend from my home town who escorted me home from market. He's like a brother, we played together as children.'

'A strange kind of brother then. His kiss did not look like a brother's kiss to me.'

She could not answer.

'When I said you could live here, it was because I trusted you, Giulia. I thought that you were a well-bred young woman who had been thrust into whoredom through no fault of her own. Don't make me have to reconsider.'

'He's just a friend, Emilio. An old friend.'

'And am I not an old friend? It seems you have more time for him than you do for me, and yet I was the one who invested the most in our friendship. You'd be in a fine predicament if it wasn't for me, yet you throw it back in my face.'

'It's not like that, Emilio. I do value your friendship, truly I do.'

'Because it suits your purposes. No, don't protest. I know it's true. I had hoped the friendship between us would grow, that you would find some affection for me, but I see now I was mistaken.'

She shook her head. 'I do have affection for you, Emilio.' But even as she said the words, she knew the small amount of esteem she had for him would never be enough for him.

His lips tightened. 'From now on, no men are to be allowed in your premises. If I hear of any man in your apartment, our arrangement will end, and your lease will be immediately terminated.'

'I understand, Emilio. You have my word.'

'Then I will let this matter pass. You may sit and read to me again. From the poetry of Tasso.'

Giulia took the book from its usual shelf and creaked open the pages. She read without hearing her own words. Her mind was half occupied with the fear of losing her workplace, and the debt she would be unable to pay.

'Did that young man find you then, the other day?' Camilla asked. She had appeared in the shop without notice again and was now prowling around the shelves.

Giulia was saved from a reply because whilst the door was

open Agnese also arrived, in a dark green gown that made her look like a bird, all glossy plumage. To her relief, there was no sign of Signora Gauci or her husband.

Agnese glanced at Camilla, who was staring at her clothes, and gave Giulia a meaningful look.

'My husband has a fever,' she said. 'Do you have something that will help?'

'Can you tell me his symptoms, please?' Giulia said, for Camilla's benefit.

Agnese looked her straight in the eye. 'Yes. He is hot, and his mouth is dry. He calls for water but cannot keep it down. Fortunately, the Manna of San Nicolo that Father Girolamo brought me seems to be effective.'

'Manna of San Nicolo?' Giulia frowned, not understanding.

'But he says his head feels as though a hundred blacksmiths are hammering on it,' Agnese said, raising her eyebrows at her.

'Ah. It sounds like the flux,' Camilla said, interrupting. 'He needs an infusion of agrimony and chamomile.'

Giulia ignored Camilla. 'I can give you a remedy for that. Wait whilst I go and fetch it.'

She extracted the parcel with Agnese's name on it from the shelf, the parcel containing more *aqua morta*, and passed it over.

'Are you sure this will help?' Agnese asked, playing innocent.

'What's in it?' Camilla asked.

'It's a tried and tested remedy of my mother's,' Giulia said, as she took the money under Camilla's watchful eye. 'And how is Signora Gauci? She is not sickening too is she?'

'No,' Agnese said, playing the game and handing over a few coins. 'She is sitting with my husband. She will not leave his side.'

'What a loyal servant, you are very fortunate.'

'Yes, aren't we?' She arched an eyebrow at Giulia and they departed.

'You're not supposed to give out medical remedies unless you are registered. I could report you to the *Sanita*.'

'It's only a remedy for an upset stomach. And anyway,' she said lightly, 'friends don't do that to each other, do they? What would Matteo think?'

Camilla scowled, but her lack of answer meant Giulia knew she had to accept it.

'What was it you wanted?'

'That tooth balm. Matteo says it helped.'

Giulia fetched more and got Bab to wrap it. 'There'll be no charge,' she said.

Camilla looked embarrassed but took the parcel without thanks. After she'd gone, Giulia pressed the back of her hand to her forehead. The *aqua morta* was working; Agnese said her husband was ill, and she knew if Agnese carried on, then he would decline and die. The shudder travelled right up her body from her feet. It was too late now to stop.

She looked up at Santa Olivia, where she stood in pride of place on the shelf in the alcove above the dispensary table. Her expression was still a slight smile, but now it seemed to hold a warning.

Antonio's men had taken part in two street fights since the one at the paper merchant's, and both had been victories. The last one had been even sweeter because his brother had been indisposed and he had found himself in command of both cohorts of men. They had responded well to Bruno's commands, and their ruthless methods had deprived his brother of funds and increased his own. That would teach him to think he could best him.

Now, Domenico had summoned him to his palazzo to talk. Outside, Antonio paused and ordered his bodyguards to wait. Then he turned to Bruno. 'This summons, I'm fairly sure it's not brotherly love – what do you think he wants?'

'For you to leave Naples, I should think,' Bruno said. 'See this scar?' He fingered his eyebrow. 'One of his men attacked me last time we were out. Tried to go for me with a rapier. Didn't like me on his territory.' He shrugged. 'I made short work of him though.'

Once through the door, Antonio stated his business and they were led up the marble staircase by a liveried servant to Domenico's apartments.

In the darkened chamber, Antonio could sense immediately that something was wrong. The shutters were drawn, and there was a sour smell of sickness in the air. There was no sign of his other brothers.

Domenico was propped up on a chair, his waxy face rimed with sweat.

'Ah, Antonio, good,' he said. His smile was more like a grimace.

Antonio exchanged pleasantries, whilst all the time thinking that his brother looked most unwell. He was shocked at the change wrought in him. This man was gaunt. Yellow circles ran under his eyes, and he didn't even attempt to stand to greet them. When he poured the customary wine his hands shook, and a female servant with a disgruntled face hovered close by with a cloth and basin.

'This evening's business,' Domenico said. 'My men are moving into the di Nido district, so I'm going to suggest you...' He paused, took a gasping breath and summoned the servant with a wave of his hand.

For a moment he hovered, his chin over the bowl, spitting bile, before the attack passed and he gestured her away. Antonio looked to Bruno, who raised his eyebrows.

'Domenico, you don't look well.' Antonio took a step away.

'I'm getting over it now,' Domenico said, though his pallor and demeanour told another story. He pointed to a table where a map lay, weighted down with lead. 'The plans, and a map. You will take the di Nido district to back up my men.'

Antonio let Bruno stride over to look, for he was barely

listening. He was thinking of his own illness, of how he was poisoned by Valentina. Since his recovery he had researched the common poisons – like *cantarella*, a kind of whitish powder with a pleasant taste. Supposedly, it looked exactly like sugar. Served in a goblet of wine at dinner, it would function with immediate effect. According to the desire of the murderer, the right dose could kill in a day, a month, or a year. Men said it was so powerful that no antidote existed.

That such a power could be held by ill-educated women was unthinkable. He fingered the bezoar stone, the antidote to poison that now hung around his neck. No such antidote was evident on his brother's person. His sharp eyes scoured the room for evidence. He could see nothing untoward, but he was sure his brother's sudden decline could only have one explanation.

This epidemic of poison, of death wrought through women's hands, must be stopped.

But should it be stopped now? A terrible but pleasing thought wormed its way into his mind.

'You see the plan?' Domenico croaked.

'I'm sure Bruno has noted it,' Antonio replied. 'I'm sorry you are unwell, Domenico. You can rely on me. I see you are indisposed, and as family we will give you every possible assistance.'

He said nothing of poison. The idea of it might lead to further investigations. These he did not want. He told himself it was because he would have a chance to trace the poisoner, so he refrained from mentioning his own experience. After all, he had told no-one of the real reason for his illness except Bruno and his housekeeper, for fear it made him look weak.

Domenico tried to stand, but his legs would not hold him and he collapsed back onto his cushions. 'My men… my men will show you where to assemble.'

'No need to worry yourself, I think we can make our own decisions about that,' Antonio said, relishing the sweetness that he was once again in control, 'once we are on the ground.'

More halting discussions on strategy followed, until it became obvious that Domenico needed to use a closet urgently. They departed hastily, nodding as etiquette demanded, and then strode from the building.

Once outside, he turned to Bruno. 'You remember when I was ill?' he said.

'You think it's the same?'

'Do you not think it strange that only a few weeks ago my brother was strutting around like a turkey cock, and now he can hardly lift his head to speak?'

'It does seem a quick decline. But then again, I think we're best to keep out of his apartments. It could be something else catching, like the flux.'

'Did you see the wife, Agnese?'

'No. I hear tell she's an attractive young thing. He used to keep her shut away in here, but of course, since he's indisposed, it's easier for her to get out now.'

'Exactly. Watch her and follow where she goes.'

'Should I suggest the female servant test his food?'

'No, no. I don't want to alarm him. But I want to know who is supplying her, if it is poison. Whether it is the daughter of the woman from Palermo. If indeed she is her daughter. The records mention no issue, only a sister. A whore who resides at the Villa Bianca. Follow Domenico's wife and see if she goes to this whorehouse.'

CHAPTER 35

THE NEXT MORNING, as instructed, Bruno was on watch outside the Palazzo del Mare. He knew Giulia would not be at the Villa Bianca, because he knew already from Isabetta that she'd been sent away for her own safety. But he was just as curious as the duke to know where Giulia Tofana was, and to get a better look at his daughter. Isabetta's revelation had made him angry, but then later, the knowledge – that something had come of their turbulent love – had warmed his heart. He had always been alone in life, and just the thought of it seemed like a small miracle, something sprung from nothing. It made him feel as if he was not such an island.

At about eleven bells, a young woman in an elaborate hooped gown left the palazzo and dismissed a serving boy that had obviously been set the task of accompanying her. By the deference of the servants, this must be Agnese de Verdi. Bronze-haired, thin as a sparrow. She looked back over her shoulder to check she was not being followed and summoned a sedan chair.

He smiled. This would make it easier. He watched as she struggled to cram her bulky skirts inside. The contraption had no windows behind, and he was fit enough to keep pace with the two porters. Keeping the bobbing green and gilded roof in his sights, he trailed it as it wove through the clustered beggars in the market square, past the clog of carriages, until it finally arrived at the old Church of San Giovanni.

There the bearers stood it down and opened the curved door to let her descend. Bruno waited around the corner in the shadow of a tall building until he saw her set off purposefully towards the most impressive building on the street. To his surprise she didn't use the front entrance but went around the back to what appeared to be a servants' entrance.

She looked behind once, then, with a knock, the door opened a crack and she spoke a few words and slipped inside. He went up to the door after her but did not go in. He read the small hand-painted sign near the door. *Aromatario Fiori – Specialist in midwifery supplies and salves for women's troubles. Open today* – and here was chalked on a sign – *eleven until two.*

So she was open when others were usually shut. He waited. After about a half hour Agnese de Verdi came out again. This time, she carried a small wrapped package. She walked back to where the sedans were queued at the side of the road.

Just before she summoned one, he placed a hand on her arm. 'Signora de Verdi?'

She startled, and a pair of panic-stricken grey eyes looked into his. 'Yes?'

'You have been to see Giulia Tofana, the apothecary?'

'What's this about?'

He maintained the grip on her arm. 'I saw you come out. The *Aromatario Fiori.*'

He could almost see the thoughts swirling in her head. Her indecision about whether to admit where she had been. Finally she said, 'So I buy perfume. What business is it of yours? Let me go.'

He released her. 'I followed you there and waited for you to come out.'

'Why? Why would you do that?' Her face had grown pale.

'Have no fear. I just need to know where Giulia Tofana lives. I have a particular reason for asking.'

Her face took on a troubled frown. She looked around her in the street, trying to catch the eye of a bearer to take a sedan and escape him. 'What reason?'

'Does she supply you with physic for your husband?'

Her guilty gaze flitted from side to side, looking for escape. 'It's only a sedative. He's ill, and I was looking for something to help him. Signorina Tofana said she might have something… but I have to be careful. You know how it is, if he should die, they always suspect the wife.'

'Quite so.' The irony was not lost on him. 'But Signorina Tofana doesn't need to know I was asking. I don't wish her any harm. I was asking for a friend, her aunt.'

'For her aunt? They don't speak. They had a disagreement.'

'Yes,' he said. 'She cares for her, wants to know how she is. But she doesn't want Signorina Tofana to know she's asking.'

'I see. She is well. Her business thrives. Oh!' Agnese de Verdi finally managed to catch a porter's eye and the sedan wobbled towards them.

'Silence is a virtue, Signora,' he said, catching her arm. 'Nobody need know of this conversation, especially Signorina Tofana.'

Signora de Verdi nodded and allowed the porters to assist her into the sedan. He watched it sway away through the streets.

Now he knew two things. Number one. Domenico de Verdi would soon die. Number two. His daughter, his own flesh and blood, would be responsible. Should he act? There was nothing he could do if he wanted Giulia to remain safe. *It's fortunate I'm used to keeping silent*, he thought. At the same time, a death in the de Verdi family could not pass without notice, and the first person to seek to avenge it would be his brother, the duke.

Agnese wished her husband could lie abed forever, hovering in a limbo between life and death. That this blessed state could go on, where she was free, with none of the mess of death or the threat of his recovery. But she knew it had to end. There was that big-boned man who had accosted her in the queue for a sedan. He knew about Giulia Tofana, and the strange look he gave her… well, it was a knowing one.

She couldn't wait any longer. She picked up the bottle with a gloved hand and held it towards the window. The Manna of San Nicolo was indistinguishable from the other engraved glass bottles of saints' elixirs that her husband favoured so much. Light glimmered through, as if no evil lurked in its viscous fluid. Slowly she turned it, and a rainbow gleam fluttered like a butterfly against the wall.

On the side table, just outside the chamber door, the bowl of broth steamed, waiting for this deadly tincture. Every day she'd added just three drops of the shining liquid and stirred it well.

Last week, physicians diagnosed a disease of the bowels, removed his hair shirt, and bled Domenico until he was as pale as milk. She was silent, despite knowing the truth of it, that only one of them could have a life, and for once, she had chosen herself.

She paused as a shadow fell over her hand, and she glanced out of the casement to the sky. A cloud, unheard of at this time of the year, had momentarily masked the sun. An omen. She felt it in her blood, the change in light. He would die today. It had come to the fatal moment, and the thought turned her knees to water.

Her gaze slid out of the window of her chamber and into the bustle of the Strada della Incoronata below. A woman in a yellow mantle was parading her tray of ripe figs, her sing-song voice calling for custom. Her freedom to come and go, the sheer carelessness of that street cry, made Agnese ache, but it also forced her into action.

Decisively she picked up the bottle.

Skirts whispering against the marble floor, she carried the bottle out of the chamber door. In the hall, the meaty smell of the broth, waiting on the lacquered tray, made her throat heave.

But now the final moment was here, the enormity of what was trapped inside the glass froze her in her shoes. In the hall, the whispers of Domenico's servants came and went below, the clatter of Signora Gauci's wooden heels, the noise of the fly-screen being pulled shut, whilst her heart leapt painfully in her chest. Yet still she hovered there, as if floating between floors, afraid to go up or down, to be the avenging angel or the ministering one.

So she waited, eyes tight shut in indecision as the steam settled on the bowl and the broth grew cold. Finally, goose-pimples visible all the way up her arm, she tilted the bottle.

One. Two. Three.

It was done.

CHAPTER 36

IN ALFONSO GARCIA'S leather shop, Alfonso and Fabio were startled as the door flew open. It was Petruchio's mother, Jacquetta. 'You won't believe it,' she said, a beaming smile on her face. 'Domenico de Verdi's dead.'

'What? No.' Garcia's expression was one of disbelief.

'When?' Fabio asked.

'This morning, that's what all the bell ringing's about. He was ill; he's been taken with some sort of flux.'

'But he was a fit man, one who never looked as if he would be prey to such things,' Garcia said. 'Are you sure?'

'You think I'd jest about this?' She slapped a fat hand down on the table. 'Go and ask anyone.'

'If that's true, then maybe we can all sleep safe in our beds,' Fabio said. 'Wait, have you heard what they'll do with Petruchio and the others now de Verdi's gone? Will they still get deported?'

'We don't know.' Jacquetta shook her head. 'It's too soon to say, but it's all over the city: people rejoicing. Never seen the streets like it. Will you come to the square? There's a keg of wine open and we're all taking a half-day off to celebrate.'

'Well, in all my born days…' Garcia said, having fallen back on his stool as if all the air had been knocked out of him. 'I just can't believe it. It's like the cloud has lifted and I can see the sun.'

'Can we take a half-day?' Fabio asked.

Garcia stood up and dragged the shutter down on the shop. 'We can have as many days as you like! Cover the fire, Fabio, grab your tankard, and we'll go celebrate with our neighbours.'

Fabio tamped the fire down and put the *couvre feu* over it.

Many had gathered in the square, tradesmen and guild men and apprentices. Everyone was smiling, some were already drunk, and most had a tankard or flagon in their hand. Fabio clinked tankards with Gallio, the wine-merchant who had supplied the keg, and took a large gulp of warm red wine.

'If you want my opinion,' Gallio said, smacking his lips, 'the wife finished him on purpose. Put poison in his food or laced his wine with something.' He nodded. 'I would, if I were her. And I'm not the only one to think so. There's rumours coming out of the servant's quarters now would make a Pope's hair stand up on end. I was talking to their kitchen maid, Cettina. She says de Verdi wore a hair shirt every day, full of thorns, and made his wife wear one too. And he beat her with a whip. What a bastard.'

'Do you really suspect poison?' Fabio said. A memory was lodged in his mind, the parcel at Giulia's apothecary. And no matter how he tried, he couldn't shake it free. 'Signora de Verdi' the label said. The name had arrested him because of his fight with de Verdi's men. He couldn't believe Signora de Verdi, wife of the most powerful man in Naples, could be one of Giulia's clients.

'It's all too quick. He was as fit as a warhorse until a week ago,' Gallio was saying. 'Mind, whoever it is that's done it, they've done us a favour. Long as they don't catch 'em. Otherwise they'll burn. Inquisition won't take kindly to their viceroy's men being picked off like that.'

The wine suddenly tasted sour. This was sounding frighteningly similar to what had happened to the Duke de Verdi in Palermo. And he'd arranged to meet Giulia, who was now calling herself Tofana, that evening. She was different from how he remembered, with a dark sultry beauty. As if she'd blossomed into a woman he didn't know. She had rebuffed him, and it had made him long for her the more.

Had she taken up her mother's trade? Claudia had warned him about her, but he'd ignored her, thought Claudia was trouble-stirring.

'What's the matter? You look like you've found a purse full of stones,' Gallio said. 'We're supposed to be celebrating. Come on, drink up, and I'll pour you another. De Verdi's dead. It means we will never have to fear a visit from his protection men again.'

Giulia was scrubbing the table with bleach when she heard the bells ring for Domenico de Verdi's passing. Every church in the city was pealing, so she knew straightaway what it meant. A tension in her stomach released, like a spring unwinding. She paused in the salve she was making and glanced to Santa Olivia. 'God grant him peace,' she said.

'Ugly noise,' Bab said, putting her hands over her ears.

'No, beautiful noise,' Giulia said.

All her thoughts were with Agnese. What would be happening there? Would she be able to act the grieving widow? She knew not to expect Agnese today, that she would not call again until all arrangements were made, but nevertheless, she was anxious to know everything that went on.

A knock at the door, and Bab brought in one of her women customers. All afternoon Bab was kept busy – many customers came that day, all bursting to tell her of the death of de Verdi. She

tried not to sound too curious; she must be aware of the consequences of every word.

She hoped Mamma would be proud. She was not the clumsy,
impetuous person she had been before Mamma's death. She was
skilled now at what she did, and she allowed herself a small glow
of pleasure at the thought. The fact she no longer had to fear de
Verdi or his men made her want to laugh, yet she knew death was
no laughing matter. Something inside her still found the idea of
what she had done sinful, but she did not dare examine that
feeling too closely. Domenico de Verdi, Domenico 'the strong',
the man who never lost a fight, was altogether powerless against
a single drop of this silky liquid.

She hoped Domenico had felt fear. That it had seized him and
squeezed his heart in its fist. She wanted him to quake and
tremble as she had that night in the Villa Bianca. She had been
afraid of so many things. Of drowning in the sea, of Vesuvius's
tongues of fire, of outbreaks of plague, of small confined spaces.
But none as much as she had feared Domenico in that moment.

She pushed the thoughts away. When the last customer went,
she carried on cleaning the table like Mamma used to do, and
remembered Agnese's words, that it was a war they were
fighting.

Bab had already retired to the bedchamber when Fabio came
that evening. The knock on the door made her startle, but
hearing his low voice call her name made her slide back the bolts
and welcome him warily in, fervently hoping Emilio hadn't seen
him outside. Their conversations recently had been strained.

'Have you heard?' Fabio said. He threw his hat down on the
table, his eyes sparkling.

'You must be about the tenth person to tell me,' she said,
laughing.

He took hold of her by the waist and swung her round. When
he put her down, he kept hold of her shoulders and drew her
towards him to kiss her on the lips.

The kiss was long and slow, and tasted of wine. It made her so breathless she felt like she was drowning and had to step away.

Lest it feel too much like a rejection, she said, 'It's good to see you, Fabio.' She took in the fact that his eye looked much better, and that he was wearing a clean cambric shirt that was only a little creased.

'Can you come out tonight? The whole city is celebrating. Alfonso thinks it will weaken the Camorra and give prosperity back to us small traders.'

'I don't know. I don't like crowds.' She turned away from him and picked up a bottle of lavender water from the table.

'I can't believe he's gone,' Fabio said.

'By all accounts, Domenico de Verdi was not a popular man,' she said.

'Nor any of his family. You knew his wife, though, didn't you?' Fabio said. I saw you had labelled something for her. What's she like?'

To her horror, her face grew hot. 'I used to give her lessons in the clavichord, in my previous employment.'

'Ah yes, I knew you could play. In Palermo we sometimes used to hear the sound of it as we passed your house, but I didn't know you taught the skill. Where did you used to work?' He had moved closer to her again, but the question had disconcerted her. She couldn't tell him she'd been a courtesan.

She hedged for an answer. 'A noblewoman's house. A distant relative.'

'I see.' An awkward pause. He fiddled with the weighing scales on the table between them. 'I saw that you had a prescription for Signora de Verdi last time I came. I don't like to bring it up, but I think you should know, there's already rumours of poison surrounding his death, and with your mother—'

She was defensive. 'There are always those sort of rumours whenever a man dies too quick or too young. It doesn't mean anything.'

'But all of this...' He gestured around the shelves. 'You must see how it looks. There have been too many men dying in this city before their time. The talk of it is on everyone's lips.'

'It's only gossip. My business is very discreet, just a few things for women's ailments. That's why I don't want to go out. I know the duke's men are still searching for me. I had hoped it would die down. I wasn't expecting him to come to Naples.'

'The de Verdi family are old blood, and they stick together. And your mother's reputation has grown. Now people are calling her the Poisoner of Palermo. It's dangerous for you, and especially in this trade. But I've thought of a solution; I was thinking as I came, now that Domenico de Verdi has gone, our trade at the leatherworker's will increase again, and Alfonso will need a woman to help in our shop. Someone to clean, make the meals, do the housekeeping. It would be regular money, and much less... much less precarious.'

'You're offering me work?'

'We could see much more of each other, see how we fettle together,' he said eagerly. He came around the table and rested a hand on her shoulder.

No. Too dangerous. She stepped back, but he moved with her.

'It's an interesting idea. But I enjoy my work,' she said. 'It's a skill that took me a long time to master.' How could she explain the drive in her soul for revenge? Or that she would never give up Mamma's legacy for such a lowly position?

He squeezed her shoulder tighter. 'But they'll come and find you if they suspect poison. If you have Agnese de Verdi as a customer, they might think you had something to do with it.'

'Do you think I did?' Her eyes challenged him, looking straight into his.

His flickered uncertainly. 'Of course I don't. I mean, I know you wouldn't. Killing a man in cold blood is wrong. No matter what he's done.'

'What about killing a woman like my mother?' She moved out

of his reach. 'She was nowhere near the duke, yet they killed her anyway. Is that not wrong?'

'Well, we have to have laws or the world would be chaos. Sometimes people just get on the wrong side of them. And it's right people should be punished if they supply the means to kill someone else.' He was looking distinctly uncomfortable.

'So fletchers and cannon makers, and swordsmiths should all be punished?' Her words came out more heated than she intended.

'Well, no—'

'Why not? Because they're for men at war? When the laws are unfair, when people are punished or oppressed because of some aristocrat's whim, you have to choose which side you're on. You made the same choice when you had a fight with de Verdi's men.'

'You've changed,' he said. 'You never used to be so argumentative.'

'Losing someone you love changes you,' she said quietly.

The silence between them grew. Giulia pressed her lips together. Even before Fabio put his hat back on, she knew the tender feeling between them was spoiled.

He stared at her a moment more as if he wished to speak but couldn't find words. He shook his head and turned to walk away. At the door he threw back the line, 'I'll be meeting the others then to celebrate; it's all right if you don't want to join us.'

The door closed behind him with a click. She had the urge to run after him but remained, as if her shoes were nailed to the spot. How could something turn sour so quickly? Only a moment before, she had been in his arms. The hurt brought back the empty sensation she'd had after Mamma's death. It made her want to lash out. Angrily, she threw the lavender bottle at the door after him.

The sharp, pungent smell filled the room. She was reminded of that time she had thrown a bottle down in Mamma's still room, and Mamma's harsh words. Had she really learnt anything? Or was she still floundering, a ship lost at sea?

On the other side of the chamber Bab appeared in her night-dress, eyes full of wonder.

'Go back to bed,' Giulia said. 'I just broke a bottle, that's all.'

DOMENICO DE VERDI'S FUNERAL, arranged in haste because of the unprecedented late summer heat, drew a large crowd. On this airless afternoon, when the sun sliced through black robes like a knife, Antonio, the Duke de Verdi, and his man Bruno filed into the new church of Santa Fina with the rest of the mourners, following the long procession of the Silk Dyers Guild in their penitential robes. More dignitaries in black shuffled after, desperate to get out of the heat.

Antonio was plagued with guilt. He knew he'd be the viceroy's favoured choice to take over the running of the city of Naples, especially since he had shown himself to be willing to step in during his brother Domenico's illness. The thought that he could have prevented his death if he'd had a mind to rusted away at his heart. The only comfort was that Domenico would be pleased, if he was looking down on them, at the way he had arranged this ostentatious Catholic burial, with the best of everything. Funerary rites were only forbidden to heretics or those who publicly decried the Church. Sinners were ignored, as long as they did not cause scandal to the Vatican in Rome.

He and Bruno positioned themselves close to the front, near

his brothers. Antonio noted with grim approval that the viceroy was in attendance, flanked by guards and hangers-on all wearing his distinctive burgundy livery.

The piercing sweetness of the boy choristers rang into the domed ceiling as Domenico's coffin arrived. *Requiem aeternam dona eis, Domine; et lux perpetua luceat eis.* – 'Eternal rest give to them, O Lord; and let perpetual light shine upon them.'

He had a panicky sense of arriving at something too late, as if he'd been running to catch a stagecoach and it had gone without him. Only on seeing the coffin did he truly understand that his brother had gone. And only then did he understand that he hated him, but he loved him too.

He watched in numb horror as the coffin was placed on a raised dais, feet pointing east, as was the tradition, with an extravagance of lighted candles flickering around it. It was covered with a heavily embroidered cloth of gold, topped by a wreath of fading lilies. They should have been white, but heat had wilted them to the colour of rotting teeth.

Officiating was Cardinal Bono, a large man resplendent in violet and black, and the right-hand man of Pope Urban VIII. His presence marked his brother's status, though Antonio knew him to be a renowned defiler of young boys. The sight of him made him want to vomit. As Bono intoned the *Subvenite*, Antonio watched the mourners file in. Behind the coffin walked his widow, Agnese, a young girl alone, supported by the ugly crone Signora Gauci, whom he had met before. The girl seemed composed under her veil, yet she was responsible for Domenico's death, he was certain.

He eyed her carefully. She gripped a black lace-edged kerchief in one hand but didn't seem to feel the need to use it, and she showed no sign of being bowed with grief. In fact, she stared straight ahead, white-faced, whereas the matron accompanying her clung to her arm and blubbed audibly, her veil pushed back as she scrubbed at her red eyes with her sodden kerchief.

Her tears made him fight back his own. He should have acted. He could have saved Domenico, but he chose not to. The thought made him grasp the front of the pew as if he would wrench it from the ground.

Bruno had followed Agnese to the Villa Bianca, the whore-house where the poisoner lived, or so Bruno said. He could have sent someone there last week, but he had hesitated. So much power over his brother's destiny had been momentarily sweet. But now the power had turned round like a monster to devour him from the inside.

Blame must lie with her. He must be seen to stamp out this rash of poisonings. A full post-mortem must be done, and Domenico's widow must not be allowed to leave Naples until he was satisfied. He scoured the congregation for the other woman he sought. Would she be here, the supplier of the poison? Giulia d'Adamo? Like mother like daughter, an ungodly conspiracy. For he was in no doubt it was she who had supplied the means to kill his brother.

The words of the cardinal and the sweet smell of frankincense penetrated his thoughts. 'Enter not into judgement with Thy servant, O Lord: for in Thy sight shall no man be justified, save Thou grant him remission of all his sins…' The altar boy swung the censer back and forth over the coffin, whilst the cardinal dipped his fingers in holy water and sprinkled it forth. 'May he be found worthy to escape the judgement of condemnation, who in this lifetime was sealed with the seal of the Holy Trinity.'

The absolution. He saw that Bruno was listening intently. They both relied on this: the knowledge that they would have the same at their Requiem. No matter what foul deeds they had done, they would be guaranteed a place in heaven with the rest, just as Domenico was.

The cardinal walked over to bless Domenico's tomb, where he would eventually lie. While this was happening, he caught a glimpse of the widow, Agnese, raising her head and turning to look among the congregation. Her glance fell on someone further back on the other side of the aisle.

A woman, taller, her features completely masked by a heavy veil, gave a brief inclination of the head. Such a small exchange, but it was enough to tell him that his brother's poisoner was indeed here, and not a stone's throw from where he was sitting. He had an intense desire to see what she looked like. He sat up straighter.

Beside the mysterious woman, a long-limbed lugubrious-looking man wept audibly. Emilio Colombo, the oil merchant, whom he hoped to do business with. Colombo turned to her and whispered something, and the dark woman nodded and passed him a kerchief. Her calmness stoked his rage.

'Show compassion to your people in their sorrow. ...Lift us from the darkness of this grief to the peace and light of your presence,' Cardinal Bono chanted.

How dare she come here, to his brother's mass? As if propelled by a force beyond his control, Antonio stood. The woman saw his movement, stiffened, and gripped her skirts with both hands.

Hardly aware of what he did, he pushed in a great hurry past Bruno Borroni. The woman had stood too, though he couldn't see her face, for her veil was thick lace over heavy voile. It didn't stop his blood and anger rising.

She saw from his intent look that he was heading straight for her, and in haste she squeezed past Emilio Colombo, and he tried to prevent her, shocked that she should interrupt the service.

Antonio was close enough to her to catch a whiff of perfume. He reached out a hand to stay her. But he was a fraction too late; his fingers brushed the cloth of her shoulder as, in a great commotion, she gathered up her skirts and floundered out of the pew. Eyes turned to look.

She fled out through the front door of the church, flinging back her veil from her face the better to see. Behind her, his footsteps slapped on the stone flags. She stole a glance behind, and he caught an impression of dark eyes, dark hair… fear. Now they were outside, she darted away like a fish swimming against the tide. The street was busy but she flung herself into the crowd of pedestrians.

Frantically he searched the crowd, and he saw a glimpse of black whisk into a narrow alley with steps leading away, dropping towards the harbour. He tried to follow, but the street was full of carriages and donkeys, and girls with baskets plying their trade. He leapt over a spread-out cloth on which a wood-carver displayed religious trinkets, only to crash into a persimmon seller carrying a tray of fruit on his head. The tray toppled down and the fruit rolled into the dirt.

'Hey! Watch where you're going.'

His frantic throwing of coins did little to assuage the fruit seller's wrath.

Where had she gone? He was panting badly and could not catch his breath. He had to lean against the alley wall to cough, a hacking cough with a wheeze to the chest. He'd thought he was getting fitter, but the exertion had drained him, the world had turned into a blur, his ears buzzed. He had to rest.

He squatted in the dust, back against a wall. A well-dressed man stopped to ask him if he was well, if there was anything he could do.

'My brother is dead,' was all he could say. 'My brother is dead.'

CHAPTER 38

IN THE DARK of the night, Giulia tossed and turned in the sultry air. Sleep was impossible. The duke chasing after her had been deeply shocking. She should not have run; it spoke too well of her guilt in the matter of Domenico de Verdi's death. And Emilio would wonder at her odd behaviour at the funeral, and why the duke had such an interest in her. One de Verdi brother's death was a wonder, a miracle even. That she might get away with another would be even more of one. She had made preparations to get inside the duke's palazzo, but now they had to be more urgent. He had seen her face.

She got out of bed, lit a candle, and opened the shutter. Insects buzzed inside to the light. She watched them hover round the flame.

That's me, she thought. *Too close to being burned.*

She feared the same fate as her mother if she was to continue, yet she could see no other way of escape. Her profession had become a straightjacket that grew tighter every day. Only one more death would do it. Without Antonio, the Duke de Verdi, she would be free, and not only free, but she would control her own life. She would be able to trade openly in this great city, fearing no-one.

She must act now. Never again would she be hounded from place to place. It would all be over.

Unable to wait, she dressed carefully in the purpling light, before the sun was rising. Last week, she had purchased material in russet and gold, and over a few nights she had made a simple skirt and bodice in the style of the duke's servants. She tied her hair tightly under a linen coif and band, and tucked the pointed end of her apron into her waistband as was the custom. Then she took a deep breath. There was no more procrastinating. Today she must go to the Palazzo de Constantin.

She made up a small pouch. A wide-mouthed bottle corked well. Arsenico, the king of poisons. Undetectable. Deadly. This, she put in the hanging pocket she had fashioned in the skirt for this purpose. *Aqua Tofana* was too slow, and besides, all his food was tested, she knew.

'You dress up?' Bab asked, rubbing sleep from her eyes. 'Look like a lady?'

'No, not a lady. A servant.'

'No sun yet,' Bab said. 'Too early. You come back soon?'

She reassured Bab she would not be gone long. 'But if by chance the sun reaches the top of the sky and I'm not back by then, go and fetch Signor Emilio. The key is on the hook by his connecting door. He'll help you.'

'I don't want you to go.' Bab clung to her arm, sensing her tension.

'I'll be back soon. Shake and turn the mattress and make the bed whilst I'm gone, then lay the fire in the brazier. I'll lock this outside door.'

She hurried through the still dark streets, keeping to the safer main thoroughfares. She didn't like to leave Bab fretting, but there was no other way. At the back gate of the yellow stone palazzo the wooden gates were still closed and guarded, but by five bells the sun was paling the sky and there were already two dozen servants waiting for admittance. Her livery wasn't quite right, so she hung back, next to a low wall, under a plane tree's shadowy dark. When the gates swung open, scraping through the deep rut in the baked ground, she followed closely behind the nearest female, head down. The guards, big men armed with halberds, continued to stare past her as if she did not exist, despite her sweating face. In through the gates and across the carriage yard, as if she did this every day.

The woman she was following knew her way through the warren of dark corridors and soon branched off towards where the clang and clatter of pans signified the kitchens and the live-in servants already busy at their work. Giulia saw some cramped wooden stairs and walked purposefully up, treading lightly so as not to draw anyone's attention. The duke, like every aristocrat, would be as far from the servants' business as possible.

At the top of the servants' stairs she was faced with a quadrangle around an inner court. To the left was a larger set of stairs with an ornate carved balustrade and a display of weaponry on the walls. In this part of the house there were no servants, only a guard pacing in the court below.

Up the long stairs to an upper floor. The duke's apartments – it must be, because a guard of two men in his livery lounged outside his door, looking bored. One was showing the other a set of luridly painted playing cards, which obviously amused him. She walked straight up to them. The cards were hastily put away.

'Maria,' she said, choosing the most obvious name for herself. She puffed out her chest, tried to look bold. 'Come to empty the night soil.'

'It was a different girl yesterday. She did it when she left His Grace the tray from the kitchen,' one of them said. 'You should do that; saves walking up twice.'

'She's sick. So they sent me. And the tray's not ready yet.'

'Rather you than me. Go on then. Don't forget the one in the manservant's room.' The men shrugged to each other and gestured her through.

The apartment was silent, the shutters still closed. She was in a long formal drawing room with many rooms off from it. The furniture was dark and solid as if it had sat there for generations. Most of the doors were open and she moved slowly, peering into each one. A manservant was here somewhere, the guards had said. She glimpsed a library, a dining chamber and another smaller parlour before seeing a door that was shut.

She turned the handle and slowly pushed it open.

'What is it?' A man in figured breeches and doublet, and rose-trimmed shoes, loomed up at her out of the dark. From his tousled hair and rumpled broad collar, she got the impression he'd been asleep.

'The night soil girl,' she whispered.

'Be quick then. And don't wake him. I want another half-hour's sleep.' He sighed and went back to his slump on the chair with his fancy shoes propped up on a padded stool. Behind him, from an area curtained off by a tapestry on an iron rail, came the sound of laboured breathing.

She hooked back the tapestry drape with a finger to see a curtained bed. Her eyes had grown accustomed to the gloom, and a gap in the bed-curtains showed the shape of a man sleeping. He was not under the sheets but fully-dressed on top of the covers, hand resting on his sword.

Curses. She'd hoped to find him in his nightclothes, the stone on a table by his bedside. But no, his face was to the gap, his mouth slightly open, his jaw slack. She took in his dark doublet with its many tiny buttons. He was still in his mourning clothes. From around his neck, the bezoar stone dangled, resting on the covers, its gold mount glinting dully. The stone that if you dipped it into tainted wine would render it harmless. 'From taint to purity' her mother had told her. Now she was to use his antidote against him.

Could she risk it? If he woke…

She had to be quick. A glance at where the chamberpot lay, beneath the bed, before she drew the pouch out from her skirt and tugged open the drawstring. Within was a single glove. She wriggled her fingers into it and drew out the wide-necked corked bottle with its glistening translucent powder.

If it worked, he would poison himself with his own antidote.

Carefully, she eased off the cork.

'Girl? What's taking you so long? Haven't you found it yet?' the manservant whispered from behind the curtain. 'It's at the top end.'

She ignored the voice, all her attention focussed on the bezoar stone where it nestled on the surface of the bedclothes. Holding her breath, lest it fall on his face and wake him, she reached out and gently lifted the stone bauble until it dangled over the bottle.

Still he did not wake, though she was leaning only inches from his face. Gently, she lowered the stone until it rested in the bottle, and slowly she turned the bottle to coat it with powder.

A sudden noise. The curtain drew back with a sharp rattle. 'What are you doing?' the manservant said.

She stood up too fast and the chain jerked at the duke's neck. His eyes opened. Met hers. She saw the flare of recognition, dropped the stone and backed away.

He scrambled to pull himself upright. His hand snatched for the bottle, but he was too clumsy and his grabbing hand knocked it from her grasp so it fell to the ground, scattering white powder. As if he'd never slept, already the duke was on his feet, stretching out a long arm towards her. 'What the devil…?'

'The night soil sir,' she said. And with a sudden lurch she ducked down, grabbed for the chamberpot and threw its contents hard at the servant.

His horrified scream made the duke look to him and gave her all the time she needed. She pelted towards the door, out through the long drawing room, past the two guards, and down to the servant's stairs.

Behind her, the duke shouted, 'Stop her.'

The guards lumbered into motion but she was already hurtling down the servants' stairs two at a time. At the bottom of the stairs a woman was on her way up with a tray. Her eyes widened as she realised Giulia was not going to stop. Not quick enough to get out of the way, she tumbled as Giulia pushed past, upturning the tray and spilling ale and bread and cheese in a splattered mess. As she fell, Giulia tripped over her outstretched leg and crashed down on top of her, but she instantly scrambled back to her feet.

She staggered onwards across the courtyard. A glance back showed the other woman blocking the guards on the stairs as she hurried to reassemble the tray.

A few moments later and she was outside the palazzo and clambering over the wall by the plane tree. She ducked out of sight. From behind it, she caught her breath. The guards lined up all the female servants in the yard as the sun bled over the horizon.

So close. A few instants more and she would have left his apartment with the chamberpot and no-one would have been any the wiser. The duke would sicken at his own hand.

Would he realise what she had done? She had to assume so. The arsenic powder was there for all to see. And he had seen her so closely, he would certainly recognise her again, but now he was doubly warned. Now he knew not only that she was in the city, but that she was intent on taking his life.

She had lost the best chance she had, and he would double his guard and double his defences. At the same time, his search for her would intensify, and it was only through some sort of uncanny quirk of fortune that he had not found her already.

CHAPTER 39

SHE WAS AWAKE EARLY AGAIN, having slept little for the second night. She could not settle to her work either. She saw the duke's eyes looking into hers as she tainted the stone, and it gave her a deep feeling of discomfort. Suppose she had succeeded? This thought was as terrifying as the regret that she had not.

She prised open a shutter and peeked out. In the cool of morning, seven or eight women were already queueing there, probably most of them sent by Father Girolamo from his confessional box. Usually they would leave with a bottle of perfume as well as the bottle labelled Manna of San Nicolo, and always she swore them to secrecy, but the secret still wove its way out – as if carried to the other women in whispers, through the air or perhaps through the dark underground labyrinth beneath their feet.

Aqua Tofana, they called it, after her name.

She turned to the side table where piles of letters lay. They were letters from women thanking her for her 'remedy'. Letters from women who had been forced into marriage with tyrant husbands, notes from girls of twelve with drooling husbands of eighty years old, grateful missives from women whose husbands were already half-dead of a palsy and who just wanted her to give them the permission, and the wherewithal, to help them leave this life.

She had to burn these every few days, those where it was all too obvious what she had done. She'd had enough of poison. How did her mother stand the strain? The feeling of being watched all the time. The feeling that every case had to be weighed on invisible scales, the scales of her heart that would tell her if it was right or no?

She told Bab to get ready and put the sign to 'Closed'. Today she would buy flowers and herbs. Nothing more.

The drought had brought swirls of dust to the streets, and they passed rich men in sedans heading for the coast for the sea breeze. Inside the city, more and more beggars had arrived from the country, and their emaciated forms cluttered every corner. She stepped around them as she entered the spice merchant, although it pained her. The fact she was thriving when they had so little made her feel guilty. She gave as much alms as she was able, whilst still leaving enough to pay her way out of Emilio's debt.

She was just loading her purchases into her basket when a familiar voice came from behind her.

'Giulia.' It was Camilla, her hair tucked neatly into a coif, a cloth hung diagonally from her waist to protect her skirts.

'Ah, Camilla. How's Matteo?'

'Better. I came out for some chamomile. He was glad to see you when you called. I told him about your shop. He was mighty pleased, though I have to say by then he'd forgotten who you were. He's back on his feet, but hobbling. They broke his ribs and it pains him mightily. He's talking of moving away to a cousin in Rome.' A sigh. 'She died ten years ago. He can't remember anything; he's just not the same man any more. Did you hear about Jacquetta?'

'What about her?'

'They're going to execute her son, Petruchio, and all those others that were caught fighting Domenico de Verdi's men. Not transportation after all, but a death sentence. Have you ever heard of anything so barbaric? The duke's adamant. He'll hear no defence, though the mothers have waited outside his palazzo wailing their pain.'

'Why the change?'

'There are so many people in the city demanding bread that the viceroy fears a riot. He's wanting to send a message that any rebellion will be met with the worst punishment, and the duke will obey him of course.'

'Is there nothing you can do?'

Camilla pulled her away from the counter and out of earshot. 'No. But you can. Do what you did with Domenico de Verdi.'

A warning tightness in her chest. 'And what was that?'

'Don't pretend you don't know. I hear it from every quarter. All the women know what you do.'

'I don't know what you mean.'

'I thought there was something about you when you first came – that knowing look,' she whispered. 'The day I caught you measuring henbane instead of hyssop.'

'It was just a mistake, Camilla.'

Camilla took hold of her wrist, her fingers gripping tight. 'Do it for Matteo's sake. You owe us it.'

Giulia shook herself free. 'I owe you nothing.'

Camilla's mouth trembled. 'He has no interest in anything but the shop. It's all he can remember. And whilst the Camorra still make us pay protection I can't reopen. It's killing him being away from his pastes and powders. He's a lost man.'

She sighed. 'When are they planning to execute the men?'

'In a few days' time, as soon as the Feast of San Gennaro is over.'

'If... if I can do something to help, then I will, but it isn't easy. The duke's palazzo is well guarded. What's more, he's a man who fears poison and has a whole army of servants to protect him.'

'But you'll try?'

'I don't know.' She was in too deep, she knew. Camilla could not have known about last night, yet she had guessed. Too many people knew about her skill. Had Mamma felt this? The slow strangulation, as if the noose were tightening all the time?

Later that day, she was thinking about Matteo as she scooped dried, powdered herbs into a flask of alcohol. She was so engrossed she didn't register the door opening until she heard a noise, and she looked up, startled to see Bab showing in a woman with hollowed-out cheeks and filthy bare feet.

Hastily, Giulia put her flask aside. 'We're closed,' she said.

'Door was open,' the woman said. She was clearly a beggar. She had a scarf swathed around her head, and she clutched a rag around a scrawny newborn baby. One stick-like arm dangled from its swaddling.

Bab probably did not understand the difference between a customer and a beggar. The woman wove unsteadily towards the counter, sunken eyes fixed on Giulia, until she could take hold of it to prop herself up. Giulia reached under the counter for her bag of coins. Now she was in here, she'd better give her a few coppers. Though she'd have to explain to Bab that beggars were to be turned away in future. She put the coins on the counter.

'No,' the woman said. 'I don't want your money. I want your remedy.'

'Oh. Pardon me, I thought…'

'I can pay. If you'll accept something in kind.'

She drew out a bag from under her shawl and laid it on the counter. 'My hair. You can sell it.' She used an emaciated hand to pull back her scarf. Her head was shorn to within a thumb-width.

Giulia swallowed. She did not want this woman's hair. 'What is it you want?'

'I heard you have a remedy. One that can send a soul from this world to the next. One that's painless and without suffering.' How had she heard? The thought fled past because the woman was continuing. 'I need it for this little one. I have no money, and there is no food. I can't feed myself, or him, and I have four other young ones to care for. He will die anyway.'

'No. You can't know that. And surely if things were to get better, would you not regret it?'

'Pah. Things won't get better soon enough. Four droughts and four bad harvests we've had, and the war in the north bleeds us of all the grain. First the Spanish soldiers take our crops, now the French. They send their armies from the north to plunder what little we have to feed their fighters. Every barn around Naples is full of nothing but dust. Birds fight for the single grains that are left.' She looked down at the infant. 'He'll starve to death, or I can send him on his way peaceful, afore he has a chance to feel the gnaw of hunger.' Her eyes were too glassy. 'Please, you can sell my hair. He's only small. A few drops will do.'

'How old is he?'

'Not even two days.'

'I can give you bread, don't do this.'

'You can give me bread today. But what of tomorrow? And I didn't come for charity, I came for a cure. I'm too tired to worry about another babe. Too bone-tired for any of it. They're shipping us all out soon.'

'What do you mean?'

'De Verdi was bad, but the duke's a devil. He's decided to clear the city of beggars and ship us all to one of the islands. It's a death sentence and he knows it. There'll be even less food there, no-one to beg from, and more hungry people.'

'Is this true?'

'He wants to clean up the city. There are rumours the roundups will start this week. I can't wait. I have no man, and I have the other children to think of.'

Giulia came round to the front of the counter. 'But things may change. I beg you, if there's another way, take it, don't do this.'

'There's no other way for women like us. And everyone does it. Newborns are easiest. Before you get to love them. In winter most of us leave them out on the mountain to die. But I can't bear it for this one. It was hard birthing him, and he's such a fighter. He doesn't deserve such pain.'

Giulia looked into the woman's face, ravaged with hunger and cold determination. She understood it was a last resort. 'Promise me,' she said, 'promise me that if I give you this remedy, you will take him first to Father Girolamo, at the old Church of San Giovanni, to bless his soul.'

'I promise.'

'Who am I doing business with?' Giulia asked.

'Marietta Spineri.'

'Wait, then, Marietta. It has to be done carefully.'

The baby began to mewl with hunger. She was dimly aware of the woman taking out a limp breast to put the baby there, but the crying continued, so weak it was barely a sound. Giulia put on her gloves and concentrated hard on siphoning three drops of the *Aqua Tofana* into a small bottle.

She sealed it with hot wax and rinsed the outside of the bottle in the pail of water before drying it carefully with a cloth. As she did so, she wondered how often her mother must have done this task, and whether Mamma was looking over her shoulder.

'There's enough here only for him,' Giulia said. 'Give it on the dropper. Let him suck. Once given, do not let anyone touch the bottle with bare hands. Wrap it in a rag, take it to the sea and wash it well. You may sell the bottle to help feed your other children.' She placed the bottle on the counter.

Marietta pushed the bundle of hair towards her.

Giulia pushed the soft package back. 'No. I don't want payment. What I do want, though, is your silence. You must never tell anyone what we have discussed here, or what you have done. Understand?'

Marietta nodded, but she did not speak.

Giulia walked around the counter and pulled back the rags to look in the baby's face. He was halfway to death already. His lips were blue, his tiny hand bony as a bird's. 'God bless you, little one,' she said. 'May you find a better welcome in heaven than you have on this earth.'

She was just turning away when she heard a slight noise. She swivelled to see the woman holding the bottle with her head-scarf. She had already broken the seal. The dropper was already in the baby's mouth.

'No!' she shouted.

The woman put the bottle back on the table. The child made a shudder, stiffened and was still.

Gently, the woman put him on the counter, kissed his fore-head and then was out of the door.

'Wait!' Giulia hurried after her, but she was already gone.

Bab was staring at the baby, where it lay still as stone.

The blood seemed to drain to Giulia's feet. She could no longer think. What could she do with the child? Panic made her breathless. Bab tiptoed over and peered in at the baby's face. Her thumb came to her mouth before she backed away.

His eyes were open. Giulia gently closed them in a numb daze.

There was only one thing she could do. She must take him to Father Girolamo.

She found a wooden box and laid him in it, with a clean sheet and a sprinkle of sweet-smelling rosemary and jasmine as Bab watched. He had no name, and this seemed terrible, that he should exist with no name. This cleansing of the city was cruel and unnecessary. She didn't want any more women like Marietta at her door. Truth be told, she could not stomach another killing like this one.

As dusk fell, she hurried through the streets carrying the box, Bab scurrying at her heels. Never had she felt such a heavy burden. The moment when he had been extinguished, like a flame at bedtime, and by something of her making, made her want to curl in a ball and never come out.

With a drooping heart, they returned home to be greeted by Agnese, who emerged like a black shadow from the shade of a neighbouring building. Giulia remembered then about the post-mortem, that it was to be rushed through because of the summer heat.

'Is the examination over?' she asked, wearily.

'Yes.' Agnese gripped her by the hands. 'They found nothing! Nothing they could attribute to me.'

'Praise God.' They hugged each other tight. 'Let's get out of sight. There are prying eyes everywhere.'

Giulia opened the door quickly, and they stepped into the cool gloom of the apartment. Bab hung at her shoulder, so she dismissed her gently, to go and turn the mattress in the bedchamber and freshen the sheets. This report would not be for her ears.

'The physicians cut Domenico open in his chamber and examined everything,' Agnese said. 'I shudder to even think of it. Thank the Lord I was not allowed to be present. My heart was beating so fast I thought it would choke me. When they first asked permission to cut the body I feigned outrage that they must doubt me, such a virtuous wife. So when they found nothing they had to apologise. And of course it helped that the physicians could testify he'd been ailing for weeks.'

'What was their verdict?'

'An infection from bad water.'

Giulia blew out slowly.

Agnese continued; 'Signora Gauci fainted when they told her; she's taken it hard; she was convinced I was at fault. She has gone back to Rome with Domenico's sister. The duke was full of rage, but he couldn't arrest me, not with the cardinal present. He says someone tried to poison him in his bed, and that they left a bottle of arsenic behind. The whole house has been scrubbed clean, every utensil, every last button.'

'So it is finally over. You look better than I thought you would,' Giulia said, embracing her again, feeling her thin shoulders in her stiff, shiny clothes. She was in mourning – a sumptuous gown befitting her station, as costly as a wedding gown but all in black. A string of expensive black coral gleamed dully at her neck,

'All morning I felt like I was standing on the mouth of Vesuvius, about to teeter over and be consumed by flame,' Agnese said. 'I'm not a good dissembler, and I was sure it would show. And now I must mourn, for I have to fulfil what is expected of me. I have cut my hair, and it will go in his coffin now the interment can proceed. And I must wear this.' Agnese brushed her fingers over her lace-edged veil, which hung to her shoulders to hide her shorn hair. 'I feel like a fraud.' Her voice was close to tears.

'Sit, take a drink.' Giulia passed her a cup of ale and turned to practical matters. 'The house – is there much left to do?'

'The lawyers are preparing the reading of the will, but they have told me all will come to me, as expected. Again, this does not please his elder brother, the duke, but they are rejoicing in the guild. They are suddenly turned flatterers. They smile and coo at me, thinking they will be able to make sweeping changes and more profits. Part of me is like a bird set free from a cage, part of me is appalled. And I'm so tired, I can barely lift my head.'

'There is nothing more you need do, surely?'

'The viceroy has replaced Domenico with the duke. After the funeral the duke sought me out. He intimated he knew what I had done and wanted to know where I had found the means, which apothecary I used, whether I had heard of a Giulia d'Adamo. Is that you?'

'I changed my name. It's a long story.'

'Of course, I put on my innocent face and feigned ignorance,' Agnese said. 'But he is not a pleasant man. He was trying to intimidate me, though he cannot do it openly.'

'A dangerous man. He wants to find me. He executed my mother and her friend Francesca for supplying the poison for an attempt on his life.'

Agnese's expression was shocked. 'I didn't know that. You never told me.'

'His wife Valentina asked them to make the fatal remedy.'

'A wife? I didn't know the duke had a wife.'

'Perhaps he executed her too. He's a cruel man. A domineering man obsessed with his own prowess. If he sends his spies to you, you must be careful. He sent a man looking for me – Bruno Borroni. A mountain of a man with a scar on his face and half an ear missing. If he comes asking questions you must tell him nothing.'

Agnese's face closed down in dismay.

'What is it?'

'Borroni. I didn't know… He knows where you live. He followed me here, to your dispensary. He told me he was looking for you on behalf of your aunt. Swore me to secrecy.' She explained about the meeting. 'Have I put us in danger?'

'I don't know. I've lived with danger too long to tell. Every day I'm alive is a gift. But you need not fear – even if the duke comes for me, I would never betray you.'

'As soon as the will is read, and I can have access to my coin, I'm leaving Naples. With the duke still here, and his savage reputation, I fear I will never be safe.'

'But where will you go?' She had never thought she might lose her friend.

'Rome, I thought. Somewhere I can live quietly. A convent, perhaps.'

'There are some nuns I know, at the Convent of Maria Assumpta in Rome; they will help you. Ask for Sister Simona – she will remember me if you mention my statue of Santa Olivia.'

The connecting door to the apartment suddenly opened. Giulia startled. Emilio had never entered without knocking before. 'Have you forgotten? It is time for our conversation,' Emilio said in a tight voice.

'Many pardons, Emilio. I'd forgotten the time. Signora de Verdi has come for a sleeping draught, and we fell to talking.'

'Ah yes. My sincerest condolences on the loss of your husband,' Emilio said. 'I know how painful it is to lose a spouse.'

Agnese bowed her head. Giulia rushed to package up a powder from the drawer and tied it with string. 'A sleeping draught,' she said. 'I hope you will have a peaceful night. Come for another dose in a few days.' She hoped this might convey that she wanted to see her before she had to leave.

With a nod to Emilio, and one long look at Giulia, Agnese took the package, went to the door and let herself out.

Emilio, who had been pacing back and forth, was already speaking. 'You made an agreement and I expect you to keep it. Please dress appropriately and I'll expect you in fifteen minutes.'

CHAPTER 40

WHEN SHE HAD WASHED and changed and arrived at his parlour, Emilio was standing before the window gazing morosely out past the faded curtains. She noticed dust on the surface of the table. The chamber was dim, no candles were lit, and it smelt of sour wine. Anna was too old to keep it in order.

'You didn't knock,' Giulia said.

'What of it?'

'I'm discomfited to find you can just come into my apartment whenever you like. You promised me privacy. You should have at least knocked before entering.'

'Why? What have you to hide?'

'Nothing, Emilio. It's the principle of it.'

'Don't think you can fool me and go back to the trade of the Villa Bianca without me knowing.'

'You know as well as I that I was never going to make a good courtesan. No, it is simply a matter of courtesy. We made an agreement and we should maintain it.' Even as she said the words she realised she had wrong-footed herself.

'In that case, you should have been here at seven bells,' he said churlishly. 'That was what we agreed.'

'I apologise, Emilio. It was unusual that a client kept me so long after hours. Agnese is so recently bereaved and I've been offering her counsel.' She refrained from saying what she wanted to say, which was that he was wallowing in his grief rather than attempting to reorder his life to his new circumstances.

'You should be offering me your counsel; after all, I have been bereaved too, and your first loyalty should be to me, your patron.'

'I am loyal, Emilio. You should at least have knocked.'

'It's my house.'

She saw she was getting nowhere. An awkward silence. 'Well I'm here now. Perhaps you'd like me to play for you.' She indicated the new clavichord standing in the corner. 'Or read some more Tasso?'

'I think not.' He was being deliberately morose because she was late.

She changed the subject. 'Have you thought any more about the development of those warehouses?'

'I'm just too tired to think of it. But at Domenico de Verdi's funeral, after you'd left in such an unseemly hurry, I met the duke again. He's still interested in investing in it and he's coming to see me tomorrow to talk about it.'

'Here? He's coming here?'

'It won't affect you. It's in business hours.'

'Don't mention that I live here, Emilio. I don't want him to know.'

'Why?'

She tried to defuse it. 'I don't want any man to know. You yourself agreed my business is with the women. I sell perfumes, midwifery supplies and simple remedies for women's ailments. There's no need for their husbands to know where they spend their time.'

'I disagree. I would have wanted to know where Elena was going, and with whom. Anyway, I'm not sure I want to start trading again. I just feel exhausted all the time. The grief still eats away at me, and I just want to sleep and sleep.'

'I could give you a tonic. I'll make you one up to strengthen the blood.'

He sighed. 'If you think it will help.'

'Why not let me do it now? Give me a quarter hour and it will be done.'

He raised a hand and flapped it in assent. She walked back through the echoing corridors of the palazzo to her door and went in. The man drained her. She pulled the jar of liverwort off the shelf and emptied a few dried leaves into the mortar, and then added a half cupful of nettle wine and turmeric, along with the herb they called *Sangre de Drago*. All the time she was thinking.

The Duke de Verdi would be here tomorrow and right on the other side of that wall. She hoped that Emilio would say nothing about her presence in the house. She should be prepared to move fast in case he said something.

But apart from the danger, this was her opportunity. She began to think more clearly. If he didn't know she was here, then perhaps she could find a way to administer something? But not the *Aqua Tofana*. She had effectively sent him a warning, so all his food and drink would be tested. Her thoughts began to whirl.

She pounded the pulp of liverwort in the mortar without seeing it. Absentmindedly, she put it into a wide-necked flask and carried it back through the house to Emilio's parlour.

'Here,' she said, passing it over.

'What's in it?' He regarded the greenish liquid with suspicion.

'Just strengthening herbs mashed in a little wine,' she said.

'Ugh.' He downed it and grimaced.

'What time does your guest arrive tomorrow?' she asked.

'Just before noon. I suggested we should talk and then we would drive down to the port where my oil ships used to dock.

He thinks the old warehouses flattened by the eruption can be put into repair.'

She wondered if she could get something into the kitchen where Anna would be preparing the meals. It would be difficult to do. What other way could there be? Everything was a risk. If she used any poison but was not there to oversee it, then Emilio might be poisoned by mistake, and she must avoid that at all costs.

Whilst they talked of small gossip about the town, her thoughts were sifting one bane from another. Finally, she had it. The perfect method. But it all depended on her entering Emilio's apartments unseen.

CHAPTER 41

THE NEXT DAY AT ELEVEN, she unlocked the door between her apartment and Emilio's, listening for the arrival of the Duke de Verdi. An hour went by before she heard the knock at the door and Anna's lop-sided hurrying feet. Men's voices echoed in the corridor, as if giving cordial greetings. She heard Anna hobble along the corridor to the vestibule adjoining her apartment and his. She hoped she was hanging the duke's cloak and hat there.

The men's voices faded away. She shut the door and began to work. She hadn't much time and the ingredients needed to be fresh. Wearing her chicken-skin gloves, she cut three thorns from a rose stem and dipped them into the greenish tincture of hemlock.

Tiptoeing on bare feet, she went out into the hall to retrieve the visitor's hat. A felted hat with a brim to keep off the heat was hanging there, with his sword and his day cloak. She picked the hat up and took it through to the workroom and laid it, crown down, on the table. The linen lining-band was easy to prise away from the crown. With iron tweezers she inserted the three thorns into the inside of the hat, thorns facing out.

Hemlock was not fatal unless it entered the blood, so Mamma's notes said. The thorns would break the skin and supply the scratch that was needed for the poison to enter. Nausea, vomiting, confusion, seizures, and death by asphyxiation should follow.

She looked at Mamma's notes again. 'Beware,' she had written. 'No antidote.'

Then further down, 'Even touching the plant may cause a severe skin reaction in susceptible people.'

She carried the hat by its brim back to the hall. She did not hang it up but let it fall on the ground. Any specks of dust would be taken as just that, dust. Until it was too late. She knew Anna would be too old and stiff to pick it up from where it lay, and he would have to pick it up himself.

It was hard to settle. She paced back and forth, and every now and then she put an ear to the door. Finally she heard voices in the hall. Three voices. Three men. Two low voices and one higher pitched. Her heart lurched.

She had thought the duke to be alone. There was only one set of garments hanging up there.

She stiffened and was still.

The men's voices receded towards the front of the villa. Seized with foreboding, she hurried out of her shop doorway and was in time to see two men climbing into the carriage. One was the Duke de Verdi, the other a man wearing the hat she had just laced with hemlock.

A wash of cold sluiced over her. What to do?

Who was the man wearing the hat? It looked like the manservant she'd thrown the night soil at.

She hurried back indoors and let herself through into Emilio's chambers.

He was where he always was, staring from the window. 'Have they gone?' she asked, her voice high-pitched and too bright.

'Oh, yes. Such a strange man, didn't even take off his hat. Still, I've agreed to sell him my warehouses.'

'Who was that with him?'

'Manservant, name of Lucio. Do you know, the duke insisted on the servant tasting the wine I offered. As if I might taint it.'

Giulia sat down, afraid her legs might no longer hold her up. The manservant must have been the duke's taster. The words in Mamma's diary played in her head. 'No antidote.'

'Excuse me,' she said, 'I feel a little unwell.' She fled from Emilio's and vomited into her washbasin. What had she done? Maybe it wouldn't work. Maybe the thorns wouldn't scratch him.

She got down on her knees. 'Mamma,' she said, 'help me.'

But no answer came. The face of the baby rose in her mind's eye, his puckered face, his milky eyes. It was bearable when she never saw the person's face, but unendurable when she'd seen them alive and breathing one moment and still as a stone the next.

How could she bear it? Two innocent lives within a week's span.

At the Palazzo de Constantin, Antonio was looking at the ground plans of Emilio Colombo's oil warehouses on a large map of the city and surrounding area. He was irritated because workmen were rehanging tapestries on the walls, and the noise of the hammering took his concentration. Since his brother's death, he'd found he couldn't bear silence, the insidious voices of his conscience, so he had decided to overhaul his living accommodation. The distraction stopped him thinking.

The warehouses that Colombo owned close to the docks and the shore would be ideal for shipping the beggars out of Naples.

He would hold them in the warehouses until he could ship them out on the old grain ships. It would solve two problems together – the lack of enough food to feed the Naples population, and the removal of these vagrants who contributed nothing to the fiscal life of the city yet hung round the city for alms.

When the viceroy next visited, he would not be harangued by urchins in the street or women plying the old trade. Those would all be gone. It would make quite an impression, this new shining city. He'd do it for Domenico. To make amends.

What was of primary concern to him, though, was the epidemic of rich men's deaths in Naples. Four more this week, all with similar symptoms. Every undiagnosed death made his stomach tighten. He remembered the queasy dread of being close to death. The young girl d'Adamo was still out there somewhere.

He was just mulling this over when a serving boy ran in. 'You'd better… you'd better come quickly, Your Excellency.'

'What's the matter?'

'Borroni wouldn't tell me. Just told me to fetch you.'

He let out a resigned breath. 'Carry on, men,' he said to the workmen who had stopped to eavesdrop on this strange exchange.

He followed the boy out and down the stairs where the boy led him to Lucio's chamber.

Bruno was just outside the door, his usually tanned face pale. 'I'm sorry, Your Excellency,' he said. 'It's Lucio. He's dead.'

Dead? He couldn't be. He'd been with him this morning at Colombo's.

'Let me see.' He threw open the door and at first saw nothing, then he saw Lucio, flat on his back, eyes still open, his face blueish around the lips, which were drawn back in what looked like a grimace. The front of his usually pristine doublet was stained and wet.

'What happened?'

'I saw him struggling to get upstairs,' Bruno said. 'It was as if his legs didn't work. I thought he'd had too much wine, but then he almost fell, so I helped him up the stairs. He protested that he just needed to sit down, but then he started drooling.'

'My God, he drank the wine before I did.'

'Do you feel well, sir?' Bruno asked.

'How long before he… before he died?'

'His legs wouldn't hold him and he lay down here, twisting and groaning, and I tried to help by fetching water. By the time I returned it was as if something was creeping up his body slowly stifling his life away. His arms twitched to hold the cup but then they stilled and went rigid. I saw the fear in his eyes but he couldn't speak, though I tried to ask him what the matter was. It had taken his tongue, made it rigid as a stick.'

'So quick?' Antonio felt his weakness return to his legs. He sat down heavily on the bed.

'It's poison, I've no doubt,' Bruno said.

'Go and check the kitchens, check they've given him nothing since he came in. If not, send a phalanx of men to check Colombo's. See if he has had any ill effects.'

He saw Bruno frown but did not reprimand him. 'And step up the search for Giulia d'Adamo. You've dragged your heels on this matter for far too long. I want her found. I give you three days. If she is not in chains by then, you will be. Do I make it clear?'

Bruno did not answer him, but he bowed and went out, his manner less obsequious than usual. Something about that bothered him.

Antonio took a moment to brace himself. He felt shaky again. It was probably the shock. Finally, he stood and walked over to Lucio and pushed him with his boot. The body, clad in matching pale blue silk breeches and doublet, was unyielding, like the trunk of a tree. Lucio's bulging sightless eyes did not flicker.

Bruno sat on the edge of his bed in his spartan chamber. He eased off his boots and stood them beside the bed. Though he hadn't thought much of simpering Lucio, he didn't deserve such a death. Was it a mistake? Was it intended for the duke?

If Giulia had administered the poison, then he'd wager it was for the man who'd killed Theofania d'Adamo – the woman who she mistakenly still believed was her mother.

His daughter, for God's sake! A daughter. And he a father. But for her to be this woman, grown tall and beautiful, but at the same time meting out death like sweetmeats, it disturbed him. Since he'd found out, he'd covertly watched fathers and daughters pass in the street, wondering at their ease and affection. But none of them seemed to be a devil of a daughter like his.

How strange to know there was flesh that was his flesh in this world. She might be the thing – the only thing – he and Isabetta had in common, and yet it was blighted before it began. He had never had any family. Plague had orphaned him at six years old and he'd had a life of fighting, of blood and death, to escape the fact he was not loved.

Except by Isabetta. They had had such passion, once. Isabetta had always been wild, but not like this. Such a daughter. He struggled to understand. What made someone rage enough to want to kill?

Should he tell her the truth of her parentage? Perhaps it might break the cycle. He wanted to know her though, wanted to unravel it all, find out what was left of himself, in her. Isabetta was right; he couldn't hand her in to the duke. And he must find a safe place for her to go. But first, he'd have to see her, and break the news to her, of who she was.

CHAPTER 42

Father Girolamo's knock was always a soft triple beat, and Bab hurried immediately to the door. She was used to his visits now, and as soon as she saw his face she let him in. Giulia smiled as he patted the top of Bab's head in affectionate blessing and handed her a sweet almond the way she supposed he did with the younger children of his congregation.

'Another twenty-five,' he said, unloading the bottles onto the counter.

'Did you bury the child?' Giulia asked him.

'I paid a man to take it out into the hills and bury it there. Pretended it had been left on my doorstep. It wouldn't be the first. Don't worry, I blessed the babe with holy water before he went.'

'Thank you, Father,' she said.

She paused a moment, rubbed the back of her aching neck before she returned to her work, mixing a paste in a mortar. She daren't let him see how much the beggar's babe had affected her.

She paused to watch Bab lift Father Girolamo's bottles onto a tray to take them to be emptied and washed. Bab was used to this routine. Afterwards she would fill them with *Aqua Tofana* and place them on open display on the bottom shelf. A second identical shelf above held genuine bottles of Manna of San Nicolo. She dreaded that she'd put the wrong bottle into the wrong hands. She wondered what the saint would make of the use of his bones, and whether he would be pleased or horrified.

'Ursula Sissipa will be coming to you,' the priest said. 'She will give you the usual greeting. She has thirteen children, and the midwife says the next will kill her. Still Signor Sissipa won't desist. Every day he wants to—'

'I understand,' Giulia said. 'She wishes to survive.'

They had arranged that women he recommended to her would ask for Manna of San Nicolo by name. The church then received a portion of the proceeds of the transaction as a donation. Of course it was not cheap, this service he offered, but the donations by thankful parishioners were generous.

'By the way, the bell's nearly finished,' he said. 'Brother Ignatio's furious. He can't understand why my church is so popular with the ladies, nor why donations have increased five-fold in the last month. But there's nothing he can do. San Giovanni's will have its new roof if we carry on like this.'

'I don't know how much longer I can go on,' she said.

'Why stop? It benefits everybody. The women can live unmolested, and the men get eternal life in heaven.'

It was too glib. She knew there was something off-kilter, for though Father Girolamo was safe in his diocese for now, the toll on her conscience was becoming hard to bear.

'Don't you ever think that what I'm doing is wrong? So wrong that I might never be forgiven?'

He paused where he was stacking bottles. 'How many have you sold this week?' he asked.

'Seven so far.'

'Only five from me. Did you tell the other women they must come to me afterwards for absolution of their sins?'

'I told them, yes. But I fear it is of little use to tell them anything until the deed is done. They are women in desperate straits, unable to think beyond ridding themselves of their troubles.'

'But that is the whole point. They must come to me. It's vital,' he said. 'You must understand I wouldn't want to be condemning anyone to the fires of hell, only to the peace of the Lord. The other two must come. Promise me you'll—'

The door opened, silhouetting a man against the light. There was no time to move before Bruno Borroni strode up to the counter.

'Good morning, Father,' he said, 'and good day to you too, Signora d'Adamo.'

Giulia backed away. Bruno Borroni was alone, yet she was still wary. 'What do you want? How did you get in?'

'The door was open,' he said.

Father Girolamo looked sheepish and shrugged.

Bruno Borroni was staring at her, yet he made no move to try to take hold or arrest her.

'Whatever you want, I have nothing to say to you.' All her instinct was to run, yet she held her ground.

'I'm alone,' he said. 'I come on my own business, not the duke's. There is nobody with me. Go and look if you like.'

She nodded to Father Girolamo, who was looking distinctly uncomfortable. He went to the door and peered out. 'Nobody there,' he said with a nervous laugh.

'To put it bluntly, there's a price on your head,' Bruno said, still staring at her in an oddly penetrating way. 'The Duke de Verdi will move heaven and earth to find you and put an end to your activities.'

'I know that already. So why is he not here with you? What is it you want?'

'I came to warn you. He's guessed you were responsible for Lucio's death and asked me to track you down. I know where you are because I followed Domenico de Verdi's widow, Agnese.'

'She told me.'

'And it isn't hard to do, to trace all the places Lucio went the day he died. If I can find you, then, eventually, he will come to Signor Colombo's and ask questions.' His face was strangely earnest, lines of worry scored his forehead. 'I've tried to protect you, but I can do no more. You must leave Naples and go somewhere else.'

'Are you trying to frighten me away?'

'No. I have no wish to harm you. But I work for the duke, and if I want to stay a free man, I must do what he says. Or at least pretend to.'

'So, he has you under his control too. You look like such a big man, yet you are cowed by the duke, just like everyone else.' She raised her chin. 'Well, I am not afraid of him.'

'Brave words, but foolish. He is a ruthless man who kills first and asks questions later. There is little time.'

Father Girolamo, who was looking more and more furtive, raised a trembling hand in farewell and scurried out. Bab merely watched them with wide eyes.

Bruno gave a hollow laugh. 'I see your friend the priest is saving his own skin at least.'

'What's it to you? Why this sudden wish to warn me?'

'I would not want you to meet the same death as your... as Signora d'Adamo.'

'How noble.'

'I couldn't have stopped it, not when she had been convicted in court of a deliberate killing—'

'And is that not what you do? You're a mercenary, aren't you? You kill people for money. So what's the difference?'

His eyes flashed briefly, but he controlled his response. 'I fight for a living, yes. And sometimes it is necessary to kill. But not in cold blood. It is different in the heat of battle.'

'And you think women are never in the heat of battle? What

about when a group of men burn a witch or abuse a woman for their pleasure, is it not battle then?'

He was silent, even puzzled, before eventually he said, 'It's not the same.'

Giulia braced her shoulders and walked around the counter. 'Bab, open the door. Signor Borroni is leaving.' She turned an icy gaze on Borroni. 'Your warning has been delivered, though I have no doubt you will tell the duke of my whereabouts as soon as you get back to his palazzo. But by then I will probably be gone.'

He did not move. 'Why did you kill Lucio? Was it a mistake?'

She was about to rebuff his accusation but then shrugged. It no longer mattered. 'The poison wasn't meant for him, it was meant for the duke. I regret it most profoundly. I never meant to kill an innocent man.' She picked up a jar and jammed the cork in tight. 'If it weren't for my mother I might have lost my resolve, but I intend to finish what she started. Tell that to your duke. Let him live in the sort of fear my mother endured at the end.'

'She was not your mother.'

The words echoed round the room. A jest. It had to be. She laughed. 'What trickery is this? Of course she was my mother, she—'

'She brought you up, yes,' he said. 'But she was not your birth mother.'

The ground seemed to fall away. Her certainty wavered. There had always been something, but surely…? 'You talk nonsense. You know nothing about me.'

'I would not have broken it to you this way if there'd been another way open to me. There is no easy way to say it. I found out from Isabetta. She's your birth mother. She bore you and handed you over to Theofania as soon as you were born. Theofania took you in and raised you as her own.'

'No. You lie. Why would she do that?'

'Because Isabetta was so young, and because she was addicted to… No. It is not my story to tell. You'll have to ask her.'

'This is some lie of Isabetta's. Isabetta hates me.'

'You're mistaken. She couldn't tell you this when Theofania was alive, for fear of breaking her trust… and when she was dead… she dare not reveal this history when you were grieving so. Why do you think she sent you away when Domenico de Verdi wanted to arrest you?'

'Because of her business! She cared more about money than me, and she feared for her livelihood.'

'Wrong. Because she feared for *you.*'

It was too much to take in; she felt as if she was drowning in falsehoods. Isabetta, her mother? Preposterous. And yet…

'I don't believe you.' Her voice was deathly quiet. 'You're making it all up. Mamma would have told me.'

He shook his head sadly, made a step towards her with outstretched arms as if to calm her. It only incensed her more.

'Get out of here with your filthy lies. You know nothing about me. Nothing!' She was shouting now.

'You can rail against it all you like, but it's the truth. And you may as well know the whole truth. She told me because… because we were lovers.' His solid figure was unmoving, but his expression held both an apology and an appeal. 'I am your father.'

'No.' It was almost a whisper. 'I have no father. It's lies, all lies. Get out.'

He shook his head and placed his high-crowned hat back on his head. When he paused at the door to look back, his eyes held a pleading that tugged in her chest. It scared her more. She slammed the door after him and slid the bolts. She found her stomach was heaving; she was panting as if she'd been running.

'Juju?' Bab stroked her arm as if stroking a distressed dog. 'Bad man gone now.'

But his words were still in her head, dark as pitch.

She saw no more clients that day. It couldn't be true, could it? And yet deep down she felt it, that her world had shifted, deep cracks in the fabric of her life, spaces that let in the ghosts of the men she'd killed. They were watching her, invisible presences, all crowding just at the corner of her eyes. Domenico de Verdi, Lucio. Even Marietta's baby stared at her with the milky eyes of death.

She took out Mamma's book and put it on the counter. She couldn't think of her as anything other than Mamma, who had loved her and scolded her in equal measure. But if Isabetta was her mother, then she was not the daughter of a poisoner at all, but the daughter of a courtesan. A memory of Isabetta sucking dreamily on her opium pipe filled her with revulsion.

Was she following a legacy that wasn't her own? She traced one of the recipes with her finger. Why had she not guessed? Why hadn't Mamma told her? But now so many things made sense, the reason why Mamma was so protective of her with men – because she was terrified Giulia might turn out like Isabetta. The fact that she didn't want to pull her into her own craft because Isabetta knew how dangerous it was and forbade it. And that was why, when things went wrong, she'd been sent to the Villa Bianca. Not away from her mother, but towards her.

Isabetta could never be a mother to her, she was certain of that, yet Bruno Borroni seemed to think she'd tried to protect her.

Bruno Borroni. The father she'd never known. A mercenary, one who killed for money. A trade she had despised, but now it seemed uncannily close to her own. Perhaps she had inherited the knack for murder from him, not Mamma at all. Icy tremors flowed up her spine.

Suddenly she snapped the book shut. Nothing made sense any more. She was hollow, as if emptied out. She'd lost her mother twice over. Once to death, and again to this. Who was she, if she was not Mamma's daughter? She was risking her life for someone who had never really been her mother at all. Her certainties collapsed like a tower of cards.

CHAPTER 43

FABIO and the other young men had crowded into Garcia's and were ranged around the shop, propped up on the workbenches, or leaning against the walls. This was their second meeting. He had called the first one directly after he had been to Giulia's. How dare she reject him like that? Who did she think she was?

He stabbed an awl into the bench. His was the proper way. Real fighting, with muscle and arms. Not this underhand business. Where would it end if women were able to just dispose of their men with a few drops of poison? Immediately he had called the men together. It was time for action. Together they would release Petruchio and the others from gaol.

At his instigation, these men were each to organise their own section, to storm the gaol and try to get the condemned men out. Word had spread. News of the planned transportations was whispered in every alley, and fear amongst the poor and hungry and dispossessed brought many to his door. He'd also gained many young men who just wanted any excuse to fight, and he had done his best to pummel them into some sort of organised force.

Fabio revelled in being spokesperson. 'Our best time is during the Feast of San Gennaro,' he said. 'The streets will be full of people. An army would have trouble stopping us if we each take responsibility for sabotaging a different part of the procession. We'll choose the busiest routes and create chaos. They'll be too busy dealing with that to send troops to the gaol.'

'Getting a riot started will be the easy part,' Alfonso said. 'How are you planning to break into the gaol?'

'Paulo from the bakery. He's smart as a whip. Says you can get anything these days if you're a baker. He bartered bread for wheel-lock pistols and two Beretta matchlocks. Don't ask where he got them from. His sons are joining us, but they're meeting in the bakery to plan from the Capuano district.' He paused, seeing Alfonso's frown. 'Six of us will be armed and will take out the guards at the gaol. The rest will act as decoys, running away through the crowd to take everyone's attention. There'll be a mass disturbance and protests which should cover our activities.'

'Is there no other way than to shoot people?' Alfonso said.

'What else would you suggest? Ask them to just give us the keys?'

'But it will bring more trouble on your heads, not less. And what about afterwards? These convicted men can't go home, can they?'

'Gallio's come round to our way of thinking and he's lending us his dray-cart. It goes south to Palermo every day.'

'Yes,' Fabio's friend Dante said with an earnest expression, anxious to back him up. Dante was always on Fabio's heels, tripping over his own feet and getting in everyone's way. Fabio hadn't the heart to ban him from their meetings though, because he saw Fabio as a kind of hero, and he had to admit it was flattering.

'Some of the biggest barrels will be empty,' Dante said, 'because Fabio got Gallio to bribe the wine gauger. We'll get them out that way, in the tun casks.'

Scepticism was written all over Alfonso's face. Fabio understood now. Alfonso just wanted a quiet life. He would keep on talking about his youth and had no inkling how much the world had changed since he was young. There were barely any firearms thirty years ago, only hand-cannon and swords. If there were going to be guns, Fabio reasoned, well he was going to be one of those that had the pleasure of using them.

'I thought we'd done with bloodshed,' Alfonso said. 'If your name gets out, they'll come here. I don't want any trouble.'

'The duke's trouble, just like his brother,' Fabio said. 'He's already tightening the bands on the traders in the Portanova quarter and demanding protection, just like his brother did. Nothing's changed. The viceroy's just switched one tyrant for another.'

Alfonso mopped his brow with a kerchief. 'I just wish our city would go back to how it was.'

'Well the only way it will is if we cause enough trouble.'

'You'll all finish up dead,' Garcia said morosely.

The duke was contemplating Bruno. Something about the man had changed, he'd swear it. Whatever it was, it made him disposable. He'd lost his unswerving loyalty, and that meant he was worthless to him. He'd send him back to Spain as a galley slave on the next outbound ship, as soon as this damned Feast of San Gennaro was over.

He called for one of his bodyguards, Alessandro.

'Ah, Alessandro,' Antonio said, putting aside his papers to give him his attention. 'Have you heard of the Villa Bianca?'

Alessandro, a young man of about thirty years, with a short thick neck and bulky shoulders, approached the desk. 'The Villa Bianca? The bordello?'

'So you know it.'

'All the men know it,' he said defensively.

'What about Bruno Borroni? Do you know if he goes there?'

'I don't know about him. But Lucio used to say he had a mistress there. It used to rile Borroni when we made jest of it.'

'Yes. He told me Bruno's mistress owns the place. Isabetta Boveri. Take a cohort of men, raid the Villa Bianca this afternoon, whilst they are sleeping, and bring in Borroni's mistress. Alive, mind you. She has a few questions to answer. And if her niece Giulia d'Adamo is there, bring her in too.'

Bruno Borroni had deceived him all along, pretending he did not know Signora Boveri, the sister of Theofania d'Adamo. But not any longer. He would be joining his lover in the interrogation cells within a few hours.

Later that afternoon Alessandro was back with news. At least one of his bodyguards was a reliable man. These days everything seemed to be such hard work. He was aware he was struggling, that fatigue often overtook him. He blamed it on the weakness from the poison. And Giulia d'Adamo would have poisoned him again had he not woken in time.

'Isabetta Boveri is in custody, Your Excellency,' Alessandro said. 'Put up a fight, but she's chained down now.'

'What about the niece?'

'Not there, sir. Boveri won't say where she is, and swears she doesn't know.'

'That tale won't last long. Have her transferred to the cells under Cardinal Bono's house. The sight of that place might loosen her lying tongue.'

Antonio paced the floor a moment more, thinking. 'When that's done, gather four men – good fighting men – and bring them here. Four more to go to Colombo's to take his wine to test for poison. Then find Bruno Borroni and send him to me. Before the end of the day.'

'What if I can't find him?'

'Find him, I said. I want it done before Naples closes down for the feast.'

Just after noon, the summons had come, as Bruno knew it would, and now here he was in the duke's chamber. Four armed guards, including Alessandro, were at the doors. He took in their presence without thinking, from force of habit. He was impassive under the duke's gaze, though inside he squirmed. He'd been avoiding him for two days, pretending there was vital work he must be doing to prepare the new warehouses for the mass transportation of the poor.

'What news on Giulia d'Adamo?' the duke asked him.

He prepared to dissemble. 'I have tried several places,' Bruno said, 'but none of them have heard of her. The aunt says that she moved on, and she swears she doesn't know where she's gone now.'

'Is that so? Unlike you, who seem to be altogether too trusting, I do not trust this whore's word. So I have had Isabetta Boveri arrested.'

'What did you say, Your Excellency?' Bruno's blood froze where he stood.

'Alessandro made enquiries and it seems she runs a bordello called the Villa Bianca. Some of the cardinal's servants are known to frequent it; even the cardinal himself, yet he has turned a blind eye to this cesspit of sin. Alessandro brought in Signora Boveri earlier this afternoon. We'll make her talk.'

'Where is she now?'

'In the cellars under Cardinal Bono's apartments. Where the

Inquisition do their work. They are used to these cases. We'll use the strappado, or the wheel. Either she gives us the information or she will die. Either way, we will have lost nothing. Whores are more numerous than pigeons in this city.'

Bruno felt himself turn rigid.

The duke narrowed his eyes, fixed him with an implacable stare. 'I know what you were doing, Bruno. Lucio told me she was your lover. It was foolish to try to protect them. You let personal considerations come above your duty to me.' He raised his eyebrows with a sardonic smile. 'I used to think you were the perfect mercenary, one who could be relied on in a crisis. Yet now I find I can no longer trust you. I treated you as a friend, confided in you, and you betrayed me.'

Bruno didn't react, though inside emotion was reeling him in, like a whirlpool.

The duke stood. 'Arrest him.'

He heard the guards' movement before he saw them. By the time he turned they were reaching for him, but anger had him in its thrall like a red flame, and he simply put his head down and charged, like a mad bull, for the door. Hands grabbed for his arm, but his weight and momentum was such that he simply barrelled through them. Down the stairs, two at a time. Shouts followed him, and the clatter of boots.

He hurtled from the door and out into the street. Which way? He shot into the road crowded with carriages and horses. One of the duke's personal bodyguards, Luigi Zito, glanced up at him as he pounded past, dodging between obstacles, but he did not stop. This was the moment when he'd chosen his own path. With the blood throbbing in his veins, he was strangely exhilarated.

After a few hundred yards, he slowed. The men had gone; he'd outstripped them. His body felt intensely alive, ready for battle. He forced himself to breathe long slow breaths. This was a temporary respite. By defying the duke, he'd signed his own death warrant. He'd have to find different clothes. Get out of the duke's livery. They'd soon be searching for him everywhere.

What to do?

His hammering on the door brought Bab, who looked small and scared and tried to close the door fast. He pushed his way in.

Seeing his face, Giulia asked, 'What is it?'

'They have Isabetta. They arrested her this afternoon.' He tried to calm himself but felt his voice rise. 'They'll force her to talk, so you won't be safe if she knows where you are.'

'Where? Is it the duke's men?'

'Giulia, does Isabetta know where you are?' He had to make her understand.

'No. She doesn't, not unless you told her.' She had put the table between them. She was still treating him like an enemy.

'No. She knows nothing from me,' he said. 'But you understand, that may be worse for her. If she denies knowing, they will kill her to force a confession from her.'

Giulia closed her eyes, swayed slightly on her feet. 'That's why she didn't let me tell her. So there'd be nothing to know.'

'She did her best to protect you, even knowing what you are.' It came out as an accusation. 'And look where it's led her.'

'It's not my fault,' she said. But he sensed the feeling writhing inside her, a discomfort that she tried to disguise by folding her arms across her chest. 'What can we do? Can we get her out?'

He shook his head. He should be taking his chance and getting away from Naples, but his heart was twisted in a knot. It crossed his mind that he could betray Giulia and perhaps that might save Isabetta. But the thought was momentary. The duke was not known for his mercy. He would execute them both, and Isabetta's need was more urgent. For the first time in years he allowed himself to feel pain.

'I don't know. I don't know if there's anything we can do. I don't think I can get inside the cardinal's house, and definitely not dressed like this. Can you find me some other clothes? Has Emilio something he can loan me?'

'Emilio and I… we're not best of friends. But I have a better idea. It's the Feast of San Gennaro tomorrow.' She remembered what Domenico de Verdi had told her about the festival. 'Naples will be at a standstill, and I know a priest who might help us. Father Girolamo.'

CHAPTER 44

THE FEAST OF SAINT GENNARO, SEPTEMBER
1633

NEITHER GIULIA nor her guest slept. She still couldn't call him her father, though she watched him warily whenever she could, looking for signs of herself in him. Bab avoided the big-boned stranger that curled on a pile of blankets where she used to sleep, his heavy feet stretched out in his worn-soled boots.

Giulia took Bab into her bed, hugged her tight, and was glad of the comfort.

The next morning Bruno was already up and supping ale, though his face was bleak. Last night, Father Girolamo, as much in the mire as they, had agreed to help. So today Bruno was wearing a cassock and surplice over his livery. It was too short for him, but she hoped in the general throng he would pass. She felt a glimmer of compassion for him as he steeled himself for a visit to the cardinal's Inquisition chambers, a place everyone in Naples knew was the closest thing to hell on earth.

They'd agreed last night that today might be his best chance of gaining entry to the cardinal's apartments. It was a risk, but both of them were used to danger. It was the one thing they shared, Giulia thought. Today, the streets would be thronging with people, men in white robes and the conical hats and masks of the guilds, along with clerics from all over the countryside, come to join in the procession and the feast. Meanwhile, she was to keep the door locked, the 'Closed' notice up, and during the festivities pack just a few essential items for a journey, in case she had to run.

When she saw Bruno set off down the street, with the leather bag over his shoulder, she almost despaired. In his borrowed robes, Bruno's stride was too long, his manner too bold. 'Slow down,' she hissed at his back. 'Stroll! It's a feast day, not a march.'

He turned, nodded, and slowed slightly, but he still walked like a military man. On his head was the rectangular biretta, the cap usually worn by clergy. Giulia wished it could have been a bigger-brimmed hat that shadowed his face and hid his scarred ear. She prayed he would find Isabetta alive. Fear for her made her realise just how much affection she held for her, despite everything. The thought that she might perish because of her, Giulia, was too hard to contemplate.

Bruno paused at the gate to the cardinal's house, a rambling building set around a square courtyard. A group of robed men were gathered there, around a trestle bearing a gold-encrusted statue of San Gennaro, dressed in real red silk, and a mitre sparkling with jewels. It seemed suddenly strange to him that they would lavish so much wealth on a figure of plaster, on a face devoid of expression, when beggars were clustered at the gates begging for bread.

He walked around the edge of the building twice to get some idea of its plan before following a carriage through the stone gates into its enclave. By now he had taken in Giulia's warning and was attempting to look more like a priest and less like a man who wanted to batter down the doors. He forced himself to breathe deeply and stroll slowly as if in contemplation. The procession wasn't ready to leave, but soon would be, so he needed to use the diversion whilst he could.

He saw that one of the side doors was open, as a group of robed guildsmen appeared carrying a smaller dais on which was a plinth bearing the holy blood in an elaborate silver vial. He stepped to the side as they staggered past to go to the front of the procession, and like quicksilver, he slipped inside the building.

A long corridor, lit by small square windows from above. He knew that prisoners were kept in the dungeons below, and that the chambers were well equipped with torture methods, though Inquisitors were prohibited by the Church to 'maim, mutilate, or draw blood'. It was a complete folly, as everyone knew that the pressing by heavy weight, the rack, and the wheel went on in these cellars, and were worse than any mutilation, because they'd all heard the screams from the street.

He followed a set of stairs down, but came to a dead end and a locked door. It looked like a storage cellar, not a prison. Hurriedly, he loped up the stairs, only to meet another cleric coming down.

'Someone's in a hurry,' the priest said, peering at him short-sightedly. 'Do I know you?'

Bruno tensed his fists automatically, ready for a fight. Then he remembered, and let go. 'I forgot something,' he said, holding up his bag, sheepishly, as if it were an excuse. With a small bow to the priest, he continued upwards. He didn't dare look back. Only a priest, he reminded himself, not a guard or a soldier.

Along the corridor again until he came to an iron door with a metal grille above. It was flanked by two guards. 'Father Bernardo,' he said to them. 'Come to give the prisoner counsel.'

'Which prisoner?' A swarthy-faced man asked.

'The woman, Isabetta Boveri.'

'The whore?' His lip curled. 'Then it'll be last rites you'll be giving, Padre.'

The other man, pale-haired and pale-eyed, laughed. 'He means she was stretched this morning.'

Bruno gripped his bag more tightly.

'What's in the bag, Father?' the pale one asked, staring at him curiously.

'A Bible, and some Manna of San Nicolo. You can look if you wish.' He unshouldered the bag and flapped open the top. The men peered in but soon lost interest.

'You've got just a few minutes,' the dark one said. 'Once the procession has left, the Inquisitors'll be back to do their work. She's been the quietest witch we've ever had, isn't that so, Roberto?'

'True. You can't go in the chamber with her, though. It's locked, and even we don't have a key. Cardinal Bono only gives it to the Inquisitors; they think we'll play at being torturer without them, don't they?'

They unlocked the metal door and opened it with a clang. Bruno felt his way down the stone stairs. Smoke from the smouldering iron torches was thick in the back of his throat.

At the bottom of the stairs the smell of burning oil mixed with the sharper smell of human excrement and misery. He stopped to peer through the iron gates that sealed the chamber from spectators. On this side of the bars were chairs and a table, on which a half-empty ale cup still stood. The corked barrel of ale stood under the table. All this he noticed as his eyes searched the gloomy chamber for any movement. A man hung from a beam in the roof by his arms. He was motionless, his flesh mottled and grey. His head had fallen to his chest, his arms, at an impossible angle, were all sinew and strain.

Then he saw her, a heap of blue fabric amongst a pile of straw. A noise, like the hush of the sea, came from her lips. Her face was bruised, her body limp, like a discarded rag.

He knew immediately he could not get her out of there. She was shackled to the wall by her ankles, and the iron gates themselves were locked. He couldn't get her out and it drew tears from his eyes.

'Isabetta,' he said softly.

At first she didn't move, but then slowly she reached one hand out to him, her white fingers stretched across the floor towards the gate. 'Bruno.'

She'd recognised his voice. 'Did you tell them where Giulia was?'

Isabetta could not stand upright. Instead, she dragged herself, handspan by handspan. Her hair was matted with blood and straw, her eyes fixed on his face. The clank of chains as she slowly moved towards him. 'No.' More forcefully. 'Never.'

'What have they done to you?' He knelt, to be closer to her level. 'I came from her house this morning. She knows everything.'

A brief acknowledgement in her eyes. 'Not much time,' she said, her words thick and slow. 'I loved her. Tell her that. Loved her right from the beginning. Never a day went by… when I did not think of her.'

'I know,' he said. 'I can't help but care, no matter what she has done. Because she's part of you,' he said simply. 'And I always held a candle for you, despite everything.'

'She is part of both of us.' Her eyes watched him closely in the dim light.

'Blood is thicker than water. I felt something for her – even when I didn't know.' It was true. There had been a feeling flowing underneath from the first time he set eyes on her in that dark alley. 'And she said something to me about the way women have to fight in a different way from men. I thought about it. It made an impression.' He reached a hand through the bars, took hold of Isabetta's cold white one. Her wrist was mangled and broken, but she didn't flinch. 'She's still safe. But who knows what they'll do next?'

She groaned and he released her hand.

'I've brought you a gift from her,' he said, 'if you want it.' He drew out the Manna of San Nicolo from his leather bag. 'I'm afraid it's not opium.'

'Bastard. Are you still keeping me from it?' A ghost of a smile.

'Something stronger. The *Aqua Tofana* – Theofania's recipe that Giulia makes.'

An almost imperceptible nod. 'She should have had her own remedy at the end. But I'm ready.'

He took a kerchief from the bottom of the bag and uncorked the bottle. The noise of the cork breaking the seal felt like his own heart breaking.

'You make a terrible priest,' she said. 'Help me. Cheat them of their afternoon entertainment.'

'Can you come closer?'

She shuffled nearer, her agony showing in every small movement. 'I should have loved you,' she said, 'whilst I had the chance.' Her breath rasped. 'But I've never liked priests.'

'Only way I could get in. The Feast of San Gennaro is today.'

'Then it's as good a day as any other to die.'

'You understand what I'm about to do?'

'Yes. Do it. For her sake.' Her eyes caught his. 'And for mine.'

She lay back, her head resting on the flagged floor. She opened her lips and he emptied the draught into her mouth. She swallowed, and her grip on his hand tightened momentarily before she let it go. He just caught her words, spoken with great effort. 'I hope our daughter's a better poisoner than she is a courtesan.'

A sudden shudder as her body convulsed before him, and then she was still. Silence filled the chamber like a breeze.

Immediately, he wished he knew the words of the absolution.

That he was a real priest and not just a man dressed up as one. Maybe his one prayer would be enough.

'God grant her peace,' he said.

Sick to his heart, he took the Bible and placed the still hand over it before turning and going back up the stairs a much poorer man than the one who went down.

CHAPTER 45

NEAR THE HARBOUR, the procession wound its way through the narrow streets, the guilds swaying along in their robes in strict order of the precedence of their *seggio* – Capuano, Montagna, Nido, Porto, and Portanova. In Capuano district the cavalcade, now almost a league in length, paused in front of the statue of Jupiter brandishing a lightning bolt, before it inched its way to the Piazza della Selleria.

In the cramped roads and passages that fed like arteries onto the main highway, Fabio and his men waited. Every doorway had a ragged man watching, every beggar was watching him for his signal, a piercing whistle through his fingers. He'd chosen this spot on purpose, because here on the front of the largest palazzo was a marble frieze of Hercules and the gods of Olympus throwing down the rebellious children of Gaia amid flames. This time, he was sure, they would unseat the gods.

Nearby, in the square of the Vicaria, the prison building was empty, except for an unfortunate debtor, his skin peeling and raw, still tied to the debtor's column. Everyone else was following the procession of San Gennaro, anxious to see the miracle of the blood and be assured of prosperity for the year to come.

At the head of the procession, after the drummers, rode the Duke de Verdi, trotting high above the crowds, his ceremonial reins gilded and hung with red silk tassels. Fabio saw him pass: a gaunt, white-faced man, rigid as a pike. As representative of the viceroy, he was followed by the other dignitaries in their plumed hats, their silks and velvets – the dukes, counts, marquises and barons. Fabio suppressed a pang of envy which quickly turned to anger.

'Bastards,' he muttered, as the chestnut stallion, the symbol of the duke's domination, passed not five yards from where he stood. He bounced on his toes, waiting for the right time to give the signal.

Meanwhile, he watched, taking note of the arms and weaponry of the ranks of helmeted Spanish mercenaries who formed the escort. Behind them came the cavalcade of forty carriages bearing the cardinals and bishops, and after that, the statue of San Gennaro himself, borne aloft as if on a vast blue sea, on the shoulders of the Silk Weavers Guild.

Fabio craned his neck as the armed escort of the dignitaries passed. From the corner of his eye he saw Dante, ready to run like a sprinter in a race. 'Hold,' he said to himself. They must wait for his signal, until most of the carriages had gone by.

A whistle.

What? Who whistled?

Dante, who was near the front of the crowd, ran forward. Seeing him move, the rest of his men leapt into movement.

'No!' Fabio shouted. 'Not yet!' But nobody could hear him for the drums.

For Christ's sake, couldn't they see? It was too soon! He was powerless to stop them once the signal had been given.

There was a surge of something cold in his veins, as two dozen men erupted from the crowd and hurled themselves towards the nearest carriage. In a moment they unshackled it from its horses and set them free. Over it went, like a beetle, complete with the clerics inside. It completely blocked the passage, and ahead, the armed men were turning, ready to fight whatever enemy was amongst them.

It should have been the last carriage! But those carriages were piling up behind. Was there time? Already, the duke's men were slashing their way back through the crowd towards him. The skirmish had already escalated, the procession full of screams and confusion.

Fabio didn't wait. He ran towards the square and the prison that sat like a rock on one side of it, its massive walls containing rows of dark windows, all with triple bars. The square, usually bustling with people, was empty. From a dozen different directions his men came running after him, men in the browns and tans of working men, like a plague of rats. In the upper storeys, slack-mouthed prisoners pressed against the bars as they saw the approaching crowd of men. Realising what was happening, they began to yell and grapple to get out.

No! He wanted to shout, *keep quiet!'*

There were fewer guards on the gates, but with the mercenaries so close behind them, would they have time? Hot with panic and anger that his signal had gone so wrong, Fabio raised his gun and shot the guard outside the door in the chest. Blood exploded from him, spattering them all. The men swarmed inside. A guard to the prison complex, who was dozing in a chair, his hat over his eyes, awoke to a pistol at his neck and a demand for keys. An instant later, his refusals were silenced by the flash of a fire-pan and more hot blood.

With the keys in hand, Fabio ran to the stairs, where a wooden wicket gate kept visitors from going in more than one at a time. Upstairs was for petty crimes like forgery or larceny. He slithered downwards, grabbing the handrail, the soles of his shoes slippery with blood.

But the keys he'd stolen were all different. His hands were trembling from the retort of the gun; he had to get Dante to hold his firearm whilst he fumbled with the keys.

'Open the doors!' Dante said.

'What the hell d'you think I'm doing?'

One by one he freed the men in the cells, relieved that Petruchio was one of the men in the third cell. But like all the others, locked away from the light, he was weak and disorientated. He had obviously suffered multiple beatings and could barely hobble down the corridor. Fabio tried to chivvy them along – the idea that the men would all be out quickly, and be joining the fight alongside him, was not the reality. 'Hurry,' he yelled, pushing at the nearest back. 'Get away from here!'

He was trying to force a key to turn when he heard the warning call, 'Out. Out! Mercenaries!'

He grabbed the gun from Dante, who was holding it as if it might bite him, and cursed as he tried to load it. His fingers wouldn't work like they usually did, but finally it was primed.

'Hey!' Rattling and clanging from the prisoners still left inside. 'Bastards!'

Gunfire outside. Dante looked to him with a frightened expression. Fabio bolted up the stairs, two at a time, and pressed through the wicket gate. Ahead of them, the released prisoners scrambled for the light. Dante cannoned into his back as he skidded to a stop. A press of bodies blocked the door, but suddenly they cleared, and Fabio and Dante erupted into the square just in time to see a group of red-sashed soldiers arrive and squat down, breastplates gleaming and arquebuses levelled at the door.

A thudding boom that seemed to shake his bones. Ahead, two men dropped, but Fabio set off at a sprint, veering right and left to keep out of range, with Dante darting at his heels.

Petruchio. One of the men on the ground was Petruchio.

No more time to think. A flash and dust spat from the walls.

Dante dropped to the ground. A moment later and he was up again, clutching his hip. Fabio grabbed him by the arm and hauled him, stumbling, down a side street. From the square, more shots.

He glanced back. The square was boiling with men fighting, the air full of smoke. The ground was already strewn with bodies. With wretched determination Fabio hauled Dante onwards; they kept on moving, down all the small passageways, in and out of peoples' tenement yards.

From the square behind them, the crack of more shots, screams, yells and the clash of steel.

He cursed himself. What a foolish signal. Who had whistled? No matter, it was done.

The men were disordered. He'd brought them out like calves to the slaughter. When at last the sounds receded, he paused, panting, his back against a wall. Dante lived on the other side of the city, too far and too risky to get to. And he couldn't go back to Alfonso's; the whole area would be full of the duke's men searching for the man who'd started this.

'Can't go on,' Dante groaned. He slumped against the wall, his legs crumpling beneath him. A red smear appeared on the stones behind him.

'You must, they'll be rounding up anyone who looks like they've been involved.'

'Then leave me here.'

Fabio looked into his pale face. He'd found him annoying, irritating. But even now, he wasn't asking for help but putting Fabio first.

'No, I'm not leaving you.' He pulled him to his feet. 'I know a place nearby where we can go.'

❧

The sound of drums and horses. The San Gennaro procession must be close now, Giulia thought.

Inside the *Aromatario Fiori*, Bab grew restless, craning to get a look from behind the shutters. 'Want to see!' she cried.

'No. We wait indoors,' Giulia said.

Would the duke be riding past, with a plumed hat and braided gold epaulettes? He had caused her so much anguish. She wished him dead. But here amongst the beat of the drums, she was oddly calm. Like her, the duke must carry all of his deeds inside him, the good and the bad. Did they chafe him like hers did, like a black tar that stuck to all her thoughts?

Mamma was dead. Nothing could bring her back. Her thoughts of revenge had evaporated, replaced with fear for Isabetta and Bruno.

An explosion nearer to home. Bab clamped both hands over her ears and cowered away from the window.

'It's all right,' Giulia soothed. 'Safe here.'

Aiming for an air of normality, she took out some sheep's grease and comfrey and asked Bab to make a paste. Soon, Bab seemed to have forgotten what was outside and was happily grinding and stirring the pestle in the mortar. But Giulia couldn't rest easy. The thud of guns and the shouting from outside made her long for news of Bruno. Had he found Isabetta? Was this unrest something to do with him? She listened intently over the noise for some inner sign, lest she should feel something change in her blood. Did either of them live?

For she knew what Bruno had taken in his bag: the Manna of San Nicolo she had prepared for Isabetta herself.

Mamma's recipe. *One drop to heal. Three drops to kill.*

She knew about the torture, about how Isabetta would have to bear it to keep Giulia safe. The thought that she would do this, for a daughter she knew so little, humbled her. So last night she had stood over the dispensing table one more time. It seemed to her that the ghosts of all the men who died because of her prescriptions were standing in the room with her. She imagined the missing faces of Lucio, of the baby, of all the men that would never see a procession again because of her, and it had choked her. Some of the faces she could picture; others were indistinct faces looming in a mist above her head.

She stood over the bottles and asked herself what Mamma would have wanted her to do.

'If you remember only one thing... Be kind.' Mamma's words came back to her, and with a heavy heart she had done what was necessary, and made this one last bottle for Isabetta, her birth mother.

She did not shed tears. But she was unsure whether, at the end of this nightmare, she'd have any family left at all.

A hammering at the door. The sharp noise dispersed the ghosts haunting her thoughts like mist rolling out to sea. Bruno? She went to it but didn't open it. She kept silent, listening.

'Giulia? It's me, Fabio. If you're there, can you let me in?'

Fabio? What did he want? She could not prevent the lifting of her heart, followed by its rapid closing down.

'Giulia. Please, if you're in there, open the door.'

She thought a moment more, then slowly unlocked the door. No sooner had the door opened a crack than two men rushed in. A stink of blood and sweat.

'Lock it,' Fabio said.

The man he'd brought with him collapsed to the ground, one leg dark with blood.

She obeyed without thinking, feeling the key grind on metal as it turned in the lock.

'We couldn't go home,' Fabio said. 'Dante wouldn't make it.'

'What's going on out there? Why are people fighting?'

'A protest. Against the famine and the transportation of the poor. But it's failed. Many, many men are dead, and they're looking for those that started it.'

'Don't tell me. And you're one of them.' She pointed to the

other man crumpled on the ground, who was panting, white-faced, clutching his shattered hip. 'Who's he?'

'Dante. Can you help him?'

'I'm a herbalist, not a physician, and it looks bad.' She pulled a cotton cloth from a basket under the table, at the same time as realising she must get him out of the shop. But there was only one bedchamber. No choice. He'd have to go in there. 'Get him to the bedchamber and staunch it with that, it's clean.' She thrust the cloth at him. 'And keep him calm.'

Out of the corner of her eye she saw Fabio hoist him up as she took down dried horsetail and plantain from the shelves. In a few moments she had pounded together a wedge of matter in a balm of witch hazel. She hoped it was suitable to plug a wound.

When she got to the bedchamber, Dante was still bleeding onto her linen counterpane. Bab was stood at his head, dabbing at his face with a damp cloth.

Bless her. How did Bab know to do that? There wasn't time to think. Together, she and Fabio peeled back the breeches from the hip. It was a glancing blow to the pelvis, but it had probably taken out a shard of bone. She sent Bab for the tweezers and did what she could to remove loose splinters. It was a gruesome job that made her heave, but it had to be done or it would fester. After-wards, she packed the wound with the blood-stopping herbs, and tried to wrap cloths tight about his hips. Blood still seeped through. It was a place hard to bandage, and with a sinking heart, she realised it wouldn't mend without rest.

After they'd done what they could, they gave Dante laudanum to help him sleep, and set to work to clean his blood from the floor. Bab refused to leave him, and rather sweetly, she sat on guard at his bedside as if he were a wounded kitten and not a gangly six foot man.

'He can't stay here,' Giulia said as she swilled the cloth in the pail of water. 'Won't his family wonder where he is?'

'I daren't go out to tell them. Anyone the duke's taken will know my name and that I was the one who started it.' In staccato bursts, he told her what had happened.

'But what were you trying to do?' she asked. 'You had no armour or proper weapons. It was madness.'

'I was angry, I wanted to get my friends out, and I thought the weight of numbers would be enough. And I believed that because we were right, that God would surely help us. That if we were fighting for good, good would be on our side.' He looked up, caught her sceptical expression. 'I know, I know. Foolish. But it all happened too early. I'd set a signal, a whistle. But someone else whistled and then... well, it was chaos.' He groaned, put his wet sleeve to his forehead. 'We should have been able to let out all the prisoners, but we didn't have time, and I didn't know how weak they'd be. They'd only been there a few weeks and you should have seen them – they were already broken men. Now they're dead. Men like Petruchio, who didn't deserve to die. And it's my fault. It's all my fault they were imprisoned in the first place. I roused them to rebel, and now they're dead.'

She couldn't say anything to ease his pain, so she just let the sound of water on wood speak for her.

'I'll need to stay here a few days,' he said. 'Until it dies down. The duke's men will go to Alfonso's, and it would put him at risk, too, if I was there.'

She stood up from her hands and knees, wiped her wet hands on her skirt. 'And I am not at risk?'

He wrung out his cloth and stood to face her. 'It is unfortunate you were the nearest friend I have.'

Friend. She had once hoped for more, but now was not the time. She hardened herself, picked up the pail of rust-stained water.

As she stood, he spoke her name. 'Giulia.' His eyes caught hers. They were sorrowful, wretched. 'Thank you. I'm sorry about... about before.'

She gave the smallest of nods. 'You'll have to sleep in the

chamber with your friend. He is your responsibility, not mine. I have done what I can for him.'

'I'll pay you for your time and your herbs, of course—'

'That's not what I meant. I have troubles enough of my own. Your arriving here has not been at the best of—'

The door again.

They both looked fearfully at it. 'Don't answer,' he ordered.

She ignored him and went to stand beside it. 'It's me, Bruno,' said a voice.

Fabio was over to her in two leaps. 'Don't,' he said. 'They'll kill us if they find us.'

'I have to. It's my father.'

His expression veered between panic and puzzlement, but he let go of her as she opened the door just a crack, enough for Bruno to push his way in. She barely registered it as Fabio's expression changed to one of rank disbelief. 'A priest?'

Bruno entered the room without saying a word and stripped off his vestments, threw them on the ground as if they contaminated him, before slumping onto a stool. His face was haggard, his eyes bloodshot.

Fabio, seeing the duke's livery, began to protest. 'I've seen him before. You said he was—'

'Be quiet, Fabio, this is not the time. You just have to trust me. Go and sit with your friend.' Something in her manner must have persuaded him, for he slunk away to the bedchamber like a dog with its tail between its legs.

'Tell me,' she said gently, going to take the stool next to Bruno at the table.

'I can't. I can't speak of it.'

'Did she take my poison?'

His lips trembled but he couldn't get out the words. His fist on the table clenched and unclenched. 'And she was my star. The guiding hope that gave some sort of meaning to this life's journey. I always hoped that one day we'd be...' The words petered out.

She felt the depth of his sorrow as if it had settled, like silt, in her own bones. Carefully, she placed a hand over his. She saw his mouth tighten as if he might cry, but instead, he closed his eyes as if to shut out the world, a big man, still as the statue of a knight on a tomb.

CHAPTER 46

THE DUKE PACED the marble floor of his chamber, feeling most unwell. He had just received the bad news that the whore from the Villa Bianca had died yesterday without giving him the answers he sought. Worse, a priest had been allowed to give her the last rites, so now she'd be in heaven, a place that, in his view, no harlot like her should ever be allowed to enter.

He had been lucky to escape with his life in that procession. He missed having the solid presence of Bruno Borroni always at his back. Why hadn't he been more on his guard before the Feast of San Gennaro? These festivals were always apt to turn into drunkenness and violence. And it irked him that Domenico's men were not as loyal to him as they'd been to Domenico. Antonio frowned. It was as if they somehow sensed his physical weakness. He'd have to stamp down on any insurrection hard.

If only he had more men.

It was like plugging a dam; the minute he sent his men one way, the leak broke out somewhere else. The work had begun of sending people to the warehouses, and his men were engaged in rounding up the poor and destitute, but of course there was resistance, and now he had to deal with riots and rebellion even on holy days. He'd heard reports of men inciting unrest by posting rebel placards in the Spanish district.

How had Domenico managed?

He hated the thought he was losing control. Naples was too sprawling; the poor seemed to be increasing, pouring in from the surrounding villages, and yet the solid citizens, the guildsmen, were dying like never before. And he was so tired. Fatigue swamped him like a blanket. He had never known a sensation like it.

He sat down at the desk, propped his head in his hands. When he came to sign the shipping orders for more transportations, his hands were shaking. He stared at them in consternation. It was making him ill again; a weakness was returning. He needed more support. He summoned Alessandro.

'Did you test Colombo's wine?'

'Yes. Nothing, sir. But Colombo was mightily annoyed that we should accuse him of tampering with it.'

He sighed. 'About the increase in deaths of our noble citizens,' he said, pulling himself upright to standing by sheer force of will. 'Did you interview the servants of all the deceased men, as I requested?

'Yes, sir.'

'And what have you found out?'

'An odd thing. Many of the women whose husbands have passed away in recent months have been seen at the Church of San Giovanni, where Father Girolamo is the priest.'

'And?'

'Well, they've all been to confession with him. I know it's not much, but it's the one link we are certain of. I'm going to talk to the priest and see if he can shed any light.'

'A priest, you say? Don't think he'll say much, and he'll be protected by the Church. But let's put a watch on where he goes.' He paced the floor a moment. 'No, wait – I have a better idea. What if we were to send a woman to this priest instead? Yes.

That's it. A young wife who confesses she wants to be rid of her ageing husband. See what happens. If you're right, then the priest will send the woman right to the viper's nest. Our men will go with her to make the arrest and bring the poisoner in as soon as she hands over the poison.'

'Where will I find such a woman?'

'I don't know. Be resourceful. A woman who can play a rich wife, of course. A courtesan might do, but choose her carefully. She has to look well bred, and speak well. We can dress her appropriately; one of the servants will see to it. And don't go and see the priest; it might warn him of our intention. Find me the right woman instead, then bring her here so I can brief her.'

Over the next two days, the men stayed in Giulia's apartment. All three men were in hiding, and Giulia thought it would be safest for all to lie low for a week or so. They kept the shutters closed and the lanterns lit. An uneasy truce had settled between Bruno and Fabio, though Bruno's weight, age and gravitas, and the fact he was so taciturn, meant he was certainly the man in charge. His mourning of Isabetta was painful to witness, and it made her feel guilty that she could not mourn her in like fashion. Her feelings around Mamma and Isabetta were still too complicated to unravel, except to leave her with a deep sense of sorrow and betrayal.

Bab was still guarding Dante as if he was her personal pet lamb, and Dante was smitten by her lavish care and attention. The one problem was of course the regular customers... and Emilio. Father Girolamo had stopped sending any more women to her after Bruno went to borrow his clothes, and he was now fearful for his life, so the number of callers was far fewer.

Nobody sat easy, though, and when a knock at the door came, late in the afternoon, Giulia leapt to her feet. Bruno pushed his head around the door of the bedchamber, sword in hand.

As Bab could no longer be persuaded to leave Dante's side, Giulia called out, 'Who's there?'

A woman's voice replied, 'Signora Caccini.'

'I'm closed,' she called.

'But Father Girolamo sent me,' said an anguished voice.

Giulia gestured at Bruno to get out of sight.

She opened the door just a small crack. 'Can I help you?' she asked.

The young woman on the threshold was well dressed, in the aristocratic fashion of the day: a tight bodice with close-fitting sleeves and embroidered skirts. 'I hope so,' she whispered, and she stepped forward into the lantern-light to reveal the face of a young woman of about twenty, with skin shining as pale as pearl and soot-black eyes. Two servants, burly men in dark russet livery, stood at a discreet distance. 'I seek Giulia Tofana, the perfumier,' she said. 'It is you?'

'Yes, but now is not a convenient time. I can't help you.'

'But Father Girolamo promised me.' She wrung her hands. 'You must see me! He promised me you would, and I trusted him.'

Giulia sighed. Father Girolamo must have thought this lady desperate if he'd decided to send her. 'You'd best enter,' Giulia said. 'But it's women only over my threshold.'

'I quite understand,' the woman said, beckoning to her maid-servant. Her voice held no accent but was soft and well-modulated. 'All right, Zito, Alessandro,' she called out to the men, 'you can both wait out here.'

She stepped inside and appraised the room with a calculating look. 'I hear you can make a special type of perfume.' She paused and trailed a hand on the table, where an array of perfume jars stood. 'They say you make a scent so potent it can send a man to another world.' She emphasised the words with a slight raise of her brows.

'I no longer trade in that kind of perfume.'

'But you must! I was told... my need's urgent. You can't turn me away.' She leant forward, her eyes intense.

'How did you hear of me?'

'A friend of mine, Agnese de Verdi. She suggested I visit Father Girolamo for confession. He said you were discreet, and that you might be able to offer me the Manna of San Nicolo. He said the saint's elixir cures all ills of this type.'

There was something about the woman that Giulia didn't like, and she seemed to be explaining too much. Usually the women were nervous, stuttering, looking over their shoulders. This one was calm, almost icy. But if she was a friend of Agnese, then she would do her best to help.

This whole business – it was like a runaway carriage, much harder to stop than she thought. Every woman deserved a life of freedom. Perhaps this woman's cold manner was a façade simply to preserve dignity.

She sighed. 'Don't worry, you're safe between these walls. You had better come through to the dispensary.'

The woman began to follow her to the curtained dispensary alcove, gesturing to her servant to attend her.

'No,' Giulia said. 'Your servant can wait there.' She indicated a rush seat chair by the parlour door.

'Oh, but Benita is very trustworthy, she—'

'She can wait outside,' insisted Giulia. The woman's mouth pursed in annoyance. Unlike her mistress, the servant did look nervous. She kept glancing to the door behind her and her eyes were never still, but she lowered herself stiffly into the chair and Signora Caccini followed Giulia into the alcove.

Giulia bade her sit opposite her at the table, and the woman removed her gloves and laid them in her lap. 'If I'm to help, you can at least tell me your husband's name.'

'My husband is Evaristo Caccini. He's a retired sugar importer.'

She had never heard of him, despite her contacts in the spice trade.

Signora Caccini was still talking in a voice of persuasion. 'He is too old now to work, and he grows more frail and incontinent each day. He can no longer walk but refuses to engage more servants. I am exhausted caring for him. He has no quality of life, and I heard that you have something that will speed his entry to the next world.'

'Yes, yes.' It was the same scenario she had heard a hundred or more times. She sighed. Would she never be free of it? Father Girolamo must need the money badly to send her at all. How could she turn this woman down when she had helped so many others? It wouldn't be fair. 'You know what it means to do this?'

'I do.'

'And do you fear it?'

'It is a last resort.'

'Then will you swear you will give him time to make his peace with God before you send him on his way? To ensure that he enters the next world shriven and anointed and ready to enter the gates of Paradise?'

'I swear it.'

'And will you go back to Father Girolamo, confess yourself to Almighty God, and throw yourself on his divine mercy?'

'I will do all in my power if you will just help me this once.'

Giulia took a bottle from the shelf. The viscous liquid glinted in the candlelight as she placed it on the table between them.

'Did Father Girolamo tell you what to pay?

'No, he must have forgotten.'

She looked as though she could afford a large fee. 'It is twenty scudi.'

Signora Caccini's gaze veered towards the door.

'I'm sure your servant will be fine,' Giulia said. 'Do not worry.'

The woman seemed to be having trouble finding her purse.

Her behaviour had changed; now she seemed distraught. Giulia saw the maidservant slip outside like an eel.

The moment the payment was in her hand the room was suddenly full of men. She shot to her feet, the coins dropping with a rattle to the table. She registered the two men in livery who had been outside the door, but there were two more soldiers there too, who crowded into the room, armed with swords.

One leapt towards her and grabbed hold of her arms. 'Take that bottle,' he said to the men in livery. 'Careful now. And pack the rest. We'll need them as evidence.'

'What is this?' she protested.

'My name is Alessandro Benedetti and you are under arrest for the attempted murder of the Duke de Verdi, his brother Domenico and—' His words stopped in his mouth as Fabio and Bruno burst out of the bedchamber.

'Borroni?' Alessandro said, confusion written all over his face.

'Let her go.' Bruno drew his sword and made a feint towards him.

Signora Caccini tried to sidle away and rush for the door, but Giulia stopped her on the threshold by grabbing for her arm. She whipped out her knife from her bodice and forced her to turn. 'Who sent you?' she said.

The woman looked round frantically for help. In that short space of time Bruno had already dispatched two of her servants; their corpses lay like washed-up driftwood on the newly scrubbed floor.

'Don't hurt me!' she begged. The other two men had made distance and were fighting back with swords and daggers.

'Who sent you?' Giulia repeated, pushing the knife towards her face.

'The duke. The Duke de Verdi.'

So now he knew where to find her. Giulia let go. The woman gave a yelp of distress and fled after her maidservant. Only now could Giulia take in the clash of metal on metal. She backed away as the fight grew more frantic in the confined space. Amid the flash of swords, bottles and jars crashed and shattered on the flagged floor.

'Be careful!' she yelled, stepping back from the spreading pool. Some of the liquids were toxic.

A groan, and she saw that Fabio, a wild light of triumph in his eyes, had finished the third man. The remaining man was backed up to the wall, his sword long gone, but his eyes were flickering left and right, searching for a way out. He held up his hands. 'Bruno, don't do this. It's me, Alessandro, your friend.'

Bruno raised his blade to keep him there. 'No. Let him go,' Giulia said. 'More will come. They know where we are already. Killing another will serve no purpose.'

Bruno let his sword drop. Fabio, who was nursing a cut to the arm, backed away.

'Friend, have you lost your reason?' Alessandro said.

Bruno shook his head. 'You heard what she said. Get out of here.'

Alessandro spat on the ground in disgust and then strode out.

'We have to leave,' Bruno said, sheathing his sword. 'That was Alessandro, a bodyguard to the duke. The duke will have every man in Naples after us as soon as word gets out. If I know him, reinforcements will be nearby and we'll have to fight our way out. You must stay close behind me. I'll do what I can to shield you. We must get to the harbour to a boat, or to the *mercato* to hire horses.'

'No,' Giulia said. 'Emilio's house has a passage into the catacombs. He dug it there in case of another eruption, to get him and his wife out of Naples. We can go that way.'

'What about Dante? I'm not leaving him behind,' Fabio said.

'You have to.' Bruno was blunt. 'He's too weak. You have to save yourself.'

'I can't. It's my fault he's injured. I'll take my chances with him.'

'No. There has to be a way,' Giulia said. 'We can carry him. And what about Bab?'

'It will be too slow,' Fabio said. 'Go with your father. It is better we split up. There will be more chance for us all if we go separately.'

'He's right,' Bruno said. 'But take heed, I know what it's like on the run. We may have to hide out a while. Have you gathered provisions? A light? Water? Bring the deathwater too, if you must. If the duke catches me, I'll be executed as a deserter, hung, drawn and quartered whilst still alive, the worst way possible. Something like it will be planned for you too. The trial is always a sham.' His face suddenly grew older.

'No,' she said. 'I'm finished with poison now. But you don't need to come with me. I will fight my own battles.'

'This is one you can't win alone.'

'I don't need saving.'

'You're still rejecting me? For God's sake, Giulia.' The battle played out on his face. Hurt, frustration, a strange pride. 'Think of Isabetta,' Bruno said. 'Think of Theofania, who raised you. Are their lives to be squandered for nothing?'

A moment before she capitulated, she hurried to fetch a flagon of water. When she returned, the bodies had been pushed under the table. The sight of them piled there made her light-headed.

'Lamps?' Bruno asked.

Woozily, she opened a cupboard and pulled out two terra-cotta oil lamps with long waxed wicks. She packed them into a leather bag. Corked bottles of oil followed.

She turned to Fabio. 'Will you make sure Bab goes with Dante? She has no-one else.'

'I will. She won't leave him anyway.'

She took hold of his hands. 'Good luck, Fabio.'

The look he gave her held so many things: yearning, guilt,

loss, regret. 'I hope we meet again someday,' he said. 'Your father is a fine fighter. I'm glad he's on your side.'

'Come, Giulia,' Bruno said, heaving the bag onto his shoulder, 'We've no more time. Alessandro and the woman will have raised the alarm by now.'

CHAPTER 47

Bruno watched as, stealthily, Giulia unlocked the connecting door. 'This way, but we must be quiet in case Emilio should hear us.'

She led him into the gloomy, echoing corridors of the palazzo, past shrouded furniture and unlit chandeliers, but the doors to the apartment stayed shut. No servant came as they made their way towards the front of the building like thieves. Finally, they came to a room with a stone-flagged floor which held the old dry well-heads under wooden covers. Giulia went to the furthest one and carefully dragged the cover aside. The scrape of wood seemed too loud.

He sucked in his breath. Dusty earth steps led downwards into a black void.

She hesitated. 'I don't know if I can.'

'Feel your way,' he urged.

'I can't,' she mouthed. 'It's too dark. And I'm afraid of small spaces.'

'You must. I swear I'll be right behind you. I'll close the lid, then we can light a lamp. Let me pass you the bag.'

Her face had drained of colour. His daughter was still a

mystery. She was capable of killing men like the de Verdis in cold blood yet she was afraid of the dark. He heard her take a few deep panting breaths before she lowered herself through, then the sound of a whimper, and loose grit and rubble as she scraped her way downwards. Her pale hands reached up for the bag. Finally, there was enough room for him to ease his legs down to follow her.

He was halfway into the hole when a voice from behind froze him where he was, half in, half out. 'Who are you? What the hell are you doing?'

A long-faced man in dark clothing was staring down at him, his face illuminated by a single candlestick. Bruno hesitated only a fraction. He couldn't fight from here. In a scramble, he clawed his way down the gritty steps to where he could unsheathe his sword. No point now to drag the cover over. 'Giulia, run,' he shouted, holding his sword towards the entrance.

Footsteps on the boards above. So the man wasn't following. Still, he'd seen them go and would no doubt send their enemies after them. He began to feel his way in the dark, a hand on each side of the tunnel, until he almost fell over her, crouched down in his path.

'We have to hurry. Someone saw me. A tall man, dark.'

'Emilio.'

They listened again. Nothing. The tunnel was cool but dry, the air still and musty.

'Please, let's light a lamp.' She thrust him a lamp from the bag.

He brought out a flint and tinder from his belt-pouch and lit it by feel. 'Now he's seen us, we need to keep moving.'

She was sitting in amongst her skirts, the bag hugged to her chest. In the flare of light her face was as pale as wax, dark shadows under her cheekbones. 'Being underground makes me feel strange,' she said, 'like drowning.'

'It opens out further along,' he said. 'There's a network of tributaries round the catacombs, first built in antiquity. In Roman times.'

'Why would anyone want to come down here?'

'They say in the past they've been used as a burial site.' Seeing her stricken face, he added, 'And for other things like storage for householders like Emilio, there are probably many that have access. There's water conduits too. I'll trim the lamp, and then we'll have a steadier flame to see by.'

'I knew of this place but I've not been down here. I thought underground Naples was a place used by smugglers and thieves, and poor beggars with nowhere to shelter.'

'I studied the map in the Duke de Verdi's chamber. I have never trusted him, and I hoped to use the tunnels to get out of Naples if he decided to send me back to gaol in Turkey. I have a vague sense of them, but I can't guarantee we won't take a wrong turn.'

'So what now?'

'We try to make our way to the harbour. If men come up behind us, you must go on without me.'

'No. You were the one who wanted us to go together, so now you'll just have to bite your tongue and live with it.'

In silence they made their way forward until the tunnel grew narrower and forked into two equal-sized passages.

'Which way?' Giulia asked, swinging the light from one side to the other. 'Doesn't look like anyone's been in either for years.'

'The harbour's to the south, so I guess the left-hand path.'

After a few hundred yards the roof grew lower until Bruno was almost in a crouch. Giulia stopped. 'We can't go any further,' she said. 'It's a dead end.'

'Are you sure?'

She passed him the lamp. 'See for yourself.'

She was right, the rock face before them was impassable. It was an unfinished tunnel. His heart sank. 'We'll have to retrace our steps.'

'I thought you said you knew these tunnels.'

'Only from paper. I'm sorry. It must be the other way. I'll lead the way back.' He feared that they would meet someone on the way back and that this mistake would cost them dearly. 'And leave the bag here, it'll only hinder us.' He began the trudge back, the noise of his boots crunching on the dry rock bed.

A small voice from behind. 'What if the other one's another dead end?'

'It won't be.'

'We might be stuck in these tunnels forever.' A few moments later she asked, 'If they come after us, will you fight them?'

'I suppose so. It's what I do best. What I'm trained to do.'

'Do you ever wish you did something else?'

The question was a leading one. He decided to be honest. 'Often. Particularly as I've got older.' He kept walking, but her silence seemed to demand more. 'When I had to fight the rebel apprentices, it didn't seem fair. I have twenty years of fighting experience, I am well armed, wise to all their crazy attacks. It seemed cruel to fight them. Unequal. Like it wasn't a fair fight. I hadn't the heart for it.'

He listened; her soft footsteps were still following. But then there was another sound, a sound like a small sob. He turned round and held up the lamp. She turned her face away. He wanted to comfort her, but he knew it was too soon for him to be a father to her. So he simply stood there and waited.

'What about the people you killed,' she asked. 'Do you ever think of them?'

'Sometimes. Like I said, the young ones. Those who had no chance, who didn't realise who I was when I was fighting. That I was not myself but someone else's weapon.'

She stared up at him and he caught the glimmer of unshed tears in her eyes before she gave him a push. 'Go on. We'd better keep moving. There may be men on our tails.'

Antonio came out of his closet and wiped his mouth. He'd been vomiting again, and the fever and chills that seemed to alternate in his blood let him have no peace. A swelling in his throat made it hard to swallow, and he was wiping his mouth when Alessandro rushed in with Signora Caccini – the woman he knew by the name of Vittoria Pugliesi, the courtesan.

Her face was apologetic, fearful and servile all at once.

'What happened?' he asked.

Alessandro broke in, 'We were outnumbered. Ambushed. She had armed men in her apartment; one of them was Bruno Borroni.'

He turned to the courtesan. 'You. Tell me what you know.'

Vittoria Pugliesi gave him a breathless summary of events that included three of his men dead. He pressed his forehead into his hands.

'Take her away,' he said to the guard at his door. 'Detain her until I tell you she's free to go.'

'Where?' the guard asked.

'I don't damn well care. Any cell or prison that will take her. And Alessandro – assemble my best fighting men. Go back to Emilio Colombo's house. If they're still there, no-one is to leave. Especially not Giulia Tofana. I want her brought here alive. Kill Borroni if you have to. If they've fled, set up a search and block all routes out of Naples. And you—' He called to a guard at the door. 'Get horses and men ready in the courtyard and I'll address them as soon as they're ready. We want to move before dark.'

When they'd gone, all he wanted to do was slump back in his chair, but he forced himself to stand. His legs felt as limp as lint. Borroni had turned against him. Even his own body had turned against him. Curse this illness. The poisoner's daughter must be giving him something, getting into his kitchen somehow. But how? No matter, she would be caught soon enough and then they would flay it out of her.

When Fabio got back to the bedchamber, Bab was helping Dante to struggle out of bed. He was testing his strength, his fearful expression replaced with one of relief. 'I heard the clash of swords but knew I'd only be a hindrance. Thank God you're alive,' Dante said.

Fabio told Dante about the fight, and that Giulia and her father, Bruno Borroni, were making their way out through the tunnel.

'She was a brave woman to help us like that,' Dante said.

'Foolish you mean.'

'She liked you.'

'No. We could never see eye to eye.' Then, after a moment's pause, 'How could you tell?'

'Just the way she looked at you, like she always wanted to say more.'

'Pah.' He gave a dismissive laugh. 'Did you know the duke's bodyguard is her father? Bruno Borroni. I never knew that. He's changed though; he's done with the duke. He was fighting for us today, but he shouldn't have let that other one go, the one who knew him. He'll bring the duke's men here. Can you manage to walk yet?'

'No, but the fever's gone and I can crawl or hop, if you help. Find a church, and you can leave me there.'

'Bab, you'll help me carry Dante, won't you? And stay with him?'

She nodded. They began to support his weight as he inched his way out of bed.

A noise behind him and the door slowly opened. A dark-clad man holding a candle stepped gingerly into the chamber.

'Who are you? What's all this?' Fearfully, he scrutinised the three faces caught in the act of manoeuvring Dante out of bed.

'Signor.' Bab let go of Dante, who grabbed the side table to support himself. She ducked a curtsey but stayed gazing at the newcomer, thumb in mouth.

His eyes caught Fabio's. 'You. You were here before, with Signorina Tofana. I told her you weren't to come here in my house again.'

'Are you Signor Colombo?' Fabio asked, stepping forward.

'Don't come any nearer! Are you responsible for the dead men littering my apartment?' Fabio was about to answer, but Colombo interrupted him with a raise of his palm. 'No. Don't tell me. I don't want a fight, but I'm warning you now, I'm calling the militia. And don't think you can go the way your friends went. I've locked the door to my storeroom.'

His light retreated from the door and they heard his footsteps go. Moments later they heard shouting.

'Hell,' Fabio said, 'he'll bring half of Naples.'

At the front of the building Emilio stood on the flagged steps, waving to attract the attention of the passing pedestrians. 'Murder!' Emilio cried. 'In my house!' Within a few moments, people had stopped and some were running to fetch help.

Alessandro was leading a cohort of men when he heard shouting, and he immediately diverted his men at a run to the front of the house, where the commotion had drawn a large throng of people.

'There's been a fight in my apartment, three dead in my house, and more felons holed up in the rear apartment. I've had nothing but trouble from the tenant, Giulia Tofana. Who knows what type of ruffians have been coming and going at all hours.'

'Don't worry, sir,' Alessandro reassured him, 'we know all

about it. I've brought reinforcements, and the woman and her friends will be arrested. The building's surrounded, they can't get out. We'll handle it now.'

'You're too late. She's gone already.'

'Where? What do you mean?'

'She went down through the stairs in my oil store. It leads to the vaults and tunnels under the city. One of your men took her.'

'One of our men?'

'In your livery.'

Borroni. It had to be him. 'This man, did he have a torn ear, a broken nose?'

'I didn't notice, but he was a big man, with a recent cut to the face.'

'Show me this tunnel,' Alessandro said. 'And fetch me lanterns. Hurry.'

In the oil store Alessandro peered down the hole into the darkness. 'Where does it go?'

Emilio shook his head. 'It joins to many other passages. But the main route leads you to the harbour. Keep to the widest part. When you come to a fork, keep right. Some of the others are dead ends to people's houses, like mine.'

Alessandro didn't relish the prospect of chasing down tunnels in the dark. 'Where are those lanterns?' he bellowed. Emilio went in search of Anna, who brought up a basket of dusty iron lanterns and a jar of oil. Alessandro ran outside and gave orders for all the exits from the catacombs and the tunnels to the harbour to be blocked.

He didn't know what Borroni was thinking. He'd always been so trustworthy before, and a good man to have at your back in a fight. Did his task efficiently without getting emotional. He didn't relish the idea of him being on the other side of his sword. Especially not down there. He craned his neck again over the dark stairs leading down under the floor. But orders were orders, and fetching this Giulia Tofana would bring him favour from the duke. Besides, he knew what happened to men who disobeyed him. Borroni wouldn't get out of this alive, no matter which way the wind blew.

Alessandro lit a lamp and led the men warily down into the tunnel.

~

Giulia could see nothing but felt her way forward, her fingers groping along the walls. They had retraced their steps and were in the right-hand tunnel, which to her relief seemed to have more headroom than the last. She had a sense of where Bruno was by his light, and she made her way slowly, following his lead, foot by foot. When her hands felt a gap, she withdrew them into her skirts, fearful of touching a corpse in the dark. Hadn't he said they were burial chambers? After it seemed like they had progressed only half a league, voices echoed behind her in the distance, and there was the clank of a sword.

She stopped, staring back into the darkness. A flicker of light. They had lanterns.

'Someone's coming.'

Bruno grabbed her hand to pull her along, but the way grew narrow and they had to stumble in single file, feeling their way on the uneven ground. He moved quicker now, and she hurried after him, a hand on his back, eyes searching for light. He suddenly turned. Left, she must go left here.

The voices were coming closer, and the scraping and rustling sound of many men's footfalls. A shadow swung out into the path behind her as they slipped sideways down the passage.

'There!' A man's voice. 'I thought I saw something move. Pass the lamp.'

Bruno dragged her back into a deep alcove set into the wall. She pulled herself tighter into it, wrapped her skirt tight to her legs. Bruno's heart thudded against her back as she pressed herself into the small space, but she did not dare breathe. Sweat trickled down between her collarbones as the scrape of boots came nearer. A light flickered against the opposite wall, showing the rough yellow texture of the passage.

'Anything?'

Low voices. 'There's nobody there.' 'They must have gone straight on.'

The noise of people moving grew further away. Bruno waited a few more moments before emerging from the alcove. She was dizzy; cramped spaces always made her faint, and she was unsteady as she groped her way forward after him. Her foot hit a loose rock. She stumbled and gave a yelp as she fell. The noise ricocheted around the tunnel.

There were shouts from the other tunnel as she scrambled up and ran blindly into the dark until she cannoned into Bruno.

'Go past me,' he said.

He was drawing his sword.

'No, Bruno!' She tugged at his belt.

Lights bobbed towards them.

'Go,' Bruno yelled. 'Get out of here.'

She saw what he was doing and would not leave him.

A man came into view, his huge shadow wavering in the lantern-light from behind. He was backed by at least six other men, forming a dense knot in the confined space. As he came into their light she knew his face. Alessandro Benedetti, who'd been at the house earlier.

'No,' she said again, but Bruno continued to stand in his path, sword glinting dully in the meagre light, his head bent to one side by the height of the roof.

'Go, Giulia,' he said. 'Run.'

Still she could not.

'Give up the girl, Bruno,' Alessandro said, 'and let's all go home. No need for any of this.'

'No. You back off. Because I'll fight you if I have to, and I don't want your blood on my hands.'

'You think you can best me?' Alessandro leapt forward, intent in the gleam of his eyes.

Bruno was fighting back now; in the passage the clash of swords was deafening. She saw he needed more room to swing his weapon and moved back. As she turned she saw another tunnel leading off to the left and, blessedly, a thin sliver of pinkish light shining down dully over rough-hewn stairs.

'There's light! This way,' she shouted.

He heard her cry and dodged the thrust that came at him from Alessandro. Shielding her from the approaching men, with an outstretched sword, he shouted, 'Go, I'll follow.'

She grasped her skirts and ran, pounding up the stairs two steps at a time. At the top was a wooden plank door, light streaming through the gaps. She shoved against it with all her might and emerged into the night air, disorientated and panting for breath. The passage opened out into a long narrow square by a well. The square was flanked by tall buildings, rosy in the low light of the evening sun which skimmed over the rooftops and dazzled her eyes.

She squinted into the light. It was then she saw them, ranged at the far end of the square.

A cohort of six soldiers with muskets, their backs to the wall, their guns pointing at the entrance. She ran backwards down the stairs but Bruno was on his way up, still holding Alessandro and his friends at bay.

There was nowhere to go. She leapt back up the stairs out of the way of Bruno's retreating back, but as she came out two more soldiers appeared from nowhere, took hold of her and dragged her sideways. Her feet were lifted from underneath her. She kicked at empty air and clawed at their hands but could not free herself from their grasp, no matter how wild her movements.

'Bruno. Go back!' she yelled, trying to warn him.

But he hadn't heard her, and a few moments later he emerged backwards from the dark belly of the passage.

As if the world had slowed, she saw the kneeling musketeer ahead of her take steady aim and a plume of dove-grey smoke drift from the barrel of the gun. A fraction after, a single crack seemed to fill a long silence. Bruno's knees sagged, then buckled, his back split into a red hole as he was propelled forwards to slam onto the earth, like a great tree felled in the forest.

The shock of the noise allowed her to break free, and she threw herself towards him with a cry of disbelief.

Dust was still settling round him.

Her knees crashed onto the ground. She reached a hand out to touch his warm head where it lay, one cheek in the dirt, his eyes still open to the setting sun.

She tried to roll him over, but in those few instants his eyes lost their spark and his body took on weight, as if filled with lead. The sun disappeared behind the buildings leaving her in a dark shadow. She took hold of his heavy hand and interlaced her fingers with his.

To her surprise, Alessandro threw down his sword in disgust and knelt with her. 'God go with him. He didn't deserve to die with such dishonour,' he said.

The sound of horses. The shot had brought the Duke de Verdi and his entourage. His men cleared the way to let him ride through. Two men took hold of Giulia again, but she did not resist. She could not find the will. She felt her fingers slowly slip from her father's grasp.

'Who's the corpse?' the duke shouted.

'Bruno Borroni, Your Excellency.' Alessandro reluctantly stood, but he would not meet his eyes.

'And is this the woman? Giulia Tofana?'

Given she was pinioned tightly, Giulia looked up at him with as much defiance as she could summon.

'I believe so,' Alessandro said.

The duke, pale-skinned and gaunt, met her eyes with a cold gaze. 'Take her to a cell in the cardinal's apartment; keep her apart from anyone else.' He turned to Alessandro. 'Good work. This has been a long time coming.'

The soldier dipped his chin in mute but surly acknowl-edgement.

The duke began to turn his horse. 'What are you waiting for? Take her away. Clear the streets.'

CHAPTER 48

THE CELL WAS WINDOWLESS, stank of urine and was unlit. The door clanged shut, leaving her alone in the impenetrable dark. There were so many different kinds of dark, and all of them made her shudder. Especially this, a damp suffocating dark that made her unable to breathe.

There wasn't a stick of furniture so she leant against the door, trying to find a sip of air, listening for the sounds outside. There were few. Once she heard the echo of a door clanging shut, but no sounds came near her, and she was left to imagine what might await her the next day. She imagined she would end the way Mamma had done. She understood it all now, and why Mamma had hidden it from her.

Numb, she leant her back against the rough stone wall and let her knees sink until she was pooled in her own skirts. She had failed to get her revenge, yet on the way she had helped many others to send their husbands to their deaths. No doubt some were like the Duke de Verdi, and, like him, their arrogance had shown every other man in Naples that he could treat women as chattels. Some, like Lucio, did not deserve their deaths. He was the only man dead at her hand; every other death was not hers to command, even though she provided the means.

She bowed her head and wondered what it was all for. Wondered at the whirlwind fire that had fuelled her with such anger that she could become an avenging angel and visit death and destruction on so many innocent men. She had felt herself an instrument, the point of something so much bigger. She couldn't say what, but the feeling had burned inside her like gunpowder on a fuse.

So much passion, but now it was all burnt out.

Bruno and Isabetta had lost their lives to give her hers, and all she could think of was that if she did not survive, their lives would be wasted. She had failed in every way possible, and her heart ached to make amends, but she couldn't see how.

She would die for this. Of that she was certain. No priest would offer her the platitudes of an absolution; instead, the fires of hell would be hers. And only now did the spectre of death begin to feel real and the first inklings of fear snake up from the base of her spine.

In the *Aromatario Ruggieri*, Camilla was watching Matteo mix a salve. She had to watch him constantly because he'd forget what ingredients he had already added. She had changed her mind and decided to open the apothecary for just one day a week, hoping it might help him remember and recover. It was hard now that he'd turned into a child again, asking her the same questions over and over.

Today was one of the days the shop was open, and they'd already had several customers. Camilla did not turn immediately when she became aware of a shadow falling over the counter. 'Wait a moment,' she called, checking she had left nothing dangerous within Matteo's reach.

'Have you heard?' said the voice.

Camilla turned to see Agnese de Verdi at her counter. She was still pale but had a more upright, assured manner than before. Her grey eyes were troubled.

'I bring good news,' she said, 'but also bad,'

'No more bad news,' Camilla said. 'I can't take it.' Petruchio and the other men had been executed just yesterday, to great unrest in the city.

'The good news then,' Agnese said. 'The Duke de Verdi is not expected to live beyond this week. They sent a messenger to me, as one of his surviving family. He sickens day by day.'

'What ails him?'

'I don't know. His brothers are suspicious of me and won't let me even inside the palazzo. Nobody is certain, but I think... that's the bad news.'

'How can it be bad news?'

'They've arrested my friend Giulia Tofana. I managed to speak to one of the servants, and she told me there was a skirmish at Emilio Colombo's house, and of course now the duke is so sick, tales of poison are flying all over the city. So from that, I can only assume—'

'Giulia managed to get inside the Palazzo de Constantin after all,' Camilla said. 'But if she is confined, will the duke not get well again?'

'They say not. They say whatever she gave him was too strong. They took books and physic from her workplace, things that prove she was skilled in the art of poison. So there's to be no trial. The duke has already found her guilty on the evidence he possesses. Her execution will be on Friday.'

Camilla's stomach dropped. Hadn't she been the one urging her to carry out this deed? But it hadn't occurred to her that it would lead to this. A young woman, a woman who had stood right here at this very table, was about to die. She shouldn't have pressed her to do it.

She swallowed. When the words came out they were gruff. 'That's terrible. It seems so unjust... so unfair, that the duke can kill any number of people and never be questioned for his cruelty at all, yet those who would try to stop him...'

'It's because he's a powerful man, from a powerful family with an army behind him,' Agnese said. 'But he only craves power because inside he is weak and must oppress people to bolster his own insufficiency. And though he might kill any number of Giulias, he will never be free of women like us.'

'Huh.' She was sceptical. 'What could women do?'

'Our time will come. The women of Naples will not be silenced forever by men like him. I wager Giulia will not be the last to take on the de Verdi family, or the other despots of this kingdom. These men should watch out, because every meal they take, every draught they swallow, might be tainted by a woman like her.' She paused for an instant. 'Or like me.'

Camilla stared at this young woman with fire in her eyes.

'Why should men be the only ones to rise up and rebel?' Agnese paused, then turned and suddenly leaned towards her, both hands on the counter. 'Listen,' she said, 'it's given me an idea. Will you help me?'

'I don't know.' Camilla glanced behind to where the scrape of the spatula could still be heard. 'I've Matteo to think of.'

'Please? Would you talk to the women you know? Those who've suffered at the hands of the duke – Jacquetta and her friends? We have a few days.' She glanced over her shoulder, then beckoned Camilla closer to the counter. She began to speak into her ear in urgent whispers.

Four days later, weakened by hunger, with only a bucket of water to sustain her, Giulia heard a heavy tread approaching. When the door clanged open, she shrank back.

'I come with a message,' Alessandro said, in his clean russet livery. 'From the Duke de Verdi. He wishes to see you. I've to escort you there.'

'Is it the trial?'

'No. There will be no trial.'

'Then I have nothing to say to him,' she said.

'You have nothing to fear. He cannot rise from his bed. He is too weak.'

Her puzzlement must have shown in her eyes. 'Nevertheless, I have no interest in his affairs.'

'You are the daughter of Theofania d'Adamo,' he said. 'Of course you have an interest.'

'Adopted daughter,' she said. 'I am the daughter of Isabetta Boveri and Bruno Borroni.'

Why did she say that? As if it mattered to this man that her whole life had been a lie. But truth seemed important now she was so near to the end.

She saw understanding dawn in his features. 'I'm sorry. You father was a fine man, a noble man. I liked him.' He paused before continuing. 'The duke, as I say, wishes to see you. It might save you if you agree to come with me. There is a carriage waiting. He said to guarantee your safety to the palazzo and your return if you should agree to come. It is a request, not an order.'

A request? This was strange, that he had not sent more soldiers to force her there. All the same, she was wary. Did he think her foolish? To walk right into the lion's jaws? 'Why?' she asked. 'What can he say to me that will make a difference?'

'He's dying. Perhaps he wants to make amends.'

She weighed this thought against all she knew of the man. Could it be possible? 'You say I'll be safe. Yet how do I know it's not a trick?'

'Whatever he is, the duke has always been a man of his word. It was what made him strong.' He held up his hands. 'Look. No weapons. Not a sword in sight.'

'And you say he's bedridden?'

'Has been for four days. He collapsed right after your arrest.'

She gave a brief nod. There was nothing more to lose in any case. Without her potions, the power was all on his side. Without a word he unlocked the door and walked ahead of her, at a slow pace so she could keep up, though she was weak and wore women's shoes. No other soldiers followed them. The sky was the brightest blue she'd ever seen. In the sun, the streets shone, as if touched by gold. If this was to be her last day, then God had gilded it for her.

At the Palazzo de Constantin there was no sign of any guards or military presence. That in itself was odd for a man in his position. A liveried domestic servant led the way up a long curved staircase to a balconied landing.

'He's in there,' Alessandro said, gesturing to the door in front of him. 'I'll announce you.'

He opened the door and led them towards a heavily draped bed at the far end of the chamber. 'Signorina Tofana,' he said.

The man in the bed stirred and half rose so he was propped on the pillows. In his cadaverous face his eyes glittered. So there was still life in him yet.

She went closer, close enough to smell camphor and eucalyptus, and to see the panoply of bottles on the side table. A quick glance revealed he was taking myrrh, angelica and Virginian snake root.

The duke was all skin and bone, his hair lankly plastered to his skull. He didn't greet her. 'What is it?' he croaked. 'How are you doing it?'

'What is what?'

'How are you poisoning me?' His voice was a rasp.

'You are mistaken, Signor. I have done nothing.'

'I knew you'd say that. But I know it's something. All my food is tested. Every glass, every knife, anything that touches my lips. Even my clothes are tested. Yet still I sicken.'

'I know. I would have poisoned you if I could. But in the end I found I could not.'

A smile briefly tightened his lips; claw-like hands grasped the linen sheet. 'I can't believe you would admit defeat, you who have poisoned half of Naples.'

'You mistake me. I did not fail through lack of skill. But I saw I was becoming sick of soul through trying. Whatever ails you now, Signor, it is a sickness in yourself. I have done nothing.'

'Tell me what you want. Gold, you shall have it. Jewels, they're yours. Look, my throat swells with your poison.' He pulled down his nightshirt to reveal an angry red and purple swelling on the front of his neck.

She could not help but see the tumour and recoil. 'This sickness is none of my doing. I can't help you. It is some infection of the humours, not poison. I have nothing more to say to you.' She shook her head. 'I have no antidote because your ill is not of my making,' she said.

'You must have something!' He pulled himself up. 'The physicians can't help me. I can't eat. I can barely breathe… They say you have the cure for any bane.'

'No. Perhaps your body poisoned itself. There's enough bad blood in you to kill a city.'

'Curse you then.' He struggled to speak the words. 'You had your chance… you will die without trial. Your mother died the way she deserved, and so will you.'

'She was not my mother. Though she was the best mother anyone could have had.' She approached him more closely and looked down at his cadaverous face. 'She died a death she did not deserve. She was trying to do good, I understand that now, though the line between good and ill is ever shifting.'

'But Domenico… you killed my brother. Though they cut him open and found nothing.'

'No. His wife, Agnese, did. He struck fear into her heart every day. He reaped what he sowed; I merely supplied the means. But if I had the choice again, then... I don't know... such work does not sit easily on my heart.'

'I could have stopped the wife sooner, did you know that?'

She turned from him, spoke to the empty room. 'Still you want to flaunt the upper hand, even though you lie in your bed and Death breathes down your neck,' she said.

He was still speaking, in a voice cracked with pain. 'Because I waited, Domenico died too soon. I keep recalling how we were as children, how we used to play soldiers together, how we laughed. I wish I could be back there, in those golden summers, swishing our sticks in the long wheatfields. He used to tell me to be careful, in case I hurt a rabbit. What turned him into such a man, a man that hated the world?' He banged a fist down on the bedcovers. 'Where does good turn into evil?' A tear leaked from the corner of his eye.

She could say nothing. She had asked herself the same question too many times.

'You have a canker of the throat,' she said eventually. 'One of my mother's patients had the same. If I'm right, there's no cure for such an ill, even with cutting.' When he did not respond, she said, 'We are both days away from death. Whatever we have done in this life will be weighed at the final reckoning, so there is no time now for blame or for ill-will. So I will do the only thing I can to help you. Did your men take the stock of Manna of San Nicolo from my workplace?'

Now his eyes turned to her in hope. 'I don't know... they brought many things, my men are testing them.'

'Find the Manna of San Nicolo. Three drops. It will provide the certain end when you need it.'

Be kind, Mamma had said.

He did not seem to have heard her. He looked through her, as if his eyes were trying to reach a place far away. Then he turned his cheek away, into the pillow. The ghastly swelling on his neck looked even more prominent.

Giulia repeated the instruction. The choice between a slow lingering death and a quick one. Mamma had never had that choice. He would not give her that choice, she knew.

She didn't look back. Telling him this secret was an admission of her guilt, and she knew he'd use it against her. If he survived long enough. But with no trial, perhaps her own death would be sooner, and now she longed for its peace.

She turned away from his bed, knowing she was done with him. As she went out of the door she was set upon by more soldiers and hustled back to the cell.

Of Alessandro, there was no sign.

CHAPTER 49

THE NOISE of a key inserted into the lock made her stagger to her feet and back away from the door, her limbs stiff and movements clumsy.

She was silent as the guards pushed her out of the cell, blinking into the bright sun, to where a cart was waiting. They shackled her to the cart and she guessed she was going to execution. But she was ready. This death would be but a moment, and she had lived so many longer, painful deaths in her heart. Her guilt was already ordained by the duke. He still survived, by force of will alone, she guessed.

When the cart creaked to a halt in the Via dei Tribunali, they unshackled her, and she was rubbing her bruised wrists when a guard grabbed her roughly by the skirts and yanked her so that she stumbled off the cart. She looked up at the building she was to enter – a huge grey stone building in the new baroque style. There were rows of small blank windows above, higher than a man's head, cells where the condemned would await execution, and a second storey where rich men leant from the iron balcony, watching the criminals arrive for trial.

They pushed her forward towards the two huge stone pillars

that buttressed the impressive door. Above it, the stone mono-gram of the Spanish double-headed eagle, in all its power and might, glared over the piazza. The ornate doors were flanked by guards.

As she was about to enter, they were forced to pause as a shiny red-topped coach, pulled by two grey horses, drew up right in front of them before the doors. A servant opened the carriage door, but she was only dimly aware of it, thinking it just an obstruction, until a familiar figure caught her eye. Agnese, alighting.

She was taken aback. What was she doing here? Had she come to watch her execution? She thought she'd fled to Rome. Now her gaze was locked on her friend, who was climbing the steps to the door, carrying something under her fringed mantle.

Agnese purposefully barred their way.

'Move aside, Signora,' the guard said.

Agnese burst into frantic motion. At first Giulia thought she was waving, but the ringing bell stopped everything around them. Agnese kept on lifting her arm, like pumping water from a well, and the clanging sound arrested everyone's attention.

The guard was about to hoist her aside when something made him turn. Something made them all turn.

A noise, like a beating of wings, or a rustling.

The sound of soft shoes running, of women's voices rising in a strange sort of war cry.

The men in front of the gates looked to each other in confu-sion. The square was filling with people. Not just people, but women. Hundreds of women. They were running into the square from all directions. A mob of women overpowered the men who were holding her by sheer numbers, scratching and clawing at them like harpies. Before she had time to make a sound, she was swept up bodily and dragged to the coach, which was still waiting by the steps.

The men were unprepared for this; they didn't know whether

to slash the women down or fight them. There were too many. It was like a tidal wave overwhelming the square.

'Get in,' shouted Agnese.

Giulia clambered in through the carriage door, and as she looked out of the window, all she could see was a sea of women; they surrounded the carriage six deep. She recognised Cettina, the duke's kitchen maid, and Camilla Ruggiero, and the faces of many women, old and young, who had come to her door.

As the carriage picked up speed and headed out of the square, there was an almighty cheer. The cheer seemed to follow them like a wave. 'What's all this?' Giulia asked, amazed. 'What have you done?'

'Not me. I have done nothing. It's you. Your reputation. I simply let it be known you'd been arrested and word spread. All the women you have ever helped wanted to thank you. The wives and daughters, and their female servants. All your mother's friends in Palermo are here somewhere. Any woman in Naples who has heard of Giulia Tofana and wants to pin your flag to their sleeve, and any woman who hates the de Verdi clan and their overbearing rule. They will form a street barrier until we're safely away.

'But where are we going?'

'I remembered what you said about your friends, the sisters at the nunnery in Rome. I wrote to them, promising them Domenico's fortune if they would help me, and in return they promised me a forgiving home and a safe haven. They know it all, and I have been at a convent close to the city since, preparing myself for the nun's life. I'm sure they will welcome you with open hearts.'

～

Giulia clung to the seat with both hands, unable to speak. The fact she was still alive and bowling through the countryside made no sense. She was astounded that so many women had even heard of her or knew who she was. Agnese seemed to understand and simply looked out of the window at the passing landscape. Giulia too fixed her eyes on the rocks and olive trees of the countryside, implacable in their silence, and which had been standing in the same places for hundreds of years, before she was even born.

They stayed the next two nights at convents on the way, where they spoke little, but took time to rest their aching bones and sleep. Their driver was an elderly man, very hard of hearing, who had been well-paid for his trouble. He obviously cared more for the horses than his passengers, as he ignored Giulia and Agnese, but made sure the horses were well-fed and rested ready for the final leg of the journey. Another tiring day of rutted roads, until the houses grew more numerous, and Giulia realised they must be approaching the outskirts of Rome. The sun had sunk lower in the sky, casting a blanket of indigo over rooftops and church towers as the horses turned into a dark cobbled road. They jolted along until they stopped at a modest whitewashed building set around a courtyard. The Convent of Maria Assumpta was housed in a series of long low colonnades with a hospital attached.

Sister Simona, who was obviously expecting them, came striding out and enveloped her in a bear hug, whilst Sister Marthe and Sister Teresa hovered waiting their turn as Agnese's servants saw to the horses. When all three had clasped her tight and showered blessings on her, they took her into the long bare refectory for a silent supper.

Even though she washed well at the pump, in the company of so many holy sisters in their homespun habits, Giulia still felt unclean, and kept her eyes cast down onto the board where bread and potage was laid out before them. Sister Simona said the Grace: *'Bless us, O Lord, and these Thy gifts, which we are about to receive from Thy bounty, through Christ our Lord. Amen.'*

Giulia could not eat. She left her plate untouched.

Sister Simona cast her a knowing look. After the meal, she came to her and said, 'Once you have had time to settle, perhaps you would like to visit the Lady Chapel to make atonement, and perhaps give thanks to those who came to your aid. Agnese will show you the way.'

So it was that in the dark of the evening she found herself in the Lady Chapel, a small square building of simple construction with a statue of the Virgin in an alcove near the altar. As she entered, she dipped her fingers in the cool stone well of holy water set into the wall and crossed herself. The beamed ceiling held two glass oil lamps suspended from beams. She was about to kneel when Agnese tapped her on the shoulder and handed her a parcel wrapped in oilskin.

'What's this?'

'I thought you might like to have her.'

Giulia unpeeled the cloth wrappings to find Mamma's little statue of Santa Olivia.

She looked to Agnese in disbelief.

'I asked Father Girolamo to fetch your things for me,' Agnese said, 'whilst you were imprisoned. I knew he had a key.'

'Was the house empty? Did he say what had happened to Fabio and Dante and Bab?'

'Father Girolamo took them in. Bab knew her way to his house and led them there. They are safe for now. He said everything in your apartment had been cleaned. The beds stripped, the shelves cleared, and that only a few unwanted things remained. This was one of them. Of course, I knew you'd want it.'

'Agnese?'

'Yes?'

'Do you ever wish you hadn't…?'

'Every single day. It is a black stain on my soul and I'll always need to pray for forgiveness, but at the same time I don't regret it. The line between good and evil is so fine and death a mystery.

I am learning to live with my deeds, with the help of the good sisters. You will too, but it takes time.'

'Do you blame me?'

'No. The sin was all in my heart, not yours.' With that, Agnese padded away, leaving Giulia alone in the flickering dark.

But she knew that the sin was shared. Things were 'not always as black and white as they seem.' Mamma's words. She placed the statue of Santa Olivia with her olive branch on the small wooden table that held the brass collecting plate. Behind the table was a tier of sandboxes with a crate of long ochre candles to light for the dead, and a living flame in a red glass.

She picked out candles for her parents – the first for Mamma, who had loved her so well and taught her all she knew. Carefully she dipped the wick in the living flame until it flared hot. With a prayer she stood it tall and proud. Two more side by side for Isabetta and Bruno, who had been family for so short a time and had protected her with such fierceness. She kept on lighting candles for those whose lives were lost. One candle after another. Only when the crate was completely empty, and Santa Olivia stood in a blaze of light, did she prostrate herself and ask for Our Lady's forgiveness.

She knelt a long time, but her heart felt lighter, as if some pressure around it had eased and floated away. She searched for one more light, and found one last candle that had fallen down behind the table. She lit this and pressed the stub of it hard into the sand. A prayer would never be wasted.

'This one's for the duke,' she said, 'may he find peace.'

Mamma's candle was burning low already, but she felt her presence, her warm weighty hand on her shoulder an invisible comforter.

She left the saint's statue where she stood, bright in her halo of light from the hundred candles, and went out into the soft evening. From the other chapel she could hear the nuns chant evensong, but she did not join them. Instead, she walked down the path towards where a few lights showed from small windows in the dark. The hospital.

Outside, she paused a moment to gaze up at the stars – at Sirius the Dog Star chasing the hare, Lepus. At the Great Bear symbolising mothers everywhere. She was so small beneath this infinity of stars, such a small pin-prick. Yet with her skills and experience, she could make a difference. She had been death's servant. Now she would be a servant to life.

She turned and lifted the heavy latch, pushed open the hospital door, and walked into the light.

'

One of the difficulties with Giulia Tofana's story is that she can easily be confused with her mother – Theofania d'Adamo, or even her eventual daughter, Girolama Spara. No portrait of her exists, though we are led to believe she was considered beautiful. Conflicting sources attribute her life and death to different dates – for example, one source says that that she died of natural causes in 1651, another that she lived on for years afterwards in a convent, dispensing her poisons through priests and nuns. Others assert that she was variously captured and executed, though they differ as to whether her actual death took place in 1659, 1709, or even as late as 1730!

There is a large amount of lore associated with her poisoning career, and like all novelists do, I have used the parts I enjoyed. For the best and most detailed analysis of the real Giulia Tofana and the facts surrounding her life, I suggest this excellent article by Mike Dash.

Nevertheless, I owe it to you, the reader, to let you know what is fact and what is fiction. One date that can certainly be nailed is the date of the death of Theofania d'Adamo, because a Palermo notary, Baldassare Zamparrone (1581–1648), gives us a contemporary description of her execution on 12 July 1633, and the manner of her death was later described by the seventeenth-century botanist Paolo Boccone.

Wikipedia states Giulia Tofana, Theofania d'Adamo's daughter, was born in 1620, but some doubt has been cast on this, because she supposedly confessed she had killed six hundred men with her poisons in Rome alone, between the years 1633 and 1651, which would give her an age of thirteen years when she began her lethal career, which is possible, but not probable. For the purposes of the novel I have made her ten years older, born in 1610. This concords with records of her activity as a poisoner in the cities of Palermo, Naples and Rome in the early seventeenth century. The first recorded mention of Aqua Tofana (literal meaning – Tofana Water) is from 1632–33.

At this time, the states of Italy, including the Kingdom of Naples, were under Spanish rule, each state controlled by the Spanish viceroy. This novel has a very narrow time frame and takes place over a four-month period in 1633, the year of Theofania's death. Later events in Giulia Tofana's life will have to wait for another book!

Do you want to know more about Giulia and Fabio? The next book in this series is called The Silkworm Keeper and a third in the series is underway.

If you enjoyed the book, a brief review or rating really helps readers searching for their next read, and reviews are invaluable to authors. The more reviews a book has, the more visible it is, and the more likely to be chosen for promotion. Thank you!

FURTHER READING

Books I have found invaluable whilst researching *The Poison Keeper* have been:

Women in Italy 1350–1650: A Sourcebook, by Mary Rogers and Paola Tinagli

Becoming Neapolitan: Citizen Culture in Baroque Naples, by John A Marino

Italy in the Seventeenth Century, by Domenico Sella

Picturing Women in Renaissance and Baroque Italy, Edited by Geraldine A Johnson and Sara F Matthews Grieco

Naples Declared: A Walk Around the Bay, by Benjamin Taylor

In the Shadow of Vesuvius, by Raleigh Trevelyan

Poisons and Poisoners: An Encyclopaedia of Homicidal Poisonings, by Michael Farrell

The Herbal Apothecary: 100 Medicinal Herbs and How to Use Them, by J J Pursell

1. What did you think of the character of Giulia Tofana?
   How did she change from the beginning of the book to
   the end?
2. Bruno, the Duke de Verdi, Fabio and Agnese all cause
   people's deaths. Discuss their different methods and
   their different attitudes to causing a death.
3. Father Girolamo has been a Catholic priest for a long
   time. Was he a good or a bad priest?
4. When Fabio suggests that the making of poison is a
   crime, Giulia asks him if the making of all weapons
   should be a crime. What do you think?
5. Emilio regrets that he did not give his wife Elena
   something that would end her life earlier. Was Emilio a
   character you liked or loathed?
6. How important is the notion of family in the novel?
   What makes someone family; is it blood or is it
   familiarity? How does this play out in the book?
7. Paracelsus says: 'Poison is in everything, and no thing
   is without poison. The dosage makes it either a poison
   or a remedy.' Discuss the different types of poison used

in the novel. Isabetta is an opium addict. Is opium a poison or a remedy?

8. In seventeenth-century Neapolitan society, women were often considered to be an underclass. Thinking about the female characters in the novel, apart from Giulia, which characters had power, and why?

9. What are the similarities between the de Verdi brothers, Antonio and Domenico? What are the differences?

10. Seventeenth-century Naples is under the control of the Mafia, in those days called the Camorra. Does power always corrupt? Is rebellion the best way to deal with an oppressive regime?

ACKNOWLEDGMENTS

My thanks go to my editor Richard Sheehan and to the online groups that have been so supportive during the publication of this book. They include Mary Anne Yarde's Coffee Pot Tweet Group, the Macmillan New Writers, and the writers I have spent time with in the Mani. Thanks to Jean Briggs for her listening ear, to Suzanne Barnhill for her helpful suggestions and to my husband John without whom no book would ever be written.

My appreciation also goes to you my readers, as without you there would be little joy in writing these books. Thanks for letting me share my stories with you.

Book cover design is by deedeebookcovers.com

MEET DEBORAH SWIFT

DEBORAH SWIFT used to work as a set and costume designer for theatre and TV. She is the author of fourteen historical novels to date. She enjoys the research aspect of creating historical fiction, something she loved doing as a scenographer. She likes to write about extraordinary characters set against the background of real historical events.

Deborah lives in North Lancashire on the edge of the Lake District in England, an area made famous by the Romantic Poets such as Wordsworth and Coleridge. When not writing, Deborah mentors other writers through The History Quill. She is a member of the Historical Writers Association and the Historical Novel Society.

FROM DEBORAH - CLAIM A FREE STORY!

Do click the link to join my community of readers and subscribe to my newsletter, The Astonishing Past. You will get a free story and be entered into a monthly giveaway. Newsletters are once a month and feature interesting snippets from our astonishing past and bargain books. See you there!

THE SILKWORM KEEPER

Rome 1638

Old sins have long shadows ~ Italian Proverb

Giulia Tofana never wanted to be a nun, but she is determined to atone for her sinful past by making her new monastery a success.

When an unexpected disaster closes the convent, Giulia is forced to turn to her old friend Fabio Pasello for help. Giulia still has intense feelings for Fabio and Fabio's passion for her has never diminished.

But they are not the same people they were before. Giulia has taken her vows, and Fabio is apprenticed to Bernini the famous sculptor, and is one of his rakish libertines. They could not be further apart.

To add to their problems, Giulia cannot escape her reputation as a poisoner, and is soon embroiled in a plot against Fabio's patron, Pope Urban VIII. Faced with the idea of murder, will Giulia renounce her vows or embrace them?

GET THE BOOK

ALSO BY DEBORAH SWIFT

The Silkworm Keeper

A Divided Inheritance

The Gilded Lily

The Lady's Slipper

The Occupation

The Lifeline

Past Encounters

Pleasing Mr Pepys

A Plague on Mr Pepys

Entertaining Mr Pepys

The Highway Trilogy for Young Adults

Don't forget your free story! A WW2 Railway Romance ideal for your coffee time reading!

GET MY STORY

Printed in Great Britain
by Amazon